国内外经典教材辅导系列·英语类

吴伟仁《英国文学史及选读》(重排版)
笔记和考研真题详解

主编：圣才考研网
www. 100xuexi. com

中国石化出版社

内　容　提　要

本书是英美文学经典教材《英国文学史及选读》（重排版）（吴伟仁主编）的学习辅导书。全书完全遵循该教材的章目编排，共分为七部分，总共40章，每章由两部分组成：第一部分为复习笔记（中英文对照），总结本章的重点难点；第二部分是考研真题与典型题详解，精选名校近年考研真题及相关习题，并提供了详细的参考答案。

圣才考研网（www.100xuexi.com）提供刘炳善《英国文学简史》辅导方案【视频课程、电子书、题库】。购书即可享受大礼包增值服务【本书电子书（电脑版、手机版）+全国名校真题详解电子书】。手机扫码（本书封底）领取本书大礼包。

图书在版编目（CIP）数据

吴伟仁《英国文学史及选读》（重排版）笔记和考研真题详解/圣才考研网主编．—北京：中国石化出版社，2016.6（2021.7重印）
国内外经典教材辅导系列·英语类
ISBN 978-7-5114-4154-6

Ⅰ．①吴…　Ⅱ．①圣…　Ⅲ．①英语-阅读教学-研究生-入学考试-自学参考资料②英国文学-文学史
Ⅳ．①H319.4：I

中国版本图书馆CIP数据核字（2016）第143575号

中国石化出版社出版发行

地址：北京市东城区安定门外大街58号
邮编：100011　电话：（010）57512500
发行部电话：（010）57512575
http://www.sinopec-press.com
E-mail：press@sinopec.com
武汉市盛宏源印务有限公司印刷
全国各地新华书店经销

*

787×1092毫米16开本13.75印张342千字
2016年7月第1版　2021年7月第2次印刷
定价：48.00元

序　　言

我国各大院校一般都把国内外通用的权威教科书作为本科生和研究生学习专业课程的参考教材，这些教材甚至被很多考试（特别是硕士和博士入学考试）和培训项目作为指定参考书。为了帮助读者更好地学习专业课，我们有针对性地编著了一套与国内外教材配套的复习资料，并提供配套的名师讲堂和题库。

《英国文学史及选读》（重排版）（吴伟仁主编）一直被用作高等院校英语专业英美文学教材，被许多院校指定为英语专业考研必读书和学术研究参考书。作为该教材的学习辅导书，本书具有以下几个方面的特点：

1．梳理章节脉络，浓缩内容精华。每章的复习笔记以该教材为主并结合其他教材对本章的重难点知识进行了整理，并参考了国内名校名师讲授该教材的课堂笔记，因此，本书的内容几乎浓缩了经典教材的知识精华。

2．中英双语对照，凸显难点要点。本书章节笔记采用了中英文对照的形式，强化对重要难点知识的理解和运用。

3．精选考研真题，补充难点习题。本书精选名校近年考研真题及相关习题，并提供答案和详解。所选真题和习题基本体现了各个章节的考点和难点，但又不完全局限于教材内容，是对教材内容极好的补充。

购书即可享受大礼包增值服务【本书电子书（电脑版、手机版）＋全国名校真题详解电子书】。手机扫码（本书封底）领取本书大礼包。

圣才考研网（www.100xuexi.com）是圣才学习网旗下的考研考博专业网站，提供考研公共课和全国500所院校考研考博专业课辅导【一对一辅导、网授精讲班等】、电子书、题库、全套资料（历年真题及答案、笔记讲义等）、国内外经典教材名师讲堂、考研教辅图书等。

考研辅导：kaoyan.100xuexi.com（圣才考研网）
资格考试：www.100xuexi.com（圣才学习网）

圣才考研网编辑部

序　言

[illegible]

目　录

第一部分　中古时期

第二部分　文艺复兴时期

第三部分　十七世纪资产阶级革命和王朝复辟时期

第四部分　英国启蒙运动阶段

第五部分　浪漫主义时期

第六部分 维多利亚时期

第七部分　二十世纪文学

第一部分　中古时期

第1章　盎格鲁-撒克逊时期

1.1　复习笔记

I. Background Knowledge—The Making of England (449—1066)	Ⅰ. 背景知识——英格兰的形成(449—1066)
1. The English Conquest	**1. 盎格鲁-撒克逊征服**
A. Brief Introduction	**A. 简介**
In the wake of the Roman invasion, three Teutonic tribes of the Angles, Saxons and Jutes from Northern Europe, made their way into Britain. A united kingdom under the name of England, also known as the land of Angles, came into being in 829.	继罗马入侵之后，来自北欧的三支日耳曼部落盎格鲁人，撒克逊人和朱特人入侵不列颠。 829年，一个统一的王国——英格兰成立了，也被称作盎格鲁人之国。
B. Influence	**B. 影响**
(1) The three tribes, whose dialects gradually merged into one single language Anglo-Saxon, also known as Old English, developed into an integrated people called the English. (2) Following the Norman Conquest was a transitional period during which the British society shifted from a tribal mode to a feudal one. (3) Having their faith in the old mythology of Northern Europe, the Anglo-Saxons were heathen people later Christianized in the 7th century.	(1) 这三支部落发展成一个统一的民族称为英国人。三种方言逐渐成为一种单一的语言，称为盎格鲁-撒克逊语言，即古英语。 (2) 诺曼征服后，不列颠社会经历了从原始部落社会向封建社会过渡的时期。 (3) 盎格鲁-撒克逊人是无神论民族，相信古老的北欧神话，但后来在7世纪被基督教化了。
Ⅱ. Literary Features of Early English Literature	**Ⅱ. 早期英国文学的特征**
(1) English Literature, categorized into the pagan and the Christian during this period, has its debut after Anglo-Saxons settled in England. (2) Introduced by Anglo-Saxons, pagan literature is the oral legends paying tribute to the ancient heroic deeds sung by the minstrels to the chiefs and warriors in the feasting hall. Alliterations and rhymes were of regular use in old English, and metaphors and understatements were common devices in poetry among which *Beowulf* is the most widely spread early poem.	(1) 盎格鲁-撒克逊人定居英国标志着英国文学的诞生。这一时期的文学可分为异教和基督教文学。 (2) 异教文学指盎格鲁-撒克逊人带来的口头传说，由游吟诗人在宴会大厅里为那些首领和勇士歌唱古时的英雄事迹。古英语中有规律地运用了头韵和韵律，同时也用到了暗喻和含蓄陈述的手法。流传最广的早期英语诗歌是《贝奥武甫》。

(3) Teachings of literate monks pushed for the development of Christian literature which, along with the extensive influence of Christianity, ushered in the language of Latin, a vital influencer on the early English prose and poetry.	(3) 基督教文学是由精通文学的僧侣发展起来的。基督教带来了珍贵的拉丁语，对早期散文和诗歌有极大影响。
Ⅲ. Literary Terms	**Ⅲ. 文学术语**
1. Anglo-Saxon Poetry	**1. 盎格鲁－撒克逊诗歌**
Poems are songs to the chiefs and warriors by Anglo-Saxon minstrels in the feasting hall to express admiration for the ancient heroic deeds. The typical work of Anglo-Saxon is *Beowulf*.	是由盎格鲁－撒克逊游吟诗人吟唱的古代英雄事迹的诗歌或者歌曲。这些诗歌或者歌曲主要是在宴会厅唱给首领或者武士们听的。代表诗作是《贝奥武甫》。
2. Alliteration	**2. 头韵**
It means the repetition of the initial consonant sounds in two or more neighboring words or stressed syllables.	就是相邻的两个或者多个单词或重音节中，开头辅音字母的重复。
3. Epic (or Heroic Poetry)	**3. 史诗**
Epic is a genre of ancient folk literature, usually referring to legends or major historical events as the subject of oral narrative poetry. Epic mainly eulogizes the struggles and heroic deeds of each nation in overcoming various difficulties, obstacles, natural disasters and resisting foreign aggression in the course of its formation and development.	通常指以传说或重大历史事件为题材的口头叙事诗。史诗主要歌颂每个民族在其形成和发展过程中战胜所经历的各种艰难险阻、克服自然灾害、抵御外侮的斗争及其英雄事迹。
Ⅳ. Major Work	**Ⅳ. 英国早期主要作品**
◆***Beowulf***	◆**《贝奥武甫》**
English literature began with the Anglo-Saxon settlement. *Beowulf* is an Anglo-Saxon poem and a national epic of the English people.	英国文学始于盎格鲁－撒克逊人的定居。《贝奥武甫》是一首盎格鲁－撒克逊诗歌，同时也是一首英格兰人民的民族史诗。
The whole epic consists of 3182 lines and is divided into two parts with an interpolation between the two. The whole song is essentially pagan in spirit and matter, while the interpolation was an obvious creation by a Christian transcriber.	全诗有3182行，分为两部分，中间有段插入部分。整首诗在精神和物质上都是异教的，但显然中间的插入部分是一个基督徒誊写员后加的。
A. The Story of *Beowulf*	**A. 《贝奥武甫》主要情节**
Beowulf is a literary recording of the deeds of Beowulf, a Teutonic hero, who fought against monsters Grendel and his mother, won the battle and protected the King of the Danes. Ascending to the throne, Beowulf's slaying a firedrake to protect his people was successful but at the price of a lethal wound causing his death after which his mound turned into a beacon for seafarers sailing along the coast.	该诗讲述了贝奥武甫这位日耳曼英雄的英勇事迹。他与怪物格伦德尔和它的母亲战斗，取得了胜利，并保护了丹麦国王。他回家成为国王后，为了保护人民，杀死了火龙，却因伤势过重而死。死后，他的墓塚变成了灯塔，为航行于此的船员指明方向。

B. Artistic Features of *Beowulf*	B.《贝奥武甫》的文学特征
(1) The most noticeable artistic feature of *Beowulf* is the use of alliteration. (2) In the poem metaphors, among which kenning was the most commonly used in old poetry (for instance, "sea" as "whale-path") and understatements are of frequent use.	(1)本诗最突出的特点是押头韵。 (2)诗中运用了很多暗喻(隐喻语在古英语诗歌中最常见，如把海洋说成鲸道)以及含蓄陈述的修辞手法。

1.2 考研真题与典型题详解

Ⅰ. Fill in the blanks.

1. *Beowulf* probably existed in its oral form as early as the ________ century and its hero and his adventures are placed in ________ and southern Sweden rather than in England.（国际关系学院 2010 研）
2. In the 8th century, Anglo-Saxon prose appeared. The famous prose writers of that period were Venerable Bede and ________.
3. The literature of the Anglo-Saxon period falls naturally into two divisions, ________ and Christian.
4. Angles, Saxons and ________ usually known as Anglo-Saxons are the first Englishmen. Language spoken by them is called ________, which is the foundation of English language and literature.
5. The ________ period witnessed a transition from tribal society to feudalism.
6. The early inhabitants on the island now we call England were ________, a tribe of Celts. From the Britons the island got its name of Britain, the land of Britons. The Britons were a ________ people.

Ⅱ. Multiple Choices

1. The history of English literature begins in the ________ century.（北二外 2009 研）
   A. 7th　　B. 6th　　C. 5th　　D. 4th
2. The Anglo-Saxons were Christianized in the ________ century.
   A. 5th　　B. 6th　　C. 7th　　D. 8th
3. *Beowulf* describes the exploits of a ________ hero, Beowulf, in fighting against the monster Grendel, his revengeful mother, and a fire-breathing dragon.
   A. Danish　　B. Scandinavian　　C. English　　D. Norwegian
4. ________ is not only a prose writer but also a king of Wessex.（北二外 2016 研）
   A. Alfred the Great　　B. Venerable Bede
   C. Adam Bede　　D. King Arthur

Ⅲ. Explain the following terms.

1. Old English period (the Anglo-Saxon period)
2. Alliteration（南开大学 2010 研）
3. epic（天津外国语学院 2007 研；厦门大学 2008 研）

Ⅳ. Short answer questions

1. What are the main characteristics of Anglo-Saxon literature?
2. What are the artistic features of Old English poetry?

Ⅴ. Essay question

What are the three parts told in the story of *Beowulf*? How is heroic ideal reflected in *Beowulf*?

参考答案及解析

Ⅰ. Fill in the blanks.

1. 6th; Denmark
   (《贝奥武甫》最早在公元6世纪开始口头传诵，故事发生在丹麦和瑞典南部，诗中并没有提及英国。)
2. Alfred the Great
   (阿尔弗雷德大帝和比德是盎格鲁-撒克逊时期的散文家。)
3. pagan
   (盎格鲁-撒克逊时期的英国文学主要是异教和基督教文学两类。)
4. Jutes; the Old English
   (盎格鲁-撒克逊人通常指盎格鲁人、撒克逊人、朱特人三个部族，他们的语言是古英语。)
5. Anglo-Saxon
   (盎格鲁-撒克逊时期，英国由部落社会步入封建社会。)
6. Britons; primitive
   (作为凯尔特一个部族的不列颠人是英格兰的早期定居者，不列颠岛也因此而得名。)

Ⅱ. Multiple Choice

1. C　英国文学始于盎格鲁-撒克逊人定居英国，即公元450年，所以是5世纪。
2. C　盎格鲁-撒克逊人在公元7世纪被基督教化了。
3. B　《贝奥武甫》讲述的故事发生在北欧斯堪的纳维亚半岛。歌颂了主人公贝奥武甫先后战胜巨怪Grendel，Grendel的母亲以及火蛇的英勇事迹。
4. A　阿尔弗雷德是英格兰盎格鲁-撒克逊时期韦塞克斯王朝的国王，也是英格兰唯一一位被授予“大帝”名号的君主。他是一个善于学习的人，鼓励教育，翻译大批古典名著，并编纂《盎格鲁-撒克逊编年史》。

Ⅲ. Explain the following terms.

1. Old English period(the Anglo-Saxon period): ①The Old English period refers to the period between the Germanic invasion into Celtic England in the first half of the fifth century and the Norman Conquest led by William the Conqueror in 1066. ②It is the conversion to Christianity in the seventh century that the Anglo-Saxons began to develop a written form of their literature.
2. Alliteration: ①Alliteration refers to the repetition of the same consonant sounds of the first letters in any sequence of adjacent words. ②Alliteration was once required in the poetry of Germanic languages such as Old English and Old Norse and in Celtic verse. ③Poetry in which alliteration is the main rhyming device is known as alliteration verse in which a vowel sound can also alliterate with any other vowels.

3. Epic: Epics are used to celebrate the heroic deeds, adventures or events, both national and foreign, in serious and grand style. Most epics focus on the exploits of a single individual, thereby adding to the integrity and unity to the composition. *Iliad* and *Odyssey* by Homer are representatives of great epics.

Ⅳ. Short answer questions

1. Anglo-Saxon literature is the type of literature largely in verse passed down orally with most of its creators unrecognized and anonymous. English poetry in the Anglo-Saxon period are categorized into the pagan and the Christian. The former is represented by *Beowulf*, and the latter is represented by the works of Caedmon and Cynewulf.

2. (1) The use of alliteration. Each full line has four stresses with several unstressed syllables, three of which begin with the same sound or letter.

   (2) The use of strong stress and the predominance of consonants. The poetry is nearly rhymeless. Each line is halved and each half has two heavy stresses.

   (3) The use of vivid poetic diction and parallel expressions for a single idea, such as the sea is called "swan-road" or "whale-path"; a soldier "shield-bearer", "battle-hero" or "spear-fighter", etc.

Ⅴ. Essay question

(1) In terms of structure, Beowulf is built around three fights: the fight between Beowulf and the monster Grendel, the battle between Beowulf and Grendel's mother revenging her son, and the confront between Beowulf and a firedrake who preys on Beowulf's subjects.

(2) As a pagan poem, *Beowulf* communicates the ideal of knighthood, kingship and heroism. At that time, life consisted of battles, so virtues such as strength and courage were indispensable for both kings and his warriors. The duty of the king was to protect his subjects and appeal to his warriors with much gentleness and generosity, who, in return, should be loyal to the king without second thoughts. The poem conveys the ideal of kingship and heroism through Beowulf's larger-than-life exploits shining with virtues of courage, wisdom, and a strong sense of commitment to his people.

第 2 章　盎格鲁 – 诺曼底时期

2.1　复习笔记

I. Background Knowledge (1066—1350)	I. 背景知识（1066 – 1350）
1. The Norman Conquest	**1. 诺曼征服**
A. Brief Introduction	**A. 简介**
The French-speaking Normans, led by Duke William, defeated the English at the Battle of Hastings in 1066 and began their rule over England.	说法语的诺曼底人在威廉公爵的带领下，在 1066 年的黑斯廷斯战役中打败了英国人，开始了对英国的统治。
B. Chief Influences	**B. 主要影响**
(1) The bringing of Roman civilization to England;	(1)将罗曼文化带到英格兰；
(2) The growth of nation state and the awareness of nationality. A strong centralized government replaced the scattered confederation of Saxon tribes;	(2)促进了国家的发展，强大的中央集权政府代替了散乱的撒克逊部落联盟；
(3) The fusion with the French language gave rise to the new English language and literature.	(3)和法国语言的融合产生了新的英语语言和文学。
II. Features of the New Literature	**II. 新文学特征**
(1) The new literature is linguistically and culturally a combination of French and Anglo-Saxon elements.	(1) 新文学是法国和盎格鲁 – 撒克逊因素的结合。
(2) There are three classes of new literature:	(2) 新文学故事的类别包括：
① Matter of France (tales about Charlemagne and his peers);	①取材于法国（查理曼大帝和他的贵族们的故事）；
② Matter of Greece and Rome (tales about Alexander and the fall of Troy);	②取材于希腊和罗马（亚历山大大帝和特洛伊毁灭的故事）；
③ Matter of Britain (tales about King Arthur and his Knights of the Round Table).	③取材于英格兰（亚瑟王和圆桌骑士的故事）。
III. Literary Terms	**III. 文学术语**
1. The Romance	**1. 传奇文学**
A. The Content of the Romance	**A. 传奇定义**
As the most popular literary genre in feudal England, romance was a long piece of literary work in verse or in prose that narrates life and adventures of noble heroes. The central character of romances was the knight, who was of blue blood, good at fighting, and celebrated for his manner and spirit of chivalry.	传奇文学是封建英国最为盛行的文学体裁。它一般是长篇作品，主要描述高尚的英雄的生平和冒险。传奇的中心人物是骑士，骑士出身高贵并且善使武器。骑士以其骑士精神著称。

Typical work is *Le Morte D'Arthur*, a collection of stories about King Arthur, translated from French by Sir Thomas Malory.	传奇典型代表作是由托马斯·马洛里由法语翻译而来的《亚瑟王之死》，是关于亚瑟王生平故事的选集。
B. The Romance Cycles	**B. 传奇分类**
The romances are divided into three groups: the "matters of Britain", "matters of France" and "matters of Rome". The "matters of Britain" deal with adventures of King Arthur and his Knights of the Round Table. The "matters of France" focuses on Emperor Charlemagne and his peers. The "matters of Rome" tells stories about Alexander the Great and so forth.	传奇可分为"英国类"，"法国类"和"罗马类"。"英国类"传奇是关于亚瑟王和他的圆桌武士的冒险。"法国类"是关于查理曼大帝和他的贵族们。"罗马类"是关于亚历山大大帝。
C. The Class Nature of the Romance	**C. 传奇的阶级本质**
Loyalty to the King is a recurring theme in legends in that loyalty was the cornerstone of feudal morality. Irrelevant to commoners, legends are written by and for nobles.	对国王和统治者的忠诚是传奇中反复强调的主题，因为忠诚是封建道德的基石。传奇与平民无关，传奇是由贵族而作也是为贵族而写的。
Ⅳ. Major Works	**Ⅳ. 中世纪主要作品**
◆*Sir Gawain and the Green Knight*	**◆《高文爵士与绿衣骑士》**
A. Content	**A. 简要内容**
The story can be divided into three parts: challenge of the Green Knight; Gawain's quest for the Green Knight in the forest; the meeting of the two in the Green Chapel and the hero's temptations.	故事可以分成三部分：绿衣骑士的战书；高文在森林里对绿衣骑士的请求；两人在绿色教堂的见面，高文受到各种诱惑。
B. Analysis of the Story	**B. 作品分析**
Gawain is concerned with the rights and wrongs of conduct. It is a series of trials on loyalty, courage, and chastity. Gawain conceals that he has earned the green belt, revealing that he cares more about his life than honesty. Yet in the end he honorably confesses, repents, and volunteers to wear the green sash henceforth as a symbol of his sin. Though he survives the quest, Gawain recognizes the problematic nature of chivalry ideals since a person must stay crystal clear of his or her own mortality and weaknesses. The theme of beheading stems from the ancient legend of plants, where trees are pruned to ensure their rebirth in the next spring. The poem aims to depict ideal characters and appears satirical, allusive, and humorous in dealing with serious moral issues.	高文是人们行为是非判断的导向。故事讲述了一系列对忠诚、勇气及纯洁的考验。高文隐瞒自己获得了绿腰带，揭示了比起诚实，他更在乎自己的生命。然而他最终令人尊敬地坦白并悔过，自愿从此带上绿腰带作为罪过的象征。尽管逃过一死，高文认识到骑士精神的理想终究不现实，因为一个人必须要先清楚自己的缺点和必有一死。砍头的主题是源于古老的植物传说，树木要剪枝以确保在下一个春天的重生。 这首诗目的在于刻画理想的角色，并且在阐述严肃道德问题时又不乏讽刺、暗指和幽默。

◆*Le Morte D'Arthur*	◆《亚瑟王之死》
Translated by Sir Thomas Malory from French, the legends of King Arthur are the foundation of *Le Morte D'Arthur* (first published in 1485). Having selected the most interesting parts such as the adventures of the Knights of the Round Table, the quest of the Holy Grail, the death of Arthur, and the dissolution of the fellowship of the Knights of the Round Table, Malory treated legends in the spirit of medieval knighthood and chivalry and told stories vividly with idiomatic English prose.	经托马斯·马洛里由法语译成,《亚瑟王之死》(1485年首次出版)是基于亚瑟王的一生的传奇。但是马洛里选择了其中最有趣的部分,例如圆桌武士的冒险,寻找圣杯,亚瑟之死,圆桌武士的志同道合的关系的消亡。马洛里的传奇体现了中世纪的骑士精,并且是用简单、惯用的英语,讲述了栩栩如生的故事。

2.2 考研真题与典型题详解

Ⅰ. Fill in the blanks.

1. ________ conquered England on October 14, 1066. From then on began the medieval period. (南开大学2008研)
2. The most magnificent prose work of the 15th century is *Le Morte D'Arthur* concerning with ________ legend.
3. The only important prose writer in the 15th century is Sir ________.
4. In 55 B. C., Britain was invaded by ________, the Roman conqueror. Along with the invasion came the ________ into Britain.
5. In the year 1066, the Normans defeated the Anglo-Saxons at the battle of ________.
6. After the ________ Conquest, feudal system was established in English society.
7. The year of ________ witnessed a famous peasant uprising led by Wat Tyler and John Ball.

Ⅱ. Multiple Choices

1. In English poetry, a quatrain is ________. (北二外2008研)
   A. a four-line stanza　B. a couplet
   C. a fourteen-line stanza　D. a terza rima
2. Knights of the Round Table are characters serving ________ in legends, which depict chivalry in early literature. (北二外2007研)
   A. Sir Lancelot　B. Sir Godwin　C. King Arthur　D. King Henry Ⅷ
3. Romance was a type of literature that was very popular in the ________. (四川大学2008研)
   A. Renaissance period　B. seventeenth century
   C. Middle Ages　D. eighteenth century
4. ________ was the greatest of English religious reformers and the first translator of the Bible.
   A. Langland　B. Gower　C. Wycliffe　D. Chaucer
5. The story of ________ is the culmination of the Arthurian romances.
   A. *Sir Gawain and the Green Knight*　B. *The Song of Beowulf*
   C. *Piers the Plowman*　D. *The Canterbury Tales*
6. After the Norman Conquest, three languages existed in England at that time. The Normans spoke

________.

A. French　　　B. English　　　C. Latin　　　D. Swedish

Ⅲ. Explain the following terms.

1. Middle English period
2. Arthurian legend
3. Romance(山东师大 2018 研)

Ⅳ. Short answer questions

1. What is the influence of the Norman Conquest upon English language and literature?
2. What are the essential features of romance in the medieval English literature?

Ⅴ. Essay question

Make comments on the romance *Sir Gawain and the Green Knight.*

参考答案及解析

Ⅰ. Fill in the blanks.

1. Duke of Normandy
   (公元 1066 年，诺曼底公爵，或者叫 William the Conqueror(征服者威廉)，占领英格兰，从此开始了中世纪时期。)
2. Arthurian
   (15 世纪左右公认的集大成作品为《亚瑟王之死》，是关于亚瑟王的传奇故事。)
3. Thomas Malory
   (15 世纪最著名的散文家是托马斯·马洛里爵士，他将众多的关于亚瑟王的传奇故事收录为集大成之作《亚瑟王之死》，是英国第一部重要的散文。)
4. Julius Caesar, Roman mode of life
   (公元前凯撒大帝率军征服不列颠。在罗马统治期间，罗马生活方式传入不列颠。)
5. Hastings
   (1066 年黑斯廷斯战役，盎格鲁 - 撒克逊人溃败，诺曼征服开始。)
6. Norman
   (诺曼征服后英国封建主义制度建立。)
7. 1381
   (Wat Tyler 和 John Ball 领导了 1381 年著名的农民暴动。)

Ⅱ. Multiple Choices

1. A　quatrain 即四行诗；a couplet 是对句；a fourteen-line stanza 是十四行诗，也就是 sonnet；a terza rima 是三韵句。
2. C　圆桌骑士是中世纪传说中亚瑟王宫廷里最高等的骑士，因聚会的桌子是圆桌而得名。
3. C　Romance 是富有浪漫色彩的恋爱故事或冒险故事，是中世纪在欧洲非常流行的一种文学体裁，著名作品如《亚瑟王之死》等。
4. C　威克里夫是一位宗教改革家，同时也是把《圣经》翻译成英文的第一人。
5. A　亚瑟王传奇由很多套诗组成，《高文爵士与绿衣骑士》可谓是巅峰之作；《贝奥武甫》是一首史诗，它主要记述了英雄贝奥武甫与格伦德尔，女妖和火龙战斗的英勇事迹；《农夫皮尔斯》是朗格兰的代表作，作者通过一系列的梦境，对 14 世纪英国的社会状况进行了生动形象的描述：《坎特伯雷故事集》是乔叟的代表作，在此作品中作者把各种各样的人聚集在一起，让处于每个社会阶层的人讲自己最喜欢的故事，以此来描述当时英国社会的生活。

6. A　诺曼征服后英国出现了三种语言鼎立的局面。国王和日耳曼的宫廷贵族使用法语；拉丁语成为教会和学校的主要语言；平民百姓使用英语。

Ⅲ. Explain the following terms.

1. Middle English period: The period between about 1150 and 1500. Middle English had its origin since the Norman Conquest in 1066, a turning point in the English history which saw radical changes in the language, life, and culture of England. Approximately around 1500, the standard literary language had become recognizably "modern English" similar to the language we use today.
2. Arthurian legend: It is a term referring to tales that developed in the Middle Ages about Arthur, semi-historical king of the Britons and his knights. The legend is a mixture of Celtic mythology with later traditions focusing on a central character with unassured historical reality.
3. 参见2.1复习笔记Ⅲ.1部分。

Ⅳ. Short answer questions

1. (1) During the period of the Norman Conquest, English, Norman-French and Latin were used in the English society. For a rather long period in the British history, French was favored and exclusively used by nobles. Latin was taught at bigger schools and also used in churches and monasteries. By contrast, people of the lower station only were limited to the English language.

   (2) In this period, English language had undergone slow but radical and extensive changes. It had borrowed heavily from French and through French from Latin and also Greek, but in the course of enriching its vocabulary, many English words disappeared. The linguistic transitional stage from Old English to Modern English has generally been known as Middle English.

   (3) Literary works covered a wide range of subjects. The Normans began to write histories or chronicles, most of which were written in Latin or French. The English feudal literature was mainly produced in the genre of romance.

   （此题主要从诺曼征服时期英语语言的变化和这一时期出现的文学形式两个方面回答。）
2. The romance, a long composition in verse or in prose about adventures of knights or other heroic deeds, was a predominant form of literature in the Middle Ages. It has the following features:

   (1) The knight takes the central place in the romance. A man born to the purple and adept at fighting battles, a knight is usually depicted as riding forth on knightly errands such as protection of religious sites, punishment of infidelity, rescue of a maiden, or challenge taking.

   (2) Romantic love has vital role to play in the plot in the romance.

   (3) It gives a larger-than-life narrative.

   (4) The structure is loose and episodic, and the language is simple and straight forward.

Ⅴ. Essay question

(1) The pinnacle of literary creation of the Arthurian romances is the story of *Sir Gawain and the Green Knight*. The romance is a long composition in verse or in prose to sing high praise to heroism and its followers.

(2) A blend of French and Saxon gave rise to the literary form of romance, which is written in an elaborate stanza combining meter and alliteration. At the end of each stanza, there is a rimed refrain.

(3) The themes of romance are tests of faith, courage, purity and human weakness for the sake of self-preservation.

(4) In addition, the romance gives the reader an engrossing story carefully told and endowed with exquisite poetry rich in artistic values. With predilection for irony and innuendo, the author tries to turn romances into an effective medium of teachings of moral virtues in which the humorous and the grotesque merges with the morally serious. Its language is simple and straightforward. This is the very enduring charm of romances through the ages.

(此题主要从《高文爵士与绿衣骑士》的写作风格和主题两方面来作答。)

第3章　杰弗里·乔叟

3.1　复习笔记

Geoffrey Chaucer(1340—1400)	杰弗里·乔叟(1340—1400)
1. Life Geoffrey Chaucer, born in or about 1343 in London, is the "father of English poetry" and one of the greatest narrative poets of England. Learned and proficient in Latin, French and Italian, Chaucer had a wide circle of acquaintances of both higher and lower station so that he was highly conscious of the workings of the world. This is especially useful in his portrayal of English society. He died in 1400 and was buried in Westminster Abbey, thus founding the "Poets' Corner".	**1. 生平** 杰弗里·乔叟于1343年(或1343年左右)出生于伦敦，他被誉为"英国诗歌之父"，也是英国最伟大的叙事诗人之一。 乔叟知识渊博。他精通拉丁语、法语和意大利语。他结交广泛且易与人深交，无论是贵族还是贫民，因此他深谙所处世事。这尤其有益于他的作品中对英国社会的刻画。 他逝于1400年，被葬在威斯敏斯特教堂，由此建立了"诗人角"。
2. Literary Career and Influence Chaucer's literary career can be divided into three periods closely related to his life experiences, the first period consists of works translated from French; the second works adapted from the Italian, as *Troilus and Criseyde*, the third period *The Canterbury Tales*, which is purely English. Chaucer's poetry paved the way for the literature of English Renaissance. The metrical form in Chaucer's poems had constructive significance in the English tonico-syllabic verse. Moreover, the Cockney dialect which he made full use was the basis of the English literary language to which Chaucer made valuable contributions.	**2. 文学生平和影响** 乔叟的文学生平可划分为三个阶段，这三个阶段与其个人生活经历有关。第一阶段乔叟的作品主要是从法语翻译过来的，第二阶段则改编自意大利语，如《特洛伊罗斯与克瑞西达》。第三阶段包括《坎特伯雷故事集》，这是纯英语创作阶段。 乔叟的诗歌为英国文艺复兴的文学开辟了道路。他诗歌的格律体为英语韵脚韵律诗体奠定基础。此外，他充分使用的伦敦方言是英语文学语言的基础，因此乔叟又为英语文学语言的形成作出巨大贡献。
3. Chaucer's Language (1) Chaucer's language belongs to Middle English and is very graphic and accurate. He was a master of constructing pictures with words. His poems are among the most fluent in the English language. (2) He introduced various French rhyming stanzas, especially the heroic couplet, to England.	**3. 乔叟的语言** (1)乔叟的语言属于中古英语，非常形象准确。他是用语言构建图画的大师。他的诗歌位列最顺畅的英语中。 (2)他将法国的各种押韵诗节(尤其是英雄双韵体)介绍到英国。

(3) Chauncer is good at the terza rima, which makes his language a high style. No other poet can match this.	(3) 乔叟善于使用三行体，这种诗体使他的语言很高雅。这是其他诗人无法匹敌的。
4. Major Works *Troilus and Criseyde* *The Canterbury Tales* (1387—1400)	**4. 主要作品** 《特洛伊罗斯与克瑞西达》 《坎特伯雷故事集》(1387—1400)
5. Selected Work **◆*The Canterbury Tales* (1387—1400)**	**5. 选读作品** **◆《坎特伯雷故事集》(1387—1400)**
A. Main Plot Thirty pilgrims set off for the shrine of Saint Thomas Becket at Canterbury. When they met at the inn, they agreed that each should tell two tales on the way to Canterbury and two more on the way back. But instead of 120 tales, the text ends after 24 tales, covering all the major types of medieval literature. Each story corresponds to the identity of the narrator, who covers people of all classes, from warriors to monks to sinning monks, etc.	**A. 主要情节** 30名朝圣者前往坎特伯雷去朝拜托马斯·贝克特。他们在酒馆相见，于是决定每个人轮流讲故事，去时和返回时各讲两个。然而最后共有24个故事，但涵盖了中世纪文学的各个方面。每个故事都与讲述者的身份相符，讲述者包罗各种阶层的人，有武士、僧侣、赦罪僧等。
B. Important Parts (1) "The Prologue": The Prologue provides a framework for the tales. The pilgrims in the Prologue included all but the royal family and the lowliest peasants in the feudal society of England. (2) "The Wife of Bath": The reader can savor Chaucer's unparalleled talent for nuanced characterization through his famous "The Wife of Bath". The heroine is the owner of a cloth factory, lighthearted, cheerful, sometimes vulgar, and very talkative. She relates the whole story of her married life. She has been married five times and wants to marry once more. Through these experiences, she has learned to control her husbands by using her body to support herself in a world where women lacked economic independence and authority. Through this Bath woman, we can understand the middle class women and their family life at that time.	**B. 重要部分** (1)《总序》:《总序》提供了故事的框架。《总序》的朝圣者中囊括了当时英国封建社会中除了皇族和最底层的农民以外的形形色色的人物。 (2)《巴斯妇人》：通过《巴斯妇人》，读者可以尽情感受乔叟细致入微的无人可比的人物塑造天赋。这位妇人是布店的经营者，为人开朗乐观，有时略带粗俗，喜欢讲话。她有五段婚史，并且还希望更多。通过这些经历，她学会了利用自己的身体来控制丈夫，从而在这个妇女几乎没有独立和权力的社会中供养自己。 通过这位巴斯妇人，我们能够了解当时中层阶级的妇女及其家庭生活。
C. Social Significances (1) It shows a true-to-life picture of Chaucer's time. (2) Chaucer opposes the dogma of asceticism preached by the Church and believes man's right to earthly happiness.	**C. 社会影响** (1) 展示乔叟时代的真实生活画面。 (2) 乔叟反对教会宣扬的禁欲主义，并且相信人们追求世俗幸福的权利。

(3) He praises man's dynamism, wisdom, resources and love of life. (4) His tales expose and satirize the evils of his time, attack degeneration of the noble, and the corruption of the Church.	(3) 他赞扬了人的力量、智慧和对生活的热爱。 (4) 他的故事展现并批判了时代的罪恶，批判了贵族和教会的堕落。

3.2 考研真题与典型题详解

Ⅰ. Fill in the blanks.

1. The English great writer Geoffrey Chaucer was born in 1343 and died in 1400. His most important work is __________, a long poem made up of a general introduction and 24 stories. (南开大学 2007 研)
2. __________ is Chaucer's longest complete poem (about 8,000 lines) and his greatest artistic achievement.
3. *The Canterbury Tales* is Chaucer's greatest work and the greater part of it was written in __________ couplets.
4. In the 14th century, the two most important writers are __________ and Langland.
5. Chaucer's work __________ gives us a picture of the condition of English life of his day, such as its work and play, its deeds and dreams, its fun and sympathy.
6. Critics tend to divide Chaucer's literary career into three periods: the __________ period, the __________ period and the __________ period.
7. When Chaucer died on the 25th of October 1400, he was the first to be buried in __________.

Ⅱ. Explain the following term.

heroic couplet (人大 2006 研；厦门大学 2007 研；北航 2010 研)

Ⅲ. Read the following quotation and answer the questions.

Questions 1 to 3 are based on the following passage of *The Canterbury Tales*. (南开大学 2009 研)

Speaking of his equipment, he (the knight) possessed
Fine horses, but he was not gaily dressed.
He wore a fustian tunic stained and dark
With smudges where his armor had left mark.

1. What does the fact that the knight owns fine horses indicate?
2. What does the clothes he wears indicate?
3. What does Geoffrey Chaucer want to show through these details?

Ⅳ. Short answer questions

1. Why is the Knight first in the General Prologue to tell a tale in *The Canterbury Tales*? (北航 2009 研)
2. What is Chaucer's contribution to the English language?

Ⅴ. Essay question

How did Chaucer's creative work reflect the changes of the English society in the second half of the 14th century? How much was Chaucer influenced by foreign authors such as Dante or Boccaccio?

What are some of the significances of such influences? (人大 2007 研)

参考答案及解析

Ⅰ. Fill in the blanks.

1. *The Canterbury Tales*

（乔叟的代表作是《坎特伯雷故事集》，是一首由一篇序言和 24 个故事组成的长诗。）

2. *Troilus and Criseyde*

（《特洛伊罗斯与克瑞西达》是乔叟最长的一首完整诗篇，长达 8000 多行。）

3. heroic

（《坎特伯雷故事集》大部分采用的是英雄双韵体。）

4. Geoffrey Chaucer

（乔叟和朗格兰是英国 14 世纪两位最重要的作家。）

5. *The Canterbury Tales*

（在《坎特伯雷故事集》中，乔叟淋漓尽致地揭露了宗教的腐败，贵族的骄奢以及当时社会的其他丑恶现象，同时也表达了他的人文主义思想。）

6. French, Italian, English

（乔叟的诗歌创作分为三个时期：①法国影响时期(1359—1372)：主要翻译并仿效法国诗人的作品。②意大利影响时期(1372—1386)：诗人接触了资产阶级人文主义的进步思想。③英语时期(1386—1400)：乔叟在这最后 15 年里从事《坎特伯雷故事集》的创作。）

7. Westminster Abbey

（乔叟死后被葬在威斯敏特教堂，从此威斯敏特教堂的一角便成为大诗人安息的“诗人角”。）

Ⅱ. Explain the following term.

heroic couplet: As a traditional form for English poetry and usually used for epic and narrative poetry, a heroic couplet refers to poems composed with a sequence of masculinely rhyming pairs of iambic pentameter lines. Such a form is best presented by Geoffrey Chaucer in *The Legend of Good Women* and *The Canterbury Tales* and later perfected by John Dryden in the Restoration Age.

Ⅲ. Read the following quotation and answer the questions.

1. The fact indicates that the knight echoes with a real knight and the ideal of a medieval Christian warrior.
2. The knight “wears a fustian tunic stained and dark with smudges”, suggesting that he has recently returned from an expedition.
3. These details imply that the knight is valiant, resourceful, pious and cautious. The Knight rides at the front of the procession described in the “General Prologue” whose his story appears first in the sequence. The Host clearly admires the Knight, so does the narrator.

Ⅳ. Short answer questions

1. Before the author gives an introduction of the pilgrims, he judges each person by their identity, opinions and arriving sequence. At that time, characters of the higher station are briefly represented by the Knight and his Squire, meaning that the Knight enjoys the highest status among them. Their nobility lies in their bravery in battles and loyalty to one woman. The Knight tells his tragic

love story which was thought highly of by people at that time. So, the Knight is the first to tell a tale, indicating a class-conscious society.

Secondly, according to Chaucer's description, the Knight is in the front of the others.

2. (1) Chaucer's language is arresting, intelligible, and concise.

(2) He introduced from France the "heroic couplet" to English poetry.

(3) With good command of French and Italian literary modes, Chaucer is the first important poet to write in the current English language. His poetic creation has vital influence on raising the status of English as the literary language of the country.

V. Essay question

(1) At that time, the feudal system had already begun to crumble. For the first time in English literature, the medieval English society was displayed to the reading public with an authentic taste and various true-to-life characters. For instance, his masterpiece *The Canterbury Tales* is a collection of stories narrated by a group of pilgrims of different identities on their journey to Canterbury. Chaucer gave a colorful characterization and truthful revelation of his society.

(2) Chaucer had received much inspiration from Dante and Boccaccio in terms of not only poetic form and content but also world value. Due to such influence, his literary creation boasted a fast period of maturation evident in *The House of Fame* and *Troilus and Criseyde*. Chaucer mainly wrote three longer poems using the heroic stanza of seven lines. On the same side of the new citizenship, Chaucer stayed positive towards love and individual happiness and against feudalism and religious abstinence.

(3) Chaucer's poetry paved way for English literature of the Renaissance period. Chaucer's poetry was prominent given its maturity, vivid characterization, and truthful presentation of human relations. His poetic creation of rhyming contributed to the English tonico-syllabic verse and had a huge impact on the London dialect.

第4章 大众民谣

4.1 复习笔记

Popular Ballads	大众民谣
1. Characteristics	**1. 特征**
(1) Ballads are oral narrative songs created and passed down by the English people.	(1) 民谣是英国人民大众创作并留存的口头吟唱的叙事歌曲。
(2) The English ballads were probably composed between 1200 and 1700 and were rarely published before the 18th century.	(2) 英国民谣很可能创作于1200至1700年间，18世纪前几乎没有出版过。
(3) A ballad usually consists of four lines in a stanza, with the second and fourth lines rhyming.	(3) 民谣通常由4行组成一节，其中第二和第四行押韵。
(4) There is a variety of ballads: historical, legendary, fantastical, lyrical and humorous.	(4) 民谣种类丰富，有历史的、传奇的、幻想的、抒情的，还有幽默的。
(5) Ballads about Robin Hood are the most important of that time.	(5) 关于罗宾汉的民谣是当时最重要的。
2. Major Works	**2. 主要作品**
◆The Robin Hood Ballads	**◆罗宾汉民谣**
A. Main Content of the Story	**A. 故事主要内容**
There are many versions of ballads about Robin Hood, but the main one is the story of Robin Hood and his companions fighting against oppressive forces, such as bishops, barons, etc.	罗宾汉民谣有很多版本与故事，但主要的就是侠盗罗宾汉与他的伙伴与某一压迫势力斗争的故事，比如主教、男爵等。
B. Analysis of Robin Hood	**B. 人物分析**
Robin Hood is a multi-faceted character: valiant, strong, resourceful, and at the same time caring and kind. He has bright eyes, good jokes and a hearty laugh. But the most important part of his personality is his hatred for cruel oppressors and his love for the poor oppressed.	罗宾汉是一个具有多面性的角色。他勇敢强壮并且机智，同时他又多情善良。他有双明亮的眼睛，爱开玩笑，笑声爽朗。但个性中最重要的就是他憎恨残暴的压迫者，热爱贫穷的被压迫者。
◆"Get Up and Bar the Door"	**◆《起来，去关门》**
"Get Up and Bar the Door" is a humorous ballad and presets a funny scene of domestic life. The story is mainly about the wife and husband's agreement that the one who began to speak first would get up and bar the door.	《起来，去关门》是一首典型的幽默民谣，展现了家庭生活中一个有趣的场景。故事主要是关于妻子和丈夫之间的一个约定：首先说话的人起来去关门。

◆***Sir Patrick Spens***	◆**《派屈克·斯宾塞爵士》**
Sir Patrick Spens is a tragic story. Sir Patrick Spens with his Scots were sent to sea by the king in the knowledge that there might be a storm, and died at in the sea.	《派屈克·斯宾塞爵士》是一个悲惨的故事。派屈克·斯宾塞爵士和他的苏格兰好儿郎接受了国王的任务，在明知可能会有风暴的情况下出海，最终葬身海底。

4.2 考研真题与典型题详解

Ⅰ. Fill in the blanks.

1. The fifteenth century has been traditionally described as the barren age in English literature. But it is the spring tide of English ________.
2. The ________ is an important stream of the British literature in the 15th century.
3. William Langland's ________ is written in the form of a dream vision.

Ⅱ. Explain the following term.

Ballad(Popular ballad)(厦门大学 2008 研；国际关系学院 2007 研)

Ⅲ. Short answer question

What are the artistic features of *Piers the Plowman*?

Ⅳ. Essay questions

1. State the social significance of William Langland's *Piers the Plowman*.
2. What is the most important department of English folk literature? And make comments on its most famous cycle: the Robin Hood Ballads.

参考答案及解析

Ⅰ. Fill in the blanks.

1. ballads

(15 世纪英国歌谣开始兴起。)

2. popular ballad

(大众民谣是英国 15 世纪重要的文学潮流。)

3. *Piers the Plowman*

(朗格兰的《农夫皮尔斯》通过一系列的梦境对当时英国社会进行了形象的描述。)

Ⅱ. Explain the following term.

Ballad (Popular ballad): ①a folk song or orally spread poem telling directly and dramatically popular stories often drawn from tragic events in history or previous legends. It has the quality of simplicity, impersonality, and vividity. ②Composed mostly in quatrains with alternating four-stress and three-stress lines, ballads have their the second lines rhyme with the fourth lines. Some ballads are in couplet form, while some others have six-line stanzas. ③Ballads were popular across Europe in the late Middle Ages but reached its utmost favor in Scotland since the 15th century down the road. Since the 18th century, educated poets not belonging to the folk-song tradition—notably Coleridge and Goethe—imitated such form and style. Coleridge's "*Rime of the Ancient Mariner*" is a typical example.

Ⅲ. Short answer question

Artistic features of *Piers the Plowman*: (1) *Piers the Plowman* is narrated in the form of a dream vision. (2) The author uses the device of allegory to relate truth through symbolism. (3) The poem satirizes the corruption of the ruling class, the ecclesiastical and the secular. (4) Alliteration is notable in this poem.

Ⅳ. Essay questions

(1) *Piers the Plowman* enjoyed wide popularity throughout the fourteenth century to the fifteenth century. Glorifying impoverished peasants and denouncing the evil of oppressors, it made vital contributions to arousing the revolutionary sentiment on the eve of the Rising of 1381 headed by Wat Tyler and John Ball.

(2) It offers a realistic depiction of medieval England. However, Piers could not count as a representative of poverty-stricken peasants as he is economically comfortable. He does not want to upset or overthrow the feudal society, but accepts the existing social hierarchy and workings. This is his limitation.

2. (1) The most important subsection of English folk literature is the ballad. A ballad is a folk song or orally spread poem telling directly and dramatically some popular stories often drawn from tragic events in history or previous legends. It has the quality of simplicity, impersonality, and vividity. Ballads are commonly treated as the entertaining literature for the commons, so they are intelligible and important for understanding people of the lower station in feudal society.

Ballads cover a wide range of subjects, such as the struggle of young lovers inflicted by their feudal-minded families, the dilemmas between love and wealth, the cruel and rippling effects of jealousy, critiques of the civil war, and class contradictions and their aftermath.

(2) Ballads about the adventures of Robin Hood are most famous. A courageous outcast and outlaw, Robin Hood is described as adept at archery and lives under the greenwood tree with his fellowmen, robbing the rich and assisting the poor, challenging bishops and archbishops, and constantly chased by sheriffs who always fail due to Robin Hood's resources.

The legend of Robin Hood and his fellowmen has its origin in the long-time struggle of peasants oppressed by landlords and the ruling class. Therefore, Robin Hood is a character combining historical and legendary quality.

The image of Robin Hood is multifaceted. Strong, valiant and resourceful, the tough man is also thoughtful and kindhearted. Nevertheless, the most significant feature of his personality is his deep hatred for cruel oppressors and pure love for the impoverished and the oppressed. In terms of religious faith, it seems that he is pious and an orthodox. Moreover, Robin Hood has great reverence for the king, who acts in the ballads as an intermediary between the outlaws and the authorities, as an amusing and thoughtful guest in the greenwood who feasts on his own stolen deer. Despite this, the Robin Hood ballads display fighting spirits, unyielding nerve, and revolutionary dynamism of the English peasantry.

(此题分两部分作答，第一部分主要分析什么是歌谣以及歌谣的写作主题；第二部分主要分析 Robin Hood Ballads 的主要内容，主题和 Robin Hood 的形象。)

第二部分　文艺复兴时期

第5章　威廉·莎士比亚

5.1　复习笔记

Ⅰ. Background Knowledge	**Ⅰ. 背景知识**
(1) England was in transition from feudalism to capitalism.	(1) 英国正处于从封建制度向资本主义制度过渡的阶段。
(2) At the beginning of the 16th century, absolute monarchy was established; during the reign of Queen Elizabeth Ⅰ, the system reached its peak.	(2) 16世纪初，君主专制政体建立，在女王伊丽莎白一世执政时达到巅峰。
(3) King Henry Ⅷ severed his relationship with the Pope and established himself as head of the Church of England, strengthening secular and religious power.	(3) 亨利八世与罗马教皇决裂，建立英国国教，并宣称自己是国教领袖，巩固了世俗和宗教权力。
(4) The gentry as a new nobility, and bourgeoisie as a new class came into being to support the monarchy.	(4) 新贵族和新兴资产阶级诞生，并且支持君主专制。
(5) England defeated the Spanish Invincible Armada and therefore achieved its dominance in world trade and on the high seas.	(5) 英国打败西班牙无敌舰队，确立了海上和国际贸易霸主地位。
(6) The conflict between the common people and the ruling classes became worse. There were lots of uprisings which were cruelly suppressed.	(6) 统治阶级与贫民的矛盾激化，发生了很多起义，但最后被无情镇压。
(7) The formation of English national state and the rise of bourgeois prompted a prosperous national culture known as the Renaissance. Humanists advocated classical literature and dedicated themselves to humans' emancipation from medieval ignorance.	(7) 新兴资产阶级地位上升和英国民族国家的形成促进了民族文化的繁荣，称之为文艺复兴。人文主义者推崇古典文学，为人类从中世纪宗教蒙昧中解放而奋斗。
Ⅱ. William Shakespeare (1564—1616)	**Ⅱ. 威廉·莎士比亚（1564—1616）**
1. Life	**1. 生平**
Renowned as the most famous playwright and poet, Shakespeare was born in Stratford-on-Avon on April 23, 1564. When he was 7, Shakespeare went to the local grammar school and learnt reading, writing, Latin and Greek there. Afterward, he became a local schoolmaster and grew familiar with theatrical performances. At the age of 18, Shakespeare married a farmer's daughter. After he moved to London, Shakespeare	莎士比亚是世界最著名的剧作家和诗人。1564年4月23日生于英格兰斯特拉福德的埃文河畔。7岁时他去了当地的文法学校，学习阅读、写作、拉丁语和希腊语。他成了当地的教师，并且渐渐熟知戏剧表演。莎士比亚18岁就和一个农夫的女儿结婚。他搬到伦敦后，和英格兰最好的剧院打过交道，做

had done business with the best theatres in England. He had became an actor, playwright and shareholder of a leading theatre. In 1612 Shakespeare returned home and purchased a house named New Palace. He died on April 23, which is his birthday, in 1616 and then was buried in Stratford Church.

过当时首屈一指的剧院的演员、剧作家和股东。1612 年，他回到家乡，买了一幢名为新宫的房子。他逝世于 1616 年 4 月 23 日，即他生日的那一天，并安葬在斯特拉特福德教堂。

2. A Chronological List of Shakespeare's Works

His literary career can be divided into three periods: the first from 1590 to 1600, the second from 1601 to 1608, and the last from 1609 to 1612.

2. 莎士比亚戏剧年表

莎士比亚的文学创作可分为三个主要阶段：第一阶段从 1590 年到 1600 年，第二阶段从 1601 年到 1608 年，第三阶段从 1609 年到 1612 年。

A. The First Period

1590 *Henry VI, Part II*
Henry VI, Part III
1591 *Henry VI, Part I*
1592 *Richard III*
The Comedy of Errors
1593 *Titus Andronicus*
The Taming of the Shrew
1594 *The Two Gentlemen of Verona*
Love's Labour's Lost
Romeo and Juliet
1595 *Richard II*
A Midsummer Night's Dream
1596 *King John*
The Merchant of Venice
1597 *Henry IV, Part I*
Henry IV, Part II
1598 *Much Ado about Nothing*
Henry V
The Merry Wives of Windsor
1599 *Julius Caesar*
As You Like It
1600 *Twelfth Night*

A. 第一阶段

1590 《亨利六世，第二部》
《亨利六世，第三部》
1591 《亨利六世，第一部》
1592 《理查德三世》
《错中错》
1593 《泰特斯·安特洛尼克斯》
《驯悍记》
1594 《维洛那二绅士》
《爱的徒劳》
《罗密欧与朱丽叶》
1595 《理查德二世》
《仲夏夜之梦》
1596 《约翰王》
《威尼斯商人》
1597 《亨利四世，第一部》
《亨利四世，第二部》
1598 《无事生非》
《亨利五世》
《温莎的风流娘们》
1599 《朱利尤斯·凯撒》
《皆大欢喜》
1600 《第十二夜》

B. The Second Period

1601 *Hamlet*
1602 *Troilus and Cressida*
All's Well That Ends Well
1604 *Measure for Measure*
Othello

B. 第二阶段

1601 《哈姆雷特》
1602 《特洛伊罗斯与克瑞西达》
《终成眷属》
1604 《一报还一报》
《奥赛罗》

1605 *King Lear*

Macbeth

1606 *Antony and Cleopatra*

1607 *Coriolanus*

Timon of Athens

1608 *Pericles*

C. The Third Period

1609 *Cymbeline*

1610 *The Winter's Tale*

1612 *The Tempest*

Henry VIII

Shakespeare had also written poems, *Venus and Adonis* (1593), *The Rape of Lucrece* (1954) and sonnets (1593—1598).

3. Selected Works

◆***Hamlet***

A. Main Plot

Hamlet, the main character, is a student at the University of Wittenberg and the prince of Denmark. The play begins with the death of Hamlet's father King Hamlet and Hamlet's mother Queen Gertrude's remarrying Hamlet's uncle Claudius, the new king. Hamlet is dismal, miserable and cynical. He hates his uncle and despises his mother for her new marriage. When Hamlet's father appears as a ghost and informs him that he has been killed by Claudius, Hamlet determined to avenge the murder of his father. During that mission, he accidentally kills Polonius, the father of Ophelia who is Hamlet's lover. After her father's death, Ophelia broke down and then drowned herself. Ophelia's death induces her brother Laertes' detesting Hamlet. In the duel between the two men, Laertes wound Hamlet when injured by the same weapon, which is poisoned by Claudius. Hamlet before his dying stabs Claudius and the queen drinks the poisoned wine made for Hamlet.

B. Analysis of Hamlet

Hamlet is wise, well-bred and shrewd. Although he's a scholar, Hamlet is courageous and reckless in action. As a

1605《李尔王》

《麦克白》

1606《安东尼与克里奥佩特拉》

1607《科利奥兰纳斯》

《雅典的泰门》

1608《佩力克尔斯》

C. 第三阶段

1609《辛白林》

1610《冬天的故事》

1612《暴风雨》

《亨利八世》

莎士比亚也写了诗歌，有《维纳斯与阿多尼斯》《鲁克丽丝受辱记》和十四行诗。

3. 选读作品

◆**《哈姆雷特》**

A. 主要情节

该剧主人公哈姆雷特是丹麦王子，威登堡大学生。戏剧开端，哈姆雷特的父亲丹麦国王刚刚逝世，他的母亲格特鲁德皇后嫁给哈姆雷特的叔叔，新任国王克劳狄斯。哈姆雷特悲痛不已、愤世嫉俗，憎恨他的叔叔，厌恶他的母亲。当父亲的鬼魂出现，告诉他自己是被克劳狄斯害死时，哈姆雷特一直想着要为父报仇。在复仇过程中，他误杀波隆尼尔，欧菲莉亚的父亲。欧菲莉亚是哈姆雷特的情人，她因父亲的死精神失常，最后溺水身亡。这引起了欧菲莉亚的哥哥雷尔提对哈姆雷特的仇恨。在两人的对决中，雷尔提用有毒的武器刺伤哈姆雷特，雷尔提自己也被同样的武器所伤。武器上的毒是克劳狄斯作为。哈姆雷特临死之际用力刺向国王，王后也喝下了克劳狄斯准备给哈姆雷特喝的毒酒。

B. 哈姆雷特人物分析

哈姆雷特是一个拥有智慧和教养，观察力敏锐的英杰。虽然身为

humanist, he doesn't hold medieval prejudices and feudal fetters. Hamlet loves good and detests evil. He cares for human beings themselves regardless of rank and wealth. He observes men and manners closely and sees through people.

Hamlet's most noticeable feature is melancholy. Revenge is in itself easy, yet Hamlet seeks more than that. It is more important for him to expose the evil in the world and to establish a just society. Therefore, his responsibility extends to a transformation of society, which has led to his melancholy and his delay in revenge.

◆*The Merchant of Venice*

A. Main Plot

Bassanio asks his friend Antonio for money in to pursue a beautiful rich woman Portia so that he can become wealthy and pay his debts. Antonio, however, has no funds at hand so he has to borrow 3000 ducats from Shylock who is a rich Jewish usurer. Shylock actually hates Antonio because the latter offers interest-free loans. Antonio accepts the agreement that if he couldn't return the loan in due course, Shylock would be able to get a pound of Antonio's own flesh. In Belmont, Bassanio picked the right lead casket and wins Portia's heart. When he hears that Antonio is not able to pay Shylock back, Bassanio returns and tries to help Antonio.

Shylock insists to exercise his right and then a trial is called. In the disguise of a law clerk, Portia impedes Shylock and claims that he must get his Antonio's flesh without causing him to bleed. Then Portia proclaims that Shylock is guilty of scheming against a Venetian citizen's life. In the end, the duke saves Shylock's life and he merely takes a fine instead of confiscating Shylock's property. Meanwhile Antonio agrees to forsake his half of Shylock's wealth as long as he promises two things. First, Shylock must convert to Christianity. Second, he must grant his entire estate to Lorenzo and Jessica after his death. So Shylock agrees and leaves. Then Nerissa and Portia make peace with their husbands. Antonio's ships also safely come back.

学者，但他行事冲动且毫无畏惧。他是位人文主义者，从中世纪的偏见和封建束缚中解放出来。他爱憎分明，关心人本身，不论贫穷贵贱。他对人事观察仔细，能够看透人心。

他最明显的性格特征是忧郁。当决心开始复仇后，他认识到重要的不只是复仇，怎样揭露现世的丑陋并建立公正的社会才是关键。因此他的责任上升到改造社会。这是他行动迟疑，表现忧郁的主要原因。

◆《威尼斯商人》

A. 主要情节

巴萨尼奥向他的好友安东尼奥借钱，去追求一个美丽富有的小姐鲍西亚，从而还清自己的债务，获得财富。可是安东尼奥没有闲钱在手，他只好向一个犹太人夏洛克借3000达克特高利贷。夏洛克十分痛恨安东尼奥，因为他借给别人钱不收利息。安东尼奥答应了夏洛克的条件，如果他期满时无法还清贷款，夏洛克就可以割去他身上一磅肉。在贝尔蒙特，巴萨尼奥选对了铅匣子，赢得了鲍西亚的爱。当他们听说安东尼奥无法偿还贷款时，巴萨尼奥赶回来试图解救安东尼奥。

夏洛克执意要割肉，因此一场审判来临。鲍西亚此时伪装成一个律师伙计，在法庭上狡辩说夏洛克割肉时不得使安东尼奥流一滴血。她又声称夏洛克因企图谋害一个威尼斯公民的生命而有罪。最终公爵赦免了夏洛克，并处罚金，而非没收财产。安东尼奥也愿放弃夏洛克的一半财产，只要他转信基督教，并在死后将全部财产给洛伦佐和杰西卡。夏洛克同意并离开了。之后鲍西亚和娜丽莎跟各自的丈夫和解，安东尼奥的船也平安返回。

B. Character Analysis As one of Shakespeare's ideal women, Portia is pretty, well-bred, courteous and she can deal with an emergency calmly. Also very powerful is the image of Shylock. Apart from being a greedy money-lender, he is pride Jew who has deep religious instincts. His detestable bond is a gesture of resisting Antonio's arrogant treatment of him. In that sense, his powerful protest against racial discrimination should not be ignored.	**B. 人物分析** 鲍西亚是莎士比亚剧中理想女性之一，她美丽，有修养，礼貌谦恭，并且在危急时刻能沉着应对。夏洛克的人物形象也很丰满。夏洛克除了是一个贪婪的借贷者外，他还是一个有自尊和深厚宗教本能的犹太人。他令人嗤鼻的合同是对安东尼奥傲慢无礼的反抗。所以他对种族歧视的高声抗议是不容忽视的。
◆Shakespeare's *Sonnets* The collection comprises 154 sonnets, generally thought to be composed between 1593 and 1599. The sonnets may be divided into three groups: number 1—17 focus on one theme. The poet persuades a handsome young man to marry and have children who will preserve his beauty, because otherwise he will lose it as he becomes old; number 18—126 are of different themes connected with a handsome young man (who is very much likely the youth of number 1—17). The poet cherishes his friendship with him and is promises to grant immortality to the young man by writing poems in his honor. The rest of the poems center around a married woman with black hair and dark complexion, whom the poet is attracted to, although he is very aware of her faults.	**◆莎士比亚《十四行诗集》** 诗集包括 154 首十四行诗，多被认为写于 1593—1599 年间。 这些诗按主题可分为三类：前 17 首是规劝一位美少年尽早结婚产生后代，来延续他的美丽，因为随着年龄增长，他的美丽会日渐消退。第 18—126 首的写作对象很可能与前 17 首相同。诗人非常珍视两人之间的友情，并且承诺要用自己的诗歌来赋予少年永生。其余诗歌描写一位黑头发黑皮肤的已婚妇女，尽管了解她的不足，诗人还是被她吸引。

5.2 考研真题与典型题详解

Ⅰ. Fill in the blanks.

1. Shakespeare's authentic non-dramatic poetry consists of two ________ and 154 ________.（国际关系学院 2009 研）
2. Cordelia is a character in ________.（大连外国语学院 2007 研）
3. ________, ________, ________, and ________ are generally regarded as Shakespeare's four great tragedies.（南开大学 2007 研）
4. Shakespeare's plays have been traditionally divided into four categories according to dramatic type: histories, ________, tragedies and ________.
5. The principal idea of Shakespeare's historical plays is the necessity for ________ under one king. These ideas were of vital interest to the Elizabethan audience.
6. William Shakespeare has been universally acknowledged to be the summit of the English Renaissance.

And of his great tragedies, __________ is considered the summit of his art.（暨南大学 2018 研）

7. "Sometime too hot the eye of heaven shines" is a line taken from "Sonnet 18" by William Shakespeare. The underlined phrase refers to __________.（首师大 2008 研）

8. Author __________ Title __________（南京大学 2008 研）

    The brightness of her cheek would shame those stars
    As daylight doth a lamp; her eyes in heaven
    Would through the airy region stream so bright
    That birds would sing and think it were not night.

9. "Hath not a Jew eyes? Hath not a Jew hands, organs, dimensions, senses, affections? Fed with the same food, hurt with the same weapons, subject to the same diseases, healed by the same means, warmed and cooled by the same winter and summer, as a Christian is?"
   The speaker is __________.（天津外国语 2013 研）

10. To what period does the following extract, poetical or prose, belong? If possible, name the author.（北师大 2007 研）

    To be, or not to be—that is the question:
    Whether 'tis nobler in the mind to suffer
    The slings and arrows of outrageous fortune
    Or to take arms against a sea of troubles.
    And by opposing end them. To die—to sleep—
    No more: and by a sleep to say we end
    The heartache, and the thousand natural shocks
    That flesh is heir to. 'Tis a consummation
    Devoutly to be wish'd. To die—to sleep.
    To sleep—perchance to dream: ay, there's the rub!

Ⅱ. Multiple Choices

1. Which of the following plays does NOT belong to Shakespeare's comedies?
   A. *Henry V*　　B. *The Merchant of Venice*
   C. *A Midsummer Night's Dream*　　D. *The Winter Tale*

2. Among the following plays, __________ is NOT written by William Shakespeare?（首师大 2009 研）
   A. *Richard II*　　B. *The Tempest*
   C. *The Winter's Tale*　　D. *Lady Windermere's Fan*

3. The author of the following sonnet is __________.（大连外国语 2007 研）
   A. William Shakespeare　　B. Geoffrey Chaucer
   C. John Donne　　D. Herbert Spencer

    When in disgrace with fortune and men's eyes,
    I all alone beweep my outcast state,
    And trouble deaf Heaven with my bootless cries,
    And look upon myself, and curse my fate,
    Wishing me like to one more rich in hope,

Featured like him, like him with friends possessed,
Desiring this man's art, and that man's scope,
With what I most enjoy contented least:
Yet in these thoughts myself almost despising,
Haply I think on thee, and then my state
Like to the lark at break of day arising
From sullen earth, sings hymns at heaven's gate;
For thy sweet love remembered, such wealth brings
That then I scorn to change my state with kings.

4. The Elizabethan age in the history of British literature represents the glory of the English theater. The greatest playwright produced in this age is ________. (天津外国语 2007 研)
   A. William Shakespeare　　B. Edmund Spencer
   C. Philip Sydney　　D. Christopher Marlowe
5. The Age of William Shakespeare is also called the second period of ________. (北二外 2008 研)
   A. Elizabethan Period　　B. Victorian Period
   C. English Renaissance　　D. James Period
6. "Shall I compare thee to a summer's day?" This is the beginning line of one of Shakespeare's ________.
   A. songs　　B. plays　　C. comedies　　D sonnets
7. With the performance of ________ in 1613, which caused the burning of the Global Theatre by the firing of the cannon at the end of Act Ⅰ, ended Shakespeare's dramatic career.
   A. *Measure for Measure*　　B. *Antony and Cleopatra*
   C. *Coriolanus*　　D. *Henry VIII*
8. "Denmark is a prison". In which play does the hero summarize his observation of his world into such a bitter sentence?
   A. *Charles I*　　B. *Othello*　　C. *Henry VIII*　　D. *Hamlet*
9. Which of the following statements best illustrates the theme of Shakespeare's "Sonnet 18"?
   A. The speaker eulogizes the power of Nature.
   B. The speaker satirizes human vanity.
   C. The speaker praises the power of artistic creation.
   D. The speaker meditates on man's salvation.
10. The works of ________ and the Authorized Version of the English Bible are the two great treasuries of the English language.
   A. Geoffrey Chaucer　　B. Edmund Spenser
   C. William Shakespeare　　D. Ben Johnson

Ⅲ. Explain the following terms.

1. Renaissance literature (人大 2006 研)
2. Tragedy (天津外国语学院 2008 研; 厦门大学 2009 研)
3. Sonnet (南开大学 2010 研)

Ⅳ. Read the following quotations and answer the questions.

Passage 1（北航 2009 研）

To be, or not to be—that is the question
Whether this nobler in the mind to suffer
The slings and arrows of outrageous fortune
Or to take arms against a sea of troubles
And by opposing end them. To die, to sleep—
No more...

Questions:

(1) From which play are these lines taken from?

(2) Who is the playwright?

(3) Who is the speaker?

(4) What does this speech show?

Passage 2

Identify each of the following quotations by giving the title of the work and the full name of the author, and explain the implications of the underlined parts. （人大 2007 研）

Make room, and let him stand before our face.
The world thinks, and I think so too,
That thou but <u>lead'st this fashion of thy malice</u>
To the last hour of act; and then, 'tis thought,
Thou'lt show thy mercy and remorse, more strange
Than is thy strange apparent cruelty;
And where thou now exacts the penalty,
Which is a pound of this poor merchant's flesh,
Thou wilt not only loose the forfeiture,
But, toucht with human gentleness and love,
Forgive a <u>moiety</u> of the principal,
Glancing an eye of pity on his losses,
That have of late so huddled on his back
<u>Enow</u> to press a royal merchant down,
And pluck commiseration of his state
From brassy bosoms and rough hearts of flint,
From stubborn Turks and Tartars, never train'd
To offices of tender courtesy.

Ⅴ. Short answer questions

1. What are the unique features of Shakespeare's sonnets?
2. Make comments on the heroines in William Shakespeare's comedies.
3. What is the central theme revealed by the conflict between the group of Christians such as Antonio, Bassanio, Portia, and the others, and the Jew Shylock in Shakespeare's comedy *The Merchant of Venice*? On which side, Antonio's or Shylock's, does Shakespeare stand and why? And

what is the progressive significance of the play?（人大 2003 研）

Ⅵ. Essay questions

1. What gives Shakespeare the unwavering reputation for greatness in age after age?
2. In Shakespeare's *Hamlet*, the tragic hero Hamlet seems to be delaying his revenge. Why? Please give your explanations by in-depth analysis with textual evidences.（北航 2012 研）

参考答案及解析

Ⅰ. Fill in the blanks.

1. long poems; sonnets

   （莎士比亚的作品除了戏剧之外，还包括两首长诗(*Venus and Adonis* 及 *The Rape of Lucrece*)和 154 首十四行诗。）
2. *King Lear*

   （Cordelia 是莎士比亚著名悲剧《李尔王》中李尔王最小的女儿。）
3. *Hamlet*, *Macbeth*, *Othello*, *King Lear*

   （莎士比亚的四大悲剧是《哈姆雷特》《麦克白》《奥赛罗》和《李尔王》。）
4. comedies; romances

   （莎士比亚的戏剧主要可以分为四种：历史剧，喜剧，悲剧和传奇剧。）
5. national unity

   （莎士比亚历史剧的一个主要观点就是国王应当维护国家统一，《李尔王》是一个很好的例证。）
6. *Hamlet*

   （《哈姆雷特》是莎士比亚所有戏剧中篇幅最长的一部，也是莎士比亚最负盛名的剧本，具有深刻的悲剧意义、复杂的人物性格以及丰富完美的悲剧艺术手法，代表着整个西方文艺复兴时期文学的最高成就。）
7. the sun

   （“天空的眼睛”指的是太阳。此句意为：有时候阳光过于炽烈。）
8. Author: William Shakespeare　　Title: *Romeo and Juliet*

   （题目节选自莎士比亚的 *Romeo and Juliet* 中 Act Ⅱ scene 2。题中诗句译文为：她脸庞的光辉，可使群星羞愧。/就像阳光可使灯光失色一般。/她的眼眸从天空穿过大气 /流泻出光亮，鸟儿们会以为夜已尽而开始歌唱。）
9. Shylock in *The Merchant of Venice*

   （题中的选段是莎士比亚著名作品《威尼斯商人》中的片段。）
10. English Renaissance; William Shakespeare

    （这段文章选自莎士比亚的《哈姆雷特》，莎士比亚是英国文艺复兴时期最杰出的艺术大师。译文：生存还是毁灭，这是个值得考虑的问题：默然忍受命运暴虐的毒箭，或是挺身反抗人世无涯的苦难，通过斗争把他们扫清，这两种行为，哪一种更高贵？死了，睡着了，什么都完了。倘若在这一种睡眠之中，我们心头的创痛，以及其他无数血肉之躯所不能避免的打击，都可以从此消失，这正是我们求之不得的结局。死了，睡着了，睡着了也许还会做梦。嗯，阻碍就在这！）

Ⅱ. Multiple Choices

1. A 《亨利五世》是莎士比亚的历史剧，不属于喜剧的范畴。
2. D *Lady Windermere's Fan*(《温德米尔夫人的扇子》)的作者是 Oscar Wilde(奥斯卡·王尔德)，其余都是莎士比亚的剧作。
3. A 题中诗句是莎士比亚的十四行诗中的第二十九首，诗中热烈地歌颂了爱情，诗歌的译文为：当我受尽命运和人们的白眼，/暗暗地哀悼自己的身世飘零，/徒用呼吁去干扰聋聩的昊天，/顾盼着身影，诅咒自己的生辰，/愿我和另一个一样富于希望，/面貌相似，又和他一样广交游，/希求这人的渊博，那人的内行，/最赏心的乐事觉得最不对头；/可是，当我正要这样看轻自己，/忽然想起了你，于是我的精神，/便像云雀破晓从阴霾的大地/振翮上升，高唱着圣歌在天门：/一想起你的爱使我那么富有，/和帝王换位我也不屑于屈就。
4. A 伊丽莎白时代最杰出的剧作家是莎士比亚。
5. C 伊丽莎白一世在位的 45 年(从 1558 到 1603 年)被认为是英国的黄金时代；维多利亚在位的 64 年(从 1837 年到 1901 年)是“日不落帝国”时期；詹姆士一世从 1603 到 1625 年在位。英国的文艺复兴主要包括伊丽莎白时代和詹姆士一世统治时期，前期的代表人物主要是斯宾塞、锡德尼和大学才子派等，莎士比亚则是把英国文艺复兴推向高潮的人物。
6. D “Shall I compare thee to a summer's day?”是莎士比亚十四行诗第 18 首的开头。
7. D 1613 年在上演《亨利八世》时剧院失火，莎士比亚的戏剧生涯也告结束。
8. D 《哈姆雷特》是莎士比亚著名的四大悲剧之一，丹麦王子哈姆雷特目睹了国家统治阶级的残暴与黑暗，人民生活在水深火热之中，由此感慨道：“丹麦就是一座监狱。”
9. C 在第 18 首十四行诗中，莎士比亚赞美了艺术作品的不朽力量。
10. C 莎士比亚的作品中用词量大，广泛采用民间语言(如民谣、俚语、古谚语和滑稽幽默的散文等)，注意吸收外来词，还大量运用比喻、隐喻、双关语，可谓集当时英语之大成。钦定版《圣经》编纂，使《圣经》成为渗透到英国各阶层的一种真正普遍性的读写文字，英语能成为当今世界最通用的语言亦是奠基于此。

Ⅲ. Explain the following terms.

1. Renaissance literature: Renaissance literature refers to a new tradition running from Petrarch and Boccaccio in Italy to Jonson and Milton in England, embracing the work of the French Pleiade and of Sidney, Spenser and Shakespeare, marked by a new self-confidence in vernacular literatures, a flourishing of lyric poetry, and a revival of such classical forms as epic and pastoral literature.
2. Tragedy: A tragedy is a story that presents courageous individuals who confront powerful forces within or outside themselves with a dignity that reveals the breadth and depth of the human spirit in the face of failure, defeat, and even death. Tragedies recount an individual's downfall; they usually begin high and end low. Shakespeare is known for his tragedies, including *Macbeth*, *King Lear*, *Othello* and *Hamlet*.
3. Sonnet: (1) A lyric poem consisting of a single stanza of fourteen iambic pentameter lines linked by an intricate rhyme scheme. (2) There are two major patterns of rhyme in sonnets written in the English language: ① The Italian or Petrarchan sonnet(named after the fourteenth century Italian poet Petrarch) falls into two main parts: an octave(eight lines) rhyming *abbaabba* fol-

lowed by a sestet (six lines) rhyming *cdecde* or some variant, such as *cdccdc*. ② Shakespearean sonnet. This sonnet falls into three quatrains and a concluding couplet: *abab cdcd efef gg*. There was one notable variant, the Spenserian sonnet, in which Edmund Spenser linked each quatrain to the next by a continuing rhyme: *abab bcbc cdcd ee*.

Ⅳ. Read the following quotations and answer the questions.

Passage 1

(1) *Hamlet*

(2) William Shakespeare

(3) Hamlet

(4) In this famous monologue, Hamlet, facing the dilemma of action and mind, is hesitating whether he should revenge for his father, which may bring him death, or he should suffer and hide his hatred for his uncle in his deep heart, which may secure his life.

Passage 2

The Merchant of Venice by William Shakespeare

"lead'st this fashion of thy malice": pretend to hate. Here it implies that the Duke hopes they will persuade Shylock to give up his original thought through saying that Shylock is kind and does not want to hurt others in his inner heart.

"moiety": a half of his property. Here it implies Shylock is so kind in the Duke's mouth.

"Enow": enough. Here it implies Duke's sympathy to Bassanio.

(译文：大家让开些，让他站在我的面前。(夏洛克)人家都以为——我也是这样想——你不过故意装出这一副凶恶的姿态，到了最后关头，就会显出你的仁慈恻隐来，比你现在这种表面上的残酷更加出人意料；现在你虽然坚持着照约处罚，一定要从这个不幸的商人身上割下一磅肉来，到了那时候，你不但愿意放弃这一种处罚，而且因为受到良心上的感动，说不定还会豁免他一部分的欠款，你看他最近接连遭逢的巨大损失，足以使无论怎样富有的商人倾家荡产，即使铁石一样的心肠，从来不知道人类同情的野蛮人，也不能不对他的境遇发生怜悯。)

Ⅴ. Short answer questions

1. (1) The Shakespearean sonnet comprises three quatrains and a final couplet, rhyming ababcdcdefefgg.

   (2) It is obvious that Shakespeare wrote his sonnets partly in conformity with the popular vogue, but we must admit also that in some of them he revealed his innermost thoughts and feelings, made topical allusions to certain contemporary events and to his own life, and above all, divulged a few of his rare comments on social evils of his time.

   (3) Generally speaking, in these sonnets, Shakespeare exalted friendship and love, sang the praises of youth and beauty, but since the numerous pieces must have been composed on different occasions, it is quite natural that they were expressions of vastly different moods and thoughts of different moments and their artistic worth was not of the same level.

2. (1) In William Shakespeare's comedies we find an expression of his ungrudging, equalitarian attitude toward women. These plays show, in different ways, William Shakespeare's respect for the dignity, honesty, wit, courage, determination and resourcefulness of women. Though there are

weariness and frailty sometimes, they never lose courage in time of danger. Portia in *The Merchant of Venice* is a best example. Portia is a woman of the Renaissance, beautiful, prudent, cultured, courteous and capable of rising to an emergency.

(2)The young heroines in William Shakespeare's comedies are always independent in character and take their own way of life, such as Julia, in *The Two Gentlemen of Verona*, and Rosalind, the heroine of *As You Like It*. Heroines like these are no longer the women who, under the yoke of feudalism, cling about the neck of a father or a husband. They are able to defend themselves.

In all, William Shakespeare's heroines belong to a new type. They are witty, brave, independent, optimistic and faithful.

(此题主要从莎士比亚对女性的态度以及其创作的新女性形象的特点等方面作答。)

3. The conflict between Shylock and the Christian characters comes to a head over the issue of mercy. The other characters acknowledge that the law is on Shylock's side, but they all expect him to show mercy, which he refuses to do. Shakespeare stands by the Antonio's side. As is seen in the drama, he praises Antonio's sense of love and generosity, and he condemns Shylock's selfishness and cold-bloodiness. The progressive significance of the play is that it makes a contrast and comparison of the Christian and the Jew. Both of them have advantages and disadvantages. The Christian is generous and sympathetic, but he only shows his generosity and sympathy within his community, i. e. to other Christians, not the Jew. The Jew, despite his selfishness and sense of hatred, is pitiable, as he is looked down upon and not treated equally by the Christian.

Ⅵ. Essay questions

1. ①First of all, living in the transitional period of the rapid decline of feudalism and the steady rise of capitalism, Shakespeare showed much antipathy towards many evil practices. And there is also the intense sympathy that his work conveys for people of every type and class, from the most exalted monarch to the humblest gravedigger or porter.

② He was a consummate artist in playwriting and in poetry. He created a whole gallery of vivid, lifelike characters. In his romantic comedies, there are many brilliant heroines of talent and ingenuity. In his history plays, he portrays his ideal king and the colorful Falstaff. In his early tragedies, Romeo and Juliet have become the celebrated as synonym for young, star-crossed lovers. And in his four great tragedies, his insuperable skill in portrayal reaches the summit in such renowned figures as Hamlet, Othello, etc.

③His most striking attainment in characterization is his ever-conscious emphasis on the psychological make-up of his major characters. His heroes and heroines not only do things and say things, but reveal to the audience and readers their thought. He uses soliloquies to show the thinking process of his characters.

④He also showed great craftsmanship in the management of plot in most of his plays. He took stories from many sources. The secrets of his success lies in his abilities to mould these borrowed source materials to the best advantages. He frequently employed dramatic irony. The use of disguise leads to mistaken identity and comic effects and pathos.

⑤He was a great poet, master of prose, and sonneteer. He has been regarded as the foremost poet and dramatist of England, and by some, of all Europe.

2. There are many reasons as to why Hamlet might be delaying the revenge.

One of Hamlet's many reasons could be that he is afraid of the consequence after killing. He worries that the killing will cause turbulence to his country. He can not decide to take such revenge. Also, Hamlet is quite religious , which can been seen in the prayer scene: "Now might I do it pat, now he is praying, and now I'll don't—and so goes to heaven, and am I reneged. That would be scanned. A villain kills my father, and for that, I his sole son do this same villain send to Heaven. " Hamlet fears the result of killing because he knows that if he kills Claudius while Claudius prays, Claudius will go to heaven, and Hamlet will have to suffer the sin of killing.

Another reason as to why Hamlet postponed the revenge, could be that he didn't want to hurt his mother Gertrude, especially after his father warned him not to hurt her in any way. "I will speak daggers to her but use non", this indicates Hamlet's protection over his mother—he will "speak in daggers", i. e. talk to her with a sharp tone, but "use non" to hurt his mother. It could be said that Hamlet didn't want to kill Claudius because he didn't want to see his mother suffer a loss of another loved one.

第6章　弗朗西斯·培根

6.1　复习笔记

Francis Bacon (1561—1626)

1. Life

Bacon was born in an aristocratic family. His father is Sir Nicholas Bacon, who was Keeper of the Privy Seal to Queen Elizabeth and an Ambassador to France. At 12, he began to study at Cambridge and he took up law after graduating at 16. Having finished his legal education, Bacon was called to the bar and became a member of the House of Commons at 23. During James I's reign, Bacon's position was promoted quickly and he was finally appointed as Lord High Chancellor, which was the head of the legal system of England. Meanwhile he became a peer with the titles of Viscount St Alban and Baron Verulam. Three years later, however, he was accused of bribery, then he lost his office and was exiled from London. He spent his last years on creating literary and philosophical works. Bacon was described by Alexander Pope as "the wisest, brightest, meanest of mankind".

2. Major Works

Bacon's works can be divided into three parts:

(1) Philosophical works—the most famous of which include the *Advancement of Learning* (1605), *Novum Organum* (1620), and *De Augmentis Scientiarum* (1623);

(2) Literary works—*Essays*;

(3) Professional works—the largest and most significant of which are the treaties named *Maxims of the Law* and *Reading on the Status of Uses*.

Of all his works, his essays are the most widely read. He constantly revised and added his essays until the final edition published in 1625, including 58 essays. His essays are quoted in textbooks as frequently as Shakespeare's plays.

弗朗西斯·培根（1561—1626）

1. 生平

培根出生于一个贵族家庭，其父为掌玺大臣尼古拉斯·培根爵士。他12岁就上剑桥大学，16岁毕业，然后从事法律事务。完成法律学习后，取得律师资格，23岁时成为众议院议员。在詹姆士一世统治时期，培根不断得到晋升，并最终被任命为大法官（英格兰法律体系的头领），同时还被晋封为维勒拉姆男爵、圣·阿本斯子爵。但是三年后他被控贿赂罪，丢了职务、被赶出伦敦。他晚年从事文学和哲学作品创作。蒲柏称他是“最聪明、最出色、最卑鄙的人”。

2. 主要作品

培根的作品可分为三类：

（1）哲学类——最著名的是《学术的进展》《新工具》《论学术的价值及其发展》；

（2）文学类——《随笔》；

（3）专业类——篇幅最长、作用最大的是《法律箴言》和《谈使用法则》。

在他的这些作品中，他的散文是被最广泛阅读的。他不断修改并增加散文，直至1625年出版的最后一版，已经包含了58篇散文。他的散文就像莎士比亚的戏剧一样经常被引用到课本中。

3. Selected Works	3. 选读作品
◆**"Of Truth"** "Of Truth" analyzes the reason of people's liking for lies, and then claims that truth is the superior virtue of human nature. Bacon quotes at the end of the essay the words of Montaigne to demonstrate: "If it be well weighed, to say that a man lieth is as much as to say that he is brave towards God and a coward towards men."	◆**《论真理》** 《论真理》首先分析了人们嗜好谎言的原因，然后表明真理是一种人性的最高美德。文章最后作者提到说谎是一种恶德，让人蒙羞，并引用了 Montaigne 的话加以说明："仔细考虑起来，要是说某人说谎就等于说他对上帝很大胆，对世人很怯懦"。
◆**"Of Studies"** "Of Studies" elaborates on the aim and functions of study, people's various views towards study and also different study methods. The essay features the employment of parallelism, the concise language and abundant wisdom.	◆**《论读书》** 《论读书》详细讨论了读书的目的和功能，世人对读书的不同态度，并介绍了读书的各种方法。文章的特点在于使用了排比的修辞手法，简练的语言以及充满了智慧。

6.2 考研真题与典型题详解

Ⅰ. Fill in the blanks.

1. The writings of Francis Bacon mainly fall into three categories: ________, purely literary and professional.
2. In Elizabethan Period, ________ wrote more than fifty excellent essays, which made him one of the best essayists in English literature.
3. "Of Youth and Age" is one of the essays written by ________.

Ⅱ. Multiple Choices

1. Which is not the intellectual energy of the English Renaissance showed itself in the achievement of Francis Bacon?
   A. The founder of English materialist philosophy.
   B. The founder of modern science in England.
   C. The first English essayist.
   D. The most gifted of the "university wits".
2. From the following, choose the one which is not Francis Bacon's work: ________.
   A. *Advancement of Learning*　　B. *The New Instrument*
   C. *Venus and Adonis*　　D. *The New Atlantics*
3. Francis Bacon, one of the most important British essayists, was active in the ________.（北二外 2010 研）
   A. Middle Age　　B. Anglo-Saxon Period
   C. English Renaissance　　D. Victoria Age
4. "Some books are to be tasted, others to be swallowed, and some few to be chewed and digested"

is one of the epigrams found in ________.

A. Francis Bacon's "Of Studies"
B. Thomas More's *Utopia*
C. John Bunyan's *The Pilgrim's Progress*
D. Henry Fielding's *Tom Jones*

Ⅲ. Explain the following terms.

1. Francis Bacon（四川大学 2011 研）

2. essay

Ⅳ. Read the following quotations and answer the questions.

Passage 1

Studies serve for delight, for ornament, and for ability. Their chief use for delight is in privateness and retiring; for ornament, is in discourse; and for ability, is in the judgment, and disposition of business. For expert men can execute, and perhaps judge of particulars, one by one; but the general counsels, and the plots and marshalling of affairs, come best, from those that are learned. To spend too much time in studies is sloth; to use them too much for ornament, is affectation; to make judgment wholly by their rules is the humor of a scholar. They perfect nature, and are perfected by experience; for natural abilities are like natural plants, that need proyning by study; and studies themselves do give forth directions too much at large, except they be bounded in by experience. Crafty men contemn studies, simple men admire them, and wise men use them, for they teach not their own use; but that is a wisdom without them, and above them, won by observation.

Questions:

(1) These words are taken from a famous essay written by ________.

(2) What is the title of this essay?

(3) What do you think of the language of this essay?

Passage 2

Identify the following quotation by giving the title of the work and the full name of the author, and explain the implications of the underlined parts.（人大 2004 研）

It will be acknowledged even by those that practice it not, that clear and round dealing is the honor of man's nature, and that mixture of falsehood is like alloy in coin of gold and silver, which may make the metal work the better, but it embaseth it. For these winding and crooked courses are the goings of the serpent; which goeth basely upon the belly, and not upon the feet. There is no vice that doth so cover a man with shame as to be found false and perfidious; and therefore Montaigne saith prettily, when he inquired the reason why the word of the lie should be such a disgrace, and such an odious charge, saith he, "If it be well weighed, to say that a man lieth is as much as to say that he is brave towards God and a coward towards men."

Ⅴ. Short answer question

What is the writing style of Francis Bacon's essays?

Ⅵ. Essay question

According to many critics, Francis Bacon is the father of the English essay while Charles Lamb, the Shakespeare of it. Make a comment the statement.（中山大学 2004 研）

参考答案及解析

Ⅰ. Fill in the blanks.

1. philosophical

（培根的著作可分为三类，即哲学类、文学类及专业类。）

2. Francis Bacon

（弗朗西斯·培根是伊丽莎白时代的散文家，一生创作了50多篇散文，1597年出版的《培根散文集》被认为是英国散文发展史的一座里程碑。）

3. Francis Bacon

（《论青年与老年》是弗朗西斯·培根创作的散文。）

Ⅱ. Multiple Choices

1. D 弗朗西斯·培根(1561—1626)，英国文艺复兴时期最重要的散作家、哲学家。他不但在文学、哲学上多有建树，在自然科学领域里，也取得了重大成就。他是英国唯物主义和现代科学的创始人；“大学才子派”是指16世纪80年代英国出现的一批受过大学教育的剧作家。这一批作家致力于英国戏剧改革，把戏剧艺术提升到了一个新高度。

2. C 《维纳斯与阿多尼斯》是莎士比亚所写的一首长诗。

3. C 弗朗西斯·培根是英国文艺复兴时期著名哲学家、思想家、作家和科学家。

4. A 选句选自培根的《论读书》。

Ⅲ. Explain the following terms.

1. Francis Bacon: Francis Bacon (1561—1626), was an English philosopher, statesman, scientist, lawyer, jurist, author and pioneer of the scientific method. He served both as Attorney General and Lord Chancellor of England. Although his political career ended in disgrace, he remained extremely influential through his works, especially as philosophical advocate and practitioner of the scientific method during the scientific revolution. His essays are famous for its brief and wise quotations and the most widely-read works are his essays "Of Studies", "Of Truth" and "Of Death".

2. essay: ① a short written composition in prose that discusses a subject or proposes an argument without claiming to be a complete or thorough exposition. A minor literary form, essay is more relaxed than the formal academic dissertation. ②The term was coined by French writer Michel de Montaigne in the title of his *Essais*, the first modern example of the form. Francis Bacon's *Essays* began the tradition of essays in English, of which important examples are those of Steele, Hazlitt, Emerson and D. H. Lawrence. The verse essays of Pope are rare exception to the prose norm.

Ⅳ. Read the following quotations and answer the questions.

Passage 1

(1) Francis Bacon

(2) "Of Studies"

(3) The language of this essay is known for its conciseness, brevity, simplicity and forcefulness. The sentences are short, pointed, incisive, and often of balanced structure.

Passage 2

"Of Truth", Francis Bacon.

"Round dealing" equals square dealing, which means honest and fair treatment.

"Embaseth" refers to "debases", which means making something or someone lose its value or people's respect. By taking the example of gold, silver and alloy, Bacon implies that falsehood in people, just as alloy devalues silver and gold, devalues people.

V. Short answer question

(1) Bacon's essays have a literary style peculiar to their own. Bacon's chief concern is to express his thought with clearness and in as few words as possible.

(2) His sentences are short, pointed, incisive, and often of balanced structure.

(3) His essays are well-arranged and enriched by Biblical allusions, metaphors and cadence. Generally speaking, Bacon's literary style has three prominent qualities: brevity, compactness and forcefulness.

(此题可从培根散文的措辞、句式结构等方面作答。)

VI. Essay question

Generally speaking, Bacon's literary style has three prominent qualities: brevity, compactness, and forcefulness. Bacon's chief concern is to express his thought with clearness and in as few words as possible. His sentences are short, pointed, incisive, and often of balanced structure. His *Essays* began the tradition of essays in English. It covers a wide range of topics, including such titles as "Of Study", "Of Beauty", "Of High Place", "Of Friendship", "Of Nature in Men." The works were much admired by his contemporaries and many of his aphorisms—such as "Cure the disease and kill the patient."—are current today. For this reason, Bacon is considered the father of the English essay.

Lamb wrote a handful of poems and made some attempts at drama. But he is known chiefly for his essays. He did much for the revival of interest in the Elizabethan drama. *Tales from Shakespeare* serves as a valuable work for the popularizing of the great plays of the great dramatist not only among children but also for many adults to whom the original Shakespearean dramas are too difficult to read. The essay "On the Tragedies of Shakespeare" is an important critical work on the great Shakespearean tragedies. In the essay, Lamb admirably pointed out the merits of these masterpieces and the impossibility of fully illustrating these merits by the performance of the plays on the stage. His criticism is a frank expression of his personal feelings; it is in the proper sense "impressionistic" criticism; and it gets its value from the quality and flavor of the author's taste and personality. In this sense, Charles Lamb could be called the Shakespeare of the English essay.

第三部分　十七世纪资产阶级革命和王朝复辟时期

第7章　约翰·多恩

7.1　复习笔记

Ⅰ. Background Knowledge (1) Monarchy hindered the development of capitalism in Britain, and the emerging bourgeoisie can no longer tolerate the domination of landlords and nobles. The conflict between feudalism and bourgeoisie had reached its peak, and the class revolution finally broke out. (2) The despotism and religious tyranny oppressed the Puritans, who advocated the divine right of the individual conscience and fought against the king's cavaliers. (3) Charles I was guillotined in 1649, and England established a Republic under Cromwell's leadership. Cromwell exercised military dictatorship in the whole country in 1653. After his death, the monarchy revived in 1660. (4) The Revolution of 1688 marked the supremacy of Parliament, opened the prelude of modern Britain, and finally won the principle of political freedom.	**1. 背景知识** (1) 君主专制已在英国阻碍了资本主义发展，而且新兴的资产阶级再也不能容忍地主贵族势力的支配。封建制度和资产阶级之间的矛盾已达到顶峰，阶级革命最终爆发了。 (2) 专制统治和宗教暴政压迫着清教徒，他们宣扬个人良知的神圣权利，与国王的骑士斗争。 (3) 1649 年查理一世被送上断头台，英格兰在克伦威尔的领导下建立共和国。1653 年克伦威尔在全国实行军事独裁，他死后君主制于 1660 年死灰复燃。 (4) 1688 年光荣革命标志着议会权力的至高无上，揭开了现代英国的序幕，政治自由原则最终取得胜利。
Ⅱ. Literary Features (1) English literature in the Puritan era was rather chaotic, because the Puritans gave up the old ideas and government and religious conventions. The medieval standard chivalry and illusory love legends disappeared. (2) The literature of the Restoration Age was often witty, clever, but immoral and cynical. Many scholars who returned from exile abandoned the shackles of old ideas and Puritanism, and were deeply influenced by the French literary style at that time.	**Ⅱ. 文学特征** (1) 清教徒时代的英国文学较混乱，这是因为清教徒们放弃了旧观念及政府、宗教的成规。中世纪标准的骑士精神和虚无缥缈的爱情传奇消失殆尽。 (2) 王政复辟时期的文学常常是机智风趣，但也较不道德和玩世不恭。许多流亡又回国的文人摒弃旧观念和清教思想的束缚，深受当时法国文学风格的影响。

(3) During this period, poetry dominated the literary field. The most famous poet is John Milton, who wrote *Paradise Lost*, *Paradise Regained* and *Samson Agonistes*. There were also two poetic schools: Metaphysical Poets and Cavalier Poets.	(3) 这一时期，诗歌在文学领域中占主导地位。最著名的诗人是约翰·弥尔顿，他创作了史诗《失乐园》《复乐园》和诗歌戏剧《力士参孙》。另外还有两个诗歌流派，即玄学派和骑士派。
Ⅲ. John Donne (1572—1631)	**Ⅲ. 约翰·多恩 (1572—1631)**
1. Life	**1. 生平**
John Donne is the founder of the Metaphysical school of poetry. Born in a Roman Catholic family, he was sent to Trinity College, Cambridge University at an early age. He experienced the rule of Queen Elizabeth, James I and Charles I. His early life was dissolute, but he became a clergyman in 1615, and soon became the dean of St. Paul's Church and the most famous missionary at that time.	约翰·多恩是玄学派的创始人。他出生在一个罗马天主教氛围浓厚的家庭，很小时就被送到剑桥大学三一学院。他经历了伊丽莎白女王，詹姆斯一世和查理一世的统治。早期生活较放荡，但在 1615 年成为神职人员，很快升为圣保罗教堂的教长和当时最著名的传教士。
2. Categories of Donne's Poems	**2. 诗歌分类**
His poems can be divided into two categories: the youthful love lyrics, published after his death as *Songs and Sonnets* in 1633, and the later sacred verses, published in 1624 as *Devotions upon Emergent Occasions*.	他的诗歌可分为两大类：青年爱情诗，代表作为 1633 年发表的《歌与十四行诗》和后期的宗教诗歌《突发事件的祷告》，于 1624 年发表。
3. Features of Donne's Poems	**3. 诗歌特点**
Donne's works are full of whimsy and exaggeration. His poetry mixes sensual enjoyment with philosophy, passion and wisdom. However, he is not only a sensory analyst, but his later poems also touched on profound religious thoughts. His prose style is complex, gorgeous and eloquent, which is a monument of brighter spirit in the early 17th century.	多恩的作品中充满奇思妙喻和夸张。他的诗歌将感官享受和哲理，激情和智慧混合在一起。但他不仅是一位感官分析者，他后期的诗歌也触及到深刻的宗教思想。他的散文风格复杂、绚丽、雄辩，是 17 世纪早期精神更加璀璨的丰碑。
4. Selected Works	**4. 选读作品**
◆"Song"	**◆《歌》**
"Song" is a love lyric written by Donne which mainly satirizes women's easy virtue. In the poem, Donne thinks it is impossible to find a loyal and beautiful woman. This poem uses a mocking tone, for example, comparing visiting a loyal and beautiful woman to pilgrimage.	《歌》是多恩写的一首爱情诗，主要是讽刺女性的水性杨花。诗中，多恩认为不可能找到一个忠诚且美丽的女人。本诗使用调侃嘲弄的语气，例如将拜会一位忠诚且美丽的女子比作朝圣。
◆"A Valediction: Forbidding Mourning"	**◆《离别辞：节哀》**
"A Valediction: Forbidding Mourning" is about the parting of two lovers. In the poem, Donne persuades his lover not to cry and be sad because of parting, because compared with	《离别辞：节哀》是一首关于爱人离别的诗。诗中多恩说服爱人不要因为离别而哭泣伤心，因为和普通人相比，他们的爱情已经升

ordinary people, their love has sublimated. Donne directly expressed his ideal of spiritual love in this poem. At the end of the poem, Donne uses two strange metaphors, "gold" and "compass", to describe spiritual love. **◆"Death Be Not Proud"** "Death Be Not Proud" is a sonnet, though rhymed abba abba cddc ee. Donne expressed his ridicule and contempt for death in his poems. He regards death as rest and sleep, from which he can get a lot of happiness. People should not fear death, but accept it, because it can make us easily escape from real life. Finally, the poet declared that death itself will die.	华。多恩在这首诗中直接表达了他对于精神上的爱情的理想，在诗的最后，多恩使用了"黄金"和"圆规"这两个奇喻来比喻精神上的爱情。 **◆《致死神》** 《致死神》是一首十四行诗，其韵式为 abba abba cddc ee。多恩在诗中表达了对死神的嘲笑和蔑视。他把死亡看作休息和睡眠，从中可以获得许多快乐。人们不应该恐惧死亡，而应接受死亡，因为它能让我们轻松地逃离现实生活。最后诗人宣告，死亡自己也必将死去。

7.2 考研真题与典型题详解

Ⅰ. Fill in the blanks.

1. John Donne is a poet of peculiar ________, having his own way of reasoning and comparison.
2. The poems of John Donne belong to two categories: the ________, and the later ________.
3. John Donne and his followers wrote what would later be called ________—complex highly intellectual verse filled with metaphors.（南开大学 2008 研）

Ⅱ. Multiple Choices

1. "One short sleep past, we wake eternally" is taken from the poem written by ________.（首都师范大学 2009 研）
   A. William Shakespeare　　B. John Donne
   C. John Milton　　D. John Keats
2. One of the most noticeable features of John Donne's poetry is his use of ________.（四川大学 2009 研）
   A. classical vocabulary　　B. conceit
   C. dramatic monologue　　D. exaggeration
3. Which of the following is NOT a religious poem by John Donne?（大连外国语学院 2008 研）
   A. "A Hymn to God the Father"
   B. "Hymn to God, My God, in My Sickness"
   C. "The Good-Morrow"
   D. "Death Be Not Proud"
4. ________ founded a new school of poetry by the name of metaphysical school.（北二外 2010 研）
   A. John Smith　　B. John Bunyan
   C. John Milton　　D. John Donne

5. The poetry of John Donne represents a sharp break from the poetry of his predecessors in the Elizabethian era. One of the outstanding features in his poetry is "conceit" which means __________.（天津外国语 2009 研）

A. irony　　B. satire

C. elaborated metaphor　　D. contrast

Ⅲ. Explain the following term.

Metaphysical poetry（南开大学 2009 研）

Ⅳ. Read the following quotation and answer the questions.

Please analyze the following poem.（北航 2010 研）

A Valediction: Forbidding Mourning

By John Donne

As virtuous men pass mildly away,
And whisper to their souls, to go,
Whilst some of their sad friends do say,
"The breath goes now," and some say, "No:"

So let us melt, and make no noise.
No tear-floods, nor sigh-tempests move;
'Twere profanation of our joys
To tell the laity our love.

Moving of th' earth brings harms and fears;
Men reckon what it did, and meant;
But trepidation of the spheres,
Though greater far, is innocent.

Dull sublunary lovers' love
(Whose soul is sense) cannot admit
Absence, because it doth remove
Those things which elemented it.

But we by a love so much refin'd,
That ourselves know not what it is,
Inter-assured of the mind,
Care less, eyes, lips, and hands to miss.
Our two souls therefore, which are one,
Though I must go, endure not yet
A breach, but an expansion,
Like gold to airy thinness beat.

If they be two, they are two so
As stiff twin compasses are two;
Thy soul, the fix'd foot, makes no show
To move, but doth, if the' other do.

And though it in the centre sit,
Yet when the other far doth roam,
It leans, and hearkens after it,
And grows erect, as that comes home.

Such wilt thou be to me, who must
Like th' other foot, obliquely run;
Thy firmness makes my circle just,
And makes me end, where I begun.

V. Short answer question

Explain the "Puritanism" during the English Revolution.

VI. Essay question

What are the different aspects between the literature of Elizabethan Period and the literature of the Revolution Period?

参考答案及解析

I. Fill in the blanks.

1. conceits

(作为"玄学派"诗人的代表，约翰·多恩是极具诗歌天赋的。他的诗采用奇特的比喻，多变的格律等，具有他独特的诗歌特色。)

2. youthful love lyrics, sacred verses

(受生活经历的影响，约翰·多恩的诗歌可分为两部分：年轻有活力的爱情诗和庄严的宗教诗。)

3. Metaphysical poetry

(约翰·多恩是英国十七世纪玄学派诗人，玄学派诗歌以奇特的意象和独具匠心的暗喻著称。)

II. Multiple Choices

1. B　这是约翰·多恩《神圣十四行诗》第十首里的一句诗。该诗是一首典型的玄学诗，主题是死亡。
2. B　作为玄学派的代表诗人，约翰·多恩以其奇妙大胆的想象和暗喻著称。
3. C　《早安》是约翰·多恩的一首爱情诗。
4. D　John Donne 是 17 世纪玄学派诗人的重要代表人物，Ben Johnson 是与莎士比亚同时代的剧作家，John Milton、John Bunyan 虽都是 17 世纪著名作家，但作品风格与玄学派大相径庭。
5. C　约翰·多恩是玄学派诗歌的代表人物，其作品中充满奇妙夸张的暗喻。

Ⅲ. Explain the following term.

Metaphysical poetry: The term "metaphysical poetry" is used to describe a certain type of the 17th century poetry. Dryden originally used the term to criticize John Donne for being too arcane and Samuel Johnson later used it to describe the specific poetic method used by poets like Donne. Metaphysical poets are generally in rebellion against the highly conventional imagery of the Elizabethan lyric. The metaphysical poetry is characterized by wits, subtle argumentations, "metaphysical conceits", and an unusual simile or metaphor.

Ⅳ. Read the following quotation and answer the questions

"A Valediction: Forbidding Mourning" is one of Donne's most famous and simplest poems and also probably his most direct statement of his ideal of spiritual love.

The nine stanzas of this Valediction are quite simple compared to many of Donne's poems, which utilize strange metrical patterns overlaid jarringly on regular rhyme schemes. Here, each four-line stanza is quite unadorned, with an ABAB rhyme scheme and an iambic tetrameter meter.

As the poem begins, the narrator talks of virtuous men that pass away and "whisper their souls to go," meaning they pass away without lamenting. The narrator is telling his lover that their parting should be the same. They should not mourn or cry because it would profane their love to show it in this way.

He further confirms this by saying that earthquakes bring fear and commotion, but celestial movements, such as the procession of the equinox, are more innocent. The narrator is saying that he and his lover have a kind of celestial love. Therefore, their parting does not need to cause commotion, like an earthquake, or a movement between more physical lovers.

The narrator then says that lovers who are more physical could not stand to be absent from each other because absence removes the very thing that love about each other, which are their physical beings. However, since the narrator and his lover have a higher kind of love, they do not care as much that they will not be together physically.

The narrator states that their two souls are one. When they depart, they will not be separating, but expanding. He uses the conceit of gold (a metal that is beautiful and desirable) because gold is a malleable substance that can be stretched far apart while still staying together.

At the end, the poem famously uses the conceit of a drafting compass to describe the strength of their spiritual love. The narrator is saying that his lover is the fixed foot of the compass and that he is the other foot. Even when one foot moves away from the other, the fixed foot will stay in one spot but lean in the direction of the other foot. This is saying that his lover will still "hearken after" him as he travels away and will still be there when he comes back. Finally, the narrator says that he must go, like the other foot of the compass. However, the firmness of his lover is what makes him return to her.

Ⅴ. Short answer question

(1) Puritanism was the religious doctrine of the revolutionary bourgeoisie during the English Revolution.

(2) It preached thrift, sobriety, hard work and unceasing labor in whatever calling one happened to be, but with no extravagant enjoyment of the fruits of labor. Worldly pleasures were con-

demned as harmful. This was precisely the outlook needed by the bourgeoisie for the accumulation of capital.

(3) The Puritans opposed the old church that squandered considerable money upon robes, candles and magnificent processions.

(4) They closed down the London theatres in 1642, not only for their extravagance and deterioration but also for the puritanic abhorrence of "worldly" pleasures in general.

Ⅵ. Essay question

There are three main characteristics in which Puritan literature differs from that of the preceding age:

(1) Elizabethan literature had a marked unity and the feeling of patriotism and devotion to the Queen, but in the Revolution Period, all this was changed. The king became the open enemies of the people, and the country was divided by the struggle for political and religious liberty. So literature was as divided in spirit as were the struggling parties.

(2) Elizabethan literature was generally inspiring. It throbbed with youth, hope and vitality. Literature in the Puritan Age expressed age and sadness. Even its brightest hours were followed by gloom and pessimism.

(3) Elizabethan literature was intensely romantic. The romantic sentiment sprang from the heart of youth. People believed all things, even the impossible. But in literature of the Puritan period, we cannot find romantic ardor.

（此题可从两个时期文学的政治态度、表达的思想、感情基调等方面作答。）

第 8 章 约翰·弥尔顿

8.1 复习笔记

John Milton (1608—16074)

1. Life

Milton was born into a wealthy, devout Puritan family. His father loved books and gave him a tutor, and his father deeply influenced Milton. At the age of 12, he went to St. Paul's, a prestigious boys' chool in London, and at 15 he entered Cambridge University, where he was known as the best scholar. After graduating, he abandoned the idea of becoming an English nationalist minister and retired to his father's country home in Horton, where he wrote poetry and studied diligently. He then traveled to France, Switzerland, and Italy, where he heard the news that there was a high probability of war between the English people and the king.

Upon his return to London, he wrote many pamphlets against the king's power and advocated for the freedom of the people. The Republican government gave Milton the important position of Secretary for Foreign Tongues. He worked hard and finally became blind. During the Restoration, he was thrown in prison and released by Charles Ⅱ. He died on November 8, 1674 surrounded by a few devoted friends.

2. Literary Career

His literary career is roughly divided into three stages: the early period (1620—1638), when he read and wrote lyric poetry; the middle period (1640—1660), when he supported the bourgeois revolution and wrote pamphlets; and the late period (1660—1674), when he wrote the most important epic poems.

3. Literary Achievements

(1) Milton composed the greatest epic poem in English literature. He and Shakespeare have always been regarded as the two types of English poetry.

(2) Milton is a master of the blank verse. He pioneered the use of blank verse in non-dramatic works.

约翰·弥尔顿(1608—1674)

1. 生平

弥尔顿出生在富裕、虔诚的清教徒家庭。他的父亲喜爱书籍，并给他请了一个家教，他父亲深深影响了弥尔顿。12 岁时，他去伦敦著名的男子学校圣保罗上学，15 岁时进入剑桥大学，并被称为最好的学者。毕业后，他放弃当英国国教牧师的想法，隐居到他父亲在霍顿的乡间住所，写诗、刻苦学习。之后，他游历了法国、瑞士、意大利，在意大利听到消息说英国人民反抗国王极可能发生战争。

回到伦敦后，他写了许多小册子反对王权、提倡人民自由。共和国政府让弥尔顿担任外语秘书这个重要职位，他工作十分努力，以致最终失明。然而王朝复辟时他被捕入狱，后被国王赦免。1674 年，弥尔顿在挚友的包围中去世。

2. 文学生涯

他的文学生涯大致分为三个阶段：早期(1620—1638)，阅读和抒情诗写作阶段；中期(1640—1660)，支持资产阶级革命，宣传册阶段；晚期(1660—1674)，最重要的史诗写作阶段。

3. 文学成就

(1) 弥尔顿创作了英国文学上最伟大的史诗。他和莎士比亚总是被视为英国诗歌的两个类型。

(2) 弥尔顿是无韵体大师。他率先将无韵体运用到非戏剧作品中。

(3) Milton is a great stylist. He is famous for his grand style, which is the result of his lifelong classical and biblical study.

(4) Milton has always been admired for his sublimity of thought and majesty of expression.

(3) 弥尔顿是伟大的文体学家。他以其高雅的文体著称，这得益于他终生对经典和圣经作品的研究。

(4) 弥尔顿向来以思想高深和表达气势宏伟著称。

4. Major Works

A. Lyric Poems

"On the Morning of Christ's Nativity"

"L'Allegro" and " Il Penseroso"

Comus

"Lycidas"

B. Pamphlets

Areopagitica

Defence of the English People

Second Defence of the English People

C. Epics

Paradise Lost

Paradise Regained

Samson Agonistes

4. 主要作品

A. 抒情诗歌

《在基督诞生的早上》

《快乐的人》和《忧思的人》

《科马斯》

《利西达斯》

B. 宣传册

《论出版自由》

《为英国人民而辩》

《为英国人民再辩》

C. 史诗

《失乐园》

《复乐园》

《力士参孙》

5. Selected Works

◆Paradise Lost

A. Main Plot

Paradise Lost is Milton's masterpiece. It is a 12-volume epic poem written in a blank verse. The story is taken from the Old Testament and covers: Genesis; Satan and his fellow angels rebel against God; Satan's defeat and expulsion from heaven and his fall into hell; the creation of the world and Adam and Eve; the fallen angels in hell plotting against God; Satan tempting Eve to steal the forbidden fruit; and Adam and Eve being expelled from the Garden of Eden.

B. Theme and Characterization

The theme of the poem is rebellion against the authority of God. God is portrayed as a selfish despot, always sitting high on the throne, surrounded by a group of foolish angels who perpetually sing praises. Satan, though defeated and suffering infernal torments, still sought revenge, and is the most striking character in the poem. Although his power is not equal to God's, he is unwilling to grovel and prefers to be independent. Adam and Eve are the embodiment of Milton's belief in human power. Their desire for knowledge adds importance to their characterization.

5. 作品选读

◆《失乐园》

A. 主要情节

《失乐园》是弥尔顿的杰作。它是一首用无韵体写的长达 12 卷的史诗。故事取材《旧约》，内容包括：创世纪；撒旦和天使同伴反叛上帝；撒旦失败并被逐出天堂，坠入地狱；世界及亚当和夏娃的创造；地狱中的堕落天使阴谋反抗上帝；撒旦诱惑夏娃偷吃禁果；亚当和夏娃被逐出伊甸园。

B. 主题和人物刻画

诗歌的主题是对上帝权威的反叛。上帝被描绘成自私的专制者，总是高坐在王位上，身边一群永久大唱赞词的愚蠢的天使。然而撒旦，虽然战败，但总是想着报复，却给人留下深刻印象。虽然力量不敌上帝，但他不愿卑躬屈膝，喜欢独立自主。亚当和夏娃是弥尔顿对人类力量信仰的化身。他们对知识的渴望使其人物性格更具重要性。

The poem's image of the many angels who are afraid to voice their opinions surrounding God contrasts with the image of Satan speaking freely with his rebellious angel friends, considered a symbol of the absolute monarchy and republican parliament.	诗中众多不敢发表自己意见的天使围绕着上帝的画面，和撒旦和他的反叛天使朋友们一起畅所欲言的画面形成鲜明对比，被认为是专制君主统治的王庭和共和议会的象征。
◆"On His Blindness"	**◆《失明述怀》**
Milton gradually lost his sight after 1652, and this poem is about his own blindness. The first eight lines of the poem constitute a turnaround from the last six lines, in which the poet is distressed by his blindness and complains to God. In the second six lines, the poet gradually returns to peace through Patience's reply.	弥尔顿在1652年后逐渐失明，而这首诗就是关于他自己的失明。诗中的前8行和后6行构成一个转折，前8行诗人对自己的失明感到痛苦，并且对上帝心存怨言。后6行通过Patience的回复，诗人逐渐归于平静。
◆"On His Deceased Wife"	**◆《梦亡妻》**
This poem is written in 1600 by John Milton to memorize his second wife Katherine Woodcock, who passed away in 1658 when delivering a baby.	本诗写于1600年，表达了弥尔顿对亡妻的怀念之情。弥尔顿第二任妻子凯瑟琳·伍德考克于1658年死于生产。

8.2 考研真题与典型题详解

Ⅰ. Fill in the blanks.

1. *Samson Agonistes* was written by __________.（大连外国语学院2007研）
2. When he was Latin Secretary to the Council of Foreign Affairs, John Milton wrote a number of pamphlets defending the English revolution. The most well-known is his controversy with the European scholar Salmasius on the Execution of __________.
3. Because of the success of *Paradise Lost*, John Milton produced in 1671 another epic, __________.
4. In 1637 Milton wrote the finest pastoral elegy in English, __________, to memorize the tragic death of a Cambridge friend.
5. John Milton wrote his masterpiece __________ during his blindness.

Ⅱ. Multiple Choices

1. The epic of *Paradise Lost* is based on the stories from __________.（北二外2009研）
   A. The New Testament　　B. The Old Testament
   C. The Ancient Greek Myths　　D. The Ancient Roman Myths
2. In addition to *Paradise Lost*, John Milton's another famous poem "Lycidas" is a __________ in which he uses some artificial imagery supplied by an idyllic shepherd's existence to bewail the loss of a friend.（天津外国语学院2009研）
   A. pastoral elegy　　B. odes　　C. cantos　　D. ballads
3. *Areopagitica* is John Milton's best-known __________.
   A. prose　　B. epic　　C. novel　　D. drama

4. John Milton wrote a number of pamphlets defending the English people. Among the following works which is not pamphlet?

A. *Defence of the English People* B. *Second Defence of the English People*

C. "L'Allegro" D. *Areoppagitica*

5. Among the following statements about *Paradise Lost*, which is not the proper one?

A. John Milton's masterpiece.

B. A great epic in 10 books.

C. Written in blank verse.

D. About the heroic revolt of Satan against God's authority.

Ⅲ. Explain the following terms.

1. *Paradise Lost* (首师大 2008 研)
2. blank verse (首师大 2009 研)

Ⅳ. Short answer questions

1. How many books does *Paradise Lost* consist of? Who are the four main characters in the epic, and what are the respective relations between them? (人大 2006 研)
2. Make a comment on the image of Satan in *Paradise Lost*.

Ⅴ. Essay questions

1. Give supporting reasons for the statement: Samson in *Samson Agonistes* is John Milton, the author himself.
2. Discuss the theme and characterization of *Paradise Lost*.

参考答案及解析

Ⅰ. Fill in the blanks.

1. John Milton

(《力士参孙》是英国作家约翰 · 弥尔顿(John Milton)的一部悲剧。)

2. Charles Ⅰ

(约翰 · 弥尔顿首先是一位革命家。他反对君主专制，并全心地为人民自由摇旗呐喊。1649 年，弥尔顿被任命为克伦威尔护国政府的拉丁文秘书，他写了很多政治小册子为英国革命辩护，其中最著名的就是对欧洲学者萨尔梅歇斯关于查理一世被处死的反驳。)

3. *Paradise Regained*

(由于《失乐园》的巨大成功，约翰 · 弥尔顿在 1671 年创作了另一部圣经题材诗《复乐园》。)

4. "Lycidas"

(《利西达斯》是英国诗人弥尔顿年轻时为溺海夭亡的剑桥同学金(Edward King)写的一首悼诗。)

5. *Paradise Lost*

(约翰 · 弥尔顿花费了 7 年的时间完成其代表作《失乐园》。整个创作期间，他已经双目失明。有时他让女儿们把他口述的内容记录下来，有时也请来探望他的朋友帮忙。)

Ⅱ. Multiple Choices

1. B 《失乐园》的故事取材于圣经旧约中 Genesis 3：1-24。

2. A 《利西达斯》是弥尔顿早年创作的一首田园挽歌，纪念在剑桥读书后来死于海难的一位同学，该诗题目源自维吉尔的《田园诗》中一位牧羊人的名字。

3. A 《论出版自由》是弥尔顿最著名的一篇散文，此书最初是1644年作者向英国国会提出的一篇演说词，也是一篇争取言论自由的战斗檄文。

4. C 约翰·弥尔顿是英国17世纪的一位诗人、政论家。英国资产阶级革命爆发后，他投身革命，创作了很多的政论小册子呼吁政治、宗教和个人自由以及为英国革命辩护。他最为著名的政论小册子包括：《为英国人民而辩》《为英国人民再辩》《论出版自由》《偶像的破坏者》等。

5. B 《失乐园》是弥尔顿的代表作，共十二册。以史诗般磅礴的气势揭露了人的原罪与堕落，同时歌颂了撒旦反抗上帝的英勇事迹。整个著作采用的是无韵诗的形式。

Ⅲ. Explain the following terms.

1. *Paradise Lost*: *Paradise Lost* is an epic poem in blank verse by the 17th-century English poet John Milton. The poem concerns the Christian story of "the Fall of Man": the temptation of Adam and Eve by the fallen angel Satan and their expulsion from the Garden of Eden. Milton's purpose, stated in Book Ⅰ, is to "justify the ways of God to men" and elucidate the conflict between God's eternal foresight and free will.

2. blank verse: Blank verse is a type of poetry, distinguished by having a regular meter, but no rhyme. In English, the meter most commonly used with blank verse has been iambic pentameter (as used in Shakespearean plays). The first known use of blank verse in the English language was by Henry Howard, Earl of Surrey. Christopher Marlowe was the first English author to make full use of the potential of blank verse, and also established it as the dominant verse form for English drama in the age of Elizabeth Ⅰ and James Ⅰ. The major achievements in English blank verse were made by William Shakespeare, who wrote much of the content of his plays in unrhymed iambic pentameter, and Milton, whose *Paradise Lost* was written in blank verse.

Ⅳ. Short answer questions

1. *Paradise Lost* consists of 12 books, the main characters in which are Satan, God, Adam and Eve. Satan and God are enemies. Adam and Eve are the first man and woman made by God. But seduced by Satan, they ate the fruits on the tree of the knowledge of good and evil, which annoyed God, finally were banished from the Garden of Eden.

2. (1) In John Milton's *Paradise Lost*, Satan, like a conquered and banished giant, remains obeyed and admired by those who follow him down to hell. He is firmer than the rest of the angels. It is he who, passing the guarded gates obstacle, makes man revolt against God.

(2) Satan is the spirit of questioning the authority of God. When he gets to the Garden of Eden, he believes in no reason why Adam and Eve should not taste the fruit of the Tree of Knowledge.

(3) Though defeated, Satan prevails, since he has won from God a third part of his angels, and almost all the sons of Adam. Though wounded, he triumphs, for the thunder which hits upon his head leaves his heart invincible. Though feebler in force, he remains superior in nobility, since he prefers independence to happy servility, and welcomes his defeat and his torments as a glory, a liberty, and a joy. In conclusion, the finest thing in *Paradise Lost* is the description of

hell, and Satan is the real hero of the poem.

（此题主要从撒旦的英勇反抗来进行分析作答。）

V. Essay questions

1. (1) *Samson Agonistes* is a poetical drama patterned on Greek tragedies. It deals with the story of Samson from the "Book of Judges" in the *Old Testament*. Samson is an athlete of the Israelites. He stands as the bravest warrior fighting for the freedom of his country. But he is betrayed by his Philistine wife Dalilah and blinded by his enemies the Philistines. Led into the temple to make them sport, he takes his vengeance upon his enemies by pulling down the temple upon them and upon himself in a common ruin. He dies but regains his dignity in death.

   (2) Samson and John Milton share much common life experiences. Like Samson the protagonist, Milton had also been betrayed by his wife, persecuted by his enemies, and suffered from blindness. And yet he holds unconquerable will.

   (3) Through Samson's miserable blindness, his agonizing longing for sight and freedom and his last terrible triumph, Milton puts forward his passionate longing that he could also bring destruction down upon the enemy at the cost of his own life. Therefore, Samson in the drama is Milton himself in life.

2. (1) *Paradise Lost* is Milton's masterpiece. Its story is taken from the Bible, about "the fall of man", that is, how Adam and Eve are tempted by Satan to disobey God by eating the forbidden fruit from the Tree of Knowledge, and how they are punished by God and driven out of Paradise. By depicting Satan and his followers as well as their fiery utterance and brave actions, Milton is showing a Puritan's revolt against the dictator and against the established doctrines of the Catholics and the Anglican Church.

   (2) God is portrayed as a selfish despot, always sitting high on the throne, surrounded by a group of foolish angels who perpetually sing praises. His long speeches are not pleasing at all. He is cruel and unjust in punishing Satan. His Archangel Raphael is only a bore. His angels are stupid. But Satan is by far the most striking character in the poem, who rises against God and, though defeated, still seeks for revenge.

   (3) Adam and Eve are the embodiment of Milton's belief in human power. God denied their craving for knowledge. It is this longing for knowledge that opens before mankind a wide road to intelligent and active life. It has been noted by many critics that Milton's revolutionary feelings made him forget religious orthodoxy. The angels who surround the God never think of expressing any opinions of their own, and they never seem to have any opinions of their own. The poem's image of the many angels who are afraid to voice their opinions surrounding God contrasts with the image of Satan speaking freely with his rebellious angel friends, considered a symbol of the absolute monarchy and republican parliament.

第9章　约翰·班扬

9.1　复习笔记

John Bunyan(1628—1688)

1. Life

John Bunyan, the son of a poor tinker, was born in Elsdo village near Bedford in 1628. With only a little education, he went to work in his father's shop, and saw a vivid picture of hell and demons among the fire and smoke of the forge. He went to church once in a while, and once he felt that the passionate missionaries made him afraid, he escaped. However, his life changed after he married a kind and poor woman. This woman brought only two religious books. After reading these two books, he often went to church, began to read the Bible slowly and difficultly, and finally became an outdoor missionary and leader of a large number of believers with strength and sincerity. After that, he was jailed for 12 years for breaking the law and preaching without the permission of the Established Church. The publication of *The Pilgrim's Progress* in 1678 made him the most popular writer, as he was already the most popular preacher in England. He died in 1688.

2. Major Work

◆ ***The Pilgrim's Progress***

It is an old-fashioned, medieval religious allegory. The allegory appeared in the author's dream, in which he saw and told the pilgrimage of a man named Christian to the Holy City. This process is divided into ten stages, vividly showing the difficulties and successes in Christian life. Every test turns into a living person.

Though an allegory, the characters in the book leave the readers with the impression of real characters. The scene depicted in the book comes from the real scene in England, and the language spoken is the image representation of the language of his time. In fact, the kingdom of heaven in the book

约翰·班扬(1628—1688)

1. 生平

约翰·班扬是一名穷苦补锅匠的儿子，于1628年出生在贝德福特附近埃尔斯多村庄。他只受了一点教育就去父亲的铺子做工，在那熔炉的烈火浓烟中看到了地狱恶魔的生动图景。他偶尔去教堂，一旦觉得那些激昂的传教士让他恐惧难受时，他就逃出来。然而，他娶了一个善良贫穷的女人后，人生从此改变。这个女人只带来了两本宗教书籍，看了这两本书后，他更经常去教堂，开始缓慢艰难地阅读圣经，最终凭借力量和真诚，成为一个户外传教士及大批信徒的领袖。之后，他因触犯法律，未经英国国教许可而布道，被打入监狱12年。1678年《天路历程》的出版让他成为最受欢迎的作家，正如他已经是当时英国最受欢迎的传道士一样。他于1688年去世。

2. 主要作品

◆**《天路历程》**

此书是中世纪古老的宗教寓言。这个寓言出现在作者的一个梦里，在梦里他看到并讲述了一名叫“基督徒”的男子去圣城的朝圣历程。这个历程分为十个阶段，生动展现了基督徒生活中的困难和成功。每个考验都化为一个活生生的人物。

虽然使用寓言体，书中的人物却留给读者真实人物的印象。书中描绘的场景来自英国真实场景，所讲语言是他那个时代语言的形象再现。事实上，书中的天国是17世

is a poor tinker's fantasy of an ideal and happy society in the 17th century, although this fantasy is hidden under the cloak of religion.	纪一位穷苦的补锅匠对理想幸福社会的幻想，尽管这个幻想掩藏在宗教外衣下面。小说中最有名的场景是名利场。班扬表现出对国王及其统治下的政府的痛恨。
3. Writing Features Bunyan is known for his vivid and concise prose style. He naturally and powerfully uses his usual daily expressions, and the simple and natural language from ordinary people and the details reflecting ordinary people's lives are the reasons for the modernity of his works.	**3. 写作特征** 班扬以他简洁而生动的散文风格著称。他自然有力地运用惯用日常表达法，来自普通群众的简朴自然的语言和反映普通人生活的细节是造就其作品具有现代性的原因。

9.2 考研真题与典型题详解

Ⅰ. Fill in the blanks.

1. Christian is a character in __________ written by __________.（大连外国语学院 2007 研）
2. After the death of Cromwell, the Parliament recalled Charles Ⅱ to England in 1660; then followed the __________ period.
3. __________ wrote his masterpiece *The Pilgrim's Progress* during his second imprisonment.

Ⅱ. Multiple Choice

1. Another school of poetry prevailing in 17th century was that of __________, i. e. those verse-writers, often knights and squires, who sided with the King against the Parliament and Puritans.
   A. Metaphysical Poets　　B. Cavalier Poets
   C. John Milton　　D. John Dryden
2. The following section describes the hero's journey in search of salvation in __________.（大连外国语 2008 研）
   A. *The Pilgrim's Progress*　　B. *Paradise Regained*
   C. *Canterbury Tales*　　D. *Utopia*

   Christian continues on his way, assisted by a new friend, Hopeful, who has been converted by Faithful's martyrdom. They hold to the high road despite many difficulties and dangers but finally, their feet being weary and the road growing hourly more hard and rocky, they are tempted to take a bypath through a pleasant meadow which seems to follow the same general route.
3. John Bunyan uses the everyday world of common experience as a metaphor for the spiritual journey of the soul toward God in his __________.（北二外 2008 研）
   A. *The Pilgrim's Progress*　　B. "Lycidas"
   C. *The Fairy Queen*　　D. *Donn Juan*

Ⅲ. Explain the following term.

Allegory（国际关系学院 2007 研；天津外国语学院 2008 研）

Ⅳ. Read the following quotation and answer the questions.

Judge: Thou runagate, heretic, and traitor, hast thou heard what these honest gentlemen have witnessed against thee?

Faithful: May I speak a few words in my own defense?

Judge: Sirrah, sirrah! Thou deservest to live no longer but to be slain immediately upon the place; yet, that all men may see our gentleness towards thee, let us hear what thou, vile runagate, hast to say.

Questions:

1. Which work is the passage quoted from?
2. Who is the author of the work?
3. Summarize the story of the passage.

Ⅴ. Short answer question

What are the main characteristics of Restoration literature?

Ⅵ. Essay question

Make an introduction of *The Pilgrim's Progress*.

参考答案及解析

Ⅰ. Fill in the blanks.

1. *The Pilgrim's Progress*, John Bunyan

(Christian 是英国作家 John Bunyan 的寓言《天路历程》中的人物。该作品被誉为“英国文学中最著名的寓言”。)

2. Restoration

(1660 年，克伦威尔死后，议会拥护查理二世回到英国，君主制死灰复燃，这一时期被称为“王朝复辟时期”。)

3. John Bunyan

(约翰·班扬是一个不信奉英国国教的清教徒，曾两次因布道被捕入狱。在第二次入狱期间他创作了代表作《天路历程》。)

Ⅱ. Multiple Choice

1. B　17 世纪上半叶的英国，在诗歌方面的主要代表是骑士派和玄学派。在内战中骑士派诗人为国王效力，反对议会和清教徒。

2. A　题目中的这段文章节选自 John Bunyan(约翰·班扬)的小说 *The Pilgrim's Progress*(《天路历程》)，描写了基督徒寻求救赎的一段旅程。

3. A　*The Pilgrim's Progress*(《天路历程》)是班扬最脍炙人口的作品。“Lycidas”(《利西达斯》)是弥尔顿的一首田园挽歌，*The Fairy Queen*(《仙后》)是斯宾塞的长诗，*Don Juan*(《唐璜》)是拜伦的一首长诗。

Ⅲ. Explain the following term.

Allegory: Allegory is a work of art in which a deeper meaning underlies the superficial or literal meaning or the representation of one meaning by another in this way. It is often referred to a work of fiction in which the author intends characters and their actions to be understood in terms other than their surface appearances and meanings, and the implied or extended meanings involve moral or spiritual concepts more significant than the actual narrative itself. John Bunyan's *The Pilgrim's Progress* and Dante's *The Divine Comedy* are typical allegories.

Ⅳ. Read the following quotation and answer the questions.

1. It is quoted from *The Pilgrim's Progress*.
2. The author is John Bunyan.
3. The passage is entitled "Vanity Fair". Christian and Faithful come to Vanity Fair where it seems that all can be bought by money. As they refuse to buy anything but Truth, they are beaten and put in a cage, and then taken out and led in chains up and down the fair and at length brought before a court. Judge Hate-good summons three witnesses: Envy, Superstition and Pick thank, who testify against him. The case is given to the jury, composed of Mr. Badman, Mr. No-good, Mr. Malice, etc. Each gives verdict against Faithful, who is presently condemned. Here Bunyan intends to satirize the state trials in the reactionary reigns of Charles Ⅱ and James Ⅱ, which are merely forms preliminary to hanging, drawing and quartering.

Ⅴ. Short answer question

(1) Restoration literature is characterized by a cliquish culture centering on the court and deeply influenced by French classical taste.

(2) There are four main characteristics of Restoration literature: ①the tendency to vulgar realism in the drama, ②a general formalism, ③the development of a simpler and more direct prose style, ④the prevalence of the heroic couplet in poetry.

(3) They are all exemplified in the works of one man, John Dryden.

Ⅵ. Essay question

(1) *The Pilgrim's Progress* is a religious allegory written by John Bunyan. It tells of the spiritual pilgrimage of Christian, who flies from the City of Destruction, meets with the perils and temptations of the Slough of Despond, Vanity Fair, and Doubting Castle, faces and overcomes the demon Appollyon, and finally comes to the Delectable Mountains and the Celestial City.

(2) In the allegory, Bunyan presents us vivid life pictures of English society, and conversations which enliven his narratives vividly repeat the language of his time. In reality, the Celestial City in *The Pilgrim's Progress* is the vision of an ideal happy society dreamed by a poor tinker in the 17th century, through a veil of religious mist.

(3) One of the remarkable passages is the one in which Vanity Fair and the persecution of Christian and his friend Faithful are described. Here Bunyan intends to satirize the state trials in the reactionary reigns of Charles Ⅱ and James Ⅱ, which are merely forms preliminary to hanging, drawing and quartering.

(4) John Bunyan cherished a deep hatred of both the king and his government. He saw and detested the injustice of law, trials and magistrates. That is why his *The Pilgrim's Progress* had won immediate success among the common people, has become one of the most popular works in the English language.

(5) His prose is admirable. It is a popular speech ennobled by the solemn dignity and simplicity of the language of the English Bible.

（此题从《天路历程》的主要内容、主题、写作风格等方面作答。）

第四部分 英国启蒙运动阶段

第10章 丹尼尔·笛福

10.1 复习笔记

Ⅰ. Background Knowledge

(1) In the wake of the "Glorious Revolution" in 1688, Britain became a constitutional monarchy with power transferred from the King to Parliament and cabinet ministers. The literature of this period was sometimes swayed by the power struggle between the liberal Whigs and the conservative Tories.

(2) The Industrial Revolution emerged as a transformative power over the socioeconomic structure of Britain, aggravating the divide between the rich and the poor.

(3) A large number of newly-opened public cafés and private clubs gave expression to the swift enrichment of public life in English cities.

(4) The Enlightenment in the 18th century, with its opposition to feudalism and emphasis on reason, looked to the goodness of human nature.

Ⅱ. Literary Style of the Eighteenth Century

(1) It became fashionable for the middle-class to discuss current affairs in cafés, giving birth to newspapers that provided information and commentary. A typical example is *The Spectator* jointly edited by Addison and Steele.

(2) Under the influence of the Enlightenment, a new school of English literature, Neoclassicism, appeared, which emphasized rationality and fixed rules for each literary genre. Writers of this school include Pope and Samuel Johnson.

(3) The English novel came into being in the 18th century and has become an important literary genre, including realistic novels, represented by Defoe, Fielding, and Swift; sentimental novels, represented by Sterne and Goldsmith; Gothic novels, such as *The Castle of Otranto*; psychological novels, such as novels by Richardson.

Ⅰ. 背景知识

(1) 1688年光荣革命后，英国从此成为君主立宪制国家，权力由国王转向议会和内阁大臣。两党之间的争权夺势不时主导着18世纪文学。

(2) 工业革命兴起，彻底改变了英国的社会经济结构，加剧了贫富矛盾。

(3) 英国城市中社会生活快速发展，例如大量公共咖啡馆和私人俱乐部的建立。

(4) 启蒙运动开始于18世纪，它反对封建主义，强调理性，相信人性本善。

Ⅱ. 十八世纪文学风格

(1) 中产阶级在咖啡馆对时事的讨论成为时尚，由此产生了提供信息和评论的报刊。典型代表是艾迪生和斯蒂尔合办的《旁观者》。

(2) 受启蒙运动的影响，英国文学出现新流派——新古典主义，他们强调理性和每个文学体裁的固定规则。新古典主义的代表是蒲柏和约翰逊。

(3) 英国小说产生于18世纪，并成为一个重要的文学体裁。包括现实主义小说，代表是笛福、菲尔丁和斯威夫特；感伤主义小说，代表是斯特恩和哥尔德史密斯；哥特小说，如《奥特兰托堡》；心理小说，代表是理查森。

(4) In the second half of the 18th century, pre-Romantic writing emerged and gradually replaced those of Neoclassicism. Blake and Burns are the forerunners of pre-Romanticism. (5) Compared with the development of the novel, drama of the 18th century was not a major genre.	(4) 18 世纪后半期，前浪漫主义产生并逐渐取代新古典主义。代表诗人是布莱克和彭斯。 (5) 与小说相比，18 世纪的戏剧没有那么重要的位置。
Ⅲ. Literary Terms	**Ⅲ. 文学术语**
1. The Enlightenment Movement (1) The Enlightenment was a progressive intellectual movement sweeping from France across Western Europe in the 18th century. (2) The Enlightenment was to bring dynamism and open-mindedness to the world in philosophical and artistic approaches. (3) The core spirit of the Enlightenment is rationality, equality, and science. It advocated universal education. Literature at the time played a popular educational role.	**1. 启蒙运动** (1) 启蒙运动是一场进步的思想运动，盛行于法国，后在 18 世纪传播到西欧。 (2) 它的目的是用现代哲学和艺术观点启蒙整个世界。 (3) 崇尚理性、平等和科学，提倡大众教育。文学在当时变成了一种非常受欢迎的公众教育的手段。
2. Neoclassicism (1) The English neoclassicism had its literary origin in both classical and contemporary French literature, conveying attitudes toward art and human existence such as ideals of order, logic, restraint, accuracy, correctness, decorum, etc. Pope and Johnson of the 18th century belong to the neoclassical school. (2) Drama is written in couplet and in compliance with the three unities of time, place, and action. It is constructed with regularity to present a certain group image rather than individual characters. (3) Poetry: According to the classification of ancient literature, poetry can be divided into lyric poetry, epic poetry, didactic poetry, allegorical poetry, and dramatic poetry. Each type should be guided by certain principles. (4) Prose should go by precision, straightforwardness, and flexibility.	**2. 新古典主义** (1) 英国新古典主义基于并源于古典文学和当代法国文学，代表了一类对待艺术和人类存在的态度：秩序、逻辑、限制、准确、正确、得体等。新古典主义者包括十八世纪的蒲柏和约翰逊。 (2) 戏剧标准：偶句诗；时间、地点和情节的统一；结构的规律性；类型刻画而非个体刻画。 (3) 诗歌标准：依照古文学分类，诗歌应分为抒情诗、史诗、教诲诗、讽喻诗和戏剧诗，每一种都应受到特定规律的约束。 (4) 散文标准：精确、直接、灵活。
3. Picaresque Novel A popular sub-genre of prose fiction, the picaresque novel often uses satire and realistic humor to describe the adventures of the roving protagonists of low social status.	**3. 流浪汉小说** 流浪汉小说是小说的一种。它常用讽刺语气和现实幽默的写法来描写社会地位低下的流浪主人公的冒险经历。

Originating in Spain, The picaresque novel gained wide popularity in Europe between the seventeenth and eighteenth centuries with a lingering influence on modern literature. Smollett's Roderick Random and Humphry Clinker are typical picaresque works.

该类小说源于西班牙。流浪汉小说在17、18世纪的欧洲盛行，并继续影响现代文学。斯莫莱特的《兰登传》和《亨弗利·克林克》是流浪汉小说的典型。

4. Sentimentalism

The term sentimentalism is used in two meanings:

(1) Overwhelmed by emotions, especially a conscious effort to work up one's emotions to enjoy it.

(2) A positive view of the innate goodness of human nature upon which The sentimental novel was developed. Laurence Sterne's *A Sentimental Journey* and Oliver Goldsmith's *The Vicar of Wakefield* are typical of the sentimental category

4. 感伤主义

感伤主义包括两层含义：

(1) 过分沉溺于情感，特别指有意识地插入情感来享受其中。

(2) 过于乐观地强调人性之善。感伤小说来源于感伤主义，代表作有斯特恩的《感伤的旅行》和哥尔德史密斯的《威克菲尔德牧师传》。

5. Pre-Romanticism

In the latter half of the 18th century, a new literary movement rose in Europe, which later generations called the Romantic Revival. The movement was characterized by a revolt against the Enlightenment and an appeal to passion and emotion, marked by a revival of interest in medieval literature. In England, this movement is represented by pre-romantic poetry, a new trend of poetic creation led by Percy, Macpherson, and Chatterton and represented by Blake and Burns.

5. 前浪漫主义

18世纪后期，欧洲兴起了一场新的文学运动，后人称之为浪漫主义复兴。这场运动以反抗启蒙主义，呼吁情感和激情为特征，以恢复对中世纪文学的兴趣为标志。在英国这场运动表现为诗歌中的前浪漫主义，其引领人为珀西、麦克菲森和查特顿，代表人物为布莱克和彭斯。

Ⅳ. Daniel Defoe (1660—1731)

1. Life

Daniel Defoe was the son of a London butcher named Foe, and later added the aristocratic prefix. Defoe was a kind of jack-of-all-trades as he was once engaged in multiple carriers. He had been a merchant, soldier, economist, politician, journalist, pamphleteer, publicist, and novelist. Born in a nonconformist family, he supported free churches in his pamphlets at the cost of imprisonment. After his release in 1704, Defoe worked for the government as a secret agent. At the age about 60, he committed himself to fiction writing to make ends meet and later retired to Newington where he lived in comfort.

Ⅳ. 丹尼尔·笛福(1660—1731)

1. 生平

丹尼尔·笛福生于伦敦，父亲是个姓福的肉商，后来他给自己的姓加上了贵族前缀。笛福是位多面手。他是商人、战士、经济学家、政治家、记者、宣传册作者、时事评论家和小说家。他也是激进的不信奉国教者。他一本有名的支持自由教会的小册子让他入了狱。1704年出狱后，他被政府雇佣为间谍或者说特工。60岁后，他转向小说写作，不久便名利双收，随后退隐纽因顿，生活十分惬意。

2. Literary Features and Achievements

(1) Puritanism has a profound influence on Defoe and his fiction with its expression in the moral teaching in Defoe's narratives.

2. 文学特征及成就

(1) 笛福对改革的清教热情是他众多作品的特征，也导致了文中随处可见的说教。

(2) He was attracted to the picturesque which he deemed as excellent materials for a "good story". His realistic stories drew on his prison experience and first-hand materials collected about criminals during his carrier as a journalist for a magazine.

(3) Boasting lingering fame for his masterpiece *Robinson Crusoe*, Defoe was one of the early practitioners of fiction, and he contributed to the popularization of novel in England. He is also credited as the pioneer of the English novel.

3. Major Works

Robinson Crusoe (1719)
Captain Singleton (1720)
Moll Flanders (1722)
Colonel Jacque (1722)

4. Selected Work

◆*Robinson Crusoe*

Robinson Crusoe is inspired by the real experience of Alexander Selkirk, who was stranded on an island off the coast of Chile and lived there alone for more than 4 years. Defoe reframed and enriched the sailor's true story with many imaginary incidents while leaving the novel as authentic as possible. Robinson Crusoe's overcoming the harsh natural environment on the deserted island constitutes the most wonderful part of the book through which Defoe extolled the brilliance of human labor and resources. Representative of the early rising of English bourgeoisie, Robinson Crusoe is a man of practicality and exactness, always religious but highly mindful of his own interests. The first word Robinson teaches Friday is "master", implying the colonial ideology of him.

（2）他对生动形象的描述有敏锐眼光，也有一种直觉能写出好故事。他现实性的小说大多借鉴了他的监狱经历和在为一家杂志社做记者期间收集到的关于罪犯的一手资料。

（3）他因《鲁滨逊漂流记》获得了不朽的名声，也是早期小说践行者之一，他推动了小说在英国的流行，甚至有人称他为英国小说的创始者。

3. 主要作品

《鲁滨逊漂流记》(1719)
《辛格顿船长》(1720)
《摩尔·弗兰德斯》(1722)
《陆军上校杰克》(1722)

4. 选读作品

◆《鲁滨逊漂流记》

笛福的杰作《鲁滨逊漂流记》是基于亚历山大·塞尔柯克的真实经历，他被困在智利海岸线外的一个小岛上，在那里独居了4年多。他用自己丰富的想象力润饰了那位水手的真实经历，因此这部小说读起来像真实发生的一样。小说最精彩的部分是鲁滨逊独自在荒岛上战胜无情自然的现实主义描述。笛福赞扬人类劳动。鲁滨逊是英国资产阶级在发展早期的代表人物，他是最为实际最为精确的一个人，永远保持宗教信仰同时对于自己的利益十分留意。"主人"是礼拜五从鲁滨逊那里学来的第一个词，这反映了殖民主义思想。

10.2 考研真题与典型题详解

Ⅰ. Fill in the blanks.

1. The __________ was a progressive intellectual movement throughout Western Europe in the 18th century.
2. The main literary stream of the 18th century was __________. What the writers described were mainly social realities.
3. The enlighteners believed that reason should be the only basis of one's thinking and action. That

is why the eighteenth century in England has been called __________.

Ⅱ. Multiple Choices

1. Modern English novel arose in the __________ century.（北二外 2010 研）

   A. 16th　　B. 17th　　C. 18th　　D. 19th

2. As a man of strongly-held religious and political convictions, Daniel Defoe published many writings, including __________.（首都师范大学 2009 研）

   A. *Of Reformation*

   B. *Areopagitica*

   C. *The Ready and Easy Way to Establish a Free Commonwealth*

   D. *The Shortest Way with Dissenters*

Ⅲ. Explain the following terms.

1. English Enlightenment（北航 2008 研）
2. British neoclassicism（南开大学 2009 研）
3. Gothic novel

Ⅳ. Read the following quotation and answer the questions.（北航 2008 研）

The Other Side of the Island

I mentioned before that I had a great mind to see the whole island, and that I had traveled up the brook, and so on to where I built my bower, and where I had an opening quite to the sea on the other side of the island. I now resolved to travel quite cross to the seashore on that side…

I saw abundance of parrots, and fain I would have caught one, if possible, to have kept it to be tamed, and taught it to speak to me. I did, after some painstaking, catch a young parrot, for I knocked it down with a stick; and having recovered it, I brought it home, but it was some years before I could make him speak. However, at last I taught him to call me by name very familiarly.

1. Identify the author and the work from which the passage is selected.
2. Why did the hero try to teach a parrot to call his name? Explain it from the historical background of the novel.
3. How do you understand his life on the island, such as hunting, capture of Friday?

Ⅴ. Short answer question

As a pioneering novelist of England, Daniel Defoe is often given the credit for the discovery of the modern novel. Does he deserve that honor? What is the title of his great work? When was the book published, and what real experiences is it based upon? What is the significance of the novel? What are some of the author's biases revealed in the novel if we examine it from a modern Critic's point of view?（人大 2006 研）

Ⅵ. Essay question

In what way does Daniel Defoe's *Robinson Crusoe* reflect the history of British colonization in the 18th century?（天津外国语 2008 研）

参考答案及解析

Ⅰ. Fill in the blanks.

1. Enlightenment

（启蒙运动是发生在17、18世纪欧洲的一场反封建、反教会的思想文化革命运动，它为资产阶级革命作了思想准备和舆论宣传。）

2. realism

（18世纪主要的文学潮流是现实主义。启蒙时期的现实主义，是文艺复兴时期现实主义的继续，但又有新的发展。它的特征在于具有更多的政论性，作家们都有意识地把他们自己的政治思想贯穿在文学作品之中。）

3. the Age of Reason

（18世纪的英国是一个启蒙主义时代，或称为理性时代。启蒙主义者宣扬理性、平等与科学。他们提出要用当代的哲学与艺术思想的晨光启迪世界，主张理性是一切思想与行动的唯一原因。）

Ⅱ. Multiple Choices

1. C　18世纪英国文学最显著的特征是现实主义小说的兴起和发展。
2. D　《与意见不同者们打交道的捷径》是笛福的作品，他曾因这本政治小册子获罪。其余都是弥尔顿的作品。

Ⅲ. Explain the following terms.

1. English Enlightenment: In the eighteenth century there emerged a wave of new ideas whose believers embraced reason, logic, eternal justice, and natural equality. The movement is termed the Enlightenment or the Age of Reason. Alexander Pope, Joseph Addison, Jonathan Swift, and Samuel Johnson are representative writers of the Enlightenment period.
2. British neoclassicism: The English Neoclassicism refers to the stylistic trend that approximately started with the Restoration and lasted till the pre-Romantic period. The term "neoclassicism" stems from beliefs that literature should follow examples of great Creek and Latin writers according to major critics of the time who also favored type over individuality, order over confusion, the three unities over other text-construction. John Dryden, Alexander Pope, and Samuel Johnson are representatives of neoclassicist writers.
3. Gothic novel: ① Also known as Gothic romance, it is a story casting terror and suspense, usually set in a gloomy old castle or monastery. ② The Gothic novel boasted growing publication in Britain between the 1790s and the 1820s with Ann Radcliffe's *The Mysteries of Udolpho* a popular literary creation to be widely imitated. ③ The Gothic novel captured the new emotional climate of Romanticism. Mary Shelley's *Frankenstein* is a successful presentation of the gothic zeal. America was also under the influence of the Gothic fervor with tales and novels by Poe, Faulkner among others.

Ⅳ. Read the following quotation and answer the questions.

1. The passage is taken from *Robinson Crusoe* by Daniel Defoe.
2. Eager to communicate and speak, Robinson tried to teach a parrot to call his name. Loneliness and isolation from human contact intensifies Crusoe's desire for company.

   In the 18th century, the religious establishments advocated that the secular had the absolute authority and power over human beings who could only abide by the holy instruction and design. However, Robinson's success in teaching the parrot to call his name is a bold proof of human creativity, knowledge, and power, suggesting the emerging bourgeois mentality of this time.
3. Though filled with difficulties at the beginning of his life on the deserted island, Crusoe adapts

himself to and finally gains dominance over the harsh environment with unremitting labor such as hunting, taming, gathering, harvesting, and making baskets and pots. Through his efforts, shelter, food, clothes, and even reading materials are available, and he is content with his life.

Later he saves a savage man and gives him the name Friday who becomes a servant and keeps Crusoe company. The story praises puritan virtues such as industry and fortitude. It is these qualities that spare him from despair and give him pride and happiness. Crusoe's adventures on the island can be deemed as colonial practice in which he acts as the conqueror of a new place with his gun and Bible. The colonial trait in Defoe's narratives is a mirror of the general colonial zeal of his time.

V. Short answer question

(1) Yes, for his novel *Robinson Crusoe* generally heads the list of modern fiction.

(2) *Robinson Crusoe.*

(3) This book was published in 1719, based on the adventures of a seaman, Alexander Selkirk, who had been marooned on one of the Juan Fernández Islands off the coast of Chile.

(4) The significance of the novel: ①The novel is a mirror of bourgeois ideal such as individualism and private property. With firm beliefs in one's capacity and potentials to advance in any environment, Robinson Crusoe is a man of the new age in which hope and confidence were mainstream qualities. ②Through Crusoe's adventures and conquering, Defoe conveyed confidence in human capacity. ③Pioneer of his age, Robinson Crusoe is ready to take control of nature, defeat his enemy, and establish his colony beyond the sea. With intense merchant spirit and interest in material gains, Robinson's every voyage is bound with some commercial enterprise. ④The novel is a fictional account of the changing climate of the English society as the rising bourgeoisie brought with them emerging zeal for individualism and colonial expansion. ⑤Friday's transformation and Crusoe's success in conquering land serve as confirmation of Defoe's recognition of colonization as part of the bourgeois merits.

(5) This novel revealed the colonialism, Negro-slavery thought, individualism, and materialism. (本题考查对丹尼尔·笛福的掌握情况。丹尼尔·笛福是英国启蒙时期现实主义小说的奠基人，被誉为“小说之父”。其作品主要为个人通过努力，靠自己的智慧和勇敢战胜困难。其代表作《鲁滨逊漂流记》闻名于世，鲁滨逊也成为与困难抗争的典型模范，因此他被视作英国小说的开创者之一。)

VI. Essay question

Robinson Crusoe can be interpreted as Defoe's idealization of colonialism and consequential improvement along with it, a general ideology shared by the rising bourgeois society in Britain. Therefore, the novel added fuel to colonial expansion by British colonizers who claimed that their adventures would spare unexplored lands from savage and backwardness. Friday, a savage man saved from hands of cannibals, is a fine example of such British concept. The colonization manifests itself first in cultural colonization. The first word Crusoe teaches Friday is "Master" which is said to be the name of Crusoe. To Crusoe, it is for Friday's sake that he learns English without taking Friday's language into account. Then, Friday is asked to convert to Christianity. By twisting Friday's identity, language, and religious faith, Crusoe takes entire control over Friday. The second level of colonization is the colonist's gun. Crusoe uses arm force to guarantee his master position in his relationship with Friday. Defoe conveyed in his novel the idea of salvation in the course of colonization which was regarded as a just cause for colonizing numerous overseas lands where terrible atrocities occurred and where the arrival of white colonizers would usher in civilization for the eventual good of local people. The care and teaching from Crusoe seem to Friday that a colonizing power can lift him out of the darkness of ignorance.

（本题考查了对《鲁滨逊漂流记》殖民主题的理解。）

第 11 章　乔纳森·斯威夫特

11.1　复习笔记

Jonathan Swift(1667—1745)

1. Life

Jonathan Swift was a satirist, essayist, political pamphleteer, poet, and cleric. At Dublin University, he detested the curriculum, reading only what interested him. He spent ten best years of his life in Moor Park, where he read extensively. However, knowing that he had more literary talent than his employer and could not stand being slighted, he quit his job, joined the Church of England, and then took up a post in a small church in Ireland.

As his satirical talent matured, he resigned from the priesthood, plunged himself into party politics, and became a literary leader. Later he became the Dean of St. Patrick's Cathedral in Dublin, where he stood beside the Irish in their fight to improve their lot. Swift has been struggling with a brain disease he suffered from since a young age. The illness eventually led to his mental disorder. After much suffering, Swift died in great pain in 1745.

2. Writing Style

(1) One of the greatest prose writers, The language of Swift features preciseness, directness, and vigor. He said, "Proper words in proper places, makes the true definition of a style."

(2) He is a master satirist as his sarcasm hits the nail on the head and is always hidden behind the surface of a cool voice.

3. Major Works

The Battle of the Books (1704)

A Tale of a Tub (1704)

Bickerstaff Almanac (1708)

Gulliver's Travels (1726)

乔纳森·斯威夫特(1667—1745)

1. 生平

乔纳森·斯威夫特是一位讽刺作家、散文家、政治宣传者，诗人和圣职人员。在都柏林大学时，他十分厌恶课程，只读自己感兴趣的书。毕业后，斯威夫特在摩尔公园度过了人生最美好的十年，博览群书。然而，他很清楚自己比雇主更有文学才能，且忍受不了被轻视，他辞了职，加入英国国教，之后在爱尔兰的一个小教堂任职。

他的讽刺才华日渐成熟，便辞去神职，投身党派政治斗争，成为文学界的领导者。后来他成为都柏林圣帕特里克教堂的教长，期间他和爱尔兰人民一起为他们的权利而战。斯威夫特一直受年轻时就患有的脑疾困扰。最后疾病导致他的精神失常，在承受巨大痛苦之后，斯威夫特于 1745 年在极度痛苦中死去。

2. 写作风格

(1) 斯威夫特是最伟大的英国散文家之一。他的语言简洁明了，充满活力。他说，在恰当的地方放上恰当的词，这就是风格的真正含义。

(2) 他是位讽刺大师，讽刺一针见血。但是他的嘲讽却总是隐藏于表面的严肃之后，不动声色的平静下面潜伏着辛辣的讽刺。

3. 主要作品

《书战》(1704)

《一只桶的故事》(1704)

《比克斯塔福历书》(1708)

《格列佛游记》(1726)

Drapier's Letters (1726)

A Modest Proposal (1729)

4. Selected Works

◆*Gulliver's Travels*

The book tells the extraordinary adventures of Doctor Lemuel Gulliver, who describes the fantastic lands he visited and the social systems, ways of living, and customs thereof in four parts.

In the first part, Gulliver narrates the shipwreck experience in Lilliput where the tallest people were six inches high. The country has two parties, divided according to the height of the heel of the shoe through which Swift satirizes the Tories and the Whigs in England. Moreover, he laughed at religious disputes through the absurd situation that Lilliput is divided according to whether the eggs should be cracked on the big side or the small side.

The second part is about the voyage to Brobdingnag. The King of Brobdingnag often asks Gulliver for his views on European affairs, and Gulliver's responses satirize contemporary politics.

The third part depicts the odd phenomenon on the flying island of Laputa where people are obsessed with abstract and dreamy speculations through which Swift criticized scholastics and philosophers.

In the last part, Gulliver's satire is the harshest. Swift depicted the bourgeoisie as man-like creatures—Yahoos to criticize the degenerating aristocracy and the English state system.

◆"A Modest Proposal"

"A Modest Proposal" is one of Swift's most important pamphlets in Ireland. Swift first presented a vivid picture of the miserable living conditions of the poor people in Ireland as a result of which he proposed a scheme that poor people should sell their babies at one year old as a delicacy for the rich. The essay is full of bitter irony, and in fact Swift is saying "the English are devouring the Irish". This article strongly condemns the cruel oppression and exploitation of people by the British ruling class, especially the oppression of poor Irish peasants by wealthy English landlords.

《布商来信》(1726)

《一个温和的建议》(1729)

4. 选读作品

◆《格列佛游记》

这本书讲述了格列佛医生非凡的冒险经历，描写了他所到的许多奇幻岛屿，其社会体系，居民的生活方式和风俗。故事分成四部分。

在第一部分格列佛描述了在一个叫利立浦特的地方海船失事。这儿的人最高的只有六英尺高。这个国家有两党，根据鞋跟高低来划分，以此讽刺英国的托利党和辉格党。利立浦特的划分是根据鸡蛋应该在大头儿砸开还是小头儿砸开，以此讽刺英国的宗教纷争。

第二部分是关于到大人国的旅行。大人国国王经常询问格列佛对欧洲事务的看法，格列佛的回答是对当代政治的辛辣讽刺。

第三部分描述了拉普他岛上的怪异现象，居民都沉迷于不切实际的空想，讽刺了学者和哲学家。

在最后一部分，格列佛的讽刺最严厉。斯威夫特将资产阶级世界形象化为令人讨厌的人型状的动物——野胡。他无情地鞭笞了堕落的贵族，讽刺了整个英国国家系统。

◆《一个温和的建议》

《一个温和的建议》是斯威夫特关于爱尔兰的最重要的小册子之一。本文首先描写了爱尔兰穷苦人民的悲惨生活。然后他建议要解决这一问题，可以让穷人出售自己一岁大的孩子给富人当作一道美味佳肴。斯威夫特通过尖锐的讽刺，实际上是在表明"英格兰人正在吞噬爱尔兰人"。本文强烈谴责了英国统治阶层对爱尔兰人民的残酷压迫和剥削，尤其是那些英国富人地主阶层对爱尔兰穷苦农民的压榨。

11.2 考研真题与典型题详解

Ⅰ. Fill in the blanks.

1. Jonathan Swift's *A Tale of a Tub* is a devastating attack on ________ and even on ________ itself. (国际关系学院 2009 研)
2. "A Modest Proposal" by Jonathan Swift is a sharp ________ against the social injustice in ________. (天津外国语学院 2011 研)
3. Author ________ Title ________ (南京大学 2007 研)

   At other times, the like battles have been fought between the Yahoos of several neighborhoods, without any visible cause: those of one district watching all opportunities to surprise the next, before they are prepared. But if they find their project has miscarried, they return home, and, for want of enemies, engage in what I call a civil war among themselves.

Ⅱ. Multiple Choices

1. Which of the following works is generally regarded as the best model of satire, not only of the 18th century but also in the whole English literary history? (四川大学 2007 研)

   A. *A Modest Proposal*　　B. *The History of Tom Jones*

   C. *An Essay on Criticism*　　D. *Robinson Crusoe*

2. In 1704, Jonathan Swift published two works together, *A Tale of a Tub* and ________, which made him well-known as a satirist.

   A. *A Tale of a Tub*　　B. *Bickerstaff Almanac*

   C. *Gulliver's Travels*　　D. *The Battle of the Books*

3. The 18th century witnessed that in England there appeared two political parties, ________, which were satirized by Jonathan Swift in his *Gulliver's Travels*.

   A. The Whigs and the Tories

   B. the senate and the House of Representatives

   C. the upper House and lower House

   D. the House of Lords and the House of Commons

Ⅲ. Explain the following terms.

1. "A Modest Proposal" (四川大学 2008 研)
2. Satire (厦门大学 2009 研; 西安交通大学 2008 研)

Ⅳ. Short answer question

What are Jonathan Swift's writing features?

Ⅴ. Essay questions

1. State the artistic features of *Gulliver's Travels*.
2. Analyze *Gulliver's Travels* to illustrate the use of satire in it.

参考答案及解析

Ⅰ. Fill in the blanks.

1. the three branches of the church; Christianity

（《一只桶的故事》表面上讲的是三兄弟背弃父亲遗嘱的故事，实际上讽刺了罗马天主教、清教和英国国教，甚至是对整个基督教的嘲讽。）

2. satire, Ireland

（1729 年斯威夫特发表的《一个温和的建议》是对英国政府对爱尔兰人民剥削压迫的极度讽刺。这一宣传册建议爱尔兰的穷人把刚满一周岁的孩子卖给富人，富人可将孩子做成美食，而穷人也将获得一笔收入。）

3. Author: Jonathan Swift　　Title: *Gulliver's Travels*

（题中文段节选自乔纳森的《格列佛游记》。其通过幻想旅行中不可置信的奇遇和体验，极其尖锐地讽刺了英国统治者的腐败和愚行，无情地揭露了社会各领域的黑暗和罪恶。）

Ⅱ. Multiple Choices

1. A　题目考查下列哪部作品被公认为不但是 18 世纪，而且是整个英国文学史上反讽艺术的典范。Jonathan Swift（乔纳森·斯威夫特）的著名讽刺散文《一个温和的建议》为正确选项。

2. D　乔纳森·斯威夫特是英国十八世纪杰出的政论家和讽刺小说家。《书战》和《一只桶的故事》是他 1704 年同时发表的两部作品。《书战》是在蒲柏"崇古非今"思想的影响下完成的。《一只桶的故事》却是一部意义深远的杰出的讽刺作品。斯威夫特这次把矛头指向教会，同时对于当时贫乏的学术、浅薄的文学批评和社会恶习也予以抨击。

3. A　18 世纪英国主要有托利党与辉格党两大政党。在其代表讽刺作品《格列佛游记》中，斯威夫特通过"高跟党"与"低跟党"的描述讽刺与批判了当时英国的两大政党。

Ⅲ. Explain the following terms.

1. "A Modest Proposal": "A Modest Proposal" is a famous satire written by Jonathan Swift. Acting like an impartial outsider concerned about the livelihood of the impoverished, the author in a calm and neutral manner suggests that children of poor Irish people be sold at one year old as food for English nobles. The pamphlet is considered Swift's most powerful response to the ruthless oppression and exploitation suffered by the Irish people and his harshest critique over the English ruling class.

2. Satire: ① Satire is a type of writing with the purpose to ridicule and criticize the weakness and wrongdoings observed by the writer. ② The ultimate goal of writing satires is to set moral standards for society and persuade the reader to see the seriousness of the problems mentioned through the force of laughter. ③ Swift's *Gulliver's Travels* is a great satire of English society unique in its style and language.

Ⅳ. Short answer question

(1) Jonathan Swift is one of the realist writers of the 18th century. All of Swift's plots are credited to his rich imagination quite different from that of Daniel Defoe whose stories are based upon the reality of human life.

(2) Swift's satire discusses serious topics with apparent coolness and sincerity which makes his satire all the more powerful and effective. His bitter satire is to criticize the bourgeoisie in general from a wider context.

(3) Swift conveyed his preference for democracy which had an enduring impact on later writers, such as George Gordon Byron and Bernard Shaw.

(4) Swift is one of the greatest masters of English prose whose writing boasts qualities of simplicity, clearness, and vigor. He said, "Proper words in proper place, makes the true definition of

a style". Removing unnecessary fancy words and keeping expressive and direct expressions, Swift is a true master of the English language and English literature.

（此题可从斯威夫特小说写作特点和散文写作特点两方面作答。）

V. Essay questions

1. ①*Gulliver's travels*, the acme of Swift's achievement in literature, is a satire on the whole English society of the 18th century. Artistically, the novel is a fantasy and a realistic work of fiction. To present an invented story with telling effect, the author used vivid language and gave as many detailed descriptions as possible. In the four parts of the book, through direct descriptions and indirect references, through contrasts and comparisons, through subtle irony and downright attacks, the satirical effect is achieved with much force.

   ②The language in this novel is simple, unadorned, straightforward, and effective. The bitter satire of the writer is well expressed through detailed account of adventures and encounters with different subjects in the story with a heavy touch of authenticity and sincerity.

   ③The narrative technique used in the work also catches attention. On the one hand, the incident begins with an accidental shipwreck, continues with man-made misfortunes, and finally ends with intended mutinies. On the other hand, the hero's attitude towards human erodes after each new adventure and finally becomes dislike. His early eagerness to return home eventually turns into complete reluctance and repulsion.

2. ①*Gulliver's Travels* satirizes the whole English society of the early 18th century, in terms of its politics, religion, legal system, military actions, scientific progress, philosophy, and literary institutions, covering almost every aspect of the society. The four parts of the book project the writer's satire in different ways.

   ②The first part is imbued with references to current politics. Lilliput is a miniature of England. Through the two parties in the countries distinguished by the use of high and low heels, Swift satires the Tories and Whigs in England. The English religious dissensions are also laughed at in the description of the controversy on the question whether eggs should be broken at the big or the small end.

   ③In the second part, the satire on Western civilization and English lords and ladies is more direct through statement of differences between Brobdingnag and the English society.

   ④In the third part, the satire is on British misgovernance of Ireland, as is reflected in the Flying Island Laputa. Via the description of the Academy of Projectors in Lagado, the author criticized the over obsession of scientific progress and twisted philosophy of his contemporary time. Moreover, false history is criticized in the episode about the Island of the Sorcerers.

   ⑤In the last part, Gulliver is in a country where horses are perfect embodiment of reason and the governing class. By contrast, Yahoos, though in the shape of man, are no better than despised beasts easily corrupted by vices such as stealing and lying. This part ruthlessly exposes the weaknesses in human character and displays a stinging satire on the English society.

第 12 章 约瑟夫·艾迪生

12.1 复习笔记

I . Joseph Addison (1672—1719)	I . 约瑟夫·艾迪生(1672—1719)
1. Life Joseph Addison, the son of a scholarly clergyman, was educated at Charterhouse School and then at Oxford University, both with Steele, his fast friend. Addison was stronger in character, the better student, quieter and more resourceful. At Oxford, Addison soon made a name for himself as a writer of verses. He was attracted to political writing and had a talent for it, so he won the patronage of some politicians to travel around Europe, learn French, and familiarize himself with the politics of European countries. Four years later, he returned home and rose to fame with a poem celebrating the English Duke of Marlborough. Soon he became a member of Parliament and later was sent to Ireland as Secretary of State.	**1. 生平** 约瑟夫·艾迪生出身于一个牧师家庭，父亲博学多识。他在查特豪斯学校和牛津大学接受教育，这两个时期都和挚友斯蒂尔一起度过。与斯蒂尔相比，艾迪生更刚强、学习更出色、更内敛和足智多谋。在牛津期间，艾迪生很快就以写诗出名。他对政治写作极感兴趣也很有天赋，因此赢得了一些政治家的资助，游历欧洲大陆，学习法语并熟悉欧洲国家的政治。四年后他回国，因一首赞扬马尔堡公爵的诗声名鹊起。不久他便成了议员，后来又去爱尔兰做国务大臣。
2. Literary Achievements Addison's major literary contributions are his essays written for *The Tatler* and *The Spectator*. He collaborated with Steele in publishing The Spectator from 1711 to 1712 which contained articles on the customs, manners, morals, literature, and other topics of the time. Steele and Addison preached temperateness, rationality, self-discipline, civility, gentility, and decent taste, which were indispensable for the newly ruling bourgeoisie to establish its social order.	**2. 文学成就** 主要文学贡献是他为《闲谈者》和《旁观者》写的文章。1711—1712 年，他和斯蒂尔合办《旁观者》。《旁观者》发表的文章与风俗、世态、道德、文学及其他时下流行话题有关。在文章中，斯蒂尔和艾迪生宣传节制、理性、自我约束、文明、文雅和高品位，这些品质都是发展中的资产阶级建立社会秩序亟需的。
3. Writing Style For over a century Addison's approachable and elegant prose remained a good literary model for most writers. Dr. Johnson described his prose as "the model of the middle style; on grave subjects not formal, on light occasions not groveling; pure without scrupulosity, and exact without apparent elaboration, always equable, and always easy, without glowing words or printed sentences."	**3. 写作风格** 艾迪生平易近人、高雅洗练的散文是一个多世纪以来大部分作家写作的典范。约翰逊博士称他的散文是"中庸风格的典范，讨论严肃的话题不正式，轻松的时候又不卑躬屈膝，纯粹而无顾虑，精确又无匠气，总是那么平和从容，毫无华丽辞藻和刻板教条"。

Ⅱ. Richard Steele (1672—1729) **1. Life** Richard Steele was born in Dublin, in the same year as Addison, and was educated at the same school and university as Addison. At Oxford, Steele dropped out of school and joined the army. Returning from wars, he tried to write a few plays and a book. In 1709, he started a paper called *The Tatler*, which contained news, gossip, stories of everyday life, and jokes on all sorts of people. Two years later, he suspended its publication and started another paper named The Spectator, combining the daily paper with the familiar essays to offer entertainment and enlightenment. **2. Analysis of Major Character in *The Spectator*** The essays of *The Spectator* presented the character and doings of Sir Roger, a simple-minded, kind-hearted, old-fashioned, and sometimes pompous country gentleman. Presented with a gentle humor, the writing displays Roger's merits of simplicity, honesty, and piety which set an example to the polite society.	**Ⅱ. 理查德 · 斯蒂尔(1672—1729)** **1. 生平** 理查德 · 斯蒂尔生于都柏林，和艾迪生同龄，并和他在同一所学校上学。在牛津期间，斯蒂尔丢掉学业，参军入伍。从战场上回来，他试着写了些剧本和一本书。1709年，斯蒂尔创办了《闲谈者》报，内容包括新闻、小道消息、日常故事和各种人的玩笑。两年后，《闲谈者》停刊，他又创办了《旁观者》，将日报和亲近人心的随笔结合，旨在娱乐和教化读者。 **2.《旁观者》主要人物分析** 《旁观者》中的随笔展现了罗杰爵士这个人物及其行为。罗杰爵士是因循守旧的老乡绅，单纯善良，爱摆架子。文章笔调幽默地描写了他的小缺点，衬托出了他单纯、诚实、虔诚的美德，为上流社会树立了榜样。

12.2 考研真题与典型题详解

Ⅰ. Fill in the blanks.

1. Joseph Addison and Sir Richard Steele are always remembered together because they started a journalistic tradition that is still alive in Britain and the United State. Their collaboration on a series of essays for *The Tatler* and ___________ strongly influenced 18th century English taste and opinion. (天津外国语 2010 研)
2. ___________ is Alexander Pope's poem which indicates the poet's political and philosophical viewpoint. It deals with man's relation to the universe, to society, to himself and to happiness.
3. Joseph Addison and Richard Steele developed the form of letter-writing to the verge of the ___________ novel.
4. ___________, i. e. the Iliad of Dunces or dullards, is a brilliant satirical poem in 4 books written by Alexander Pope, provoked by Theobald's criticism of his edition of Shakespeare.
5. Alexander Pope's ___________ is a manifesto of English neo-classicism in which Alexander Pope put forward his aesthetic theories. It was a comprehensive study of theories of literary criticism.

Ⅱ. Multiple Choices

1. *An Essay on Criticism* is a didactic poem written in ___________.
   A. alliteration B. heroic couplet C. sonnet D. blank verse
2. In the 18th century, satire was much used in writing, and English literature of this age produced

some excellent satirists, such as the following writers except ________.

A. Alexander Pope　　B. Jonathan Swift

C. Henry Fielding　　D. Daniel Defoe

3. ________ was the most important English poet in the first half of the 18th century.

A. Richard Steele　　B. Joseph Addison

C. Alexander Pope　　D. Samuel Richardson

Ⅲ. Explain the following term.

British neoclassicism（南开大学2009研）

Ⅳ. Read the following quotation and answer the questions.（南开大学2007研）

All nature is but Art, unknown to thee;
All Chance, Direction, which thou canst not see;
All discord, Harmony not understood;
All partial Evil, universal Good;
And, spite of Pride, in erring Reason's spite,
One truth is clear, Whatever is, is right.

1. What idea do these lines indicate that the poet has?
2. What philosophy do these lines express? Do you agree with the writer's idea that "whatever is, is right"? Why or why not?

Ⅴ. Short answer questions

1. Why is Alexander Pope known as representative of the Enlightenment?（国际关系学院2007研）
2. What great work did Joseph Addison and Richard Steele do for English literature?

Ⅵ. Essay question

Comment on the features of the neoclassical literature.

参考答案及解析

Ⅰ. Fill in the blanks.

1. *The Spectator*

（约瑟夫·艾迪生和理查德·斯蒂尔是英国著名的散文家，两人最重要的贡献是创办两份著名的杂志《闲谈者》与《旁观者》。）

2. *An Essay on Man*

（《人论》是蒲柏的一首哲理诗，在这首诗中蒲柏表达了他的政治哲学思想。）

3. epistolary

（约瑟夫·艾迪生和理查德·斯蒂尔经常一起被提起，两人最重要的贡献是创办两份著名的杂志《闲谈者》(*The Tatler*)与《旁观者》(*The Spectator*)以及发展了书信体写作形式。）

4. *The Dunciad*

（《群愚史诗》共四册，是亚历山大·蒲柏最优秀的讽刺作品。他讽刺了同时期所有与蒲柏为敌的文学人士。）

5. *An Essay on Criticism*

（《批评论》是亚历山大·蒲柏对文学批评理论的全面研究，叙述了古典主义诗歌的原理，对同时期的作家们产生了深远的影响，倡导了古典主义标准，在英国普及了新古典主义。）

Ⅱ. Multiple Choices

1. B 《批评论》是蒲柏著名的诗歌，阐明了自己的文学观点，全诗采用了英雄双韵体。
2. D 亚历山大·蒲柏是18世纪英国最伟大的诗人；杰出的启蒙主义者。他的诗作《夺发记》和一些讽刺诗被称为讽刺诗的最高境界；乔纳森·斯威夫特为英国18世纪杰出的政论家和讽刺小说家，写了很多具有代表性的讽刺文章。其代表作是《格列佛游记》，一部杰出的游记体讽刺小说；亨利·菲尔丁是18世纪最杰出的英国小说家，戏剧家。他的许多作品讽刺和抨击当时的社会陋习；丹尼尔·笛福是一位英国作家，新闻记者，小册子作者。英国启蒙时期现实主义小说的奠基人，被誉为“小说之父”。他的作品反映当时追求冒险，倡导个人奋斗的社会风气。
3. C 蒲柏是18世纪上半期英国最主要的新古典主义诗人；理查德·斯蒂尔和约瑟夫·艾迪生是新古典主义时期齐名的散文家；塞缪尔·理查森是新古典主义时期重要的小说家。

Ⅲ. Explain the following term.

British neoclassicism: The English Neoclassicism refers to the stylistic trend that approximately started with the Restoration and lasted till the pre-Romantic period. Critics of neoclassicism emphasized that literature and literary criticism should follow the steps of ancient Greek and Latin writers and they favored type over individuality, strict observation of the three unities over loose structure, regularity over disorder. John Dryden, Alexander Pope, and Samuel Johnson are representatives of neoclassicist writers.

Ⅳ. Read the following quotation and answer the questions.

1. As a classical poet in the period of English Enlightenment, Alexander Pope highlighted the human capacity to think and reason and expressed concern over the conditions of human life and nature in the poem.

   （题目中的诗歌节选自英国启蒙时期的伟大诗人亚历山大·蒲柏的 *An Essay on Man*（《人论》）的第一章。《人论》是首哲理诗，反映了诗人的哲学、伦理观点，表现了启蒙思想家的思想特点。）

2. These lines deal with God's design of order and human's role in it. As God's purposes are unknown to man, he cannot complain about his position in the Great Chain of Being and must accept that “Whatever is, is right”.

   In my opinion, this assumption could be right if it is based on an underlying assumption that people do everything according to the order of the nature. Otherwise, it is a fallacy.

   （本题考查节选诗句中所包含的哲学思想，即：存在的即是合理的，因为造物主所创造的一切都有其内在的秩序与和谐，只是人类不能理解和领悟。答题时可以根据自己的理解对这种哲学思想进行评价。参考译文：整个自然都是艺术，不过你不领悟 /一切偶然都是规定，只是你没有看清；/一切不协，是你不理解的和谐 /一切局部的祸，乃是全体的福。/高傲可鄙，只因它不近情理 /凡存在的都合理，这就是清楚的道理。（王佐良译））

Ⅴ. Short answer questions

1. Alexander Pope was among the first to write on rationalism in Britain. To his mind, universal education is necessary, especially that of social morality, classic culture, and scientific knowledge.

As a typical neoclassical writer, he also sang high praise for traditional civilization which embraced virtues of reason, classical learning, sound art, good taste, and civism. He considered his duty to "correct" and enlighten people who went astray through his poetry. His *An Essay on Man* is an important work of enlightenment.

2. ①Addison and Steele's chief contribution to English literature is the two periodicals: *The Tatler* and *The Spectator* whose popularity and success helped promote the development of periodical literature in England.

   ②Their essays offered a new code of social morality for the rising bourgeoisie. The general propose was "to enliven morality with wit, and to temper wit with morality". In their articles, virtues such as moderation, rationality, self-discipline, gentility, civism and good taste are advocated as necessary for the newly ruling bourgeoisie to establish its social order.

   ③They presented the social life in the eighteenth-century England with vividity. *The Spectator* contains an extensive and expressive account of members of a club Spectator, which represented the contemporary social types. The periodical also records their visit to the exchanges, theaters, coffee-houses, and many other popular places.

   ④The English essay had completely established itself as a literary genre. There are prominent features such as humor, intimacy, and elegance shown in their essays and the English familiar essay. The approach of character-sketching and storytelling used in essays provided new literary treatment and contributed to the birth of modern English novel.

Ⅵ. Essay question

(1) Neoclassicism in literature refers to the style of writing with particular emphasis on reason and order, following the literary principles derived from the best ancient Greek and Roman authors. There is a strong tendency to go back to tradition among Neoclassical writers who showed great respect for classical writers and took classical works as the literary models.

(2) Neoclassical writers tended to follow the models and rules in Greek and Roman works in which rimed couplets, the three unities of time, place, and action, regularity, and types were considered as standards of drama. Poetry, including popular forms such as mock epic, romance, satire, and epigram, was structured elegantly with serious, earnest, and didactic tone. In terms of the overall diction, prose should be accurate, straightforward, and flexible.

(3) In terms of style, neoclassical writings are noted for qualities such as politeness, complaisance, humor, and intellect as writers pursued regularity and unity in structure and an overall sense of harmony and grace.

(4) Literature at that time was of heavy didacticism and moralization and served as a very popular means of public education.

第13章 亨利·菲尔丁

13.1 复习笔记

Henry Fielding(1707—1754)	**亨利·菲尔丁(1707—1754)**
1. Life	**1. 生平**
Fielding was born on April 22, 1707 in the family of General Fielding. He was educated at the Eton School and took a degree in letters at the University of Leiden in 1728. Later, he made a precarious living by writing plays, farces, and buffooneries for the stage. He went to Lisbon in 1754 to recuperate, but died within the year.	菲尔丁于1707年4月22日出生，父亲是菲尔丁将军。他就读于伊顿公学，1728年在莱顿大学拿到文学学位。之后，他靠给剧场写剧本、闹剧、滑稽剧为生，很不稳定。为了疗养身体，他于1754年去里斯本，但年内就去世了。
2. Literary Achievements	**2. 文学成就**
Fielding is the greatest novelist of the 18th century. He was energetic, not only as a novelist, but also as a dramatist, essayist, and political commentator. He was called "Father of English novel".	菲尔丁是18世纪最伟大的小说家之一。他精力充沛，不仅是小说家，而且是戏剧家，散文家和评论政治时事的作家。他被称为英国小说之父。
3. Writing Style	**3. 写作风格**
Fielding's style is direct, vigorous, hilarious, and even vulgar. He told the story of a vagabond life simply to "laugh men out of their follies". So, his story always has a strong sense of authenticity.	菲尔丁的风格直接、强有力、非常滑稽、甚至有些粗俗。他讲述流浪汉的生活，只是为了"取笑人们的愚蠢"。所以他的故事总是给读者很强的真实感。
4. Major Works	**4. 主要作品**
Shamela (1741)	《莎美拉》(1741)
Joseph Andrews (1742)	《约瑟夫·安德鲁斯》(1742)
Jonathan Wild (1743)	《乔纳森·威尔德》(1743)
The History of Tom Jones, a Foundling (1749)	《弃婴汤姆·琼斯的故事》(1749)
Amelia (1751)	《阿米丽亚》(1751)
5. Selected Work	**5. 选读作品**
◆***The History of Tom Jones, a Foundling***	◆**《弃婴汤姆·琼斯的故事》**
Tom Jones is a foundling discovered in the bedroom of a very kind, wealthy landowner, squire Allworthy. The squire takes him in, and Tom grows into a vigorous, mischievous, but kind and honest young man. He falls in love with his neighbor Sophia. But both Sophia's father and Allworthy object to the relationship because Tomis a bastard. Blifil, the son of	汤姆·琼斯是一个弃儿，被发现在富裕的乡绅奥尔华绥的卧室里。乡绅收养了他，汤姆长成一个精力充沛、淘气但心地善良且诚实的年轻人。他爱上了邻里索菲亚。但是索菲亚的父亲和奥尔华绥都反对两人之间的恋情，因为汤姆是个

Allworthy's sister and adopted by the squire after his parents' death, has always coveted his uncle's fortune and secretly hates Tom. By Bliffy's design, Tom is kicked out of the house. Tom has a series of adventures and affairs in London before he is proved to be the son of Mr. Allworthy's sister, which is withheld by Blifil. At last, Mr. Allworthy reconciles with Tom, and makes him his heir, while Blifil gets his deserved punishment. Sophia forgives Tom's youthful mistakes and Sophia's father gives his consent to their marriage.	私生子。布力菲是奥尔华绥妹妹的儿子，在父母去世后由乡绅收养，他一直觊觎舅舅的财产，并且暗恨汤姆。在布力菲的设计下，汤姆被扫地出门。汤姆在伦敦经历了一系列的冒险和情事。后来真相大白，汤姆也是奥尔华绥妹妹的儿子，他和乡绅和好如初，乡绅立汤姆为继承人。布力菲得到应有的惩罚。索菲亚的父亲同意两人的婚事。

13.2 考研真题与典型题详解

Ⅰ. Fill in the blanks.

1. Henry Fielding has been regarded as "__________", for his contribution to the establishment of the form of the modern novel.（吉林大学 2007 研）

2. As a dramatist, __________'s dramatic theory and practice were in conformity with the theory of "a return to nature" and the principle that "the stage should be a school of morality" in the Enlightenment Period.

Ⅱ. Multiple Choices

1. The author of the following selection is __________.（大连外国语 2007 研）

   A. William Thackeray　　B. Mark Twain

   C. Henry Fielding　　D. Elizabeth Gaskell

   Tom could by no means divine what had incensed Mr. Allworthy, for of Master Blifil he had not the least suspicion. However, as his friendship was to be tired out by no disappointments, he now determined to try another method of preserving the poor gamekeeper from ruin.

   Jones was lately grown very intimate with Mr. Western. He had so greatly recommended himself to that gentleman, by leaping over five-barred gates, and by other acts of sportsmanship, that the squire had declared Tom would certainly make a great man if he had but sufficient encouragement. He often wished he had himself a son with such parts; and one day very solemnly asserted at a drinking bout, that Tom should hunt a pack of hounds for a thousand pound of his money, with any huntsman in the whole country.

2. Of all the 18th century novelists, __________ was the first to set out in theory and practice, to write specially a "comic epic in prose", and the first to give the modern novel its structure and style.

   A. Daniel Defoe　　B. Samuel Richardson

   C. Henry Fielding　　D. Oliver Goldsmith

3. Which of the following is NOT a character in the novel *The History of Tom Jones, a Foundling*?

   A. Blifil　　B. Sophia　　C. Mr. Allworthy　　D. Amelia

4. Henry Fielding's first novel __________ was written in connection with *Pamela* of Samuel Rich-

ardson. But after the first ten chapters, Henry Fielding became so interested and absorbed in his own novel as to forget his original plan of ridiculing *Pamela*.

A. *Tom Jones* B. *Joseph Andrews* C. *Jonathan Wild* D. *Amelia*

5. Which of the following novels is not epistolary novel? ________.

A. *Clarissa* B. *Pamela*

C. *The History of Sir Charles Grandison* D. *Tom Jones*

Ⅲ. Explain the following term.

Picaresque novel

Ⅳ. Read the following quotations and answer the questions.

Passage 1

The hero of this great history appears with very bad omens. A little tale of so low a kind that some may think it not worth their notice. A word or two concerning a squire, and more relating to a gamekeeper and a schoolmaster.

As we determined, when we first sat down to write this history, to flatter no man, but to guide our pen throughout by the directions of truth, we are obliged to bring our hero on the stage in a much more disadvantageous manner than we could wish; and to declare honestly, even at his first appearance, that it was the universal opinion of all Mr. Allworthy's family that he was certainly born to be hanged.

Indeed, I am sorry to say there was too much reason for this conjecture; the lad having from his earliest years discovered a propensity to many vices, and especially to one which hath as direct a tendency as any other to that fate which we have just now observed to have been prophetically denounced against him: he had been already convicted of three robberies, viz., of robbing an orchard, of stealing a duck out of a farmer's yard, and of picking Master Blifil's pocket of a ball.

The vices of this young man were, moreover, heightened by the disadvantageous light in which they appeared when opposed to the virtues of Master Blifil, his companion; a youth of so different a cast from little Jones, that not only the family but all the neighbourhood resounded his praises. He was, indeed, a lad of a remarkable disposition; sober, discreet, and pious beyond his age; qualities which gained him the love of every one who knew him: while Tom Jones was universally disliked; and many expressed their wonder that Mr. Allworthy would suffer such a lad to be educated with his nephew, lest the morals of the latter should be corrupted by his example.

1. Identify the author and the work from which the passages are selected.
2. How do you understand the comments at the beginning of each chapter?
3. What is the relationship between the structure of the story and titular protagonist's growing process of gaining knowledge?
4. What are the author's contributions to the theory of novel?

Passage 2

But well says a certain author, no man is wise at all hours; it is therefore no wonder that a boy is not so. A difference arising at play between the two lads. Master Blifil called Tom a beggarly bastard. Upon which the latter, who was somewhat passionate in his disposition, immediately caused that phenomenon in the face of the former, which we have above remembered.

Master Blifil now, with his blood running from his nose, and the tears galloping after from his eyes, appeared before his uncle and the tremendous Thwackum. In which court an indictment of assault, battery, and wounding, was instantly preferred against Tom; who in his excuse only pleaded the provocation, which was indeed all the matter that Master Blifil had omitted.

It is indeed possible, that this circumstance might have escaped his memory; for, in his reply, he positively insisted, that he had made use of no such appellation; adding, "Heaven forbid such naughty words should ever come out of his mouth."

Tom, though against all form of law, rejoined in affirmance of the words. Upon which Master Blifil said, "It is no wonder. Those who will tell one fib, will hardly stick at another. If I had told my master such a wicked fib as you have done, I should be ashamed to show my face."

"What fib, child?" cries Thwackum pretty eagerly.

"Why, he told you that nobody was with him a shooting when he killed the partridge; but he knows, (here he burst into a flood of tears) yes, he knows; for he confessed it to me, that Black George the gamekeeper was there. Nay, he said, —yes you did, —deny it if you can, that you would not have confessed the truth, though master had cut you to pieces."

At this the fire flashed from Thwackum's eyes; and he cried out in triumph: "Oh ho! This is your mistaken notion of honor! This is the boy who was not to be whipped again!" But Mr. Allworthy, with a more gentle aspect, turned toward the lad, and said, "Is this true, child? How came you to persist so obstinately in a falsehood?"

Tom said, "He scorned a lie as much as anyone; but he thought his honour engaged him to act as he did; for he had promised the poor fellow to conceal him; which," he said, "he thought himself farther obliged to, as the gamekeeper had begged him not to go into the gentleman's manor, and had at last gone himself in compliance with his persuasions." He said, "this was the whole truth of the matter, and he would take his oath of it;" and concluded with very passionately begging Mr. Allworthy to have compassion on the poor fellow's family, especially as he himself had been only guilty, and the other had been very difficultly prevailed on to do what he did. Ind"eed, sir," said he, "it could hardly be called a lie that I told; for the poor fellow was entirely innocent of this whole matter. I should have gone alone after the birds; nay, I did go at first, and he only followed me to prevent more mischief. Do, pray sir, let me be punished; take my little horse away again; but pray sir, forgive poor George."

Mr. Alloworthy hesitated a few moments, and then dismissed the boys, advising them to live more friendly and peaceably together.

Questions:

1. In this passage, what characteristic traits can be found in Tom Jones and Master Blifil?
2. What does the passage say about the relation between Tom and Blifil?
3. Comment on Fielding's narrative features as is reflected in the passage.

V. Short answer questions

1. Why is "Tom Jones" a successful novel? (北航 2008 研)
2. Analyze the character of Tom Jones in *The History of Tom Jones, a Foundling*.

Ⅵ. Essay question

Discuss the artistic features of Henry Fielding's novels.

参考答案及解析

Ⅰ. Fill in the blanks.

1. Father of the English Novel
（亨利·菲尔丁被誉为"英国小说之父"。）
2. Henry Fielding
（亨利·菲尔丁是18世纪最杰出的英国小说家、戏剧家。其代表作品《弃婴汤姆·琼的故事》对后世影响极大。菲尔丁谴责文明世界的伪善和庸俗，赞扬纯朴的人的善良，与启蒙时期"回归自然"的思想相似。）

Ⅱ. Multiple Choices

1. C　题中片段选自英国18世纪现实主义小说的代表人物菲尔丁的代表作《弃婴汤姆·琼斯的故事》(*The History of Tom Jones, a Foundling*)。
2. C　在18世纪的小说家中，亨利·菲尔丁第一次在理论和实践上开创了喜剧性散文体史诗，并且第一次创作了现代小说的结构和风格。
3. D　前三项均为《弃婴汤姆·琼斯的故事》中的人物，其中Blifil为主人公Tom的同母异父兄弟，也是和Tom相对的人物。Sophia是Tom的恋人，Mr. Allworthy是Tom的养父。而Amelia则是作者菲尔丁的另一部小说《阿米丽亚》(*Amelia*)的主人公。
4. B　亨利·菲尔丁的第一部小说《约瑟夫·安德鲁斯》是对塞缪尔·理查森的《帕米拉》中含糊不清的道德标准及造作的伤感情调的嘲讽。
5. D　《克拉丽莎》《帕米拉》《查尔斯·格兰迪森爵士的历史》都是由塞缪尔·理查森创作的书信体小说；《汤姆·琼斯》是亨利·菲尔丁的代表作。

Ⅲ. Explain the following term.

Picaresque novel: ① A genre of novel that was created in the middle of the 16th century based on the description of the city's lower life as the center and on the analysis of all kinds of social phenomena, usually in a humorous style and in concise and fluent language. In it the author exposes evils and social problems of the day. ② Well-known examples of the picaresque novel are Cervantes' *Don Quixote* (1605) and Henry Fielding's Tom Jones (1749).

Ⅳ. Read the following quotations and answer the questions.

Passage 1

1. Henry Fielding, *Tom Jones*
2. Each book of this novel begins with a long chapter of detailed discussions of the character's motives, so that the chapters, if culled and put together would make a good volume on the art of fiction.
3. This novel is a long story of 18 books in three sections of six chapters each. The structure of the novel is well balanced and symmetrical: the first six are set in the Allworthy estate, books Ⅶ—Ⅷ relate events on the road to London, and the last six, the climax, is set in London. The structure coincides with the different stages of the protagonist's growing process of gaining knowledge.
4. Fielding was an innovator in the craft of fiction and a conscious literary artist. His literary theory

is well integrated and expostulated in his novel Tom Jones. Fielding's literary genius embraces a wide range of subjects, including the definition of novel as a genre, faithful descriptions of life, formal characteristics, and the qualities of a novelist. He was the first ever to define novel as a prose epic which enjoys qualified status as an epic poem. Fielding regarded the novel as an effective agent for moral teaching and true reflection of life and nature. In his fiction, Fielding probed into the psychic reality which contributed to the growth of psychological realism. Regarding the form of the novel, sequential movements, priority, and probability are given much thought by Fielding. In terms of the qualification of a novelist, Fielding deemed it necessary for a writer to have four basic qualities—originality, adequate learning, rich experience of life, and kindness.

Passage 2

1. ①Tom Jones is a kind-hearted, righteous, and frank youth. Though he at first denies the fact that the gamekeeper is with him when he kills the partridge, he lies with good intentions. He'd rather be punished by Mr. Allworthy than betray others. Besides, he shows great sympathy for the impoverished. Nevertheless, sometimes he is weak in disciplining his passions. When delighted, or grieved, or angry, he is apt to fall into fits of frenzied excitement. His impulsiveness leads him to break the nose of Master Blifil.

   ②Blifil is a real hypocrite who pretends to be selfless and extremely moral. He always comes up with tricks and plays them upon other people in order to get what he wants but professes the purest motives for his ill deeds. He denies that he has called Tom "'a beggarly bastard", even with tears in his eyes. Obviously, it is he that lies and wants to get the upper hand in the fight with Tom by lying and cheating.
2. They do not get along very well with each other. Master Blifil takes Tom Jones as his rival, and he always competes with Tom for his uncle's favor. He even inflicts injuries upon Tom for his own benefit.
3. ① This passage is about the fight between Blifil and Tom. Fielding assumed a mock-epic tone which gives an impression of seriousness in presenting the scene. He used formal words and expressions such as "provocation", "appellation", and some legal terms like "indictment" and "assault and battery". With these words, Fielding seemed to create a scene in the court.

   ②Fielding depicted the incident as if it were a serious confrontation to give a sense of mocking and humor with exaggerated expressions. The portrayal of Blifil's tears "galloping after from his eyes" highlights Blifil's parochial small-mindedness. Fielding used irony here: Blifil intentionally conceals the fact, while the narrator says: "It is indeed possible, that this circumstance might have escaped his memory..." Blifil's hypocrisy is fully exposed here.

V. Short answer questions

1. Henry Fielding's *Tom Jones* is one of the great comic masterpieces of English literature and contributes to the overall development of the novel.

   Tom Jones gives a broad presentation of Tom Jones's life experiences from infancy to his marriage to Sophia Western. Through Tom's growing-up story, Fielding casted heavy satire on the hypocrisy and vanity of most of his supporting cast. The growth of Tom lies in his success not only in overcoming external difficulties and obstacles but also in realizing and correcting his weaknesses in character to win love and make fortunes.

Tom Jones brings its author the name of "Prose Homer." With scores of different places and a whole gallery of about 40 characters, the novel provides a superb panoramic view of the eighteenth-century English country and city life.

Fielding wrote in clear and supple language with excellent design of plot. Its eighteen books of epic form are divided into three sections, 6 books each, clearly marked out by the change of scenes: in the country, on the highway and in London. With this, Fielding has indeed achieved his goal of writing a "comic epic in prose".

2. ①Tom, a frank, righteous, and kind youth, may sometimes be very impulsive and commit rather serious mistakes, particularly in his relations with women. Despite this weakness in character, he is always ready to help others and never intends to hurt anyone for selfish purposes.

   ②Tom Jones is an antihero, who embodies the author's view of human nature that it is a combination of good and evil. It shows that even a good man may commit mistakes and be easily led astray, but by virtue of his innate goodness, he will eventually triumph over corruption and overcome his weaknesses.

Ⅵ. Essay question

①First of all is his approach to accounting a story. Fielding started "the third-person narration", with which he could tell the external behavior of characters which readers can easily "see" themselves but also the inner world of them. Fielding frequently communicated with readers at the beginning of his novel about his opinions of literary creation and criticism.

②Also, Fielding used satire extensively in his novels. There are two kinds of satire: humorous satire and grim satire. The former is meant to instruct and correct; the latter is used to attack the cardinal evils and corruption of the ruling class.

③Fielding is a master of style. He wrote in easy and approachable style but also presented stories with vigor and vividity by virtue of his excellent linguistic command. Sentences in his novels are always logical and rhythmical. Moreover, Fielding would set his story in balanced structure with dramatic dialogues pertaining to each character and use theatrical devices such as suspense, coincidence, and surprise. The skillful use of these techniques contributed to the juicy storyline and presentation of his novels.

第 14 章　托马斯·格雷

14.1　复习笔记

Thomas Gray (1716—1771)	托马斯·格雷(1716—1771)
1. Life Thomas Gray was brought up in poor health, and his unhappy childhood caused his melancholy which is noticeable in all his poems. He graduated from Cambridge and lived a life of serenity as a professor of history and modern languages at Cambridge. Gray was a poet of transition from neoclassicism to Romanticism.	**1. 生平** 托马斯·格雷从小体弱多病，他不幸的童年造成了他的忧郁，这种忧郁在他的诗中随处可见。他毕业于剑桥，后作为历史和现代语言教师任教于剑桥，过着平静的生活。他是新古典主义过渡到浪漫主义时期的诗人。
2. Major Works "Elegy Written in a Country Churchyard" "Ode on a Distant Prospect of Eton College" "Hymns to Adversity"	**2. 主要作品** 《墓园挽歌》 《伊顿远眺》 《逆境颂》
3. Selected Work **◆"Elegy Written in a Country Churchyard"** The natural scene chosen at the beginning of the poem brilliantly creates a somber atmosphere without losing classical precision and elegance. The poem expresses respect for the hard and useful work of ordinary people as well as sympathy for their obscure lives. The poem also reminds us that we are all destined to die, no matter how much we enjoy and possess in our lifetime.	**3. 选读作品** **◆《墓园挽歌》** 诗歌开篇选取的自然景象绝妙地渲染了一种阴沉忧郁的氛围，同时又不失古典主义的精确与优雅。这首诗表达了对普通人民辛勤有益的劳动的尊重，以及对他们默默无闻的一生的同情。这首诗也提醒我们人固有一死，不论在世时享尽多少荣华富贵。

14.2　考研真题与典型题详解

Ⅰ. Fill in the blanks.

1. Thomas Gray's highly-praised poem ________ shows the poet's sympathy for the poor, and condemns the great ones who despise the poor and bring sufferings to the common people.
2. The 18th century produced the first English novelists, who fall into two groups, one is the sentimental novelists; the other is the ________ novelists.

Ⅱ. Multiple Choices

1. The sentence of "The plowman homeward plods his weary way, /And leaves the world to darkness and to me" is written by ________.

   A. William Cowper　B. George Crabbe　C. Thomas Gray　D. William Blake

2. ___________ found its representative writers in the field of poetry, such as Edward Young and Thomas Gray, but it manifested itself chiefly in the novels of Laurence Sterne and Oliver Goldsmith.

A. Pre-romanticism B. Romanticism C. Sentimentalism D. Naturalism

Ⅲ. Explain the following term.

Graveyard school of poetry

Ⅳ. Short answer questions

1. How do images help to convey the poet's idea in "Elegy Written in a Country Churchyard"?
2. What are the features of Thomas Gray's poetry?

Ⅴ. Essay question

What are the three stages of the Enlightenment?

参考答案及解析

Ⅰ. Fill in the blanks.

1. "Elegy Written in a Country Churchyard"

(托马斯·格雷是"感伤主义"诗派中一位重要诗人。《墓园挽歌》是格雷最优秀的诗篇，在诗中，他抒发了对穷人与无名卒的同情，并嘲讽了那些轻视穷人并给穷人带来苦难的"伟人"。)

2. realist

(18 世纪英国小说家可分为：感伤主义小说家和现实主义小说家。)

Ⅱ. Multiple Choices

1. C "耕种的人拖着疲惫的身体脚步踉跄地走在回家的路上 ⁄把整个世界留给了我与黄昏"是托马斯·格雷《墓园挽歌》的诗句。

2. C 感伤主义是 18 世纪中叶英国新诞生的一个文学流派，它的诞生主要源自某些启蒙运动家对社会现实的极大不满。感伤主义在诗歌领域的代表人物是：爱德华·扬和托马斯·格雷，小说领域则是：劳伦斯·斯特恩和奥利弗·哥尔德史密斯。

Ⅲ. Explain the following term.

Graveyard school of poetry: (1) It refers to a group of eighteenth-century English poets who already did not strictly follow the literary principles of neoclassicism such as objectivity and detachment but emphasized subjectivity, mystery, and melancholy. (2) Writers of this school wrote meditative poems usually set in graveyards and dealt with themes of death, mortality/immortality with melancholy appeal. Thomas Gray's "Elegy Written in a Country Churchyard" is the most famous example.

Ⅳ. Short answer questions

1. ①"Elegy Written in a Country Churchyard" is regarded as the best poem by Thomas Gray and it established his poetic fame.

②In this poem, the poet meditates on death, human suffering, and the mysteries of human life with a touch of melancholy. The poem presents rich images of gloom, desolateness, and melancholy and images that show the close of a day as a symbol of the end of life: The bell returning at night, the weary farmer returning home, the jingling of the sleep-inducing bells under the necks of cows, and the insects appearing in the dusk.

③These images highlight the predominant atmosphere of gloom and the central feeling of melancholy, contributing to the poet's lamentation and meditation.

2. ①Thomas Gray's poems are generally sentimental and melancholy. The subjects are often common people who are ideal subjects to convey the poet's central idea that human life, transient and mysterious, is inflicted by endless suffering and inevitable demise. ②His poems leave an impression of seriousness in mood and weight in style, burdened with personification and poetic diction. ③His poems are rich in images and biblical and mythological allusions. All these traits can be easily found in "Elegy Written in a Country Churchyard".

V. Essay question

(1) The early period of the Enlightenment, known for the flourishing neoclassic poetry, lasted from the "Glorious Revolution" to the end of the 1730s. Alexander Pope was a representative. Meanwhile a new prose literature appeared in the essays of Jonathan Swift and in the first realistic fiction of Daniel Defoe.

(2) The second period, the mature period of the Enlightenment, lasted from the 1740s to the 1750s. Important works that appeared during this period were chiefly the novels of Samuel Richardson, Henry Fielding, and Tobias Smollett, with the last two writers vigorously attacked existing social conditions.

(3) The last stage of the Enlightenment covered the last decades of the 18th century during which new literary tendencies of sentimentalism and Pre-Romanticism, both served as protests to social injustice of the day. Representative writers of sentimentalism are poets represented by Edward Young and Thomas Gray and novelists represented by Laurence Sterne and Oliver Goldsmith. Pre-Romantic writers are represented by William Blake and Robert Burns. The chief realistic dramatist of the century is Richard B. Sheridan.

（此题主要从每个阶段的主要文学流派及代表人物等方面作答。）

第 15 章 奥利弗·哥尔德史密斯

15.1 复习笔记

Oliver Goldsmith(1730—1774)

1. Life

Oliver Goldsmith was born in Ireland, the son of a poor Anglican curate. He was disabled due to smallpox in his early years, so his face was ugly and his figure was awkward. He was obviously stupid and useless when he was a child. However, in 1749 he graduated from Trinity College Dublin with a Bachelor of Arts degree. Later, he received medical education, but eventually became a hired writer for *Monthly Review*. Goldsmith was a versatile essayist, poet, novelist and playwright.

2. Major Works

The Citizen of the World (1762)
The Traveller (1764)
The Vicar of Wakefield (1766)
The Good-Natured Man (1768)
The Deserted Village (1770)
She Stoops to Conquer (1773)

3. Selected Work

◆*The Vicar of Wakefield*

The story is told by Dr. Primrose, the kind-hearted vicar. His family suffers successive misfortunes. He loses all his property, and the family is forced to move to a new residence with funding from the squire Thornhill. But Thornhill is a scoundrel with no conscience. He lures the vicar's eldest daughter Olivia and then abandons her. The vicar is also thrown into prison for debts to the squire. The youngest daughter Sophia is forcibly taken hostage by an unknown villain. At this time, a gentleman who seemed to be bankrupt rescues Sophia, and then he explains that he is the uncle of the Thornhill Squire. Finally, the evil deeds of the squire are exposed. All now ends happily. Sir William marries Sophia. Olivia is found out and the squire is made to marry her. The vicar's fortune is restored to him.

奥利弗·哥尔德斯密斯(1730—1774)

1. 生平

奥利弗·哥尔德史密斯出生于爱尔兰，是一个贫困的英国国教乡村牧师之子。他早年因得天花而残疾，面部丑陋，身形笨拙。小时候他显然十分愚笨无用。然而，1749年他从都柏林三一学院毕业，获得文学学士学位。后来他又接受医学教育，但最终转行做了《每月评论》的雇佣写手。哥尔德史密斯多才多艺，是颇有建树的散文家，诗人，小说家和剧作家。

2. 主要作品

《世界公民》(1762)
《旅游人》(1764)
《威克菲尔德牧师传》(1766)
《好心人》(1768)
《荒村》(1770)
《屈身求爱》(1773)

3. 选读作品

◆《威克菲尔德牧师传》

故事由好心的乡村牧师普里姆罗斯本人讲述。不幸接连降临牧师一家。牧师失去了所有财产，全家被迫搬到新住所，得到乡绅桑希尔的资助。但是桑希尔是个道德低下的坏蛋，他引诱牧师的大女儿奥利维亚又抛弃了她。牧师也因欠乡绅的债被投入狱。小女儿索菲亚被不知名的恶棍强行挟持。这时牧师家之前认识的一位貌似破产的绅士救了索菲亚，后他说明自己就是桑希尔乡绅的舅舅。最后乡绅的恶行被揭发。结局完满，威廉爵士和索菲亚喜结连理，乡绅被迫娶奥利维亚为妻，牧师的财产也被返还。

15.2　考研真题与典型题详解

Ⅰ. Fill in the blanks.

1. *The Deserted Village* was written by ________.（大连外国语 2008 研）
2. The only novel of Oliver Goldsmith is ________, which gives a detailed account of the numerous misfortunes befalling the central character and his family.
3. *She Stoops to Conquer* is the best-known comedy written by ________.

Ⅱ. Multiple Choices

1. ________ found its representative writers in the field of poetry, such as Edward Young and Thomas Gray, but it manifested itself chiefly in the novels of Laurence Sterne and Oliver Goldsmith.

   A. Pre-romanticism　B. Romanticism　C. Sentimentalism　D. Naturalism
2. In the early 18th century, English writers of the neo-classic school does not include ________.

   A. Alexander Pope　B. Joseph Addison　C. Richard Steele　D. Oliver Goldsmith

Ⅲ. Explain the following term.

Sentimentalism(人大 2007 研)

Ⅳ. Short answer question

What are the essential features of sentimentalism?

参考答案及解析

Ⅰ. Fill in the blanks.

1. Oliver Goldsmith

   （奥利弗·哥尔德史密斯，英国诗人、剧作家、小说家。《荒村》是他的一首感伤主义诗歌。）
2. *The Vicar of Wakefield*

   （奥利弗·哥尔德史密斯(Oliver Goldsmith)是 18 世纪著名的英国剧作家，《威克菲尔德牧师传》(*The Vicar of Wakefield*)是他唯一的一部小说。）
3. Oliver Goldsmith

   （《屈身求爱》是哥尔德史密斯最出名的喜剧。）

Ⅱ. Multiple Choices

1. C　感伤主义是 18 世纪中叶英国新诞生的一个文学流派，它的诞生主要源自某些启蒙运动家对社会现实的极大不满。感伤主义在诗歌领域的代表人物是：爱德华·扬和托马斯·格雷，小说领域则是：劳伦斯·斯特恩和奥利弗·哥尔德史密斯。
2. D　18 世纪早期英国新古典主义的代表人物是：约瑟夫·艾迪生、理查德·斯蒂尔、亚历山大·蒲柏；奥利弗·哥尔德史密斯是 18 世纪中叶诞生的感伤主义的代表。

Ⅲ. Explain the following term.

Sentimentalism: Sentimentalism is one of the most important trends in English literature of the middle and later decades of the 18th century, presenting a new view of human nature which prized feeling over thinking, passion over reason, and personal instincts of "pity, tenderness, and benevolence" over social duties.

Ⅳ. Short answer question

①Sentimentalism was popular in English literature in the middle and late 18th century. It is closely related to the drastic social and ideological changes that occurred in the UK at that time.

②Sentimentalists criticized the cruel and serious social injustices of the capitalist relations brought about by the bourgeois revolution and the industrial revolution in 1642 and 1688, but they did not affirm the inevitability of the industrial revolution and the progressive nature of this huge social change.

③Sentimentalism takes the countryside as its background, which is in sharp contrast with neoclassicism. The works are marked by sincere sympathy for poor and land-expropriated farmers.

第16章　理查德·布林斯利·谢里丹

16.1　复习笔记

Ⅰ. 18th Century Drama

British drama in the 18th century did not achieve the same achievements as novels. The Licensing Act passed in 1737 drove Fielding out of the theater. It also restricted the freedom of expression by playwrights. But playwrights in this period showed great interest in Shakespeare, so did the criticism and editions. Only the plays of Goldsmith and Sheridan have high literary value and are still adapted into performances.

Ⅰ. 18世纪戏剧

18世纪英国戏剧没有取得与小说一样的成就。主要原因之一便是1737年通过的戏剧审查法案，这一法案将菲尔丁赶出戏剧领域，同时也限制了剧作家的言论自由。但是这一时期的演员、评论和选集对莎士比亚的作品表现出极大的兴趣。只有哥尔德史密斯和谢里丹的剧作有较高的文学价值，至今仍被搬上舞台。

Ⅱ. Richard Brinsley Sheridan(1751—1816)

1. Life

Richard Brinsley Sheridan, the son of Thomas Sheridan (an Irish actor and author), was a dramatist and politician. He was educated at Harrow. After eloped with the daughter of a composer in 1773, he began writing for the theater. In 1776, he became a partner and manager of Lane Theatre. In 1780, Sheridan became a Whig Congressman. In 1787, Sheridan gave a famous speech and impeached the first Governor of India, Warren Hastings. He opened a new theater in 1794, but it was destroyed by fire in 1809. Sheridan was arrested for debts in 1813 and suffered from brain disease in his later years. He died in 1816 and was grandly buried in Westminster Abbey. His plays are generally considered to be a bridge between the classics of Shakespeare and Bernard Shaw.

2. Major Works

The Rivals (1775)
A Trip to Scarborough (1777)
The School for Scandal (1777)
The Critic (1779)
Pizarro (1799)

Ⅱ. 理查德·布林斯利·谢里丹(1751—1816)

1. 生平

理查德·布林斯利·谢里丹是爱尔兰演员和作者托马斯·谢里丹之子，是一名戏剧家和政治家。1773年与一位作曲家女儿私奔后，他开始为剧院写作。1776年成为车道剧院合伙人和经理。1780年，谢里丹投身政界成为一位辉格党议员。1787年谢里丹发表了著名演讲，弹劾了第一届印度总督沃伦·黑斯廷斯。他在1794年开了新剧院，但在1809年就被火烧毁。1813年谢里丹因欠债被捕，晚年则患有脑病。他于1816年去世，被隆重地葬在威斯敏斯特教堂。他的戏剧通常被认为是莎士比亚和萧伯纳经典著作的桥梁。

2. 主要作品

《对手》(1775)
《斯卡伯勒之行》(1777)
《造谣学校》(1777)
《批评家》(1779)
《皮萨罗》(1799)

3. **Selected Work**	3. **选读作品**
◆***The School for Scandal***	◆**《造谣学校》**
The School for Scandal has been called a great comedy of manners. It describes and satirizes the British high society. The play consists of five acts. There are two main lines in the work: one being Lady Teazle's loss of innocence and growth and the other is the process by which Sir Surface chooses an heir between his two nephews, Charles and Joseph. In the play, Mrs. Sneerwell spreads rumors about others for personal gain. Peter accidentally discovers that Joseph is the one who wants to seduce Mrs. Peter. And Sir Surface is impressed by Charles's kindness to his poor relation and finds that Joseph is stone-hearted towards the poor relation and is treacherous and selfish. Finally, Sir Surface appoints Charles as his heir.	《造谣学校》被认为是一部伟大的风尚喜剧。它描写并讽刺了英国上流社会。这部戏剧由五幕组成。书中有两条主线：第一条是梯泽尔夫人从失足到成熟的过程；另一条是萨费思爵士在两个侄子——查尔斯和约瑟夫之间选择继承人的过程。剧中，史尼威尔夫人为谋取私利到处散播别人的谣言。彼得偶然间发现约瑟夫才是想要勾引彼得夫人的人。萨费思爵士被查尔斯对穷亲戚的善良打动，而约瑟夫的铁石心肠、阴险狡诈以及自私自利的真面目也暴露出来。最后萨费思将查尔斯立为继承人。

16.2 考研真题与典型题详解

Ⅰ. Fill in the blanks.

1. __________ was the most important playwright of the 18th century.
2. __________ is R. B. Sheridan's masterpiece which has been known as a great comedy of manners.

Ⅱ. Multiple Choices

1. Sheridan is considered usually as a great __________ writer.（北二外 2009 研）
   A. comedy　　B. tragedy　　C. essay　　D. short fiction
2. In Sheridan's *The School for Scandal*, "sentiment" refers to __________.（大连外国语 2007 研）
   A. intense religious emotion　　B. erotic love
   C. aesthetic refinement　　D. a hypocritical statement of a moral platitude
3. From the character Mrs. Malaprop, in __________ by Richard Brinsley Sheridan, is derived the term "malapropism" which means a ridiculous misusage of big words.
   A. *The Rivals*　　B. *The School for Scandal*
   C. *The Beggar's Opera*　　D. *The London Merchant*

Ⅲ. Read the following quotation and answer the questions.

Identify each of the following passages by giving the title of the work and the full name of the author, and explain the implications of the underlined parts of the passage.（人大 2006 研）

Snake: They were, madam; and, as I copied them myself in a feigned hand, there can be no suspicion whence they came.

Lady Sneer: Did you circulate the report of Lady Britle's intrigue with Captain Boastall?

Snake: That's in as fine a train as your ladyship could wish. In the common course of things, I think it must reach Mrs. Clackitt's ears within four-and-twenty hours; and then, you know, the business is as good as done.

Ⅳ. Short answer question

Analyze the theme of the play *The School for Scandal*.

参考答案及解析

Ⅰ. Fill in the blanks.

1. Richard Brinsley Sheridan

（谢里丹是18世纪英国剧作家，他代表了18世纪英国戏剧艺术的最高成就。）

2. *The School for Scandal*

（《造谣学校》是谢里丹的名篇，讲述了史尼威尔夫人等一群贵族男女以造谣生事为乐，专门破坏别人的名誉和家庭幸福的故事。被世人称为风尚喜剧。）

Ⅱ. Multiple Choices

1. A　谢里丹是18世纪英国一位伟大的喜剧家。

2. D　谢里丹的《造谣学校》描写了史尼威尔夫人等一群贵族男女以造谣生事为乐，专门破坏别人的名誉和家庭幸福，抨击了英国上层社会的虚伪、贪婪和虚荣。剧中的“感伤”，是指对道德的陈词滥调的一种虚伪说法。

3. A　谢里丹是英国最为著名的喜剧作家。他代表了18世纪英国戏剧艺术的最高成就。在《情敌》中，通过马拉普洛普夫人诞生了“文字误用”一词，即荒谬地使用大词。

Ⅲ. Read the following quotation and answer the questions.

The School of Scandal, Richard Brinsley Sheridan.

in a feigned hand: in a disguised handwriting.

Lady Britle's intrigue with Captain Boastall: Rumor about the love affair between Lady Britle and Captain Boastall.

the business is as good as done: the same as done, practically accomplished.

（参考译文：

史尼威尔夫人：史内克先生，你是说，那几段文字都加插进去了？

史内克：加插进去了，夫人；都是我亲自仿抄的，所以不会让别人怀疑是哪儿来的。

史尼威尔夫人：你散播碧桃女士和鲍士托上校两人的绯闻了吗？

史内克：一切都如夫人您预期的一般巧妙。照一般事情的发展来看，我相信一定会在二十四小时内传到克雷奇特太太的耳朵；到时候，您知道，事情就圆满达成了。）

Ⅳ. Short answer question

（1）*The School for Scandal* is Sheridan's masterpiece and one of the most brilliant comedies in the English language.

（2）It is a satire of the moral degeneration of the English aristocratic bourgeois society in the 18th century. It shows the vices of creating vicious scandals among the idle rich, abnormal marriage relationships, and the luxury life of the upper class, thereby exposing the immorality and hypocrisy under the cover of the upright life and the noble moral principles.

第 17 章 威廉·布莱克

17.1 复习笔记

William Blake(1757—1827)

1. Life

William Blake, born on 28 November 1757, was the son of a London haberdasher. Apart from learning to read and write, he had no formal school education. He only went to painting school and later studied at the Royal Academy of Arts. From the age of 14, he worked as an apprentice with a famous sculptor for 7 years, reading extensively in his spare time and trying to write poetry. In 1800, Blake moved to Felpham and was funded by William Hayley. He wanted to make Blake traditional, and Blake hated it. In 1803, Black was framed for inflammatory speech, but was later found not guilty. In 1827 Black died in obscurity and poverty. Although he was not understood and recognized by his contemporaries in his life, Blake's talent was recognized by future generations.

2. Literary Achievements

Blake's outstanding achievement lies in his opposition to the classicist tradition of the time. His lyric poems show the romantic spirit. Romanticism emphasizes that natural emotions and individual originality are the basics of literary creation. Blake and Shelley have similar revolutionary feelings. There are many similarities between the two. The application of imagery and symbolism in Shelley's revolutionary poems, as well as the underlying revolutionary spirit, find the most direct response in Blake's prophetic poems.

3. Major Works

Poetical Sketches (1783)
Songs of Innocence (1789)
Songs of Experience (1794)
The Book of Thel (1789)
The Marriage of Heaven and Hell (1790)
America a Prophecy (1793)

威廉·布莱克(1757—1827)

1. 生平

威廉·布莱克生于1757年11月28日，是伦敦一杂货商之子。除了学习读写，他从未接受过正式的学校教育。他仅上过绘画学校，后来又在皇家艺术学院学习过。14岁起，他在一个著名雕刻家那里做了7年的学徒，闲暇时广泛阅读，并试着写诗。1800年，布莱克移居费尔法姆，受威廉·海利资助，他一心想让布莱克变得传统，却使布莱克很厌恶。1803年，布莱克被陷害发表煽动性言论，不过后来被判无罪。1827年布莱克在默默无闻和贫困交加中死去。虽然一生得不到同时代人的理解和认可，布莱克的才华得到后世子孙的承认。

2. 文学成就

布莱克的突出成就在于他反对当时的古典主义传统。他的抒情诗歌显示出浪漫气息，浪漫主义强调自然情感和个体的原创性是文学创作的基本。布莱克与雪莱有相似的革命情怀。两人之间存在着许多共同点，雪莱的革命诗歌中意象的应用和象征主义手法以及潜在的革命精神在布莱克的预言诗中找到了最直接的呼应。

3. 主要作品

《诗的素描》(1783)
《天真之歌》(1789)
《经验之歌》(1794)
《赛尔记》(1789)
《天堂与地狱的婚姻》(1790)
《亚美利加》(1793)

Milton (1804—1808) *Jerusalem* (1804—1820)	《弥尔顿》(1804—1808) 《耶路撒冷》(1804—1820)
4. Selected Works	**4. 选读作品**
◆***Songs of Innocence* and *Songs of Experience***	◆**《天真之歌》和《经验之歌》**
Songs of Experience was in marked contrast with *Songs of Innocence*. The gloomy and mysterious tone, as well as the evil forces of the former replaced the latter's optimism. Both embodied the resistance to the shackles of the norms and exudes love. The two poems address the same issue of the chimney sweeper, but from a different perspective. The child in *Songs of Innocence* lives in miserable conditions with a dream of promised happy afterlife. However, the child in *Songs of Experience* understands that the oppression of religion and government causes his misery, as is said "And gone to praise God and his Priest & King, /Who make up a heaven of our misery".	《经验之歌》与《天真之歌》迥然不同，前者阴郁神秘的基调和邪恶势力取代了后者的乐观。两者都体现了对准则束缚的反抗，流露出了爱。两首诗都探讨了"扫烟囱的小孩"这同一话题。《天真之歌》中的小孩生活凄苦却抱有来世幸福生活的幻想，而《经验之歌》中的小孩已经明白了宗教和政府的双重压迫造成了他的悲惨，就像诗中所说的："就跑去赞美了上帝、教士和国王，/夸他们拿我们的苦难造成了天堂。"
Both "London" and "The Tyger" are selected from *Song of Experience*. "London" depicts a real world full of sin and poverty. "The Tyger" focuses more on the good side. The tiger was created by God and symbolizes flames, strength, passion and courage. This poem also expresses the duality between beauty and evil.	《伦敦》和《老虎》均选自《经验之歌》。《伦敦》描绘了一个充满罪恶和贫穷的现实世界。《老虎》这首诗更侧重好的一面。老虎由上帝创造，象征的是烈焰、力量、激情和勇气。这首诗也表达了美和恶之间的双重性。

17.2 考研真题与典型题详解

Ⅰ. Fill in the blanks.

1. In the 18th century, __________ found its expression chiefly in poetry. The most important representative poets are William Blake and __________.
2. As a poet, William Blake's fame has been chiefly resting upon two volumes of poems, __________ and *Songs of Experience*.
3. The author of *The Tyger* is __________.
4. In __________, we find particularly Blake's hate of the church and the clergy. In the poem "A Little Boy Lost", he attacks religious persecution.

Ⅱ. Multiple Choices

1. __________ is not written by William Blake.

   A. *Poetical Sketches*　　B. *Songs of Innocence*

   C. *Songs of Experience*　　D. "Auld Lang Syne"

2. The realist novelists of the 18th century do not include __________.

   A. Daniel Defoe　　B. Jonathan Swift　　C. Henry Fielding　　D. William Blake

Ⅲ. Read the following quotations and answer the questions.

Passage 1

The Chimney Sweeper

(from *Songs of Experience*)

A little black thing among the snow
Crying "'weep! 'weep!" in tones of woe!
"Where are thy father & mother? say?"
"They are both gone up to the church to pray.

"Because I was happy upon the heath,
And smil'd among the winter's snow;
They cloth'd me in the clothes of death,
And taught me to sing the notes of woe.

"And because I am happy, & dance & sing,
They think they have done me no injury,
And are gone to praise God & his Priest & King,
Who make up a heaven of our misery."

Questions:

1. What is the "little black thing" in the poem?
2. When the young child speaks of his "father and mother", whom does he refer to?
3. What is the theme of the poem? How does the poet convey his view?

Passage 2

I wander thro' each charter'd street,
Near where the charter'd Thames does flow,
And mark in every face I meet
Marks of weakness, marks of woe.

In every cry of every Man,
In every Infant's cry of fear,
In every voice, in every ban,
The mind-forg'd manacles I hear:

How the Chimney-sweeper's cry
Every black'ning Church appalls;
And the hapless Soldier's sigh
Runs in blood down Palace walls.

But most thro' midnight streets I hear
How the youthful Harlot's curse

Blasts the new born Infant's tear,
And blights with plagues the Marriage hearse.

Questions:

1. Identify the author of the poem and give the title of it.
2. What is the rhythmical pattern of the poem?
3. Repetition is the most striking formal feature of the poem. What role does it play?
4. What does the speaker mean when he says "The mind-forg'd manacles I hear"?
5. What does the "blackening Church" suggest? What does the palace represent?
6. Why does the poet use the phrase "Marriage hearse"? What kind of plague would be associated with the harlot's curse?
7. What is the main idea of the poem?

Ⅳ. Short answer questions

1. Comment on William Blake's *Songs of Innocence* and *Songs of Experience*.
2. What is William Blake's position in English literature?

参考答案及解析

Ⅰ. Fill in the blanks.

1. Pre-Romanticism; Robert Burns
   （18 世纪的英国诗歌中开始出现浪漫主义的痕迹，最具代表性的诗人是：威廉·布莱克、罗伯特·彭斯。）
2. *Songs of Innocence*
   （威廉·布莱克是 19 世纪诗人，英国第一位重要的浪漫主义诗人。主要诗作有诗集《天真之歌》《经验之歌》等。早期作品简洁明快，中后期作品趋向玄妙晦涩，充满神秘色彩。）
3. William Blake
   （威廉·布莱克是 19 世纪诗人，英国第一位重要的浪漫主义诗人。《老虎》是他的诗作之一。）
4. *Songs of Experience*
   （威廉·布莱克一生都保持着宗教、政治和艺术上的激进倾向。《经验之歌》中布莱克表达了他对教堂和牧师的憎恨。《一个小男孩丢失了》抨击了宗教迫害。）

Ⅱ. Multiple Choices

1. D　威廉·布莱克是 18 世纪的浪漫主义诗人，他的早期作品简洁明快，中后期作品趋向玄妙晦涩，充满神秘色彩。创作的作品有：《诗的素描》《天真之歌》《经验之歌》《天堂与地狱的婚姻》等；《友谊地久天长》则是罗伯特·彭斯的作品。
2. D　18 世纪是英国现实主义小说迅速发展的时期，这一时期的现实主义小说家有：亨利·菲尔丁、丹尼尔·笛福、乔纳森·斯威夫特等；威廉·布莱克是 18 世纪末浪漫主义诗人的代表。

Ⅲ. Read the following quotations and answer the questions.

Passage 1

1. The "little black thing" is a little boy who is a chimney-sweeper. It is chimney-sweeping that has made him look black.

2. He may refer to his own parents who are ignorant of his misery. More likely he is referring to all the people who have pushed him into this sort of life, for he expresses that they feel no remorse for their maltreatment of him. His condition results from widespread social wrongs, not mere family irresponsibility.
3. ①This poem exposes the hypocrisy and cruelty of the ruling-class people. The political and religious leaders, represented by God, Priest and King live an extravagant life, but ignore the suffering of poverty-stricken groups. Through the child's simple statement, the poet intends to attack them for their indifference and ruthlessness.

   ②The poet employs many contrasts to convey the bitter tone. There is the contrast between the color white and black, which emphasizes the polarity of opposing positions. There is a contrast between the dancing and singing and the notes of woe, and between the praising of God and the weeping. Finally the last line shows the contrast between heaven and a miserable existence on earth. All of these contrasts point out the inequality between the lives of the rich ruling class and lives of the miserable poor.

Passage 2

1. William Blake, "London"
2. Iambic tetrameter
3. The repetition of the words, "chartered", "Mark" reinforce the sense of the speaker's uncomfortable feelings upon entering the city. Similarly, the repetition of "every" in the second stanza emphasizes the prevalence of misery and horror among the people in London, hence reflects the suffocating atmosphere of the city.
4. The "mind-forg'd manacles" implies that the manacles are made by the minds of the reactionary rules. The poet here suggests that the basic cause of the various forms of oppression he mentions is a kind of mental enslavement.
5. Literarily, every London church grows black from soot and hires a chimney-sweeper, a small boy, to help clean it. The poet suggests that by profiting from the suffering of the child laborer, the church is soiling its original purity. The church represents the clergy, while the palace represents the government. Obviously, the poet employs the device of synecdoche, that is, the institutions are rendered by mention of the places in which they reside.
6. ①The phrase "Marriage hearse" involves the use of oxymoron, which is used here satirically to compare the wedding to a funeral.

   ②The young prostitute's curse brings calamity upon the tearful new-born baby and ruins with malignant disease the newly-wed lovers. Thus the "Marriage hearse" serves as a vehicle in which love and desire combine with death and destruction.
7. The speaker wanders through the streets of London and comments on his observations. He sees despair in the faces of the people he meets and hears fear and repression in their voices. The whole picture of the miseries of the common people in the English capital is reflected in all its bareness. This is the greatest lyric in which the poet utters his social criticism. He reveals the evils of the commercial capitalism and attacks certain institutions like the clergy, the king and the government.

Ⅳ. Short answer questions

1. (1) The poems in the two books are all short and lyrical, assume childlike tone and use simple language. They deal with similar subject matter, but the tone, emphasis and conclusion differ.

   (2) *Songs of Innocence* is a lovely volume of poems, presenting a happy and innocent world, though not without its evils and sufferings. His poems are very attractive to children, and most of the poems in the series have a peculiar and simple beauty in terms of theme, language, verse form and rhythm. Also in this book, Blake frequently uses symbolism.

   (3) *Songs of Experience* is a much more mature work than *Songs of Innocence*. It paints a different world, a world of poverty, suffering, war, misery and repression with a melancholy tone. In this collection, the poet revealed the evils and vices of the world. Especially striking is the fact that a number of the poems in *Songs of Innocence* are either rewritten or considerably revised in *Songs of Experience*, with the result that the joyful atmosphere or the harmonious ending is in each case changed into a bitter mood or a sad story.

2. Blake's outstanding achievement lies in his opposition to the classicist tradition of the time. His lyric poems show the romantic spirit. Romanticism emphasizes that natural emotions and individual originality are the basics of literary creation. Blake and Shelley have similar revolutionary feelings. There are many similarities between the two. The application of imagery and symbolism in Shelley's revolutionary poems, as well as the underlying revolutionary spirit, find the most direct response in Blake's prophetic poems.

   (此题从布莱克诗歌创作理念角度入手作答。)

第 18 章 罗伯特·彭斯

18.1 复习笔记

I. Robert Burns(1759—1796)	I. 罗伯特·彭斯(1759—1796)
1. Life Robert Burns was born in 1759, Scotland. His father was a poor and honest Scottish farmer who worked hard all day to keep the family. Burns did not receive a good education, but his father taught him to teach himself. At the age of 15, he worked like an adult. In 1786, he decided to go to Jamaica to find a job. So he published a collection of poems which he wrote after a day's work, earning some travel expenses. His collection of poems was praised by some critics in Edinburgh, who hoped that Burns would publish a second edition. So Burns gave up going to Jamaica and went to Edinburgh to compile a new edition of poetry, which was published in 1787. He married in 1788 and rented a farm in Dumfries. However, the farm was not profitable, so he went to seek a livelihood from famous people. Then he became a tax officer. Burns died miserably in 1796 at the age of 37 and was buried in Dumfries County.	**1. 生平** 罗伯特·彭斯于1759年生于苏格兰。父亲是一位贫苦忠厚的苏格兰农民，整日劳作辛苦持家。彭斯没怎么上过学，但父亲教会了他自学。15岁时，他已经像大人一样干活了。1786年，他决定去牙买加找份工作，便出版了农余时写的诗集，挣点路费。他的诗集受到爱丁堡一些批评家的赞扬，他们希望彭斯再出第二版。于是彭斯放弃去牙买加，去爱丁堡编纂新版诗集，于1787年出版。1788年彭斯结婚，在敦夫里斯郡租住了一个农场。然而农场并没有盈利，他便去向有名望的人求得谋生之计。之后他做了税务官。1796年彭斯凄惨地死去，享年37岁，被葬于敦夫里斯郡。
2. Literary Achievements Burns is the national poet of Scotland. He is not only a poet of ordinary people, but also a peasant poet. The rich Scottish folk songs inspired him, and his poems became the wealth of the Scottish people.	**2. 文学成就** 彭斯是苏格兰的民族诗人。他既是普通人民的诗人，更是一位农民诗人。丰富的苏格兰民谣给予他灵感，他的诗也成为苏格兰人民的财富。
3. Major Works *Poems Chiefly in Scottish Dialect* (1786) "A Red, Red Rose" "To a Mouse" "Holy Willie's Prayer" "My Heart's in the Highlands" "Auld Lang Syne" "To a Louse" "The Twa Dogs"	**3. 主要作品** 《主要用英格兰方言写的诗集》 《一朵红红的玫瑰》 《致小鼠》 《威利长老的祈祷》 《我的心在高原》 《友谊地久天长》 《致虱子》 《两只狗》

4. Poetic Style

Burns is memorized mainly because of his extensive themes and poems written in Scottish dialects. The romantic feelings expressed in these poems move people's hearts. His poems cover nature, religion, love, humanistic spirit, rural life, and social criticism. Some poems are humorous and pleasant.

His great success was also largely due to his profound knowledge and understanding of the ancient folk song tradition. He often revised old ballads and transformed them into masterpieces through a series of improvement methods such as omission, condensing and adding.

5. Selected Works

◆"My Heart's in the Highlands"

The poem is mainly about the beautiful hometown of Scotland, expressing Burns' patriotism and homesickness. Each line in the poem consists of 11 syllables. Through the extensive use of long vowels and diphthongs, the poem has a strong musicality.

◆"John Anderson, My Jo"

This poem celebrates the love of an elderly couple who grow old together. Although the young man has become a gray-haired old man, their love has not changed. In the poem, the old lady still calls her husband "John Anderson, my jo". "My jo" means my sweetheart.

◆"A Red, Red Rose"

This is one of Burns' most famous love ballads written in Scottish dialect. Its simple rhythm, strong emotion and hidden wisdom are the reasons why it has been passed down through the ages.

◆"To a Mouse"

Part of the original poem is written in Scottish dialect. In his poem, Burns made an analogy between animals and the human world, and the experience of mice reminded him of his own situation. In 1937, John Steinbeck published his novel *Of Mice and Men*, of which the title is derived from this poem.

4. 诗歌风格

彭斯主要因为自己主题广泛的以苏格兰方言写成的诗歌为大家熟记，这些诗歌所抒发的浪漫感情打动人心。他的诗歌涵盖自然、宗教、爱情、人文精神、乡村生活、社会批判。一些诗则以幽默和愉快为特色。

他巨大的成功很大程度上也归功于他对古老歌谣传统的渊博知识和杰出把握。他经常对古老的歌谣进行修改，通过一系列诸如省略、浓缩和增加的改善手段将它们转化为杰作。

5. 选读作品

◆《我的心在高原》

该诗主要是关于美丽的家乡苏格兰，抒发了彭斯的爱国情怀和思乡之情。诗中的每行包括 11 个音节，通过大量使用长元音和双元音，使得诗歌具有很强的音乐性。

◆《约翰·安徒生，我的爱人》

该诗歌颂了一对老年夫妇白头偕老的爱情。虽然当年的小伙已经成为白发苍苍的老人，但是他们的爱情没有变化，诗中老妪仍然深情地呼唤她的丈夫为"John Anderson, my jo"。"my jo"的意思为我的爱人。

◆《一朵红红的玫瑰》

这是彭斯用苏格兰方言写成的最为知名的爱情歌谣之一。它简单的韵律、浓郁的感情以及内中隐藏的智慧正是其流传千古的原因。

◆《致小鼠》

《致小鼠》原诗版本中部分使用了苏格兰方言。彭斯在诗中把动物和人类世界进行了类比，而小鼠的遭遇让他想到了自己的境况。1937 年，约翰·斯坦贝克出版了小说《人鼠之间》，其小说标题来源于本诗中的句子。

◆"Auld Lang Syne"

Inspired by an ancient folksong, Burns composed this universal parting song. The poet recalled a happy childhood and friendship with his partners, and lamented that the cruel reality had ruthlessly separated them.

◆《友谊地久天长》

受一首古老民间歌谣的启发，彭斯写下了这首广为流传的离别歌谣。其中诗人回忆了快乐的童年及和伙伴结下的友谊，哀叹残酷的现实无情地把他们分离。

【笔记补充说明：本章对以下作家介绍不多，但是这些作家在英语专业考研试题中也经常涉及，故这里对他们作简要补充。】

Ⅱ. Alexander Pope (1688 – 1744)

1. Life

Alexander Pope was born in London on May 21, 1688. His father was a businessman who believed in Roman Catholicism. Pope first received tutoring from a pastor and then went to a Catholic school, but he taught himself mostly. Pope was very clever. He knew Latin, Greek, French and Italian as a child. Because he was a Catholic, Pope could not go to university. In 1705, he unfortunately suffered from tuberculous spondylitis, which caused lifelong disability. When he was in his early 20s, he often went to London and met local literati. When he was only 22, his poem *An Essay on Criticism* was published, and from then on he was looked up to as a great master of verse in England and in Europe. His later satirical works won praise as well as attracting attack from those he satirized. Pope died at Twickenham on May 30, 1744.

2. Major Works

An Essay on Criticism (1711)

The Rape of the Lock (1714)

The Dunciad (1728—1742)

An Essay on Man (1732—1734)

Imitations of Horace (1733—1738)

Epistle to Dr. Arbuthnot (1735)

3. Poetic Style

(1) Pope was the representative of 18th century Neoclassicism. He perfected the heroic couplet.

(2) His style is direct and compact. Many commonplaces become household saying under his pen. Pope was a diligent

Ⅱ. 亚历山大·蒲柏（1688—1744）

1. 生平

亚历山大·蒲柏于1688年5月21日生于伦敦。父亲是一个信奉罗马天主教的商人。蒲柏先是接受一个牧师的家教，后来上了天主教学校，但他基本上都是自学。蒲柏早熟，小时候就认识拉丁文、希腊文、法文和意大利文。由于是天主教徒，蒲柏不能上大学。1705年，他不幸患了结核性脊椎炎，导致终身残疾。20岁出头时，他就经常去伦敦，结识了当地的文人。年仅22岁，他就发表了《批评论》，从此以后他成为在英国乃至欧洲受人敬仰的诗歌大师。他后来的讽刺作品既受到赞扬，也招致了来自被讽刺者的攻击。1744年5月30日，蒲柏在特威克纳姆去世。

2. 主要作品

《批评论》(1711)

《夺发记》(1714)

《群愚史记》(1728—1742)

《人论》(1732—1734)

《仿贺拉斯》(1733—1738)

《致阿伯诺斯特医生书》(1735)

3. 诗歌风格

(1) 蒲柏是18世纪新古典主义的代表。他完美使用了英雄双韵体。

(2) 他的风格直接简洁。许多他笔下的平常话都变成了街知巷闻

reader. Pope's style also depends upon his great patience in elaborating his art.

(3) He was at his best in satire and epigram. He was an example of conscious literary artist. But he lacked the lyrical gift. And in his endeavour for finish and compactness, he sometimes became artificial and obscure.

的谚语。蒲伯是位勤奋的读者。他的风格也有赖于他对自己艺术加工的无比耐心。

(3) 他最擅长讽刺和警句。他是一个有意识的文学艺术家。但是他缺乏抒情天赋，而且在追求完整和紧凑时略显矫饰和晦涩。

Ⅲ. Samuel Richardson (1689—1761)

1. Life

Samuel Richardson was born in 1689, his father was a carpenter. Because his family was poor, his education was limited. In 1707 he became an apprentice as a printer in London. Thirteen years later, he became a stationer and printer. He opened his own shop as a leading businessman in London. Richardson's literary career began when the publishing industry was already booming. At that time, two booksellers suggested that he should compile a letter writing manual for young men and women who could not write. In the process of editing, Richardson had a whim and began to write novels. Several letters from a daughter who went out to work to his father asking how to avoid the entanglement of the employer constituted the novel *Pamela*. The novel was a big success as soon as it was published. He became famous for his novels' popularity. He died in 1761 and was buried in St. Brad's Church in London.

2. Major Works

Pamela, or, Virtue Rewarded (1740—1741)
Clarissa, or, The History of a Young Lady (1747—1748)
The History of Sir Charles Grandison (1753—1754)

3. Literary Style

Richardson is famous for his emphasis on detail, his psychological probe into women, and his dramatic technique. But he is also accused of being a verbose and sentimental storyteller.

Ⅲ. 塞缪尔·理查森(1689—1761)

1. 生平

塞缪尔·理查森出生于1689年，父亲是一位木匠。因为家里贫穷，他接受教育有限。1707年他在伦敦成为一个印刷工的学徒。13年后他成了一个文具商和印刷工，开了自己的店，是伦敦商人翘楚。理查森的文学生涯始于出版事业已蒸蒸日上的天命之年，当时两位书商建议他编纂一本面向不会写信的青年男女的书信写作手册。在编辑的过程中，理查森突发奇想，开始写起了小说。其中几封外出做工的女儿写给父亲征求如何避开雇主纠缠的书信构成了小说《帕米拉》。这本小说一经面世就大获成功。他因小说广受欢迎而名声大噪。他死于1761年，被葬在伦敦的圣布莱德教堂。

2. 主要作品

《帕米拉》(1740—1741)
《克拉丽莎》(1747—1748)
《查尔斯·格兰迪森爵士的历史》(1753—1754)

3. 文学风格

理查森因其对细节的强调，对女性心理的挖掘和戏剧化技巧而闻名。但他也被指责是一个啰嗦、多愁善感的小说家。

Ⅳ. Sameul Johnson (1709—1784)

1. Life

Sameul Johnson, son of a bookseller, was born in Lichfield, Staffordshire. Johnson was a poet, a lexicographer, a translator, a journalist and essayist, a travel writer, a biogra-

Ⅳ. 塞缪尔·约翰逊(1709－1784)

1. 生平

塞缪尔·约翰逊是书商之子，生于斯塔福德郡的利奇菲尔德。约翰逊是诗人、词典编纂家、翻译家、

pher, and a critic. He was educated at Lichfield Grammar School and spent a brief period at Oxford University, but was forced to leave due to lack of money. Unable to find a teaching job, he moved around and started writing. In 1735, he married Elizabeth Porter, a widow more than 20 years older than him. In 1737, Johnson moved to London and worked hard. He wrote all kinds of essays to maintain his life and gradually gained fame. It took him 8 years to compile the *Dictionary of the English Language*, which was published in 1755. Johnson later became the leader of London's literary circles. He died in 1784 and was buried in Westminster Abbey.

报纸撰稿人、散文家、游记作者、传记作者和批评家。他在利奇菲尔德语法学校上学，在牛津大学待过短暂时间，但因为缺钱不得不辍学。找不到教书工作，他辗转开始写作。1735 年，他娶了伊丽莎白·波特，一个比他大 20 多岁的寡妇。1737 年，约翰逊移居伦敦，努力投稿，写各种杂文维持生活，渐渐声名鹊起。他花了 8 年时间编纂成了《英文词典》，在 1755 年出版。之后约翰逊成了伦敦文学界的领袖。他死于 1784 年，被葬在威斯敏斯特教堂。

2. Major Works

London (1738)
The Vanity of Human Wishes (1749)
The Rambler (1750—1752)
The Prince of Abissinia: A Tale (1759)
The Plays of William Shakespeare (1765)

2. 主要作品

《伦敦》(1738)
《人类欲望之虚幻》(1749)
《漫步者》(1750—1752)
《阿比西尼亚国拉塞拉斯王子传》(1759)
《莎士比亚集》(1765)

V. Tobias Smollett (1721—1771)

1. Life

Smollett was born in Scotland. He was the son of a judge and landowner, and was educated at the University of Glasgow, qualifying as a surgeon. He studied medicine at the University of Glasgow, but he preferred literature. He died in Italy in 1771. Smollett was poor all his life. He was a critic, historian, critic, medical writer, poet and brochure writer. Most of his novels were created based on his own experience, and the characters he was familiar with were the prototypes of the characters in the works.

2. Major Works

The Adventures of Roderick Random (1748)
The Adventures of Peregrine Pickle (1750)

3. Selected Works

◆ ***The Adventures of Roderick Random***

The story is dictated by the protagonist Langdon in the book. It is an autobiographical novel based on Smollett's

V. 托比亚斯·斯莫莱特(1721—1771)

1. 生平

斯莫莱特生于苏格兰，父亲是一位法官和地主。他在格拉斯哥大学学医，然而他更喜欢的是文学。他 1771 年逝于意大利。斯莫莱特一生贫穷潦倒。他曾经是评论家，历史学家，批评家，医学作者，诗人和宣传册作家。他的小说大部分是根据自身经历创作，他自己熟悉的人物是作品中的人物原型。

2. 主要作品

《兰登传》(1748)
《皮克尔传》(1750)

3. 选读作品

◆《兰登传》

该故事为书中主人公兰登口述。它以斯莫莱特在军舰行医的历史为背景，是一部带有自传体性质

medical practice on warships. Like Smollett, Random is a Scot and a doctor. Random leaves home and goes to London to make a fortune. After being bullied and deceived, Random becomes the assistant of a French apothecary, and then he is seized by the press gang to become a naval surgeon's mate in the war. He has experienced the cruel war and shipwreck. And then he is robbed. He returns to London penniless and is thrown into a debtor's prison. His uncle Tom Bowling obtains his freedom for him, and they go abroad on a trading voyage, in the course of which they meet a Spanish gentleman, immensely rich, who turns out to be Random's father. Smollett mercilessly attacked the regime in the English fleet.

的小说。如同斯莫莱特，兰登也是名苏格兰医生。他前往伦敦谋生。经历欺凌欺骗后，他成为一位法国药剂师的助手。后来他被捉上船，成为外科医生的助手。在海上他经历了海战的残酷，后来船失事，他遭人抢劫。之后他回到伦敦但由于身无分文被投入欠债者监狱。这时，他的叔叔将他从狱中救出。他们一同登上去往国外的商船，在期间他们结识了一位十分富有的西班牙绅士，结果这位老人被证明是兰登的父亲。斯莫莱特无情地抨击了英国舰队的体制。

◆***The Adventures of Peregrine Pickle***

The novel tells of Peregrine's upbringing, education at Oxford, journey to France, his debauchery, bankruptcy, jailing at the Fleet, unexpected succeeding to the fortune of his father, his final repentance and marriage to his beloved Emilia. Smollett exposed all kinds of political crooks and mocked the state system, as well as many prejudices and conventions. He also praised the generosity, kindness and sense of humor of ordinary people.

◆《皮克尔传》

小说主要讲述派瑞格林的成长，在牛津的教育，法国之旅，他的堕落、破产、监禁及意外地继承父亲的遗产，和他的悔过和迎娶深爱着的爱米莉亚。斯莫莱特揭露了各类政治骗子，嘲讽了国家体制、各种偏见和成规。他也赞扬了普通人民的慷慨、善良和幽默感。

Ⅵ. Laurence Sterne (1713—1768)

Ⅵ. 劳伦斯·斯特恩(1713—1768)

1. Life

Laurence Sterne was born in Ireland, the son of an officer in the army. In 1733, he entered Jesus College of Cambridge University as a reduced fee student. In 1740 he received a master's degree in literature. He didn't start writing until nearly 50 years old. As the most outstanding figure of English sentimentalism, his literary career is represented by two works, *Tristram Shandy* (1760—1767) and *A Sentimental Journey* (1768). He died from consumption in 1768.

1. 生平

劳伦斯·斯特恩生于爱尔兰，是一位陆军军官之子。1733 年作为减费生进入剑桥大学耶稣学院。1740 年获得文学硕士学位。直到年近 50，他才开始写作。他的主要作品是《项狄传》(1760—1767)和《感伤的旅行》(1768)。1768 年斯特恩死于肺痨。

2. Major Work

◆***Tristram Shandy***

The book is an iconic novel in the history of English literature. It is an excellent example of Sterne's humorous and playful approach to the form of the novel (a full page of black ink for a death; rows of asterisks and dashes; blank pages and lines). The author is no more serious in his treatment of the

2. 主要作品

◆《项狄传》

该书是英国文学史上一部具有标志性意义的小说。他是斯特恩以幽默戏谑方式处理小说形式的绝佳例证(一张黑页代表死亡；成排的星号，破折号；空白的页、行)。作者不再像标题显示的那样以严肃

subject matter suggested by the title: Tristram himself is not born until the fourth volume and by the end of the novel is not out of his infancy. The novel has no plot, just a series of thoughts and events narrated by Tristram, which are about his noisy and eccentric family and eccentric friends. The style and structure of the book is completely irrational, revealing a purely emotional approach to life on the part of the narrator. This novel can be regarded as the forerunner of stream-of-consciousness novels.	的方式处理主题：主角特利斯特拉姆在第四卷才出世，而到结尾的时候才刚刚到穿裤子的年龄。小说没有任何情节，只是一系列由特利斯特拉姆讲述的想法和事件，它们关乎他那喧闹古怪的家庭和古怪朋友。本书的风格和结构完全不是理性的，它揭示了叙述者对待生活的纯情感的方式。这部小说可以看成是意识流小说的先导。

18.2 考研真题与典型题详解

(一)

Ⅰ. Fill in the blanks.

1. __________ wrote some patriotic poems, in which he expressed his deep love for his motherland, such as "My Heart's in the Highlands".
2. __________ is undoubtedly the greatest poet Scotland has ever produced. His *Poems Chiefly in Scottish Dialect* is of great significance.

Ⅱ. Multiple Choices

1. Many of Robert Burns' songs deal with friendship, __________ has long become a universal parting song of all the English-speaking countries.

   A. "A Red, Red Rose" B. "Auld Lang Syne"

   C. "My Heart's in the Highlands" D. "John Anderson, My Jo"

2. In the last twenty years of the 18th century, England produced two great romantic poets. They are __________.

   A. Samuel Johnson and William Blake B. Thomas Gray and Edward Young

   C. Alexander Pope and Oliver Goldsmith D. William Blake and Robert Burns

Ⅲ. Read the following quotations and answer the questions.

Passage 1（北航 2009 研）

O, my love's like a red, red rose.
  That's newly sprung in June;
O, my love's like the melodie
  That's sweetly played in tune.

As fair art thou, my bonnie lass.
  So deep in love am I;
And I will love thee still, my dear.
  Till a' the seas gone dry.

Questions:

1. Who wrote this poem?

2. What is the title of the poem?

3. The odd-numbered lines are iambic tetrameters, what about the even-numbered lines?

4. What is the rhyme scheme?

5. What do you know about the poem?

Passage 2

He was the eldest son of a poor Scotch peasant family. From childhood he had to struggle with poverty and toil in the fields day and night. He got only a little schooling. He had a great passion for Scottish folk songs and an intimate knowledge of Scottish poets and their works. He is remembered mainly for his songs written in the Scottish dialect on a variety of subjects.

Questions:

1. Who is the poet mentioned above?

2. His poetry falls into several groups according to the subject matters, what are they?

Ⅳ. Short answer question

What does Robert Burns' poetry mainly deal with?

Ⅴ. Essay question

What are the features of Robert Burns' poetry?

(二)

Ⅰ. Fill in the blanks.

1. *Pamela* is written in the form of a __________ novel.

2. *Joseph Andrews* is Henry Fielding's first novel. He wrote the novel with the intention of ridiculing Samuel Richardson's novel __________.

3. *Clarissa* is the second epistolary novel written by __________. And it is also his masterpiece.

4. __________ is a good humorist. He used the form of picaresque novel. His humor is better shown in *Humphrey Clinker* than anywhere else.

5. One of the special features of *Tristram Shandy* is its art of __________. It seems that Laurence Sterne tried to catch the actual flow of human mind and sentiment in ordinary life, in the manner of a modern novelist.

6. *A Sentimental Journey* is a narrative of __________'s personal experience of travel in France.

7. Laurence Sterne's fame rests chiefly on his two books, __________ and *A Sentimental Journey*, especially the former.

Ⅱ. Explain the following term.

Epistolary novels(北师大 2008 研)

Ⅲ. Read the following quotation and answer the questions.

The novel of *Pamela* was written in the form of a series of letters from the heroine to her parents and two friends, telling them in great detail her adventures at her master's house.

Questions:

1. Who is the author of this book?

2. Are there any new things in this book?

Ⅳ. Short answer questions

1. What is the significance of *Pamela* in English literature?

2. What are the features of Laurence Sterne's novels?
3. How much do you know about the novel of *Pamela, or, Virtue Rewarded*?
4. What are the features of Samuel Richardson's novels?

参考答案及解析

(一)

Ⅰ. Fill in the blanks.

1. Robert Burns
(罗伯特·彭斯是苏格兰民族诗人。他的诗歌充满了激进的民主、自由的思想。他的诗歌歌颂了故国家乡的秀美，抒写了劳动者纯朴的友谊和爱情。例如，《一朵红红的玫瑰》《友谊地久天长》《我的心在高原》等。)
2. Robert Burns
(罗伯特·彭斯是一位苏格兰诗人，被认为是苏格兰的民族诗人，1786 年他出版了《主要用苏格兰方言写的诗集》(*Poems Chiefly in Scottish Dialect*)，彭斯的名气由此大增。)

Ⅱ. Multiple Choices

1. B 《友谊地久天长》("Auld Lang Syne")赞美了人类的友谊，在世界各国广为传唱。《一朵红红的玫瑰》和《约翰·安徒生，我的爱人》歌颂了爱情的美好，《我的心在高原》则以思念家乡、赞美家乡为主题。
2. D 罗伯特·彭斯和威廉·布莱克是18 世纪末浪漫主义诗人的代表；爱德华·扬和托马斯·格雷则是18 世纪中叶诞生的感伤主义诗歌的代表，奥利弗·哥尔德史密斯是感伤主义小说的代表；亚历山大·蒲柏是18 世纪早期英国新古典主义的代表。

Ⅲ. Read the following quotations and answer the questions.

Passage 1

1. Robert Burns
2. "A Red, Red Rose"
3. Iambic trimeter
4. ABCBDEFE
5. "A Red, Red Rose" is a love poem written to be sung. Robert Burns based it on a folk version of a song he heard on his travels. Burns completed the poem in 1794 in an English dialect called Scots for publication in collections of traditional Scottish ballads. Burns clearly states and restates the theme: The speaker loves the young lady beyond measure. The only way he can express his love for her is through vivid similes and hyperbolic comparisons.

Passage 2

1. Robert Burns.
2. According to the subject matters Robert Burns' poetry falls into several groups:
(1) Lyrics on love and friendship with a great charm of simplicity such as "A Red, Red Rose" and "Auld Long Syne";
(2) Poems to express his hatred for the oppression of the ruling class and his love for freedom, such as "A Man's A Man for A' That";
(3) Patriotic poem with the expression of his deep love for his motherland, such as "My

Heart's in the Highlands";

(4) Verse-tales based on old Scottish legends and the best example of these poems is "John Barleycorn".

Ⅳ. Short answer question

Robert Burns' poems deal with diverse themes and are written in different forms, including many songs and many verse-epistles, and mostly in the Scottish dialect. Generally speaking, they fall into three groups:

①Most of Burns' poems deal with the themes of love and friendship. The thoughts in these songs are quite simple, but they are expressed with very strong emotions and in effective words and rhythm. "A Red, Red Rose" is a famous love poem. "Auld Lang Syne" are good poems on friendship.

②The second group concerns with Scottish life, especially the rural life of the Scottish peasants. His patriotic poems on Scotland's struggle for its freedom are associated with this group. He shows his sympathy for the peasants with satire on the social evils. "My Heart's in the Highlands" is a typical one.

③The third group deals with some forceful lyrics on the principles of liberty, equality and fraternity, especially those written under the influence of the American Independence and the French Revolution. The best known is "A Man's A Man for A' That.

Ⅴ. Essay question

Robert Burns is one of the greatest song writers in the world. He is the national poet of Scotland. Burns is memorized mainly because of his extensive themes and poems written in Scottish dialects. The romantic feelings expressed in these poems move people's hearts. His poems cover nature, religion, love, humanistic spirit, rural life, and social criticism. Some poems are humorous and pleasant.

His great success was also largely due to his profound knowledge and understanding of the ancient folk song tradition. He often revised old ballads and transformed them into masterpieces through a series of improvement methods such as omission, condensing and adding.

In his poems he always shows his affection and closeness to the people and expresses his hatred toward the hypocrisy and egoism of the ruling class. He also calls national independence for Scotland and liberty, equality and fraternity for all the people in the world.

(此题可从彭斯诗歌的主题、语言风格等方面作答。)

(二)

Ⅰ. Fill in the blanks.

1. epistolary

(《帕米拉》是18世纪英国小说家塞缪尔·理查森(Samuel Richardson)的第一部书信体小说。)

2. *Pamela*

(亨利·菲尔丁的第一部小说《约瑟夫·安德鲁斯》是对塞缪尔·理查森的《帕米拉》中含糊不清的道德标准及造作的伤感情调的嘲讽。)

3. Samuel Richardson

(《克拉丽莎》是塞缪尔·理查森的第二部书信体小说，也是其代表作。)

4. Tobias Smollett

(斯莫莱特是一个极具幽默感的作家，他运用流浪汉小说的形式创作。在其作品《享弗利·克林克》中，幽默到处可见。)

5. digression; stream-of-consciousness

(劳伦斯·斯特恩是英国小说家，他写的《项狄传》打破传统小说叙述模式，写法奇特。例如采用现代主义作家使用的"意识流"，书中充满长篇议论和插话，并出现乐谱、星号、省略号等。)

6. Lawrence Sterne

(《伤感的旅行》是斯特恩借约里克牧师的名义叙述的他在欧洲大陆的旅行。)

7. *Tristram Shandy*

(劳伦斯·斯特恩从46岁时才开始创作，主要以两部小说闻名：《项狄传》(*Tristram Shandy*)和《感伤的旅行》(*A Sentimental Journey*)。)

Ⅱ. Explain the following term.

Epistolary novels: Epistolary novels are novels written in the form of a series of letters exchanged among the characters of the story, with extracts from their journals sometimes included. A form of narrative often used in English and French novels of the 18th century, it has been revived only rarely since then, as in John Barth's *Letters*. Important examples include Richardson's *Pamela* and *Clarissa*, Rousseau's *La Nouvelle Heloise* and Laclos's *Les Liaisons dangereuses*.

Ⅲ. Read the following quotations and answer the questions.

1. Samuel Richardson.

2. The novel of *Pamela* was a new thing at that time for the following reasons.

(1) First, the author firstly used psychoanalysis and presented the secret thoughts and feelings of the characters in detail.

(2) Secondly, it discarded the "improbable and marvelous" accomplishments of the former heroic romances, and pictured the life and love of ordinary people.

(3) Thirdly, its intention was to afford not merely entertainment but also moral instruction.

(4) It was an epistolary novel.

Ⅳ. Short answer questions

1. (1) Samuel Richardson's first book *Pamela* is the first epistolary novel in the English language. It tells of a virtuous servant girl's resistance to the attempts of her young master and her final reward of honorable matrimony with the man.

(2) The chief contribution of this novel to the development of the English novel lies in the penetrating psychological study of the heroine employed for the first time in the English prose fiction.

(3) In this novel for the first time Richardson gave a detailed description of the English family life in the 18th century. There is not much action in the story, but the author chiefly describes and analyses the thoughts and especially the feelings of the heroine in great detail.

2. (1) Laurence Sterne was the representative of sentimentalism in the 18th century. To him sentiment was more important than reason.

(2) Laurence Sterne gave detailed descriptions of the characters' inner thought and feeling. His deep psychological analysis was a good example for later writers.

(3) Laurence Sterne's characters are ordinary persons. Sterne described the unimportant interest of the character ironically and humorously. They are like real persons with faults and merits.

(此题可从劳伦斯·斯特恩写作手法、人物刻画等方面作答。)

3. This novel is a series of letters from the heroine to her parents and two friends, telling in detail about her adventures in the host's house. The first part of the novel tells us that Pamela is a young maid who works in a wealthy family. After the death of the mistress, her son Mr. B. wants to seduce this beautiful young girl. Pamela rejects him angrily. To avoid more trouble, she leaves the house. Because of Pamela's virtues, Mr. B begins to have true love for the girl and decides to marry her.

The second part deals with Pamela's life after marriage. The heroine tells that she manages to bear the burden of a profligate husband and how she does all her best to reform him.

In this novel, Samuel Richardson, for the first time, gave a detailed description of the English family life in the middle of the 18th century. The chief contribution of this novel to the development of the English fiction lies in its penetrating psychological study of the heroine. Moreover the novel criticizes the bourgeois moral standards and moral hypocrisy.

(此题可从《帕米拉》这部小说的故事情节、写作手法、意义等方面作答。)

4. (1) Samuel Richardson is the first novelist of sentimentalist tradition. His novels have a moral purpose. His chief object in most of his works is to inculcate virtue and good deportment.

(2) Samuel Richardson is an outstanding novelist because he had much sympathy for women in their inferior social status and entered into detailed psychological study of female characters, and he not only showed the conflict between the helpless women and the social evils around her, but also laid bare the moral hypocrisy of the aristocratic-bourgeois society of his day.

(3) All of his novels are written in the form of letters. He was the master of writing epistolary novels.

(此题可从塞缪尔·理查森小说创作的主题、写作手法、文体等方面作答。)

第五部分　浪漫主义时期

第19章　威廉·华兹华斯

19.1　复习笔记

Ⅰ. Background Knowledge (1) After the Industrial Revolution, Britain became the "workshop of the world" and was unrivalled in national strength. The English bourgeoisie was the ruling class, though the aristocracy still retained some importance in politics and society. (2) The Enclosure Movement forced many farmers dispossessed of their lands to work in factories and become wage labors, forming a proletariat mercilessly exploited. There existed an ever-expanding gulf between the rich and the poor, aggravating social unrest. (3) The slogan of the French Revolution, "Liberty, Equality, and Fraternity," was supported by the working class and progressive literati. The British government compromised to carry out some social reforms. (4) Against the backdrop of the Industrial Revolution, American and French Revolution, Romanticism came into being and flourished in England as a main literary trend. English Romanticism began with the publication of the *Lyrical Ballads* (1798) and ended with Walter Scott's death (1832). **Ⅱ. Literary Style of the Romantic Period** The Romantic Period saw the poetical revival. Romantic poets are generally divided into two groups: the elder generation, or the passive romanticists (Wordsworth, Coleridge, and Southey, also known as Lake Poets), and the younger generation, or the active romanticists (Byron, Shelley, and Keats). The elder generation preferred the merry and idealized old England and showed negative attitudes toward capitalism. The younger generation expressed the aspirations of the laboring classes with hatred for capitalism and love for liberty. It should be noted that the term "Romanticism" was a later coinage.	**Ⅰ. 背景知识** (1) 工业革命之后，英国一举成为"世界工厂"，综合国力无可匹敌。资产阶级成为统治阶级，贵族在政治和社会上仍保留一些重要性。 (2) 由于圈地运动，许多失去土地的农民去工厂做工，成为雇佣工人，形成了无产阶级，被无情地剥削。贫富差距拉大，社会动荡加剧。 (3) 法国大革命的口号"自由、平等、友爱"受到工人阶级和进步文人的支持。英国政府被迫进行一些社会改革。 (4) 在英国工业革命，美国和法国大革命的影响下，浪漫主义应运而生并且繁荣发展成为主要的文学潮流。 1798年《抒情歌谣集》的出版标志英国浪漫主义时期的开始，1832年沃尔特·司各特的去世则宣告浪漫主义时期的结束。 **Ⅱ. 浪漫主义时期文学风格** (1) 浪漫主义时期是诗歌复兴时期，是诗歌的时代。浪漫主义诗人主要分为两类：早期浪漫主义诗人(也叫消极浪漫主义诗人)和晚期浪漫主义诗人(也叫积极浪漫主义诗人)。前者包括华兹华斯、柯勒律治和骚塞，这三个人也被称作湖畔诗人。后者包括拜伦、雪莱和济慈。早期浪漫主义诗人反对资本主义，诉诸于快乐而理想的旧英格兰时代。晚期浪漫主义诗人则表达

Representative writers of this period would not call themselves Romantics as they considered each as very much different from the others. Therefore, they would think of "Romanticism" or any generalization of literary style as inappropriate.

(2) The Romantics consciously declared a break with neoclassicism, emphasizing free expressions of imagination and feelings, the relationship between man and nature, the use of symbolism and myths, and literary originality and spontaneity.

(3) The Romantic literature presents strong-willed heroes, grand images, thrilling events, tragic situations, strong emotional conflicts, and exotic pictures.

(4) Women novelists emerged in this period and for the first time occupied an important place in English literature. Renowned female writers include Ann Radcliffe and Jane Austen.

了劳动阶级的抱负、对资本主义的仇恨和对自由的热爱。需要注意的是，"浪漫主义"一词是后来人们对这一时期文学风格的称呼，但这一时期的主要作家并不认为他们是"浪漫主义作家"。他们认为彼此之间差异甚大，不能用一个词笼统概括。

（2）浪漫主义者自觉地宣称与新古典主义分道扬镳，他们强调自由表达情感和想象、人与自然的关系、使用象征主义和神话、文学的创新性和自发性。

（3）浪漫主义者的作品充满了意志坚强的英雄、宏大的意像、惊心动魄的事件和悲剧情景、强烈的感情冲突、奇异的画面。

（4）女性小说家出现，并且首次在英国文学中占据重要地位，包括安·拉德克里夫和简·奥斯丁。

Ⅲ. Literary Terms

1. Romanticism

(1) In the late 18th and early 19th centuries, under the influence of the British Industrial Revolution and the French Revolution, Romanticism emerged as a reaction against neoclassicism.

(2) Romanticism prevailed in England from 1798 to 1832. The co-authored book *Lyrical Ballads* published in 1798 by poets William Wordsworth and Samuel Taylor Coleridge marked the beginning of romanticism, while the death of Walter Scott in 1832 declared the ending of it.

(3) Romanticism in literature is represented by the great achievement of poetry. Romantics emphasized emotion, intuition, and imagination. The common feature of their works is the expression of dissatisfaction with the capitalist society. Romanticists were more attracted to the inner world of man. Nature appears as a power of transcendence, harmony, and unity in their works.

2. Lake Poets

Wordsworth, Coleridge, and Southey are known as Lake poets, or passive romantic poets because they lived in the Lake District in the northwest of England and shared similar literary

Ⅲ. 文学术语

1. 浪漫主义

（1）18 世纪末 19 世纪初，在英国工业革命和法国大革命的影响下，反对新古典主义的浪漫主义应运而生。

（2）1798 年华兹华斯和柯勒律治共同编写的《抒情歌谣集》标志浪漫主义时期的开始，1832 年沃尔特·司各特的去世则宣告英国浪漫主义时期的结束。

（3）浪漫主义时期是诗歌复兴时期，是诗歌的时代。浪漫主义者强调的是情感，直觉和想象。他们作品的共同特征是表达对资本主义社会的不满。他们更注重意的是人的精神和感情生活层面。在他们的作品中自然有超验、和谐和统一一切的力量。

2. 湖畔诗人

华兹华斯，柯勒律治和骚塞，这三个人被称作湖畔诗人，或消极浪漫主义诗人 因为他们都住在英

and social outlook. Having high expectations of the French Revolution, they were disappointed and horrified by the disorder and violence instead of freedom and harmony. Dismayed, they turned conservative, missing the old feudal society and the ideal life of the Middle Ages as a reaction to the development of capitalism.

格兰西北部的湖区，并且在文学和社会见解上有着一致性。原本对法国大革命抱有期待的他们见证了大革命后的血腥和暴力而非自由与和谐，因此倍感失望的他们后来变得保守，诉诸于旧的封建主义社会和中世纪的理想生活，来反抗资本主义发展。

3. Byronic Heroes

(1) As a variant of the Romantic Hero, the Byronic hero is a charismatic and mysterious character first exemplified in Lord Byron's semi-autobiographical epic *Childe Harold's Pilgrimage*(1812—1818).

(2) Although this type of hero is superior to the average person in intelligence, self-esteem, and sensitivity, the Byronic hero has many dark qualities and is usually a social misfit, an outcast born emotional or passionate about a particular issue.

(3) The Byronic hero can be found in the works of many contemporary writers and 19th-century novelists, such as Captain Wentworth in *Persuasion* by Jane Austen(1818), Heathcliff from Emily Brontë's *Wuthering Heights*, Rochester from Charlotte Brontë's *Jane Eyre* (1847), and James Steerforth from Charles Dickens's *David Copperfield*(1849—1850).

3. 拜伦式英雄

（1）作为浪漫主义英雄的一个变体，拜伦式英雄是有魅力且神秘的人物，首先出现在拜伦的拟自传体史诗《恰尔德·哈罗德游记》中。

（2）虽然这类英雄在智力、自尊和反应上面都比普通人优秀，但是他们有自己的“黑暗”品质。他经常与社会格格不入，像是一个被放逐者。而且这类英雄生来情绪化，对某一件事情很有激情。

（3）拜伦式英雄在很多同时代作家和19世纪的小说家的作品中都有所体现，如简·奥斯丁《劝导》中的温特华斯，艾米莉·勃朗特《呼啸山庄》中的希斯克里夫，夏洛特·勃朗特《简·爱》中的罗切斯特和查尔斯·狄更斯《大卫·科波菲尔》中的詹姆斯·斯蒂福思等。

Ⅳ. William Wordsworth(1770—1850)

1. Life

William Wordsworth, the representative of the early Romanticism, was born in 1770. The beautiful landscape of the Lake District aroused his love and reverence for nature. He studied at Cambridge from 1787 to 1791. At the time he was an ardent supporter of the French Revolution, which he dreamed would give birth to an ideal republic. However, his financial situation took a turn for the worse and the Revolution ended in failure, which depressed him and dampened his revolutionary enthusiasm. In 1797 he made friends with Coleridge. In 1798 they jointly published *Lyrical Ballads*. Coleridge's contribution was his masterpiece "The Rime of the Ancient Mariner". The majority of the poems in this collection were written by Wordsworth.

Ⅳ. 威廉·华兹华斯(1770 –1850)

1. 生平

威廉·华兹华斯是早期浪漫主义代表，生于1770年。湖区优美的风景激发了他对自然的热爱和崇敬。1787年到1791年，他在剑桥学习。当时他是法国大革命的热心支持者，曾幻想革命会孕育一个理想的共和国。然而，他的经济状况急转直下，大革命也以失败告终，让他十分沮丧，并浇灭了他的革命热情。1797年，他与柯勒律治结识。1798年，他们共同出版《抒情歌谣集》，其中大多数诗歌是华兹华斯所作。柯勒律治的贡献是他的名著《古舟子咏》。

2. Wordsworth's Principles of Poetry in the Preface to the *Lyrical Ballads*

(1) Wordsworth held that "all good poetry is the spontaneous overflow of powerful feeling". He regarded personal feelings, such as pleasure, excitement, enjoyment, and sorrow, as the foundation of the creation and appreciation of poetry.

(2) Wordsworth advocated the use of "common speech". The function of poetry is to bring to the familiar commonplace, the events, and situations of everyday life with unexpected grandeur. He wrote that poets should write like a "man talking to man".

(3) He objected to the contemporary hierarchy that placed epic poetry above lyric poetry.

3. Poetic Style

Wordsworth's language is simple and pure. The subject of his poems is common people and common things in ordinary life. He was a great lover of nature, and his descriptions of all kinds of natural scenery are exquisite.

4. Major Works

"Lines Composed a Few Miles above Tintern Abbey" (1798)

Lyrical Ballads (1798)

The Prelude (1805—1806)

Miscellaneous Sonnets (1807)

The Excursion (1814)

5. Selected Works

◆ *The Prelude*

Wordsworth's most famous work, *The Prelude* is an autobiographical poem and considered to be the crowning achievement of English Romanticism. It honestly records the poet's spiritual life and growth of mind during his childhood, school days, first impressions of London, first visit to France, residence in France during the Revolution, and reaction to these experiences.

◆ "Lines Composed a Few Miles above the Tintern Abbey"

This poem is the last poem in *Lyrical Ballads*. In 1793, Wordsworth visited the Wye valley and the Tintern Abbey by himself. Five years later, he revisited the place together with

2. 华兹华斯在《抒情歌谣集》的序言中阐释的诗歌原则

(1) 他认为"好诗都是强烈情感的自然流露"。他将个人情感，如愉悦、兴奋、享受、痛苦等，视为诗歌创作和鉴赏的基础。

(2) 他支持使用"日常语言"。诗歌的功能在于它能给熟悉平常的事物、日常生活中的事件和情景赋予意想不到的壮美。他写道诗人写作应该是"人与人之间谈话"般。

(3) 他反对当时将史诗置于抒情诗之上的等级。

3. 诗歌特征

华兹华斯的诗歌语言简练纯粹。诗歌的主题是普通生活中的平常人和平常事。他是一个极其热爱自然的人，他对各种自然风光的描写十分精湛。

4. 主要作品

《丁登寺旁》(1798)

《抒情歌谣集》(1798)

《序曲》(1805—1806)

《十四行诗集》(1807)

《远足》(1814)

5. 选读作品

◆《序曲》

华兹华斯最著名的作品《序曲》，是华兹华斯的自传体诗歌，也被公认为英国浪漫主义的最高成就。《序曲》记录了诗人的思想，真实反映了他对一些经历的情感及他的情感发展历程。这些经历包括童年、学校时光、对伦敦的第一印象、第一次法国之旅、大革命期间在法国的居住等。

◆《丁登寺旁》

该诗是《抒情歌谣集》中最后一首压轴之作。1793 年，诗人独自游览了丁登寺，5 年后同妹妹一

his sister and then composed this poem. In this poem, the poet looks back on the past, examines the present and looks forward to the future, expressing complex feelings of revisiting the old place and the infinite longing for returning to nature.	起再次故地重游，因此写下了本诗。该诗中诗人回顾过去、审视现在、展望未来，表达了故地重游的复杂心情和对大自然的无限向往之情。
◆"She Dwelt among the Untrodden Ways"	**◆《她住在人迹罕至的地方》**
This poem is the first and probably the best known of Wordsworth's Lucy Poems. The poem describes a beautiful but poor Scottish girl named Lucy. In the last stanza of the poem, the poet uses the contrast between life and death. The reader is moved by Lucy's obscurity and her importance to the poet.	这首诗是华兹华斯"露西组诗"中的第一首诗，可能也是最为人所知的一首。这首诗描写了一个美丽而贫穷的苏格兰女孩露西。诗的最后一节，诗人使用了生与死的对比，露西的不为世人所知和她对诗人的重要性让读者闻之动容。
◆"I Travelled among Unknown Men"	**◆《我在陌生人中孤独旅行》**
This poem is the fifth and final poem of Wordsworth's Lucy Poems. In this poem, the poet realizes his great love for his native England when he is living abroad. Similarly, he understands his feelings for his beloved Lucy. The character of Lucy later appears in the poem and is associated with the landscape of England as if the landscape of nature mourned for Lucy as much as the poet.	这是华兹华斯"露西组诗"中的第五首，也是最后一首。本诗中，当诗人旅居海外时才意识到对家乡英格兰的无比爱恋。类似地，他也明白了自己对珍爱的露西的感情。诗的后半部分才出现露西这一人物，并且是与英格兰的景色相联系，好像大自然的景色也和诗人一样在为露西而哀悼。
◆"I Wandered Lonely as a Cloud"	**◆《我好似一朵流云独自漫游》**
Written in 1804, the poem is an artistic recording of the poet's own experience meditated over in tranquility. Wordsworth in the poem discusses the harmony he felt in relation with nature and the harmonious existence of all life in the universe. It is written in iambic tetrameter, with the rhyme scheme of "ababcc" in each stanza.	该诗创作于 1804 年，是诗人于宁静之中对独自漫游时光的回忆。在本诗中，诗人歌颂了自然事物之间的和谐以及诗人自己与自然之间的融洽。本诗采用抑扬格四音步，每一小节的韵脚为"ababcc"。
◆"Composed upon Westminster Bridge"	**◆《登威斯敏斯特大桥》**
This poem is written in Italian sonnet form. In the first eight lines, Wordsworth paints a detailed picture of London in the early morning. And through the last six lines, the poet compares London of this moment to the wonder of nature. London in sleep is a peaceful scene. In this poem, personification is used.	该诗是一首意大利体式的十四行诗，也称作彼特拉克十四行诗。华兹华斯在前八行中描绘了清晨伦敦的细节景象；而通过后六行诗，诗人把这一时刻的伦敦比作大自然的奇迹。沉睡中的伦敦属于大自然景色中的一幕。本诗中运用了拟人化的修辞手法。
◆"London, 1802"	**◆《伦敦，1802 年》**
The poem, written immediately after Wordsworth's return from France to London in 1802, is an Italian sonnet. The first eight lines of the poem show the poet's dissatisfaction with	该诗写于华兹华斯 1802 年从法国回国之后不久，是一首意大利体式的十四行诗。诗的前八行展现了诗人对于英国社会的不满，后六

English society, while the last six lines extol the virtues of Milton and call for them to be used to counter the ongoing decay. The poet speaks in the second person voice, as if he were confiding in Milton (1608—1674), the late English poet of the time. **◆"The Solitary Reaper"** "The Solitary Reaper" is a ballad by Wordsworth. The poet uses "Behold her", "Stop here, or gently pass!" and "O listen!" to request the listeners to behold and listen to the solitary young maiden reaper without disturbing her.	行诗中诗人高度赞扬了弥尔顿所具有的美德，呼唤用这些品质去对抗现有的腐化衰退。诗人使用了第二人称的口吻，仿佛在跟弥尔顿(1608—1674)这位当时英国已故的诗人吐露心声。 **◆《孤独的割麦女》** 《孤独的割麦女》是华兹华斯的一首民谣。诗人使用了祈使语气的句子"看她"、"停住吧，或者悄悄走过去!"及"听啊!"来引起听者在视觉和听觉上的注意，并且让听者不要打扰到她。

19.2 考研真题与典型题详解

Ⅰ. Fill in the blanks.

1. Two English poets, __________ and __________ published a book of poems *Lyrical Ballads*.(国际关系学院 2009 研)
2. "I Wandered Lonely as a Cloud" is a poem written by the romantic poet __________.(首师大 2008 研)
3. The publication of __________ by William Wordsworth and Samuel Taylor Coleridge marked the beginning of the Romantic Age in English literature.(南开大学 2008 研)
4. Author __________ Title __________ (南京大学 2009 研)
   Ten Thousand saw I at a glance,
   Tossing their heads in sprightly dance.
5. The Romantic Age began in 1798 when William Wordsworth and Samuel Taylor Coleridge published their joint work __________ and came to an end in 1832 when the last Romantic writer __________ died.
6. Women as __________ appeared in the romantic age. It was during this period that women took, for the first time, an important place in English literature.

Ⅱ. Multiple Choices

1. In "Preface to Lyrical Ballads", Wordsworth gives his definition for good poetry "for all good poetry is the __________ overflow of powerful feelings. "(四川大学 2011 研)
   A. natural　　B. spontaneous　　C. impulsive　　D. Artless
2. The writer of "The Solitary Reaper" also wrote __________.(大连外国语学院 2008 研)
   A. "Holly Willie's Prayer"　　B. "The Defense of Poetry"
   C. "Lucy Poems"　　D. "The Fall of Bastille"
3. Which of the following poems written by Wordsworth is called his "lyrical hymn of thanks to nature"?
   A. "Lines Written in Early Spring".

B. "I Wandered Lonely as a Cloud".

C. "Lines Composed a Few Miles above Tintern Abbey".

D. "To the Cuckoo".

4. Which of the following is NOT a typical feature of Romanticism in England? (四川大学 2008 研)

A. Spontaneity in expressing feelings.
B. Emphasis on reason.
C. Worship of nature.
D. Simplicity in language.

5. __________ was made poet laureate in 1813. But most of his works, according to modern critics, are "the product of literary industry, not of literary creation."

A. William Wordsworth
B. Samuel Taylor Coleridge
C. Robert Southey
D. George Gordon Byron

6. __________ was the first critic of the Romantic school.

A. William Wordsworth
B. Samuel Johnson
C. Samuel Taylor Coleridge
D. Wordsworth and Coleridge

Ⅲ. Explain the following terms.

1. tercet (人大 2006 研)
2. Romanticism

Ⅳ. Read the following quotation and answer the question. (大连外国语学院 2007 研)

V

Our birth is but a sleep and a forgetting:
The Soul that rises with us, our life's Star,
Hath had elsewhere its setting,
And cometh from afar:
Not in entire forgetfulness,
And not in utter nakedness,
But trailing clouds of glory do we come
From God, who is our home:
Heaven lies about us in our infancy!
Shades of the prison-house begin to close
Upon the growing Boy,
But He beholds the light, and whence it flows,
He sees it in his joy;
The Youth, who daily farther from the east
Must travel, still is Nature's Priest,
And by the vision splendid
Is on his way attended;
At length the Man perceives it die away,
And fade into the light of common day.

VI

Earth fills her lap with pleasures of her own;
Yearnings she hath in her own natural kind,

And, even with something of a Mother's mind,
And no unworthy aim,
The homely Nurse doth all she can
To make her Foster-child, her Inmate Man,
Forget the glories he hath known,
And that imperial palace whence he came.

VII

Behold the Child among his new-born blisses,
A six years' Darling of a pigmy size!
See, where' mid work of his own hand he lies,
Fretted by sallies of his mother's kisses,
With light upon him from his father's eyes!
See, at his feet, some little plan or chart,
Some fragment from his dream of human life,
Shaped by himself with newly-learned art;
A wedding or a festival,
A mourning or a funeral;
And this hath now his heart,
And unto this he frames his song:
Then will he fit his tongue
To dialogues of business, love, or strife;
But it will not be long
Ere this be thrown aside,
And with new joy and pride
The little Actor cons another part;
Filling from time to time his 'humorous stage'
With all the Persons, down to palsied Age,
That Life brings with her in her equipage;
As if his whole vocation
Were endless imitation.

VIII

Thou, whose exterior semblance doth belie
Thy Soul's immensity;
Thou best Philosopher, who yet dost keep
Thy heritage, thou Eye among the blind,
That, deaf and silent, read'st the eternal deep,
Haunted for ever by the eternal mind, —
Might Prophet! Seer blest!
On whom those truths do rest,
Which we are toiling all our lives to find,

In darkness lost, the darkness of the grave;
Thou, over whom thy Immortality
Broods like the Day, a Master o'er a Slave,
A Presence which is not to be put by;
To whom the grave
Is but a lonely bed without the sense or sight
Of day or the warm light,
A place of thought where we in waiting lie;
Thou little Child, yet glorious in the might
Of heaven-born freedom on thy being's height,
Why with such earnest pains dost thou provoke
The years to bring the inevitable yoke,
Thus blindly with thy blessedness at strife?
Full soon thy Soul shall have her earthly freight,
And custom lie upon thee with a weight,
Heavy as frost, and deep almost as life!

Question:

The above excerpt is taken from "Ode: Intimations of Immortality from Recollections of Early Childhood" by Wordsworth. Analyze the excerpt with reference to the entire poem. Write about 200—300 words.

Ⅴ. Short answer question

List four of the main points made by Wordsworth in the preface to *Lyrical Ballads*. (人大2006研)

Ⅵ. Essay question

What are the general features of English Romanticism?

参考答案及解析

Ⅰ. Fill in the blanks.

1. William Wordsworth; Samuel Taylor Coleridge
(1798年，华兹华斯和柯勒律治联合出版了《抒情歌谣集》，标志着英国浪漫主义的诞生。)
2. William Wordsworth
(《我好似一朵流云独自漫游》，或译《水仙》，是英国著名浪漫主义诗人华兹华斯的名作。)
3. *Lyrical Ballads*
(1798年，华兹华斯和柯勒律治共同出版了《抒情歌谣集》，标志着英国浪漫主义文学的开端。)
4. Author: William Wordsworth　　Title: "I Wondered Lonely as a Cloud"
(题目选自Wordsworth的名诗《我好似一朵流云独自漫游》。威廉·华兹华斯被封为"桂冠诗人"并享有"自然诗人"的美誉。1798年他同柯勒律治合作出版了有名的《抒情歌谣集》(Lyrical Ballads)，该诗集第二版的"序"被认为是英国浪漫主义的宣言。)
5. *Lyrical Ballads*; Walter Scott
(英国的浪漫主义时期一般被认为始于1798年，标志为威廉·华兹华斯(William Words-

worth)和塞缪尔·泰勒·柯勒律治(Samuel Taylor Coleridge)的《抒情歌谣集》的出版，结束于1832年，标志为沃尔特·司各特(Walter Scott)的去世。)

6. novelists

(浪漫主义时期英国女性小说家开始在英国文坛崭露头角并在英国文学界占有重要地位。)

Ⅱ. Multiple Choices

1. B　Wordsworth(华兹华斯)的 *Lyrical Ballads* 突破了18世纪经典主义的诗歌传统，标志着浪漫主义在英国的复兴。在其序言中，华兹华斯阐述了其诗作的原则，与经典主义诗歌不同，强调个人的即时感受。
2. C　"The Solitary Reaper"(《孤独的割麦女》)是英国著名浪漫主义诗人华兹华斯的名诗，他的其他重要诗歌还有："Lucy Poems"(《露西组诗》)，"To a Skylark"(《致云雀》)，"I Wandered Lonely as a Cloud"(《我好似一朵流云独自漫游》)和"Lines Composed a Few Miles above the Tintern Abbey"(《丁登寺旁》)等。
3. C　华兹华斯在他的长诗《丁登寺旁》里表达了大自然给他的安慰和灵感。
4. B　18世纪的启蒙思想家们强调理性，而浪漫主义恰恰表达了对理性的一种反抗，所以选项B是错误的。著名浪漫主义诗人华兹华斯曾经说过："诗歌是强烈感情的自然流露"；浪漫主义诗人们歌颂自然，崇尚自然，抛弃华丽的藻饰，用最简洁的语言表达最优美的思想。
5. C　罗伯特·骚塞是英国湖畔派诗人之一。诗人曾一度激进，后反对法国革命，于1813年被国王封为桂冠诗人。
6. C　塞缪尔·泰勒·柯勒律治(Samuel Taylor Coleridge)英国浪漫主义时期的第一位文学评论家。他于1817年完成了重要的散文作品《文学传记》(*Biographia Literaria*)。这部作品是一系列的自传体笔记以及多篇主题丰富的学术论文和文学评论。

Ⅲ. Explain the following terms.

1. tercet: Tercet refers to a poem of three-line stanzas, usually rhyming either with each other or with adjacent lines.
2. Romanticism: (1) It refers to the literary and artistic movements of the late 18th and early 19th century in Europe. (2) It emerged as a reaction against neoclassicism which advocated rationality, order, balance, and objectivity. By contrast, Romanticism emphasized individuality, subjectivity, imagination, spontaneity, originality, irrationality, transcendence, and sensitivity. (3) English Romanticism began with the publication of Lyrical Ballads in 1798 and declined with the death of Walter Scott in 1832. The English Romantic period is an age of poetry. Blake, Wordsworth, Coleridge, Byron, Shelley, and Keats are commonly known as "the Big Six" male poets who boasted dominant influence upon poetic creation in this period.

Ⅳ. Read the following quotation and answer the question.

This poem is philosophical in the sense that it covers the Platonic theory of pre-existence and Wordsworth's insight into childhood wisdom that adults lack. The poem is written in anisometric verse, with lines of varied iambic stresses.

The poem is a meditative reflection on the poet's relationship with nature and his spiritual maturation. The poet's understanding of and response to nature has shifted from childhood innocent following of nature's lead to a soberer one. Though nature does not change in its beauty, the authority and glory of nature is no longer felt by the poet. Then, the poet tries to figure out the reason behind this shift in the excerpt.

He argues that man has pre-existence. In Stanza V, Wordsworth is lost in meditation. "Our birth is but a sleep and a forgetting," he says, for our souls originate in a purer, more glorious realm: heaven itself. Small children retain some memory of paradise, which glorifies their experiences on earth, but as people grow up, they are distracted by secular worries until they entirely forget such memory and glory (Stanza VI).

Next, the speaker observes a six-year-old boy mimicking adult behavior in his play, "as if his whole vocation / Were endless imitation." In Stanza VIII, the speaker addresses the child, wondering why he, "thou best Philosopher" and "Mighty Prophet," imitates adult behavior as though he were eager to hasten "the inevitable yoke" of earthly cares and customs ("freight").

Nevertheless, in the following stanzas, the poet comes to realization that as adults, we do not simply lose our memory as a result of which we can still feel nature and attain happiness from it. It is because of the secular experiences that man can see nature in depth and sobriety.

"Intimations of Immortality" is Wordsworth's masterpiece that conveys the poet's faith that earthly existence is derived from an earlier, purer one shortly preserved in childhood and then transformed and likely lost on life's journey.

V. Short answer question

The four main points made by Wordsworth in the preface to *Lyrical Ballads* are:

(1) Emphasis on nature;

(2) Good poetry is "the spontaneous overflow of powerful feelings recollected in tranquility";

(3) Emphasis on the usage of common language;

(4) Emphasis on imagination and originality.

VI. Essay question

(1) Expressiveness: The Romantics valued expressions of personal feelings, imagination, and originality over simple and direct portrayal of nature. In contrast to the neoclassical emphases on rationality and observation of established rules by ancient Greek and Roman masters, Romantic poetry demonstrates the original, the visionary, and the subjective. It is a pure expression of the self.

(2) Imagination: Romantic poets attached great importance to the role of imagination as means of seeking truth otherwise unattainable.

(3) Singularity: Romantic poets have a strong love for the remote, the unusual, the strange, the supernatural, the mysterious, the splendid, the picturesque, and the illogical, which finds its expression in their wild imagination. These features also manifest in the gothic novel of this time.

(4) Worship of nature: For Romantic poets, nature reveals universal truth and brings together the universe (the idea of "one life" in Coleridge's theory). The transcendental power of nature is highly respected and admired by poets of this time. In many romantic poems, the poets or subjects experience spiritual healing and peace in their contact with nature.

(5) Simplicity: In Wordsworth's poetics, poetic language is the language that man used to speak to man. That is, the decorated poetic diction favored by neoclassical poets must be replaced by simple and clear expressions.

(6) Dominant poets in this period are Blake, Wordsworth, Coleridge, Byron, Shelley, and Keats.

第20章　乔治·戈登·拜伦

20.1　复习笔记

George Gordon Byron (1788—1824)

1. Life

George Gordon Noel Byron, the sixth Baron Byron, was born on 22 January 1788 in London. In 1812 the first two cantos of *Childe Harold's Pilgrimage* were published. Byron rose to fame overnight. However, his failed marriage in 1816, scandalous affairs, and huge debts put on him so much pressure that Byron left England in April 1816 and never returned. In 1823, he went to Greece to fight a war of independence against the Ottoman Empire. However, he died from fever at Missolonghi.

2. Literary Achievemnts

Byron is one of the most distinguished and influential English Romantic poets. The Byronic hero, full of passion, genius, and defiance, pervades Byron's works and had a profound influence on the work of later Romantic poets. His literary career is closely related to the struggle and revolutionary movements of his age. His poems expressed great strength, vitality, courage, and passion. His resistance to oppression and love of freedom inspired young people and the working class.

3. Major Works

English Bards and Scotch Reviewers (1809)
Childe Harold's Pilgrimage (1812, 1816—1818)
The Giaour (1812)
"She Walks in Beauty" (1814)
"When We Two Parted" (1819)
Cain (1821)
Don Juan (1819—1824)

4. Selected Works

◆"When We Two Parted"

This poem mainly describes the scenes and feelings of his separation from his lover: When we parted, we were in silence

乔治·戈登·拜伦（1788—1824）

1. 生平

乔治·戈登·拜伦，第六任拜伦男爵，1788年1月22日生于伦敦。1812年，《恰尔德·哈罗尔德游记》前两章出版。拜伦一举成名。然而，他1816年离婚，陷入多件风流韵事，又欠下巨额债款，面对如此多的压力，拜伦1816年4月离开英国，再也没回去。1823年，他去希腊参加反抗奥斯曼帝国的独立战争，却因患热病在梅索朗吉昂去世。

2. 文学成就

拜伦是最杰出、最有影响力的英国浪漫主义诗人之一。拜伦式英雄，充满激情、才华和反抗精神，遍布他的作品，并且对后世浪漫主义诗人影响深远。他的文学生涯和当时的革命斗争运动息息相关。他的诗表达了强大的力量和活力，胆量和激情。他反抗压迫，深爱自由，激励了年轻人和劳动阶级。

3. 主要作品

《英国诗人和苏格兰评论家》(1809)
《恰尔德·哈罗德游记》(1812，1816—1818)
《海盗》(1812)
《她走在美的光彩中》(1814)
《当初我们两分别》(1819)
《该隐》(1821)
《唐璜》(1819—1824)

4. 选读作品

◆《当初我们两分别》

本诗主要描述了他与爱人分别的场景和感受，及后来的心情：当

and tears. However, you gradually changed and forgot me. At last, the poet says, "If I should meet thee/ After long years, /How should I greet thee? /—With silence and tears."	我们分别时，我们默默无言流着泪，然后你逐渐改变并且把我忘记，最后诗人说到，"如果很多年以后/我们又偶然会面，/我将要怎样招呼你？/只有含着泪默默无言。"
◆"She Walks in Beauty"	**◆《她走在美的光彩中》**
Bryon wrote his most quoted poem the morning after he had seen his beautiful cousin, Mrs. Wilmot, wearing a black mourning gown brightened with spangles at Lady Sitwell's party in June 1814. The poem extols the lady's elegance and innocence.	拜伦这首最常被引用的诗写于1814年6月，在他见到美丽的表妹的第二天早上。当时在西特韦尔夫人的聚会上，他的表妹身着饰有亮片的黑色丧服。这首诗赞美了表妹简单的优雅脱俗和纯真。
◆"Sonnet on Chillon"	**◆《咏锡雍》**
This sonnet served as a poetical introduction to the poem *The Prisoner of Chillon*. The theme of "Sonnet on Chillon" is to acclaim liberty and those who remain true to the spirit of freedom even in imprisonment and persecution by oppressors.	这首十四行诗是长诗《锡雍的囚徒》的简介。《咏锡雍》的主题是歌颂自由，赞美那些即使处于统治者的监禁和迫害，仍然忠于自由精神的人们。
◆*Childe Harold's Pilgrimage*	**◆《恰尔德·哈罗德游记》**
This long poem contains four cantos. It is written in the Spenserian stanza. The poem tells of Childe Harold's travels across Europe. Harold is an aristocratic young man whose world-weary attitude shows his dissatisfaction with the upper classes of English society, so he flees from England. Though seemingly indulged in solitude and melancholy, Harold is a gloomy, earnest, and suffering young man with ardent feelings, keen understanding, and thirst for freedom. Byron's own outlook on philosophy and politics is conveyed through Childe.	这篇长诗包括四个篇章。全诗用斯宾塞体写成。诗歌讲述了恰尔德·哈罗德在欧洲的游历。哈罗德是一位贵族青年，他的厌世态度表明他对英国上层社会的不满，因此他逃离了英国。哈罗德孤独而忧郁。但是掩藏在他的忧郁下的是一个伤心、认真而又痛苦的青年人，他有着热烈的感情和对自由的深刻理解和强烈热爱。诗中通过哈罗德表达了拜伦自己的人生观和政治观。
◆*Don Juan*	**◆《唐璜》**
It has 16,000 lines in 17 cantos, written in ottava rima, but remains unfinished. Each stanza contains eight iambic pentameter lines, and the rhyme scheme is abababcc. Don Juan is a young Spaniard of noble descent. The long poem describes the ups and downs of his life and adventures in many counties. Through the hero's experiences in many historical events, we can get a panoramic insight into the social life at that time. The poem also poignantly satirizes the vanity and hypocrisy of the English ruling class through the dislike of Don Juan.	本诗共有1.6万，分为17篇，用八行体写成，但是并没有全部完成。每一节包含8个五步抑扬格，韵律是abababcc。唐璜是一个有贵族血统的西班牙青年。这首长诗描述了他人生的起伏和在许多国家的冒险经历。唐璜见证了很多历史事件，因此我们可以看到当时社会生活的全景。这首诗也通过唐璜的厌恶之感，辛辣地讽刺了英国统治阶级的虚荣和虚伪。

20.2 考研真题与典型题详解

Ⅰ. Fill in the blanks.

1. Byron is chiefly known for his two long poems, one is *Childe Harold's Pilgrimage*, the other is __________.（中国人民大学2006研）
2. "When We Two Parted" is a poem by __________.

Ⅱ. Multiple Choices

1. George Gordon Byron was a staunch champion of the people's cause. He raised his voice in defense of the oppressed workers in his well-known __________.
   A. *Song for the Luddites*　　B. *The Prisoner of Chillon*
   C. *The Vision of Judgement*　　D. *The Revolt of Islam*
2. The following statements are about *Childe Harold's Pilgrimage*. Which statements is not true?.
   A. George Gordon Byron used his own experiences as the material of the long poem.
   B. The first canto deals with the hero's journey in Portugal and Spain.
   C. The second canto describes Albania and Greece.
   D. The fourth canto describes Greek.

Ⅲ. Explain the following term.

Byronic hero

Ⅳ. Short answer question

Please analyze Byron's *Don Juan*.

参考答案及解析

Ⅰ. Fill in the blanks.

1. *Don Juan*
   （拜伦的代表作有《恰尔德·哈罗德游记》(*Childe Harold's Pilgrimage*)和《唐璜》(*Don Juan*)两首长诗。）
2. Byron
   （《当初我们两分别》是拜伦的诗。）

Ⅱ. Multiple Choices

1. A　拜伦一生反对压迫奴役，讴歌自由解放。他的《卢德工人之歌》是反映现实阶级斗争的诗作，是一篇他为被压迫的工人阶级辩护的诗作。
2. D　《恰尔德·哈罗德游记》是拜伦根据自己的游历创作的，共四个诗章。第一诗章描写的是主人公在葡萄牙和西班牙的游历，第二诗章是主人公在阿尔巴尼亚和希腊的游历，第三诗章讲述的滑铁卢之战，第四诗章则是主人公在意大利的经历。

Ⅲ. Explain the following term.

Byronic hero: "Byronic hero" refers to a kind of characters in the works of the British romantic poet Byron in the 19th century. They are proud, energetic, stubborn, dissatisfied with reality, indominable in will, and rebellious against any kind of tyranny. But at the same time they appear melancholy, lonely, pessimistic, isolated from others and cannot find the right way out. Usually a social outcast, the Byronic hero is in constant war with authorities and social conventions.

Ⅳ. Short answer question

The comedic poem, also a satirical epic, is composed according to the legend of Don Juan. Written in ottava rima, each stanza contains eight iambic pentameter lines, and the rhyme scheme is abababcc. Don Juan is a young Spaniard of noble descent. The long poem describes the ups and downs of his life and adventures in many countries. Through the hero's experiences in many historical events, we can get a panoramic insight into the social life at that time. The poem also poignantly satirizes the vanity and hypocrisy of the English ruling class through the dislike of Don Juan.

第21章　珀西·比希·雪莱

21.1　复习笔记

Percy Bysshe Shelley (1792—1822)	珀西·比希·雪莱（1792—1822）
1. Life Percy Bysshe Shelley was born on 4 August 1792 near Horsham in Sussex. Shelley received education at Eton and Oxford University, where he read works of radical writers such as Tomas Paine and William Godwin. In 1811, he was thrown out school because he published a pamphlet in support of atheism. Shelley then eloped with 16-year-old Harriet Westbrook to Scotland, causing a serious rift with his family. In 1814, Shelley lost his heart to Mary, the 16-year-old daughter of writers William Godwin and Mary Wollstonecraft. In 1818, Shelley took his family to Italy. Two of Shelley's children died, and Mary herself was afflicted with mental breakdown. On 8 July, Shelley returned from a visit to his friends Lord Byron and James Leigh Hunt with his boat capsized and himself drowned.	**1. 生平** 珀西·比希·雪莱于1792年8月4日在苏塞克斯郡的霍舍姆出生。雪莱在伊顿公学和牛津大学接受教育，在牛津开始阅读激进作家的作品，如托马斯·潘恩，威廉·戈德温。1811年，他因出版一本小册子支持无神论被赶出学校。随后雪莱和16岁的哈丽雅特·维斯布鲁克私奔到苏格兰。由此产生的丑闻使雪莱和他的家人决裂。1814年，雪莱又爱上威廉·戈德温和玛丽·沃斯通克拉夫特的女儿，16岁的玛丽。1818年，雪莱带着家人去意大利。其中两个孩子去世，玛丽也精神崩溃。7月8日，雪莱看望过朋友拜伦和亨特后返程时，船倾覆而被淹死。
2. Poetic Style Shelley's writings contain inexhaustible sources of social, political, and philosophical concerns. His use of myths and language is extremely complex, subtle, and closely related to his cultural background. Shelley symbolizes the human spirit of freedom. His ideas challenge people's subservience to authority and inspire us to achieve lofty ideals of self-improvement and social perfection.	**2. 诗歌风格** 雪莱的作品包含社会、政治、哲学问题的永不枯竭的源头，同时他使用的神话和语言极其复杂微妙，跟他的文化背景密切相关。雪莱象征着人类自由翱翔的精神。他的思想挑战着人们对权威的卑躬屈膝，也激励着我们去实现完善自我和社会的崇高理想。
3. Major Works *The Necessity of Atheism* (1811) *Queen Mab* (1813) *Prometheus Unbound* (1819) "Ode to the West Wind" (1819) "To a Sky Lark" (1820)	**3. 主要作品** 《无神论的必要性》(1811) 《麦布女王》(1813) 《解放了的普罗米修斯》(1819) 《西风颂》(1819) 《致云雀》(1820)

4. Selected Works

◆*Queen Mab*

(1) *Queen Mab* is Shelley's first long poem of importance which embraces nearly all of Shelley's ideas concerning society and politics. Written in the form of a fairy-tale dream, it tells the story that fairy Queen Mab, through whose mouth the poet discusses philosophy, religion, morality, and social problems, carries off the beautiful and pure maiden Ianthe in her celestial chariot and shows her the past, present, and future of mankind.

(2) *Queen Mab* is a revolutionary poem that condemns tyranny, exploitation, and unjust wars that the cruel ruling class waged to plunder wealth. However, Shelley in this poem only demonstrated his utopian ideal of a perfect future for man with no willingness to achieve it by means of revolution or violence.

◆*Prometheus Unbound*

(1) Shelley's masterpiece is *Prometheus Unbound*, a lyrical drama in four acts. The poem is derived from Greek mythology. Prometheus steals fire from heaven and gives it to earth because of which he is punished by Zeus, the head of the gods. Zeus bounds him to a rock in chains. Eagles come by day and eat Prometheus' liver, which grows again at night. So the torture is endless.

(2) In Shelley's poem, Prometheus is the embodiment of a noble revolutionary, while Zeus is the incarnation of the counter-revolutionary. Prometheus may be chained to a rock, but he has a large alliance. Encouraged, Prometheus faces his suffering with equanimity. Finally, Demogorgon, the god of change and revolution, overthrows Zeus. Prometheus is at last set free by Hercules.

◆"Ozymandias"

In this poem a traveler tells of seeing a broken statue of Ozymandias, the Greek name for Ramses II of Egypt. The broken statue stands in the empty desert with the words "My name is Ozymandias, King of kings…". Shelley used the

4. 选读作品

◆《麦布女王》

(1)《麦布女王》几乎包含了雪莱所有的社会政治观点。该诗采用神话故事和梦境的形式。麦布女王用双轮马车载着美丽纯真的女孩艾安西，并向她描述人类的过去、现在和未来。通过这位神话女王之口，诗人阐述了他本人对于哲学、宗教、道德和社会问题的看法。

(2)《麦布女王》是一篇革命诗，谴责了剥削阶级的残暴专制以及他们为了掠夺财富发动的非正义战争。然而，雪莱只是一个乌托邦的社会主义者，盼望人类美好的未来，但是拒绝走暴力革命道路。

◆《解放了的普罗米修斯》

(1)《解放了的普罗米修斯》是雪莱的杰作。它是一首抒情戏剧，共分四幕。该诗取材于希腊神话。普罗米修斯从天上偷来火种给人间，结果遭受众神之首宙斯惩罚。宙斯用锁链将他绑在巨石上，白天有鹰来啄食普罗米修斯的肝脏，而肝脏在晚上又会长出。所以折磨是永无止尽的。

(2) 在雪莱的诗中，普罗米修斯是高尚的革命者的化身，而宙斯则是反革命的代表。普罗米修斯虽然被锁束缚在巨石上，但是他有广大的同盟。受到鼓舞的普罗米修斯沉着面对自己的苦难。最后变化和革命之神德摩根将垂死反抗的宙斯的统治推翻。普罗米修斯最终被大力神赫拉克勒斯解救出来。

◆《奥西曼迪亚斯》

这首诗中一个旅行者讲述了他看到埃及国王拉美西斯二世破损雕像的情景。破损的雕像站立在空荡的沙漠中，其底座写着"我的名字是奥西曼迪亚斯(拉美西斯二世的

alliteration of "boundless and bare" and "lone and level" to illustrate the smallness of Ozymandias, who has nothing but the ambition to claim his own imperial power.

拉丁文名字），乃万王之王……"。雪莱通过使用"boundless and bare"和"lone and level"这两组押头韵的词组来修饰沙漠，从而反衬出奥西曼迪亚斯的渺小：除了声称自己王权的野心外别无他物。

◆"A Song: 'Men of England'"

(1) Shelley wrote this poem at a time of upheaval in England, hoping to bring about a proletarian revolution. As the poet had hoped, the poem has become a hymn of the British labor movement.

(2) In the song, "men of England" refers to the laborers in England who build the city. The first four stanzas put forward a series of questions and ask "Why work for those oppressors who exploit you?", and then the fifth stanza states the fact that the fruits of a worker's labor only benefit others. In the last three stanzas, Shelley calls upon all working people of England to rise up, or otherwise perish.

◆《给英格兰人的歌》

（1）雪莱在英格兰动荡的时候写下了这首诗，希望迎来一场无产阶级的革命。正如诗人所期望的，这首诗成为了英国工人运动的赞歌。

（2）诗歌中，"英格兰人"指的是英格兰的建造者，英格兰的工人。诗的前四节是一系列的发问，"为什么要为那些压迫自己的人工作?"诗的第五节指明事实：工人的劳动成果只是让别人获利。诗歌的最后三节，雪莱呼吁英格兰的工人们奋起反抗，否则只会灭亡。

◆"Ode to the West Wind"

(1) This poem is prophetic, full of fighting spirit and lyrical beauty. It deals with themes of death and rebirth. Shelley was very much concerned with his own spiritual and poetic renewal and the political revival of Europe.

(2) It consists of 5 stanzas. The first stanza discusses the dual role of the west wind as both destroyer and preserver. Stanza two focuses on the power of the west wind to disperse clouds and bring storms. The third stanza tells of the influence of the west wind on the sea. The fourth stanza expresses the poet's affection for the west wind, which makes him yearn for his free youth. The last stanza reveals the poet's plea to the wind to help spread the words of his poem among mankind, predicting that spring will come after winter. The ending note of the poem is uplifting and expectant.

◆《西风颂》

（1）该诗具有预言性，富有斗争精神和抒情的美感。该诗以死亡和重生为主题。雪莱非常关心他自己在精神上和诗才上的新生和欧洲政治上的复苏。

（2）诗歌由五个诗节组成。第一诗节描写了西风作为毁灭者和保护者的双重作用。第二诗节着重描写了西风的力量：驱散乌云，带来风暴。第三诗节讲述了西风对海洋的影响。第四诗节表达了诗人对西风的感情，这样的情感使他怀念自由的少年时光。最后的诗节表达了诗人对西风的请求，希望它将这首诗在人类中传播开去，并预言春天会跟着冬天的脚步而来。诗的结尾是振奋期待的。

◆"The Cloud"

This poem is about the cloud in nature, portrayed as a rebellious character who pursues freedom and happiness. The rhyme of this poem is special. For the odd lines, the last word

◆《云》

本诗是关于自然界的云，云被描述成一个追求自由和幸福的具有反叛性格的人物形象。本诗押韵别

is rhymed with the word in the middle, like "showers" and "flowers" in the first line. Of the even lines, the last words are rhymed, like "streams" and "dreams" in the second and fourth lines.	致，奇数行押内韵，每行诗中间的一个单词于行尾的单词押韵，例如第一行的"showers"和"flowers"。诗歌的偶数行押尾韵，如第二行的"streams"和第四行的"dreams"。
◆**"To a Sky-Lark"** "To a Skylark" is written in 1820 by Shelley. Through the image of skylark and its songs, Shelley shows his artistic ambition: "Such harmonious madness /From my lips would flow /The world should listen then—as I am listening now." The poem consists of 21 stanzas, each of which consists of four short iambic trimester lines and one long iambic hexameter lines, designed to mimic the song of a lark—with a long ending after a short series of calls.	◆**《致云雀》** 《致云雀》写于1820年。雪莱通过云雀的形象及其歌声，展现了他的艺术抱负，即"和谐、炽热的激情/就会流出我的双唇，/全世界就会像此刻的我——侧耳倾听。" 这首诗包括21节，每一节由四个三步抑扬格的短的诗行和一个六步抑扬格的长的诗行组成，这一设计是为了模仿云雀的歌声——在一串短促的鸣叫后拖带一长声尾音。

21.2 考研真题与典型题详解

Ⅰ. Fill in the blanks.

1. *Prometheus Unbound*, a lyrical drama in four acts, was written by ________.（大连外国语学院2008研）
2. The main idea running through the dramatic poem *Prometheus Unbound* is that of ________.
3. *Queen Mab*, Percy Bysshe Shelley's important poem, is written in the form of a ________.

Ⅱ. Multiple Choices

1. ________ can be found among Shelley's love lyrics.
   A. "One Word is Too often Profaned" B. "When We Two Parted"
   C. "A Red, Red Rose" D. "Song to Celia"
2. Among the following, ________ is an elegy.
   A. *Lamia* B. *Isabella* C. *Adonais* D. *Queen Mab*
3. Which is Percy Bysshe Shelley's masterpiece?
   A. *Queen Mab* B. *Prometheus Unbound*
   C. *Prometheus Bound* D. *The Revolt of Islam*
4. Which is Percy Bysshe Shelley's work of literary criticism?
   A. *An Essay on Criticism* B. *A Defence of Poetry*
   C. *The Necessity of Atheism* D. *Of Studies*

Ⅲ. Short answer question

How is Shelley's *Prometheus Unbound* different from the traditional Greek interpretation? What is the significance of this difference?

参考答案及解析

Ⅰ. Fill in the blanks.

1. Shelley

（雪莱，全名为 Percy Bysshe Shelley。《解放了的普罗米修斯》是雪莱的著名诗剧，取材于古希腊罗马神话。）

2. freedom

（诗剧《解放了的普罗米修斯》（简称《普罗米修斯》）是雪莱的代表作，它表达了雪莱的哲学思想和社会理想，塑造了一个为自由而斗争、毫不妥协的英雄形象。）

3. fairy-tale dream

（《麦布女王》是珀西·比希·雪莱（Percy Bysshe Shelley）最早的长诗。这部长诗富于哲理，以梦幻的方式，表达了年轻的诗人对于人类最终摆脱愚昧和专制统治，走向光明未来的憧憬和信念。）

Ⅱ. Multiple Choices

1. A 《有一个被人经常亵渎的字》是雪莱的一首爱情诗。《当初我们两分别》是拜伦的一首爱情诗，《一朵红红的玫瑰》是彭斯的爱情诗，《致西利娅》则为本·琼森所作。

2. C 《阿多尼》（*Adonais*）是雪莱为悼念济慈而作，《拉米亚》（*Lamia*）是济慈的一首抒情诗，《伊莎贝拉》（*Isabella*）是济慈的一首叙事诗，《麦布女王》（*Queen Mab*）是雪莱的一首叙事长诗。

3. B 雪莱的代表作是诗剧《解放了的普罗米修斯》，《麦布女王》（*Queen Mab*）和《伊斯兰的反叛》（*The Revolt of Islam*）是他两首重要的长篇诗作；《被束缚的普罗米修斯》是希腊悲剧家埃斯库罗斯的剧作。

4. B 雪莱的文学评论作品是《诗辩》（*A Defence of Poetry*）；《批评论》是新古典主义时期亚历山大·蒲柏的文学批评著作；《无神论的必要性》是雪莱的散文作品；《论学习》是培根的一篇著名的散文。

Ⅲ. Short answer question

（1）The plot of Shelley's drama is a literary reference to Aeschylus's *Prometheus Bound* in which Prometheus finally makes peace with Zeus, an ending intolerable to Shelley. Therefore, Shelley adapted the story with his own interpretation as he changed the ending compromise to struggle which leads to the liberation of the oppressed. With strong support from Earth, his mother, Asia, his bride, and Demogorgon, and Hercules, Prometheus is unbound, while Zeus steps down from the throne.

（2）In this poem Prometheus is the embodiment of a noble revolutionary, while Zeus is the incarnation of the counter-revolutionary. The ending is a declaration of man's success in his struggle against tyranny and oppression, suggesting Shelley's faith in the ultimate victory of man.

第22章 约翰·济慈

22.1 复习笔记

John Keats (1795—1821)

1. Life

John Keats was born in London in 1795. At the age of eight he went to a small country school in Enfield where he began a love of literature. At the age of 15 he was apprenticed to a surgeon. He then studied medicine in London, passing the medical examination, but finally quit medicine for literature in 1814.

The introduction of Keats to the literary circle by Leigh Hunt, then editor of *The Examiner*, greatly encouraged and inspired Keats. In May 1816, Hunt helped him publish his first poem in a magazine. A year later Keats published about thirty poems and sonnets printed in the volume *Poems*. Absorbed in love and poetry, in the autumn of 1819 Keats tried a common job as a way to detach himself from literature. However, an unmistakable sign of consumption in February 1820 shattered all his plans for the future. On the night of 23 February 1821, Keats died and was later buried in the Protestant Cemetery. He had requested that the stone bear no name, only the words "Here lies one whose name was writ in water."

2. Poetic Style

The artistic goal of his poetry is always to create a beautiful world of imagination detached from the secular. Beauty is the finest expression and embodiment in his poetry. His leading principle is: "Beauty is truth, truth beauty". He made it clear that he is also part of nature. His poetry is distinguished by sensual and formal integrity. Some of his poems deal with the politics of the time in which he conveyed his dissatisfaction with the capitalist society and empathy with the poor oppressed.

约翰·济慈（1795—1821）

1. 生平

济慈于1795年生于伦敦。济慈8岁时到恩菲尔德的小乡村学校上学，在那里他开始渐渐培养起对文学的热爱。15岁时，他做了一个外科手术医生的学徒。之后他在伦敦学医，通过了医学考试，但最终在1814年弃医从文。

时任《观察家》编辑李？亨特将济慈引入文学圈，济慈初出茅庐的才华得到极大鼓励。1816年5月，亨特帮他在杂志上出版了第一首诗。一年后，济慈出版了《诗集》，包括30首诗和十四行诗。因为深陷爱情和诗歌中，他耗尽了自己的精神，在1819年的秋天，济慈试着做一份普通工作来从文学中抽离。然而1820年2月确切的肺痨迹象，打破了他对未来所有的规划。在1821年2月23日，济慈去世，随后被葬在新教徒公墓。他临死前要求墓碑上不刻姓名，只刻"这里安息着一个人，姓名写在水上的人。"

2. 诗歌风格

济慈诗歌的艺术目标就是创造充满想象的、与俗世不同的美丽新世界。他试图在他所有的诗歌里都体现美。他的原则就是"美是真理，真理就是美"。就像他描写的那样，他也是大自然的一部分。他的诗歌可以通过感官和形式的完整性来区分。他的一些诗歌也触动到了当时的政治。他的诗歌中表现出了对社会的不满以及对穷苦人民的描写。

3. Major Works *Endymion* (1818) *Lamia, Isabella, The Eve of St. Agnes, and Other Poems* (1820) "Ode on a Grecian Urn" (1819) "Ode to Autumn" (1819) "Ode on Melancholy" (1819) "Ode to a Nightingale" (1819) "On First Looking into Chapman's Homer" (1819) "Bright Star" (1819)	**3. 主要作品** 《恩底弥翁》(1818) 《拉米亚，伊莎贝拉，圣阿格尼斯之夜，和其他诗歌》(1820) 《希腊古瓮颂》(1819) 《秋颂》(1819) 《忧郁颂》(1819) 《夜莺颂》(1819) 《初读查普曼译荷马史诗有感》(1819) 《明亮的星》(1819)
4. Selected Works ◆***Endymion*** The poem is 4,000 lines long and was written in memory of Thomas Chatterton. The story is based on Greek mythology but heavily adapted by the poet. Endymion is a handsome shepherd loved by the moon goddess Cynthia who seduces him and leads him to eternal life. This story is mingled with other legends, including one about Venus and Adonis. So the effect of the poem is like a fairy journey to beauty.	**4. 选读作品** ◆**《恩底弥翁》** 该诗有四千行，是为纪念托马斯·查特顿而作。故事来源于希腊神话，但作者本身将其作了进一步发展。恩底弥翁是一个英俊的牧羊人，月神辛西娅爱上了他。后月神引诱了他并将他带向永生。故事当中还穿插着其他神话，其中一个有关维纳斯和阿多尼斯。全诗达到了通往美丽的仙境之旅的效果。
◆***Isabella*** Isabella, the daughter of a wealthy Florence family, is in love with a poor servant named Lorenzo. After her two brothers find out their love affair, they trick Lorenzo away, murder him, and bury his body in a forest. The heartbroken Isabella finds the body of her beloved, buries the head in a flower pot planted with basil, and takes care of it all day. Having noticed Isabella's unusual obsession with the basil, her brothers steal the pot and figure out the truth. As a result, they dsipose of Lorenzo's head, which is Isabella's last consolation. The desperate Isabella finally dies of sorrow. The main theme of *Isabella* is sympathy for oppressed people and disgust for the heartless rich.	◆**《伊莎贝拉》** 伊莎贝拉是佛罗伦萨富人家的女儿，她爱上了穷仆人洛伦佐。她的两个哥哥发现之后，设计将洛伦佐骗走，后将他无情地杀掉，并将尸体埋在森林里。伤心的伊莎贝拉找到尸体后将爱人的头骨放在种有紫苏的花盆里，每天守护着它。她的两个哥哥发现她珍视着那个花盆，发现实情后将花盆拿走，发现了头骨。失去了最后的安慰后，伊莎贝拉心碎而死。《伊莎贝拉》的基本主题是对受压迫人民的同情和对无情的富人的厌恶。
◆***Lamia*** Lamia, a serpent-maiden, falls for young Lycius who is attracted by her beauty and marries her. To show his extreme happiness, he makes a bridal feast. Among the guests, however, comes the sophist Apollonius who sees through Lamia's disguise and calls her name. Thereupon, Lamia and the house all vanish in an instant.	◆**《拉米亚》** 拉米亚，一个由蛇变成人形的少女爱上了凡人利休斯，后者被她的美貌吸引结了婚。为了给自己的幸福锦上添花，利休斯结婚时大摆筵席。然而宾客之中有位智者阿波罗尼亚斯看穿了拉米亚的真身，当他叫到拉米亚的名字时，拉米亚和房子一起消失不见了。

The poet argues in the poem that though Lamia is a serpent in disguise, she trully loves Lycius and means him no harm, while Apollonius, with his "sophist's eye", is none other than a destroyer of beauty and love with his rigid principles and philosophy.	通过诗歌诗人想表达的是虽然拉米亚是蛇精，但她真心爱着利休斯，并且不会伤害他。而那位智者，用他世人的眼光和冰冷的原则作出不人道的事，摧毁了别人的幸福。
◆"On first Looking into Chapman's Homer" This poem was written in 1816 by Keats after he was first introduced to Homer through the translation of George Chapman, an Elizabethan dramatist, translator, and poet who published his translation work *The Whole Works of Homer* in 1616.	**◆《初读查普曼译荷马史诗有感》** 本诗写于1816年济慈首次通过乔治·查普曼的翻译接触到荷马的作品。乔治·查普曼是伊丽莎白时期的剧作家、翻译家和诗人，他在1616年出版了译作《荷马全集》。
◆"Ode to a Nightingale" The ode is one of Keats' masterpieces that consists of eight stanzas of ten lines each. The first stanza expresses the poet's contradictory feelings of happiness and pain after he hears the nightingale singing. The second stanza indicates the poet's desire to get drunk and escape into the forest with the bird. Stanza three continues with the thought of escapism, in which the poet mourns for the merciless workings of the world. Stanza five is about the poet's imagination of himself intoxicated by the music of the nightingale and the fragrance of forest plants. Stanza six conveys the writer's despair and his desire to die comfortably and escape the misery of the human world. He imagines what will happen after his death. The seventh stanza contrasts the pain of life to the eternal joyful music of the nightingale. In the last stanza states the poet describes that as the bird's song fades, his thoughts return to reality.	**◆《夜莺颂》** 该诗歌是济慈的代表作之一。这首颂歌由每节十行诗句的八个诗节组成。 第一节表达了诗人在听到夜莺歌唱后幸福又痛苦的矛盾心情。第二节表达了诗人想喝醉以及想和夜莺逃往森林的欲望。逃避主义继续在第三节体现。诗人表达了生活在这个残酷世界的无限悲伤。第五诗节描写了诗人想象自己在夜莺的鸣叫声和森林植物的香气中陶醉。第六诗节表达了诗人绝望的情绪，想舒适地死去逃脱人世间的悲惨，此外还想象自己死后的情景。第七诗节把生活的痛苦和夜莺永恒的鸣叫相比较。最后一个诗节描述了鸟的鸣叫的逝去和诗人的意识回归现实。
◆"Ode on a Grecian Urn" The ode suggests that the poet's imagination runs wild when looking at a Grecian urn. He reckons the urn as a symbol for the joy of eternal life and for the immortalizing power of art and imagination.	**◆《希腊古瓮颂》** 《希腊古瓮颂》透露出诗人在面对希腊古瓮时的万千思绪。诗人把古瓮当作永恒生活的幸福的象征，也是艺术和想象力的不朽力量的象征。
◆"To Autumn" The poem, written in 1819, marks the final moment of Keats' career as a poet. The poem personifies and animates the image of autumn by describing its shape, view, and sound. And the natural progression from late summer to early winter hints at the progression of life: from birth to maturity to death.	**◆《秋颂》** 本诗写于1819年，是济慈诗人生涯的最后一首诗。 诗歌中，通过描述秋天的形态、景色和声音，让秋天这一形象人格化并生动起来。而从夏末到初冬这一自然进程也暗示着生命的进程：从出生、成熟到死亡。

◆"Bright Star"	◆《明亮的星》
"Bright Star" is a love sonnet by John Keats. In the poem, Keats interwove issues of love, death, and eternity. This poem is usually associated with Fanny Brawne with whom Keats falls in love.	《明亮的星》是济慈的一首爱情十四行诗。诗中济慈把爱情、死亡和永恒交织在一起。这首诗通常与芬妮·勃劳恩联系在一起。芬妮·勃劳恩为济慈的恋人。

22.2 考研真题与典型题详解

Ⅰ. Fill in the blanks.

1. John Keats wrote a number of well-known odes. In one of his famous odes he declares his idea of beauty. He claims that beauty is truth and truth is beauty. The title of this famous ode is __________. (天津外国语学院2007研)
2. "Ode on an Grecian Urn" shows the contrast between __________ and __________.

Ⅱ. Multiple Choices

1. __________ is a poem of 4,000 lines, "inscribed to the memory of Thomas Chatterton", the young forerunner of the Romantic Movement.

   A. *Isabella*　　B. *The Eve of St. Agnes*

   C. *Endymion*　　D. *Lamia*

2. Which of the following poems is based on Baccaccio's *Decameron*?

   A. *Isabella*　　B. *The Eve of St. Agnes*

   C. *Endymion*　　D. *Lamia*

Ⅲ. Explain the following term.

Ode

Ⅳ. Short answer question

Please analyze the theme of Keats' "Ode to a Nightingale".

Ⅴ. Essay question

Make a comment on John Keats.

参考答案及解析

Ⅰ. Fill in the blanks.

1. "Ode on a Grecian Urn"

   (济慈写过很多著名的颂，其中在《希腊古瓮颂》中他表达了自己的审美观点：美就是真，真就是美。)

2. the permanence of art, the transience of human passion

   (济慈的《希腊古瓮颂》("Ode on a Grecian Urn")展示了永恒的艺术与短暂的人类热情之间的对比。)

Ⅱ. Multiple Choices

1. C 《恩底弥翁》(*Endymion*)是济慈于1818年5月发表的长诗，描写了希腊神话中月亮女神与凡人恩底弥翁相爱的故事，为的是纪念浪漫主义运动的先驱托马斯·查特顿

(Thomas Chatterton)。

2\. A 《伊莎贝拉》(*Isabella*)是济慈根据薄伽丘的《十日谈》(*Decameron*)创作的叙事诗。《恩底弥翁》(*Endymion*)是济慈于1818年5月发表的长诗，描写了希腊神话中月亮女神与凡人恩底弥翁相爱的故事；《圣阿格尼斯之夜》(*The Eve of St. Agnes*)和《拉米亚》(*Lamia*)是继《伊莎贝拉》后陆续出版的诗作。

Ⅲ. Explain the following term.

Ode: Ode is a poetic form in which the poet elaborately eulogizes some people or events in length.

Ⅳ. Short answer question

In the ode, the speaker touches upon themes of creative expression and morality through his observation of transient passage of time and human life.

The nightingale's song carries the writer's thoughts far away. He imagines that he has flown away into the forest with the singing emissary. The beautiful song even makes the poet think about death as a beautiful experience free from earthly concerns and pain at some point. The poet is intoxicated by the song so much that when the bird's singing fades away, he could not even tell whether he is in dream or reality.

Ⅴ. Essay question

(1) John Keats is a representative of the second-generation English Romantic poets.

(2) John Keats got inspiration in poetic art mainly from poets of the English Renaissance such as Edmund Spenser and William Shakespeare, John Milton, and Italian poet Dante.

(3) John Keats was a bit different from his contemporary poets. Keats always created a imaginary world of beauty as reaction to the secular one impaired by filth and ugliness. As a poet of beauty, he is known for his assertion that "Beauty is truth, truth beauty."

(4) Keat described his sensory experiences and sensual satisfaction in his poetry in delicate form. So Keats has always been known as a sensuous poet. He has such unique appreciation of senses and talent to write them out with refined language.

(5) Some of Keats's poems respond to the worrying political and social situations in his time, expressing his concern over poor sufferers and outrage against the capitalist society.

第 23 章　沃尔特·司各特

23.1　复习笔记

Walter Scott (1771—1832)

1. Life

Walter Scott was born in Edinburgh in 1771. Sickly and frail as a child, Scott was taken to his great-grandfather's farm at the age of three, where he heard the legend of the frontier war, the spirit of which became woven into Scott's poetry. In 1778, he returned to Edinburgh improved in health, but with an incurable slight lameness. In 1783, he entered the University of Edinburgh and read prodigiously about travels, romances, poetry, and traditional plays. He went bankrupt in 1826 but bravely decided to pay his debts with his pen. He worked hard, publishing novels, tales and histories one after another. But his health was severely damaged.

2. Literary Achievements

Walter Scott is the pioneer and master of the historical novel. His chief achievement is the 20 novels he wrote, guaranteeing his unique place in literary history. He brought huge changes to the English novel by elevating its theme, expanding its content, and refining it with artistic beauty. With his historical novels Scott pushed forward the development of the realistic novel in the nineteenth century.

3. Literary Style

(1) Scott's historical novels offer a panoramic view of the rise and fall of feudal society, covering the period from the Middle Ages to the 18th century. The novels describe different periods of this era, including the Crusades, the rise of absolute monarchy, the bourgeois revolution, and the Restoration.

(2) He described people and natural landscape brilliantly. Scott has a remarkable gift for bringing the past to life, combining historical fact with romantic imagination.

沃尔特·司各特(1771—1832)

1. 生平

沃尔特·司各特于 1771 年出生于爱丁堡。司各特小时候体弱多病，三岁时被带到曾祖父的农场，在那里听到边境战争的传说，其精神被融入到司各特的诗歌中。1778 年他回到爱丁堡，身体有所好转，但落下终身不治的轻微跛脚。1783 年他进入爱丁堡大学，博览游记、传奇、诗歌、古代戏剧等。1826 年他破产了，随后勇敢地决定靠写作偿还债款。他辛勤写作，接连出版小说、故事、历史故事，但是身体健康受到严重损害。

2. 文学成就

司各特是历史小说的开创者和大师。司各特的主要成就是他所著的 20 部小说，使他在文学史上占据独特地位。他革新了英国小说，表现在提升了其基调，开阔了其范围，使其具有艺术性。他的历史小说为 19 世纪现实小说的发展铺平了道路。

3. 文学风格

(1) 司各特的历史小说展现了封建社会从兴起到衰落的全景，涵盖了从中世纪到 18 世纪这一时期。这些小说描述了这一时代的不同阶段，包括十字军东征、君主专制的兴起、资产阶级革命和王政复辟。

(2) 他极其出色地描绘了人物和自然景观。司各特具有将过去生动复活的杰出天赋，把历史事实和浪漫想象相结合。

(3) His novels have a clear class stance. Although he yearned for the aristocracy, he was also deeply attracted to the fate of ordinary people and depicted the erosion of their lives by industrial capitalism.

(4) The protagonists of his novels are heroic young men, often of noble birth, who have been made poor by persecution. By fighting alongside ordinary people, they overcome difficulties and eventually regain their titles and return to prosperous life.

(3) 他的小说有明确的阶级立场。尽管他向往贵族阶级，他也对普通人民的命运极感兴趣，并描绘了工业资本主义对他们生活的腐蚀。

(4) 他小说的主人公是英勇的年轻小伙子，通常出身高贵却因受到迫害变得贫穷。他们通过和普通百姓并肩作战，战胜困难，最终恢复了头衔，重回繁华生活。

4. Major Works

A. Poems

The Minstrelsy of the Scottish Border (1802—1803)
Marmion (1808)
The Lady of the Lake (1810)

B. Novels

Waverley (1814)
Guy Mannering (1815)
The Antiquary (1816)
Rob Roy (1817)
The Heart of Midlothian (1818)
Ivanhoe (1820)
Kenilworth (1821)
The Fortunes of Nigel (1822)
Woodstock (1826)
Quentin Durward (1823)
St. Ronan's Wells (1823)

4. 主要作品

A. 诗歌

《苏格兰边区歌谣集》(1802—1803)
《玛米恩》(1808)
《湖上夫人》(1810)

B. 小说

《威弗利》(1814)
《盖·曼钠令》(1815)
《古董家》(1816)
《罗伯·罗伊》(1817)
《米德洛西恩的监狱》(1818)
《艾凡赫》(1820)
《肯纳尔沃斯堡》(1821)
《尼格尔的家产》(1822)
《皇家猎宫》(1826)
《昆廷·达沃德》(1823)
《圣罗南之泉》(1823)

5. Selected Works

According to the content described, Scott's historical novels can be divided into three categories: those describing the history of Scotland, those describing the history of England, and those describing the history of European countries. Novels on Scottish history include *Waverly*, Rob Roy, and *Old Morality*. English-subject novels include *Ivanhoe*, *The Fortunes of Nigel*, and *Woodstock*. Novels on the history of European countries include *Quentin Durward*. And *St. Ronan's Wells* is the only one of Scott's novels that deals with his contemporary life.

5. 选读作品

司各特的历史小说根据所描写的内容可以分为三大类：描写苏格兰历史的、描写英国历史的、描写欧洲国家历史的。描写苏格兰历史的包括《威弗利》，《罗伯·罗伊》和《清教徒》。描写英国历史的包括《艾凡赫》，《尼格尔的家产》和《皇家猎宫》。描写欧洲国家中最有名的是《昆廷·达沃德》。唯一一部描写与作者同时代的作品是《圣罗南之泉》。

◆***Ivanhoe*** The story of the novel takes place at the end of the twelfth century, when the people of England, the Anglo-Saxons, are living a miserable life under the rule of the Normans. In the novel, Richard is depicted as a chivalrous, brave, and upright monarch who represents the far-sighted Norman nobles, who sympathizes with the Saxons' desire for peace, and who is willing to reach a compromise with them. Meanwhile, Prince John, the opposite of his brother Richard, is devious and plots to take over the throne. Ivanhoe, a Saxon aristocrat, helps Richard against Prince John. The novel also tells of Ivanhoe's feelings and other life experiences.	◆**《艾凡赫》** 小说的故事发生在十二世纪末，当时的英国人民，即盎格鲁－撒克逊人，在诺曼人的统治下过着苦难的生活。在小说中，理查德被描写成具有侠士风范，勇敢，正直的君主，他代表了有远见的诺曼贵族，并且同情撒克逊人渴望和平的愿望，愿意与撒克逊人达成妥协。同时，与理查德相反的是他的弟弟约翰王子，他阴险狡诈，密谋夺取哥哥的王位。出身为撒克逊人贵族的主人公艾凡赫，帮助理查德对抗约翰王子，小说同时讲述了艾凡赫的感情和其他人生经历。
◆***Rob Roy*** *Rob Roy* describes the 1715 uprising of the Scottish Highlanders against the English yoke. Francis Osbaldistone, the son of a rich London merchant, lives with his uncle. Previously an honest cattle-dealer, Rob Roy is now the leader of the Scottish Highlanders against the English rule. Francis witnesses the struggle between the Scottish people and the English troops. Finally, Rashleigh, the sixth son of Francis's uncle and a malicious man, attempts to get rid of Francis and seize his father's property, but is killed by Rob Roy.	◆**《罗伯·罗伊》** 《罗伯·罗伊》描述了1715年苏格兰高地人为反抗英国政府的奴役而爆发的起义。弗朗西斯·奥斯巴蒂斯通是位富商之子，住在叔叔家。罗伯·罗伊原来是一个诚实正直的贩牛人，现在则领导苏格兰高地人民反抗英国的统治。弗朗西斯亲眼目睹了苏格兰人民和英国军队的战争。拉什利是弗朗西斯叔叔的第六个儿子，一个心地恶毒的人，一心想要除掉弗朗西斯，夺取父亲的家产。拉什利被罗伯·罗伊杀死。

23.2 考研真题与典型题详解

Ⅰ. Fill in the blanks.

1. *Waverley* was written by __________. （大连外国语学院2007研）
2. Scott is considered "the father of __________" which opens up to fiction the rich and lively realm of history.
3. __________ marked the transition from romanticism to the period of realism which followed it.

Ⅱ. Short answer question

What are the major features of Scott's historical novels?

Ⅲ. Essay question

Please briefly comment on Walter Scott's *Ivanhoe*. （四川大学2009研）

参考答案及解析

Ⅰ. Fill in the blanks.

1. Walter Scott

（《威弗利》是英国诗人、小说家 Walter Scott 的第一部历史小说。）

2. the historical novel

（司各特以其历史小说闻名，开创了欧洲历史小说的先河，被称为“历史小说之父”。）

3. Walter Scott

（沃尔特·司各特(Walter Scott)是英国浪漫主义时期的最后一位作家，他是英国文学由浪漫主义向现实主义过渡的标志。）

Ⅱ. Short answer question

Scott's historical novels provide us with a panoramic view of feudal society from its early stages to its downfall from the period between the Middle Ages and the 18th century. Scott has a remarkable gift for bringing the past to life, combining historical fact with romantic imagination. His novels have a clear class stance. Although he yearned for the aristocracy, he was also deeply attracted to the fate of ordinary people and depicted the erosion of their lives by industrial capitalism. The protagonists of his novels are heroic young men, often born to purple, who have been made poor by persecution. By fighting alongside ordinary people, they overcome difficulties and eventually regain their titles and return to prosperous life.

Ⅲ. Essay question

The story of the novel takes place at the end of the twelfth century, when the people of England, the Anglo-Saxons, are living a miserable life under the rule of the Normans. In the novel, Richard is depicted as a chivalrous, brave, and upright monarch who represents the far-sighted Norman nobles, who sympathizes with the Saxons' desire for peace, and who is willing to reach a compromise with them. Meanwhile, Prince John, the opposite of his brother Richard, is devious and plots to take over the throne. Ivanhoe, a Saxon aristocrat, helps Richard against Prince John. The novel also shows Ivanhoe's feelings and other life experiences.

In *Ivanhoe*, as in Scott's other novels, people from different backgrounds and social class are given detailed depiction. *Ivanhoe* is reputed for the realistic description of life in feudal England. The novel's plot is structured in balance with proper language in accordance with different situations. Despite its fictional feature, the general political events depicted in the novel are accurate. *Ivanhoe* helps increase interest in the Middle Ages in 19th century Europe and America.

第24章 简·奥斯丁

24.1 复习笔记

Jane Austen (1775—1817)

1. Life

Jane Austen was the seventh child of Reverend George Austen, rector of Stevenson, and was born in the parsonage of the village in 1775. She passed her life peacefully and happily amid the petty domestic affairs of the country. She was home-schooled and began writing at an early age. But her works were not taken seriously by publishers. It was not until Walter Scott's publishing an anonymous article praising *Emma* that Austen began to be known by the public. Austen was a bright and attractive woman averse to publicity and popularity. She died, quietly as she had lived, at Winchester in 1817, and was buried in the cathedral.

2. Literary Style

(1) Austen is a realist novelist. In her works, she vividly depicted the reality of ordinary country life.

(2) Austen's novels are full of humor, wit, quiet irony, and concise and detailed analyses of characters.

(3) Her characters are true to life with both weaknesses and virtues.

(4) Her writing is natural and fluent, untainted by worldly slang and empty talk, making her works the perfect reading materials for a genteel lady. Her dialogue is equally authentic.

3. Major Works

Sense and Sensibility (1811)
Pride and Prejudice (1813)
Mansfield Park (1814)
Emma (1815)
Persuasion (1818)
Northanger Abbey (1818)

简·奥斯丁（1775—1817）

1. 生平

简·奥斯丁是乔治·奥斯丁，史蒂文森教区牧师的第七个孩子。她在乡村琐碎的家庭事务中平静愉快地度过了一生。她在家接受教育，很小就开始写作。但是她的作品并没有受到出版方的重视。直到司各特发表了一篇匿名文章，赞赏《爱玛》，奥斯丁才渐渐为人熟知。奥斯丁开朗迷人，对出名十分厌恶。她于1817年在温彻斯特平静地离世，被葬在教堂。

2. 文学风格

(1) 奥斯丁是现实主义小说家。她在作品中生动描绘了普通乡村生活的真实图景。

(2) 奥斯丁的作品充满幽默、机智、冷静的反讽，和对人物简洁细致的分析。

(3) 她小说中的人物活灵活现，跟真实的人一样既有美德，又犯些错误。

(4) 她的文风自然流畅，丝毫未受现世的俚语和空话的污染，是文雅淑女的完美读本。她的对话同样真实自然。

3. 主要作品

《理智与情感》(1811)
《傲慢与偏见》(1813)
《曼斯菲尔德庄园》(1814)
《爱玛》(1815)
《劝导》(1818)
《诺桑觉寺》(1818)

4. Selected Work	**4. 选读作品**
◆*Pride and Prejudice*	**◆《傲慢与偏见》**
Pride and Prejudice is a love story between the rich proud young man Darcy and the ordinary but beautiful and intelligent Elizabeth Bennet. At first, Elizabeth has a prejudice against Darcy because of a series of misunderstandings and refuses his proposal for his behavior towards her family and friends. In Elizabeth's eyes, Darcy is too proud to appreciate the good in people. But after a series of things, Elizabeth sees the nobility and kindness in Darcy. In the end, they are happily united.	小说主要讲述了富有的年轻人达西和家境一般却美丽聪慧的伊丽莎白·班尼特之间的爱情故事。起先，伊丽莎白因为一系列事情对达西产生了偏见，从而讨厌他并拒绝了他的求婚。在她眼里，达西永远一副瞧不起她家人和朋友的形象。但经过许多事情之后，她了解到达西的善良和高尚，最终两人走到一起。

24.2 考研真题与典型题详解

Ⅰ. Fill in the blanks.

1. The English Romantic period produced two major novelists: __________ and __________.
2. Jane Austen wrote the novel __________ when she was 21 in 1797, and the work was rewritten and published under the title *Pride and Prejudice* in 1813.（武汉大学2015研）

Ⅱ. Multiple Choices

1. *Pride and Prejudice* is noted for its vividly depicted characters who are revealed through comparison and contrast with each other. Of the following pairs of characters __________ are NOT in contrast.

   A. Darcy and Wickham　　B. Elizabeth and Charlotte
   C. Elizabeth and Jane　　D. lady Catherine and Mr. Collins

2. Which one of the following novels is not written by Jane Austen?

   A. *Sense and Sensibility.*　　B. *Pride and Prejudice.*
   C. *North and South.*　　D. *Northanger Abbey.*

Ⅲ. Read the following quotation and answer the questions.（大连外国语学院2007研）

It is a truth universally acknowledged that a single man in possession of a good fortune must be in want of a wife.

However little known the feelings or views of such a man may be on his first entering a neighbourhood, this truth is so well fixed in the minds of the surrounding families, that he is considered as the rightful property of some one or other of their daughters.

"My dear Mr. Bennet," said his lady to him one day, have you heard that Netherfield Park is let at last?"

Mr. Bennet replied that he had not.

"But it is," returned she; "for Mrs. Long has just been here, and she told me all about it."

Mr. Bennet made no answer.

"Do you not want to know who has taken it?" cried his wife impatiently.

"You want to tell me, and I have no objection to hearing it."

This was invitation enough.

"Why, my dear, you must know, Mrs. Long says that Netherfield is taken by a young man of large fortune from the north of England; that he came down on Monday in a chaise and four to see the place, and was so much delighted with it that he agreed with Mr. Morris immediately; that he is to take possession before Michaelmas, and some of his servants are to be in the house by the end of next week."

"What is his name?"

"Bingley."

"Is he married or single?"

"Oh! Single, my dear, to be sure! A single man of large fortunes; four or five thousand a year. What a fine thing for our girls!"

"How so? How can it affect them?"

"My dear Mr. Bennet," replied his wife, "how can you be so tiresome! You must know that I am thinking of his marrying one of them."

"Is that his design in settling here?"

"Design! Nonsense, how can you talk so! But it is very likely that he may fall in love with one of them, and therefore you must visit him as soon as he comes."

"I see no occasion for that. You and the girls may go, or you may send them by themselves, which perhaps will be still better, for as you are as handsome as any of them, Mr. Bingley might like you the best of the party."

"My dear, you flatter me. I certainly have had my share of beauty, but I do not pretend to be anything extraordinary now. When a woman has five grown-up daughters, she ought to give over thinking of her own beauty."

"In such cases a woman has not often much beauty to think of."

Questions:

1. This excerpt is taken from the novel entitled ___________ by ___________.
2. Comment on the characters of Mr. and Mrs. Bennet.
3. What methods are used to depict the characters of Mr. and Mrs. Bennet?
4. This excerpt is taken from a chapter that has been highly praised as an opening chapter. Do you consider such praise justified? Give reasons for your answer.

Ⅳ. Short answer question

State briefly the artistic features of Jane Austen.

Ⅴ. Essay question

In *Pride and Prejudice* Jane Austen put forwards three kinds of motivations of marriage. Try to make a brief comment on her attitude towards these motivations with specific examples from the novel.

参考答案及解析

Ⅰ. Fill in the blanks.

1. Walter Scott; Jane Austen

(英国浪漫主义时期的代表作家是：沃尔特·司各特(Walter Scott)和简·奥斯丁(Jane

Austen)。前者是英国小说史上第一位重要的历史小说家；后者虽然对浪漫主义有深刻的认识，但文中表现的道德意识和写作风格都带有极强的18世纪的烙印。）

2. *First Impressions*

（简·奥斯汀21岁时写成她的第一部小说，题名《最初的印象》，她与出版商联系出版，没有结果。十几年后，《最初的印象》经过改写，换名为《傲慢与偏见》，得以出版。）

Ⅱ. Multiple Choices

1. D 在《傲慢与偏见》中，几位人物都形成了鲜明对比，比如：达西(Darcy)和威克汉姆(Wickham)一起长大，但一个正直善良一个谎话连篇；伊丽莎白(Elizabeth)和夏洛特(Charlotte)是闺中密友，但一个有胆识有远见，不屈于富贵，一个软弱，屈服于钱财；伊丽莎白和姐姐简(Jane)虽都很善良，但一个有主见，一个没有自己的主意。在书中，唯独凯瑟琳夫人(lady Catherine)和柯林斯(Mr. Collins)没有形成鲜明对比。

2. C 《南方与北方》是盖斯凯尔夫人的小说。

Ⅲ. Read the following quotation and answer the questions.

1. *Pride and Prejudice*; Jane Austen

2. Mr. Bennet is a man of complex personality and quick wit. His daily sarcastic jokes on his wife and life cannot be understood by her, an empty-headed, simple, talkative, and na? ve woman.

3. First, Mr. and Mrs. Bennet are shown in contrast in both manners and language. Mrs. Bennet talks nonstop, while Mr. Bennet is reserved and addresses his mildly sarcastic statements. The irony and satire in Austen's language give the novel additional amusement.

4. The excerpt is lucid and graceful in style and humorous in language. The vivid and authentic conversations bring characters to life.

Ⅳ. Short answer question

(1) Jane Austen was much attracted to personal relationships, especially love affairs of young men and women.

(2) Austen's characterization is vivid and authentic with detailed depiction of daily activities and events.

(3) One virtue of her novels is the touch of authenticity through ordinary language and daily conversations.

(4) She pays much attention to the formal qualities of composition and to design. Her plot appears natural and unforced.

(5) However, the subject of Austen's novels is quite limited to genteel life in the countryside. She also created a narrow range of characters with single moral standard. The plots in her novels are set in the provincial or village life of the 19th-century England, with only three or four landed gentry families involved.

Ⅴ. Essay question

In this novel, three kinds of motivations of marriage are presented.

First, some characters in the novel marry for money, fame, and social rank. For instance, Miss Bingley's pursuit of Darcy, Lady de Bourgh's intention to marry her daughter to Darcy, and Charlotte Lucas's marriage to Mr. Collins are examples of this kind. The first two set their goals to satisfy their vanity and pride, while the latter shows practical purpose of the poor to raise their station.

Second, some in the novel marry simply for beauty and passion without economic considerations or concerns over the personality of their marrying subject. The learned and skeptical Mr. Bennet marrying beautiful but shallow-minded Mrs. Bennet and their youngest daughter Lydia marrying to handsome but morally weak and penniless Wickham are of this kind. Their unhappy marriage life proves that blind and careless marriage only leads to tragic results.

Lastly, the ideal marriage is one between couples with matching personal merits and economic conditions. The marriage of Darcy and Elizabeth and that of Mr. Bingley and Jane are of this kind. Nevertheless, such perfect marital combination is somewhat dramatic.

In this novel Jane Austen reminds the reader of what a good marriage should be like: it is not built on attraction of the other sex or impulse, but one built on mutual love, complimentary personal merits, and matching economic conditions. Of the three types, she prefers the last one which is best represented by the marriage between Darcy and Elizabeth.

第25章　查尔斯·兰姆

25.1　复习笔记

Charles Lamb (1775—1834)	查尔斯·兰姆(1775－1834)
1. Life Charles Lamb was born and spent his youth in the Inner Temple, London. Lamb attended Christ's public school and became lifelong friends with Coleridge. In 1796, Lamb's sister Mary killed their mother in a fit of insanity. As Mary suffered from intermittent mental illness, he began to take care of his sister, who was very fond of him. He himself was mentally deranged from 1795 to 1796. In 1833, he and Mary moved to Edmonton, where Lamb died and was buried.	**1. 生平** 查尔斯·兰姆出生于伦敦的内殿律师学院，并在那里度过青年时光。兰姆在基督公学上学，并和柯勒律治成了终生好友。1796年兰姆的姐姐玛丽因发疯杀死了他们的母亲。由于玛丽患有间歇性精神病，他开始照顾姐姐，玛丽也对他十分怜爱。1795至1796年间，兰姆自己也有些精神错乱。1833年，他和玛丽搬到爱民顿，兰姆去世并被埋葬于此。
2. Literary Career Lamb's literary career can be divided into three periods: (1) Early literary compositions, including 4 sonnets, the best-known poem "The Old Familiar Faces", a romance, a poetical drama, and an unsuccessful play. (2) Literary criticism on Shakespeare's plays, Wordsworth's *The Excursion*, etc.; stories based on classical works with the most popular one being *Tales from Shakespeare*. (3) Observation of life, essays published in *The London Magazine*.	**2. 文学生涯** 兰姆的文学生涯可以被分为三个阶段： (1) 早期文学创作，包括四首十四行诗、最著名的诗《熟悉的老面孔》、一部传奇剧、一首诗剧和一部失败的戏剧。 (2) 文学批评，关于莎剧、华兹华斯的《远足》等；基于经典名著重写的故事，最著名的是《莎士比亚戏剧故事集》。 (3) 生活观察，出版在《伦敦杂志》上的散文。
3. Literary Style (1) The calm, unsophisticated style of Lamb's prose is appealing. (2) The essays are intensely personal and is refined demonstration of himself and his humanity. (3) The greatest characteristic of Lamb's prose is its humor which is mixed with tears and sadness. (4) His essays are full of long and strange words, frequent exclamations, and parentheses.	**3. 文学风格** (1) 兰姆散文的风格平和古朴，十分吸引人。 (2) 他的散文关乎个人，很好地展现了兰姆本人和人性。 (3) 兰姆散文最大的特点就是文中的幽默。他的幽默是笑语夹杂着泪水，幽默背后隐藏着悲伤。 (4) 他的散文中到处是冗长和奇特的词语，还经常插有感叹和插入语。

4. Major Works *Tales from Shakespeare* (1807) *Essays of Elia* (1823) *Last Essays of Elia* (1833) **5. Selected Work** ◆***Essays of Elia*** The pen name "Elia" was borrowed from an old clerk and Lamb's colleague in the Sea House. In his collection of more than 50 essays on a variety of subjects, Lamb was frank with the reader. This form of personal essays allowed Lamb to showcase his life experience as a clerk, his study of literary masters, his imagination, his wit and humor, his love for London, and his whole personality. "Dream-Children: a Reverie" and "Poor Relations" are selected from *Essays of Elia*.	**4. 主要作品** 《莎士比亚戏剧故事集》(1807) 《伊利亚随笔集》(1823) 《伊利亚随笔续编》(1833) **5. 选读作品** ◆《伊利亚随笔集》 笔名伊利亚来自兰姆在海关工作的同事，一个老职员的名字。书中收集了50多篇主题多样的散文，兰姆在文中直抒胸臆，同读者娓娓闲谈。这种私人随笔的形式能让兰姆充分展示他的职员经历，他对文学大师作品的研究，他的想象，智慧和幽默，他对伦敦的热爱以及他自己的个性。《梦中的儿女：一首幻想曲》和《穷亲戚》均选自本散文随笔。

25.2 考研真题与典型题详解

Ⅰ. Fill in the blanks.

1. With __________, the essay is no longer chiefly a mode of intellectual inquiry and moral address. Rather, the essay becomes a medium for a delightful literary treatment of life's small pleasures and reassurances.
2. *Tales from Shakespeare* is written by __________ and Mary Lamb.

Ⅱ. Multiple Choices

1. Charles Lamb wrote a series of miscellaneous essays, collected in 1823 as the __________.
   A. *Tales from Shakespeare*　　B. *Rosamund Gray*
   C. *Dream Children*　　D. *Essays of Elia*
2. Which is not Charles Lamb's work?
   A. *Tales from Shakespeare*　　B. *Essays of Elia*
   C. *Last Essays of Elia*　　D. *Woodstock*

Ⅲ. Explain the following term.

Charles Lamb (四川大学2007研)

Ⅳ. Short answer question

What is the writing style of Lamb's essays?

参考答案及解析

Ⅰ. Fill in the blanks.

1. Charles Lamb

（兰姆的随笔不同于以往用来阐明知识和道德说教的散文模式，而是以生活中的细小乐趣为出发点，把城市生活中的琐碎话题写得妙趣横生，把平凡的事物点化得鲜活生动。）

2. Charles Lamb

（兰姆和姐姐共同重写了基于经典名著的故事集《莎士比亚戏剧故事集》。）

Ⅱ. Multiple Choices

1. D　查尔斯·兰姆(Charles Lamb)的主要成就是散文，他创作的散文被收录在其1823年出版的《伊利亚随笔集》里面。

2. D　*Woodstock*《皇家猎宫》是沃尔特·司各特(Walter Scott)的小说。

Ⅲ. Explain the following term.

Charles Lamb: Charles Lamb was an English essayist and author of *Essays of Elia* and children's book *Tales from Shakespeare* collaborated with his sister Mary Lamb. He made great contributions to English essays.

Ⅳ. Short answer question

Lamb's essays are gentle, personal, and attractive in style with intense humanistic care. Lamb also displayed humor mingled with tears. Sadness is felt through his humor. In his essays there are long and curious words, and his sentences are often interrupted by frequent exclamations and parentheses.

第六部分　维多利亚时期

第 26 章　查尔斯·狄更斯

26.1　复习笔记

Ⅰ. Background Knowledge	**Ⅰ. 背景知识**
(1) The Victorian period represents the Queen Victoria's reign(1837—1901). But this new era really began with the passing of the Reform Bill in 1832 and closed at the end of Boer War in 1902.	(1) 维多利亚时期指女王维多利亚统治期(1837 年至 1901 年)。这个新时代真正始于 1832 年《改革法案》的通过，终于 1902 年布尔战争结束。
(2) Democracy became the established order, and the House of Commons became the ruling power in England. The suffrage was rapidly extended.	(2) 民主成为既有秩序，下议院在英国成为统治力量。选举权极大扩展。
(3) The reformed parliament made some legislative achievements including the emancipation of slaves in British dominions, colonial administration, religious tolerance, pauperism, sanitation, free trade, etc.	(3) 改革后的议会取得了一些立法成就，包括在英国领土上解放奴隶、殖民地管辖、宗教宽容、贫困、卫生、自由贸易等。
(4) The main social conflict was the labor-management conflict. As the working class grew stronger, their self-confidence increased. But their lives became more miserable, and the Chartist Movement broke out at 1832. This movement lasted until the 1850s.	(4) 主要社会冲突是劳资冲突。由于工人阶级力量壮大，自信提升，而生活越发凄惨，1832 年至 50 年代早期爆发了宪章运动。
Ⅱ. Literary Style of the Victorian Period	**Ⅱ. 维多利亚时期的文学风格**
(1) Chartist literature showed the growing strength of the working class. In the Chartist movement, chartist writers introduced a new literary theme, that is, the proletariat's struggle for rights. Famous representatives of chartist literature are Ernest Jones, Thomas Cooper and William James Linton.	(1) 宪章文学展现了工人阶级的日益强大。在宪章运动中，宪章作家引进了一种新的文学主题，即无产阶级为权利斗争的主题。著名的宪章文学代表有欧内斯特·琼斯，托马斯·库柏和威廉·詹姆斯·林顿。
(2) Critical Realism of the 19th century flourished from the 1840s to the early 1850s. The realist writers criticize the capitalist society and sympathize with the laboring people. The most excellent realists are Dickens and Thackeray.	(2) 批判现实主义文学在 19 世纪 40 年代至 50 年代早期繁荣。这些现实主义作家批判资本主义社会，同情劳动人民。最具代表性的批判现实主义小说家是狄更斯和萨克雷。
(3) There were more and more outstanding female writers, including the Bront? Sisters, Mrs. Gaskell, and George Eliot.	(3) 出现了越来越多卓越的女性作家，包括勃朗特姐妹，盖斯凯尔夫人和乔治·艾略特等。

(4) A group of outstanding poets appeared in the second half of the 19th century, including Alfred Tennyson, Robert Browning, and Algernon Charles Swinburne.

(4) 19 世纪后半叶出现了一批杰出的诗人，包括阿尔弗雷德·丁尼生，罗伯特·勃朗宁和阿尔杰农·查尔斯·斯温伯恩。

Ⅲ. Literary Terms

Ⅲ. 文学术语

1. Critical Realism

1. 批判现实主义

(1) Critical realism reveals the bad influence of money supremacy on human nature. Critical realists not only satirically described the bourgeoisie and other ruling classes, but also showed deep sympathy for the general public.

(1) 批判现实主义揭示了金钱控制一切对人性的恶劣影响。批判现实主义者不仅讽刺地描述了资产阶级和其他统治阶级，还表现了对普通大众的深切同情。

(2) But the critical realists failed to find a way to eliminate the social evils they were familiar with. They strived for reform rather than revolution. Their work usually powerfully revealed the ugliness of the capitalist world at the beginning, but ended with compromise and reconciliation.

(2) 但是批判现实主义者们并没有找到消除他们熟知的社会罪恶的办法。他们力争改革而不是革命。他们的作品通常是在开始时强有力地揭示了资本主义世界的丑恶，但最后只是无力的妥协与和解。

2. Chartist Movement

2. 宪章运动

(1) The British Chartist Movement was a reform movement led by the working class from 1838 to 1848 to strive for social justice and improve lives, which included manhood suffrage, payment of Members of Parliament, equal electoral districts, annual parliaments, voting by ballot, and the abolition of property qualifications for MPs. Though the movement had failed, it was "the first broad, really mass, politically formed, proletarian revolutionary movement."

(1) 英国宪章运动是 1838 年至 1848 年由工人阶级领导的，争取社会公正、改善生活的改革运动。它要求男性公民选举权，议员缴款，平等选区，年度议会，投票表决，废除为取得议员资格应具备的财产资格。宪章运动虽然失败了，但是它是第一个广泛的、真正群众参与的、有政治组织形式的无产阶级革命运动。

(2) The author of chartist literature introduced a new literary theme, namely the struggle of the proletariat for rights. The writers mainly include Ernest Jones, Thomas Cooper and William James Linton. Writers include Ernest Jones, Thomas Cooper, and William James Linton.

(2) 宪章文学作者引入了一种新的文学主题，即无产阶级为权利的斗争。作家主要包括欧内斯特·琼斯，托马斯·库柏和威廉·詹姆斯·林顿。

(3) All important events of the Chartist Movement, especially the class conflicts can also be found in the novels of critical realists like Dickens, Charlotte Brontë and Mrs. Gaskell.

(3) 宪章运动的所有重要事件，特别是阶级冲突都可以在批判现实主义作家的小说中找到，如狄更斯，夏洛蒂·勃朗特和盖斯凯尔夫人。

Ⅳ. Charles Dickens (1812—1870)

Ⅳ. 查尔斯·狄更斯(1812—1870)

1. Life

1. 生平

Charles Dickens was born in a small town in Hampshire

查尔斯·狄更斯于 1812 年出生

in 1812. His childhood was very difficult, which became the material in his future novels. His education was haphazard, but he supplemented it with constant reading. At the age of 12, his father was thrown into debtor's prison, so he worked in a warehouse and lived a miserable life. At the age of 15, he became a fellow in a law firm, and in his free time he went to the British Museum to study. In 1833, his first book, *Sketches by Boz*, was published. In the same year, he got married and meanwhile was writing *The Pickwick Papers*, which helped Dickens rise to fame at 25. This book made him famous at the age of 25. Dickens kept writing with great energy. He wrote novels, autobiographies, travel books, wrote and performed plays, edited periodicals, and administered charitable organizations. After separating from his wife, he read his works to the public to make money. But this job made him more tired and damaged his health. In spite of repeated warnings to stop, while working on the unfinished *The Mystery of Edwin Drood* in 1870 at his country house, he suffered a stroke of apoplexy and died a day later. Following his will, the funeral was simplified, and he was buried in Westminster Abbey.

在汉普郡的一个小城。他的童年过得很艰辛，这也成为他日后小说中的素材。狄更斯的教育杂乱无章，但他通过不断阅读来弥补。12 岁时，他的父亲被投入债务人监狱，因此他就在一个仓库做工，过着凄惨的生活。15 岁时，他成了律师事务所的小伙计，空闲时则去英国博物馆读书。1833 年，他的第一本书《博兹札记》出版。同年，他结了婚并且开始写《匹克威客外传》。这本书使他在 25 岁时一举成名。狄更斯笔耕不辍、精力旺盛。他写小说、自传、游记、既写又演戏剧、编辑期刊，管理慈善组织。和他的妻子分居后，他开始向公众阅读他的作品，来增加收入。但这份工作使他本已繁重的写作雪上加霜，损害着他的健康。他不听劝阻继续写作，1870 年正在写《艾德温·德鲁德之谜》时，他患中风，一天后就去世了。遵循他的遗嘱，葬礼从简，之后他被葬在威斯敏斯特教堂。

2. Literary Style

(1) Dickens was a great British realist novelist. The most memorable thing about him is his vivid and extraordinary characters, with exhaustive descriptions of social classes, customs, and values.

(2) Dickens's works are humorous and ironic. Micawber in *David Copperfield* is a well-known comedy figure in world literature, and another representative figure is the hypocrite Mr. Pecksniff.

(3) In the structure of his novels, the main clue is usually interspersed with several secondary clues. This will not only introduce more interesting secondary characters, but also describe broader life scenes.

2. 文学风格

(1) 狄更斯是伟大的英国现实主义小说家。他最令人难忘的是生动非凡的人物，对社会阶级、习俗、价值观详尽无遗的描述。

(2) 狄更斯的作品幽默而具有讽刺意味。《大卫·科波菲尔》中的米考伯是世界文学中出了名的喜剧人物，另一代表人物是具有讽刺意味的伪君子佩克斯列夫。

(3) 在小说结构上，通常是主线索穿插着几个次要线索。这样既能介绍更多的有趣的次要人物，还能描述更广的生活场景。

3. Major Works

1836　*Sketches by Boz*

1836—1837　*The Pickwick Papers*

3. 主要作品

1836　《博兹札记》

1836—1837　《匹克威克外传》

1837—1838 *Oliver Twist*
1838—1839 *Nicholas Nickleby*
1840—1841 *The Old Curiosity Shop*
1841 *Barnaby Rudge*
1842 *American Notes*
1843—1844 *Martin Chuzzlewit*
1843 *A Christmas Carol*
1844 *The Chimes*
1845 *The Cricket on the Hearth*
1846—1848 *Dombey and Son*
1849—1850 *David Copperfield*
1852—1853 *Bleak House*
1854 *Hard Times*
1855—1857 *Little Dorrit*
1859 *A Tale of Two Cities*
1860—1861 *Great Expectations*
1864—1865 *Our Mutual Friend*
1870 *The Mystery of Edwin Drood*

4. Selected Works

◆*The Pickwick Papers*

This is the work that first made Dickens famous as a popular writer of novels. The novel tells a series of adventures of Mr. Pickwick. Pickwick is a wealthy retired businessman and the founder and chairman of a strange Pickwick club.

Written in the picaresque form of Don Quixote, the book depicts a panoramic view of British society and presents readers with various images of petty bourgeoisie. Although the author attacked the ugly side of the political system at the time, the story was still full of joyful laughter from young people. The funny plot contained in the whole story is very interesting, funny, and true.

◆*Oliver Twist*

Oliver Twist tells the story of an orphan boy, whose life experience reflects the life of the lower class in London. Oliver was born in a workhouse and does not know who his parents are. After a very unfortunate apprentice life in the coffin shop, he fled to London and fell into the hands of a group of thieves.

1837—1838《雾都孤儿》
1838—1839《尼古拉斯·尼克尔贝》
1840—1841《老古玩店》
1841《巴纳比·卢杰》
1842《美国札记》
1843—1844《马丁·瞿述伟》
1843《圣诞颂歌》
1844《钟声》
1845《炉边蟋蟀》
1846—1848《董贝父子》
1849—1850《大卫·科波菲尔》
1852—1853《荒凉山庄》
1854《艰难时世》
1855—1857《小杜丽》
1859《双城记》
1860—1861《远大前程》
1864—1865《我们共同的朋友》
1870《艾德温·德鲁德之谜》

4. 选读作品

◆《匹克威克外传》

该书是狄更斯的成名作。小说围绕匹克威克先生的一系列冒险展开。匹克威克是一位富有的退休商人，同时也是一个奇怪的匹克威克俱乐部的创始人和主席。

故事以类似堂·吉诃德的冒险故事形式写成。书中描绘了英国社会的全景，给读者呈现了各种各样的小资产阶级人物形象。虽然作者攻击了当时政治制度丑陋的一面，故事仍然充满了年轻人的欢乐的笑声。整个故事包含的滑稽情节非常有趣、滑稽、形象真实。

◆《雾都孤儿》

《雾都孤儿》讲述了一个孤儿奥利弗·特维斯特的故事，他的生活经历反映了伦敦下层社会的生活。奥利弗出生在济贫院，不知道自己的父母是谁。在棺材店过了一段非常不幸的学徒生活后，他逃到

After a series of adventures, Oliver was rescued and adopted by Mr. Brownlow. In the novel, the author makes readers aware of the brutality of urban life under the capitalist system. Through vivid descriptions of the thieves and the underworld in London, the author successfully aroused the readers' sympathy for the trampled people in the lower class. The main defects of the novel are the unreliability of the plot, and the incredibility of some characters. Toward the end of the novel, the plot gets to be very intricate and the reader is simply mystified. Oliver can always get help from others at critical moments, and these people are finally confirmed to be his relatives. Fagin and Bill Sikes are too inhuman to be true, while the rich Mr. Brownlow is simply pictured as benevolent and good.	伦敦，落入一群贼的手里。经历了一系列的冒险后，奥利弗被从贼窝里救出来，并被布朗罗先生收养。 在小说中，作者使读者意识到资本主义制度下城市生活的残暴。在生动描写贼窟和伦敦的黑社会时，作者很成功地唤起了读者对下层社会中被践踏的人民的同情。小说的主要缺点是小说情节的不可靠性，人物性格也有些不可靠。小说结尾处，情节过于扑朔迷离。而奥利弗在关键时刻总能得到贵人相助，这些贵人最后又经证实是他的亲属。费根和赛克斯太过凶残，好人布朗罗先生又只是单一的好心。
◆*The Old Curiosity Shop* It is a story of the sufferings and hardships of an old man and his granddaughter, Nell. The grandfather and grandson live in an antique shop, but driven by hardship and poverty, the two flee to central England to make a living by begging. But bad luck still follows them, and they die far away from home.	**◆《老古玩店》** 这篇小说讲述了外祖父和他的外孙女内尔两人的遭遇和艰难。祖孙二人以一家古玩店为生，但是在苦难和贫困的驱使下，两人逃往英格兰中部地区，靠乞讨为生。但是坏运气依然跟随他们，他们死在远离家乡的地方。
◆*Great Expectations* The novel tells the life experience of the protagonist Pip. Estella is the heroine of the book and the girl Pip likes. She wants to enter the upper class, so she looks down on Pip. This makes him very hurt. Irritated by this, Pip determines to become a gentleman and he gets financial aid from a secret donator Magwitch, who turns out to be the convict and dies in the prison. Then Pip loses the money to support him. Pip's dream of a great future is shattered, and after experiencing more things, both he and Estella become mature.	**◆《远大前程》** 小说围绕主人公匹普的人生经历(童年、青年、中年)展开。埃斯特拉是书中的女主人公，也是匹普喜欢的女孩，她一心想要进入上流社会，因此根本瞧不起匹普，这使得他很受伤害，这时有一位神秘的捐助者马格维奇使匹普进入了上层社会。但是马格维奇是个罪犯，最后死在监狱里，匹普的远大前程之梦破灭，最后经历过更多事情后，他和埃斯特拉都变得成熟了。

26.2 考研真题与典型题详解

Ⅰ. Fill in the blanks.

1. The Victorian Age in English literature was largely an age of prose, especially of the __________. (人大 2006 研)
2. Mr. Peggotty and Steerforth are two characters in Dickens's novel __________. (人大 2006 研)

3. The title __________ is not merely the name of one novel written by Dickens and a house, but is also an apt description of the society in which the action takes place. The main butt of satire in the novel is aimed at the abuses of the English __________.

4. In the basic plot of *A Tale of Two Cities*, the fate of Dr. Manette is closely interwoven with the development of the __________.

5. As a novelist, Charles Dickens is remembered first of all for his __________.

Ⅱ. Multiple Choices

1. In __________, common sense and moral propriety took the place of the principle of Romanticism and became the predominant preoccupation in literary works.（北二外 2009 研）
   A. Renaissance　　B. the Elizabethan period
   C. the gilded age　　D. the Victorian period

2. "Of all my books," wrote Dickens, "I like this the best." Which work does it refer to?
   A. *A Tale of Two Cities.*　　B. *David Copperfield.*
   C. *Pickwick Papers.*　　D. *Oliver Twist.*

3. The three most eminent novelists who represent the three phases of the Victorian novels are Charles Dickens, Thomas Hardy and __________.（天津外国语学院 2008 研）
   A. George Moore　B. Louis Stevenson　C. James Joyce　D. George Eliot

4. The English novel as a genre began to prosper in the __________.（天津外国语学院 2007 研）
   A. 16th century　B. 17th century　C. 18th century　D. 19th century

5. In 1859, Charles Dickens published his historical novel of the French Revolution entitled __________.（大连外国语学院 2008 研）
   A. *Hard Times*　　B. *Bleak House*
   C. *A Tale of Two Cities*　　D. *Our Mutual Friend*

6. The statement "It reveals the dehumanizing workhouse system and the dark, criminal underworld life" may well sum up the main theme of Dickens's __________.
   A. *David Copperfield*　B. *Bleak House*　C. *Great Expectations*　D. *Oliver Twist*

7. The pride of wealth, or "purse-pride", is the theme of the novel __________.
   A. *Dombey and Son*　　B. *A Tale of Two Cities*
   C. *Little Dorrit*　　D. *Bleak House*

8. Which of the following is NOT directly related to the literature of Victorian Age in England?（四川大学 2013 研）
   A. The growth of urban population resulted in the appearance of a new reading public.
   B. Many libraries were set up so that books were now available to readers who could not afford to buy them.
   C. The plot of novels is unfolded against a social background which is broader than what it had been in previous novels.
   D. Most of the novels were not first published in serial form, that is, by installment, before they were fully published in a single book.

Ⅲ. Explain the following terms.

1. English critical realism

2. Victorian period

Ⅳ. Short answer questions

1. Make a brief comment on the English poetry in the Victorian Age.
2. Please make a brief comment on *David Copperfield*.

Ⅴ. Essay questions

1. Analyze the theme of social class in Dickens's *Great Expectations*.（北航 2009 研）
2. What is the strength and weakness of English critical realism?

参考答案及解析

Ⅰ. Fill in the blanks.

1. novel

（在维多利亚时期，英国的文学表现形式主要是小说。）

2. *David Copperfield*

（Mr. Peggotty 和 Steerforth 是狄更斯的小说《大卫·科波菲尔》中的两个人物。）

3. *Bleak House*; courts

（在《荒凉山庄》(*Bleak House*)中，狄更斯批判揭露了英国社会法律体系的漏洞和极力搜刮客户腰包的无耻企图。）

4. French Revolution

（《双城记》(*A Tale of Two Cities*)中，莫奈特医生的命运与法国大革命息息相关。正是法国大革命爆发，巴士底狱被革命者攻陷，莫奈特医生才重新获得自由。）

5. character-portrayal

（查尔斯·狄更斯以其人物塑造而出名。他笔下的人物类型多种多样，各种人物形象既具备典型化的特点，又分别拥有自己与众不同的独特性。）

Ⅱ. Multiple Choices

1. D　在维多利亚时代，道德和理性取代了浪漫主义原则，重新回到了文学主流当中。
2. B　《大卫·科波菲尔》(*David Copperfield*)是半自传体的小说，它的成就超过了狄更斯所有其他作品，被狄更斯称为他“心中最宠爱的孩子”。
3. D　维多利亚时期小说以 Charles Dickens, Thomas Hardy 和 George Eliot 三个人为代表。
4. D　英国小说开始进入繁荣期是在 19 世纪。
5. C　《双城记》发表于 1859 年，是一部以法国大革命为背景的小说，也是狄更斯的代表作。
6. D　狄更斯在小说《雾都孤儿》中揭露许多当时的社会问题，如救济院、童工、以及帮派吸收青少年参与犯罪等，描写了资本主义社会穷苦儿童的悲惨生活，无情地鞭挞了资本主义社会的黑暗和虚伪。
7. A　《董贝父子》描写了董贝父子公司的盛衰史。董贝是个贪得无厌的大资本家，妻子儿女都成了他追逐利润的工具和摆设。公司经理卡克尔是个奸诈小人，骗取了董贝的信任后又一手造成了他的破产。在现实的教训中，董贝的思想发生了转变。最后，虽然他已无法重整家业，却成全了真正的家庭幸福。
8. D　维多利亚时代的小说大多先以连载的形式出版，然后才以一本书的形式完全出版。它们最初出现在小册子、期刊或报纸上，查尔斯·狄更斯的作品和威廉·萨克雷的《名利场》就是以连载的方式出版的。故选 D。

Ⅲ. Explain the following terms.

1. English critical realism: ① English critical realism of the 19th century flourished in the forties and in the early fifties. The critical realists described with much vividness and artistic skill the chief traits of the English society and criticized the capitalist system from a democratic viewpoint. ②The greatest English realist of the time was Charles Dickens. With striking force and truthfulness, he pictured bourgeois civilization, showing the misery and sufferings of the common people. Another critical realist, William Makepeace Thackeray, was a no less severe exposer of contemporary society. Thackeray's novels were mainly a satirical portrayal of the upper strata of society. ③ Critical realism reveals the bad influence of money supremacy on human nature. Critical realists not only satirically described the bourgeoisie and other ruling classes, but also showed deep sympathy for the general public. But the critical realists failed to find a way to eliminate the social evils they were familiar with. They strived for reform rather than revolution. Their work usually powerfully revealed the ugliness of the capitalist world at the beginning but ended with compromise and reconciliation.
2. Victorian period: ① Chronologically the Victorian period roughly coincides with the reign of Queen Victoria who ruled over England from 1836 to 1901. The period has been generally regarded as one of the most glorious in the English history. ② In this period, class struggle was very tense. As a result, a new literary trend—critical realism appeared. The criticism of the 19th century flourished in the forties and in the early fifties. The critical realists described with much vividness and great artistic skill the chief traits of the English society and criticized the capitalist system from a democratic view point. In this period, the novel became the most widely read and the most vital and challenging expression of progressive thought. The Victorian age also produced a host of great prose writers. The poetry of this period was mainly characterized by experiments with new styles and new ways of expression. ③ Victorian literature, as a product of its age, naturally took on its quality of magnitude and diversity. It was many-sided and complex, and reflected both romantically and realistically the great changes that were going on in people's life and thought.

Ⅳ. Short answer questions

1. (1) Victorian Age covers the years from 1837 to 1901. The age of English poetry had come to an end. The Victorian Age was largely an age of prose, especially of the novel.

   (2) However, the development of English poetry did not stop. Poetry was no longer a major art intended to change the world, as that of George Gordon Byron and Percy Bysshe Shelley. It now seldom touched on the serious social problems, but mainly concerned itself with the poets' purely personal tastes or spiritual questionings.

   (3) The most important poets of the age was Alfred Tennyson, Robert Browning and his wife Mrs. Browning.
2. ①Charles Dickens' *David Copperfield* is an autobiographical novel to some extent, but it has far great significance.

   ②In the novel, Dickens makes good use of his experience to attack the social evils of the day that were prevalent in Victorian England. Therefore, the novel is not just a personal record, but a broad picture of the society of the author's day. Dickens' own experience was turned to good account likewise in the creation of a number of very vivid characters.

③In this novel, there is the eulogy of simple people, their joys as well as sorrows. Dickens gives his usual contrast between the selflessness and mutual helpfulness of the simple folk and the immorality of the upper classes. He makes his condemnation of the so-called civilized, respectable members of the upper classes of his time.

④The novel was written at a time when his creative powers had reached their height. All these give the book a combination of verisimilitude, familiarity and artistic maturity seldom met with in his other novels.

V. Essay questions

1. Throughout *Great Expectations*, Dickens explores the class system of Victorian England, ranging from the most wretched criminals (Magwitch) to the poor peasants of the marsh country (Joe and Biddy) to the middle class (Pumblechook) to the very rich (Miss Havisham). The theme of social class is central to the novel's plot and to the ultimate moral theme of the book—Pip's realization that wealth and class are less important than affection, loyalty, and inner worth. Pip achieves this realization when he is finally able to understand that, despite the esteem in which he holds Estella, one's social status is in no way connected to one's real character. Drummle, for instance, is an upper-class lout, while Magwitch, a persecuted convict, has a deep inner worth.

   The most important thing about the novel's treatment of social class is that the class system it portrays is based on the post-Industrial Revolution model of Victorian England. Dickens generally ignores the nobility and the hereditary aristocracy in favor of characters whose fortunes have been earned through commerce. Even Miss Havisham's family fortune is made through the brewery that is still connected to her manor. In this way, by connecting the theme of social class to the idea of work and self-advancement, Dickens subtly reinforces the novel's overarching theme of ambition and self-improvement.

2. Critical realism reveals the bad influence of money supremacy on human nature. Critical realists not only satirically described the bourgeoisie and other ruling classes, but also showed deep sympathy for the public. Hence humor and satire abound in the English realistic novels of the 19th century. Humorous scenes set off the actions of the positive characters, and the humor is often tinged with a lyricism which serves to stress the fine qualities of such characters. Here lies the essentially democratic and humanistic character of critical realism.

   But the critical realists failed to find a way to eliminate the social evils they were familiar with. They strived for reform rather than revolution. Their work usually powerfully revealed the ugliness of the capitalist world at the beginning but ended with compromise and reconciliation. Here we see the strength and the weakness of critical realism.

第 27 章 威廉·梅克比斯·萨克雷

27.1 复习笔记

William Makepeace Thackeray (1811—1863)	威廉·梅克比斯·萨克雷(1811—1863)
1. Life Thackeray was born in 1811, in Calcutta, India. His father was a British civil servant in the Indian government. After his father's death in 1817, he returned to England and went to many preparatory schools. He was tired of this experience. Then he went to the public school at the Charterhouse and was bullied and beaten. Six years later, he entered Trinity College, Cambridge. He contributed to The Snob, and became friends with Tennyson, Edward Fitzgerald, and William Brookfield. But he only stayed for more than a year and left without getting a degree. He squandered his inheritance due to extravagant waste and irrational investment, and in 1834, he had to do his own work. In 1836, he married an Irish girl who went crazy after giving birth to her third child. Thackeray had to raise his daughter alone and leaded a lonely life. He found relief at his friend Brookfield's house, but was forced to end the friendship because he fell in love with the mistress. *The Book of Snobs* made him a social satire. Afterwards, his literary lectures were welcomed. By 1859, he was on par with Dickens. In 1860 he became the first editor of the *Cornhill Magazine*. He had been in poor health for ten years and died suddenly in Kensington, London in 1863.	**1. 生平** 威廉·梅克比斯·萨克雷于1811年生于印度加尔各答，父亲是印度政府的英国公务员。1817年父亲去世后，他回到英国，辗转多所预备学校，他十分厌恶，之后又到了卡尔特修道院的公立学校，被欺负鞭打。6年后，他进入剑桥大学三一学院，为《势利者》投稿，并和丁尼生、爱德华·菲茨杰拉尔德、威廉·布鲁克菲尔德成为朋友。但是他只待了一年多就离开了，没有拿到学位。他因奢侈浪费和不理性投资把遗产挥霍一空，1834年不得不自力更生。1836年，他与一个爱尔兰女孩结婚，这个女人在生了第三个孩子后就疯了。萨克雷不得不独自抚养女儿，过着孤独的生活。他在朋友布鲁克菲尔德家找到宽慰，但因单纯地深爱上女主人，被迫结束了这段友谊。《势利者集》使他成为社会讽刺家。之后他的文学讲座受到欢迎。到1859年，他已经和狄更斯平起平坐了。1860年他成了《康希尔杂志》的第一任主编。十年来他一直身体欠佳，1863年在伦敦的肯辛顿突然去世。
2. Major Works *The Book of Snobs* (1848) *Vanity Fair* (1847—1848) *Pendennis* (1848—1850) *The Newcomes* (1853—1855) *The History of Henry Esmond* (1852) *The Virginians* (1857—1859)	**2. 主要作品** 《势利者集》(1848) 《名利场》(1847—1848) 《彭登尼斯》(1848—1850) 《纽克姆一家》(1853—1855) 《亨利·埃斯蒙德的历史》(1852) 《弗吉尼亚人》(1857—1859)

3. Selected Work	**3. 选读作品**
◆***Vanity Fair*: *A Novel without a Hero***	◆**《名利场》**
The sub-title of the book, "A Novel without a Hero" emphasizes the fact that the author did not intend to describe the individual, but the entire bourgeoisie and aristocratic society. The title was taken from Bunyan's The Progress, and the "vanity fair" means a fair where all kinds of vanity are sold, such as houses, lands, honours, preferment, titles, lusts, pleasures and delights of all sorts.	书的副标题"一部没有主人公的小说"强调了这样一个事实：作者没有打算描写个人，而是描写整个资产阶级和贵族社会。"名利场"一词来自班扬的《天路历程》，书中对名利场的描述是这样的：它是一个售卖各种名利的地方，出卖的物品有房子、土地、荣誉、升迁、头衔、欲望、欢喜和各种各样的与享乐有关的东西。
A. Main Plot	**A. 主要情节**
The plot is built around the fates of Amelia Sedley and Rebecca (Becky) Sharp. Becky wants to be in the upper society. Later, she achieves this goal through some despicable means, living like a lady. Emilia also experienced the ups and downs of her life. Out of gratitude, she marries Dobbin who has loved her all her life.	书中故事是围绕艾米丽亚·赛特笠和利蓓加·夏泼(又叫贝基)展开的。贝基一心想要跻身上流社会，后来通过一些拙劣的手段她达到了这个目的，像贵妇一样地生活着。而艾米丽亚也在经历过了人生的跌宕起伏后，出于感激，嫁给了爱了她一生的多宾。
B. Analysis	**B. 分析**
The novel describes the life of the ruling classes of England in the early 19th century. Thackeray ruthlessly attacked the superficial values and pseudo-ethics of the British upper class, and satirized people's persistent pursuit of wealth and status. This novel is an excellent study of treacherous and hypocritical, and it is also a mirror of today's society. Becky Sharp is a classic example of the money-grubbing instinct. The only wish in her life is to obtain wealth and status by unscrupulous means. Thackeray did not write Rebekah as a special character. She is a typical representative of that era: everyone wants something in the Vanity Fair. There are few positive characters in the book.	小说描写了19世纪早期英国统治阶级的生活。萨克雷无情抨击了英国上层阶级浅薄的价值观和伪道德，也讽刺了人们对财富地位的执拗追求。他敏锐地揭示了荒唐和弱点。这部小说极好地研究了奸诈和虚伪，也是审视当今社会的明镜。利蓓加·夏泼是获取钱财的一个典型代表。她生命中唯一的愿望就是不择手段地获地财富和地位。萨克雷没有把利蓓加写成是一个特殊的人物，她是那个时代的典型代表：每个人都希望在名利场中得到些什么。书中几乎没有正面人物。

27.2 考研真题与典型题详解

Ⅰ. Fill in the blanks.

1. William Makepeace Thackeray's first literary success came with a series of satirical sketches entitled __________, published between 1846 and 1847.
2. In 1847, William Makepeace Thackeray published his masterpiece __________, which marks

the peak of his literary career.

3. __________'s popularity as a social satirist rivaled that of Dickens by 1859.

4. The title of the novel *Vanity Fair* is taken from __________.

Ⅱ. Read the following quotation and answer the questions.

On nothing per annum then, and during a course of some two or three years, of which we can afford to give but a very brief history, Crawley and his wife lived very happily and comfortably at Paris. It was in this period that he quitted the Guards, and sold out of the army. When we find him again, his mustachios and the title of Colonel on his card are the only relics of his military profession.

It has been mentioned that Rebecca, soon after her arrival in Paris, took a very smart and leading position in the society of that capital, and was welcomed at some of the most distinguished houses of the restored French nobility. The English men of fashion in Paris courted her, too, to the disgust of the ladies their wives, who could not bear the parvenue. For some months the salons of the Faubourg St. Germain, in which her place was secured, and the splendours of the new Court, where she was received with much distinction, delighted, and perhaps a little intoxicated Mrs. Crawley, who may have been disposed during this period of elation to slight the people—honest young military men mostly—who formed her husband's chief society.

But the Colonel yawned sadly among the Duchesses and great ladies of the Court. The old women who played écarté made such a noise about a five-franc piece, that it was not worth Colonel Crawley's while to sit down at a card-table. The wit of their conversation he could not appreciate, being ignorant of their language. And what good could his wife get, he urged, by making curtsies every night to a whole circle of Princesses? He left Rebecca presently to frequent these parties alone; resuming his own simple pursuits and amusements amongst the amiable friends of his own choice.

The truth is, when we say of a gentleman that he lives elegantly on nothing a year, we use the word "nothing" to signify something unknown; meaning, simply, that we don't know how the gentleman in question defrays the expenses of his establishment.

Questions:

1. This passage is taken from a famous novel entitled __________.
2. The novel takes its title from that fair described in John Bunyan's work entitled __________, where all sorts of cheats are displayed for sale.
3. This novel is __________ masterpiece.
4. The subtitle of the novel is __________. Why?
5. What do you know about Rebecca (Crawley's wife)?
6. What is the main idea of this passage?

参考答案及解析

Ⅰ. Fill in the blanks.

1. *The Book of Snobs*

(随着一系列名为"英国的势利小人"的讽刺故事于1846—1847年间出版，萨克雷的文学事业首告成功，这些故事后来被收录在一本名为《势利者集》的书里。实际上，《势利者集》用讽刺的口吻描写了英国统治阶级不同的阶层。)

2. *Vanity Fair*

(《名利场》是英国十九世纪小说家萨克雷的成名作品，也是他生平著作里最经得起时间考验的杰作，是英国较著名的讽刺性批判现实主义小说。)

3. Thackeray

(到 1859 年，作为社会讽刺家的萨克雷已经和狄更斯平起平坐了。)

4. Bunyan's *The Pilgrim's Progress*

(“名利场”一词来自班扬的《天路历程》。)

Ⅱ. Read the following quotations and answer the questions.

1. *Vanity Fair*
2. *The Pilgrim's Progress*
3. William Makepeace Thackeray's
4. *A Novel without a Hero*. The subtitle indicates that the novel is concerned principally not with individual heroes but with the society as a whole. It is also possible to interpret the subtitle as meaning that there are only heroines but no heroes.
5. Rebecca or Becky Sharp is crafty, unscrupulous, resourceful, and all in all "sharp". She lives in a world where money grubbing is the main motive for all members of the ruling classes. She is a classic example of those money-grubbing instinct. The only wish in her life is to obtain wealth and status by unscrupulous means. She flirts and carries on illicit relations with all rich and powerful men, young and old, within her reach, for the sole purpose of living a comfortable life. Of course she has her vanity also of outrivaling other women in beauty and in her power over men, and of gaining admittance into high society, but all such vanity is inseparably bound up with the greed for wealth.
6. This passage talks about Becky's adventures in Paris. It satirizes on cheatings of all sorts prevalent in the high society in Paris. But here also may be seen the author's cynicism as he tries to indicate that such vices are too common in the world and that therefore the offenders like Becky and her husband are not to be blamed too severely.

第 28 章　乔治·艾略特

28.1　复习笔记

George Eliot (1819—1880)	乔治·艾略特(1819—1880)
1. Life George Eliot was the pseudonym of Mary Ann Evans. Her father was a wealthy farm agent, and she spent her childhood in the rural area of Warwickshire in central England. From the age of 5 to 16, Mary Ann went to the boarding school. Because of her shy and unsocial personality, she devoted herself to hard reading. She believed in the Anglican religion as a child and turned to rationalism as an adult. After the death of her father, she became the assistant editor of *The Westminster Review*. Later she fell in love with a married man George Henry Lewes and they lived together as true husband and wife. From 1856, Mary Ann began to write novels. By 1876, she had achieved a reputation unmatched by any female writer. Eliot and Lewes were so famous, and no one talked harsh gossip about them. They gathered around celebrities and friends in their last days. After Lewes's death in 1878, she married John Cross in 1880, who was more than 20 years her junior. Soon she caught a chill at a concert and died after four days of illness.	**1. 生平** 乔治·艾略特是玛丽·安·埃文斯的笔名。她父亲是一个富有的农场代理人，她在英国中部沃里克郡的农村度过了童年。5 至 16 岁之间，玛丽·安在寄宿学校上学。由于她性格腼腆，不善交际，于是便全身心投入到刻苦的阅读中。她童年信仰英国国教，成年后转向理性主义。父亲去世后，她成了《威斯敏斯特评论》的助理编辑。后来，她爱上了有妇之夫路易斯，他们犹如真正的夫妻一般生活。从 1856 年起，玛丽·安开始写小说。到 1876 年，她取得了任何女性作家难以企及的声望。艾略特和路易斯名声大噪，没人再说刻毒的闲话。他们俩最后的日子身边名人好友云集。路易斯 1878 年去世后，艾略特于 1880 年嫁给了比她小 20 多岁的约翰·克罗斯。不久她在一场音乐会中染上风寒，4 天后因病去世。
2. Literary Style (1) The focus of her work is always the moral position of the protagonist in the world, which is somewhat homiletic. (2) She is a genius who shows the psychological development of characters. She depicts the rural scenery and the lives of ordinary rural people. (3) But in other respects, her work is also a retrogression. She shifted the focus of the novel from social issues to religious and moral issues, because she believed that human nature and friendship could eliminate the evils of capitalism.	**2. 文学风格** (1) 她作品的侧重点总是主人公在世上的道德立场，多少有些说教。 (2) 她是展现人物心理发展，描绘乡村景色、普通乡村人们生活的天才。 (3) 但是在其他方面，她的作品也是一种倒退。她把小说的重心从社会问题转移到宗教和道德问题上，因为她相信人性和友爱可以消灭资本主义的罪恶。

3. Major Works

Adam Bede (1859)

The Mill on the Floss (1859—1860)

Silas Marner (1861)

Romola (1862—1863)

Middlemarch (1871—1872)

Daniel Deronda (1876)

4. Selected Works

◆*Adam Bede*

A. Main Plot

Adam Bede is a country carpenter, an upright and hard-working young man. He falls in love with Hetty Sorrel, a beautiful woman with strong vanity. She wants to improve her social status through marriage, so she wants to marry the young squire, Arthur Donnithorne, a frivolous and selfish person. After seducing Heidi, Arthur ends the relationship with Hetty. The heart-broken Hetty agrees to marry Adam who loves her. But just before the wedding, she finds out that she is pregnant. Hetty goes to find Arthur, but in vain. She leaves her newborn child in the woods, and then the child died when she comes back. Therefore, she is convicted of murdering a child. While in prison, Dinah Morris comes to visit and preach for her. Before the execution, Hetty is pardoned and sentenced to exile.

B. Analysis

Adam Bede is full of moral conflicts, showing the collision between personal desires and moral obligations. The two pairs of lovers, Arthur and Hetty on the one hand, and Adam and Dinah on the other hand, are described in contrast to each other. The first two care only for their own interests, regardless of the life or death of others, but the latter two have high moral sentiments. The book also combines typical Elliott-style moral teachings with social injustice.

◆*The Mill on the Floss*

A. Main Plot

Most of the first few chapters are the author's autobiography. The author describes the fate and tragedy of a young girl

3. 主要作品

《亚当·贝德》(1859)

《弗洛斯河上的磨坊》(1859—1860)

《织工马南》(1861)

《罗慕拉》(1862—1863)

《米德尔马契》(1871—1872)

《丹尼尔·德龙达》(1876)

4. 选读作品

◆《亚当·贝德》

A. 主要情节

亚当·贝德是个乡村木匠，一个正直且勤奋的年轻人。他爱上了海蒂·苏洛，一位美丽但是虚荣心强的女人。她一心想着通过婚姻提升自己的社会地位，因此她想嫁给年轻乡绅亚瑟·唐尼桑恩，一个轻浮、自私的人。在引诱了海蒂之后，亚瑟结束了与海蒂之间的关系。心碎的海蒂同意嫁给爱着她的亚当，但就在婚礼前夕，她发现自己怀孕了，于是海蒂前去寻找亚瑟，结果徒劳，她将刚出生的孩子放在树林里，再回来时孩子已经死了。因此海蒂被判谋杀孩子罪名，在监狱时，黛娜·莫里斯前来看望并为她布道。在行刑前，海蒂被赦免，判以流放。

B. 分析

《亚当·贝德》这部小说充满了道德冲突，展现了个人欲望和道德义务之间的碰撞。小说中的两对爱侣——亚瑟和海蒂，亚当和黛娜——形成鲜明对比。前两人只顾自己利益，不管别人死活，后两人却拥有高尚的道德情操。书中也将典型的艾略特式的道德教导和社会不公糅合在一起。

◆《弗洛斯河上的磨坊》

A. 主要情节

小说的前几章大部分是作者的自传。作者描写了一个年轻姑娘的

whose noble pursuit is incompatible with the vulgarity and bigotry of the people around her. The protagonists of the novel are Tom and Maggie, who are the children of the wealthy miller Tulliver. Tom drives Maggie out of the house because Maggie falls in love with her cousin's suitor and almost elopes with him but she stops herself timely. In a flood, Maggie rows the boat to rescue Tom who is trapped. The boat is overturned by the flood, and the reconciled siblings are eventually submerged.	命运和悲剧，她的高尚追求和周围人的庸俗和偏执互不相容。小说主人公是汤姆和麦琪，他们是富有的磨坊主托利佛的孩子。汤姆因为麦琪爱上了表妹的追求者并险些与之私奔而将麦琪赶出家门。在一次洪灾中，麦琪摇船去救被困的汤姆，船被洪水打翻，和解了的兄妹俩最终被淹没。
B. Analysis	**B. 分析**
The author's moral preaching can be seen from Maggie's character. The tragic fate of the heroine actually expresses the irreconcilability of a gifted and noble person and the reality of the bourgeoisie.	从麦琪的性格中可以看出作者的道德说教。女主人公的悲剧命运实际上表现了一个有天赋的、心灵高尚的人和资产阶级现实的不可调和性。
◆*Middlemarch*	**◆《米德尔马契》**
Dorothea Brook is an idealistic and wealthy young lady. To everyone's surprise, she is married to Edward Casaubon, a middle-aged pedantic scholar. Dorothea wanted to find a sense of accomplishment by sharing her husband's wise life, but she finds disappointment. At the same time Dorothea forms a friendship with Casaubon's young nephew Will Ladislaw. Casaubon dies, leaving a will stating that Dorothea should not marry Ladislaw, and his property would belong to Dorothea. In the end, Dorothea breaks through the bondage and marries Ladislaw.	多萝西娅·布鲁克是一个怀有理想主义的富有的小姐，出乎众人意料的是她嫁给了爱德华·卡苏朋，一个中年迂腐的学者。多萝西娅想要通过分享她丈夫的充满睿智的生活来找到成就感但找到的却是失望。同时多萝西娅和卡苏朋的年轻侄子威尔·拉德斯拉形成了友谊。卡苏朋死了，留下一份遗嘱声明只有多萝西娅不嫁给拉德斯拉，他的财产才归多萝西娅所有。最后，多萝西娅冲破了遗嘱对自己的束缚，和拉德斯拉结合。
Silas Marner	**《织工马南》**
The novel tells the story of a weaver, Silas Marner. One day Marner adopts a little girl who comes to his house and named her Eppie. Godfrey has a secret that threatens his relationship with Nancy, a young woman who is well-bred: He married a low-born woman who smoked opium, Molly. But now the two have no feelings. Molly freezes to death in the snow while holding the baby to find Godfrey. The child is Eppie who is adopted by Marner. Sixteen years later, Eppie has become a girl that everyone in the town is proud of. She and Marner also have a very deep relationship. Godfrey confesses to his wife Nancy about the past. Godfrey and his wife, who have no children, come to Marner's house to return Eppie,	小说讲述了一位纺织工赛拉斯·马南的故事。有一天马南收养了一个来到了他家门前的小女孩，并起名为爱贝。戈弗雷怀有一个威胁到他与一个出身教养都很好的年轻女子南希的恋情的秘密：他娶了一个出身低下且吸食鸦片的女人，莫利。但是现在两人已经没有感情。莫利在抱着孩子寻找戈弗雷的路上冻死在雪地里。孩子就是被马南收养的爱贝。16 年过去了，爱贝出落成全镇人都感到骄傲的亭亭少女。她跟马南也有了非常深厚的

but Eppie will not leave Manan. After she marries a local guy, the couple live happily with Marner.	感情，戈弗雷向妻子南希坦白交代之前的往事，没有子嗣的戈弗雷夫妇前往马南家想要回爱贝，但是爱贝不会丢下养育自己的马南，她嫁给当地一位小伙后，夫妻二人跟马南幸福地生活着。

28.2 考研真题与典型题详解

Ⅰ. Fill in the blanks.

1. *Daniel Deronda*, written in 1876, is __________'s last novel. The mastery of the subtler complexities of psychological analysis is revealed thoroughly.
2. George Eliot was the pseudonym of __________.
3. In the novel *Adam Bede*, Adam falls in love with a village girl called __________ who is seduced and deserted by a squire.

Ⅱ. Multiple Choices

1. __________, the pioneering woman, according to D. H. Lawrence, was the first novelist that "started putting all the actions inside".
   A. George Eliot　　B. Jane Austen
   C. Charlotte Brontë　　D. Emily Brontë
2. George Eliot's __________ tells the story of a weaver, who has taken refuge in an isolated hut.
   A. *Adam Bede*　　B. *The Mill on the Floss*
   C. *Silas Marner*　　D. *Romola*

Ⅲ. Essay questions

1. Please analyze the character Adam in *Adam Bede*.
2. Please analyze the theme of marriage in *Middlemarch*.

参考答案及解析

Ⅰ. Fill in the blanks.

1. George Eliot
   (《丹尼尔·德龙达》(1876)是乔治·艾略特的最后一部小说。在书中，艾略特做了细致的人物心理分析，展现了丰富的人物内心世界。)
2. Mary Ann Evans
   (乔治·艾略特是英国维多利亚时期与狄更斯和萨克雷齐名的一位女作家，她的本名是玛丽·安·埃文斯。)
3. Hetty Sorrel
   (《亚当·贝德》是乔治·艾略特的第一部长篇小说。小说中木匠亚当爱上了农家姑娘海蒂(Hetty Sorrel)，而海蒂却被一个庄园主的孙子诱骗并被抛弃。)

Ⅱ. Multiple Choices

1. A　在塑造文学形象的时候，乔治·艾略特十分注重内心世界与外部环境的结合，由此开创了一种新型的现实主义，并且进一步向着自然主义与心理分析小说发展。在作品中，她致力于表现人们内心深处的斗争，揭示那种对人类行为起支配作用的动机、冲动和遗传因素。因此，劳伦斯称赞她为第一位“探究所有行为的内心活动”的小说家。

2. C　乔治·艾略特的《织工马南》(*Silas Marner*)讲述了一位纺织工赛拉斯·马南的故事。

Ⅲ. Essay questions

1. Adam is the imperfect hero of the novel. At first, he is a proud man who considers himself a good carpenter and a hard worker. But he is judgmental toward his father, whose death causes him to examine his heart. Adam has a soft spot for all helpless creatures. However, he has no tolerance for evil because he cannot understand temptation. Blinded by her physical beauty, he cannot see that Hetty is really a shallow, vain young girl. Upon finding out the affair between Hetty and Captain Donnithorne, Adam blames Captain Donnithorne and continues to believe only the best about Hetty, even to the point of proposing to her in spite of her tarnished honor. But Hetty's arrest for murdering her infant nearly crushes Adam. After he recovers from the shock of Hetty's crime, Adam's character is mellowed by the experience. His pride is largely humbled, and he is less judgmental of others.
2. Eliot did her best to portray the reality of marriage. Most of the characters in the novel marry for love rather than duty, but marriage still appears negative and unromantic. Marriage and its pursuit are the central issue of the novel, but unlike many novels at that time, marriage is not regarded as the ultimate source of happiness. Two examples are the failed marriages of Dorothea and Lydgate. Both Rosamond and Lydgate think of courtship and romance in terms of ideals taken directly from conventional romance. Dorothea's marriage fails because of her youth and her disillusions about marrying a much older man, while Lydgate's marriage fails because of irreconcilable personalities. Mr. and Mrs. Bulstrode also face a marital crisis due to his inability to tell her about the past, and Fred Vincy and Mary Garth also face a great deal of hardship in making their union. As none of the marriages reach a perfect fairytale ending, *Middlemarch* offers a clear critique of the usual portrayal of marriage as romantic and unproblematic.

第 29 章 夏洛蒂·勃朗特和艾米莉·勃朗特

29.1 复习笔记

Ⅰ. Lives of The Brontë Sisters

The three Brontë sisters: Charlotte, Emily, and Anne were all engaged in literature. They were very talented and died young. As the daughters of a poor pastor in a small village in Howards, Yorkshire, in the north of England, they grew up into wild children, with independent personalities and deep sisterhood, but they were very suspicious of outsiders. In 1824, all the girls except the youngest Annie were sent to a charity school, which was a veritable prison. The two eldest sisters died there. Charlotte and Emily returned home and were educated by their father. The family education was very rough, but they read widely and wrote many stories. For a while, they worked as tutors in rich people's homes. In 1842 Charlotte went to Brussels to work as a tutor with her aunt's support. But she fell in love with her married employer and returned within a year. The Brontë sisters write poems in private. In 1846, Charlotte published their poems at her own expense, but they were not welcomed. Later they began to write novels. In 1847, *Jane Eyre* was published and was an immediate success. However, later a joint book appeared, containing Anne's *Agnes Grey* and Emily's *Wuthering Heights*, without attracting much attention. In 1848, Emily died of pneumonia, and Anne died of tuberculosis six months later. Charlotte lived longer than the brothers and sisters. Charlotte married her father's assistant pastor in 1854, but died of pneumonia a few months later during her pregnancy.

Ⅰ. 勃朗特姐妹生平

勃朗特三姐妹：夏洛蒂，艾米莉和安妮都从事文学，很有才能，英年早逝。她们是英国北部约克郡霍华斯镇一个小村庄里穷牧师的女儿。她们都长成了野孩子，性格独立，姐妹情深，但对外来者疑心很重。1824 年，除了最小的安妮，其他所有的女孩都被送到了一个慈善学校，那是个名副其实的监狱。两个最大的姐姐死在那里，夏洛蒂和艾米莉回到家由父亲教育。家庭教育很粗略，但她们广泛阅读，写了很多故事。她们有一段时间在有钱人家里做家庭教师。1842 年夏洛蒂在姑姑的资助下去布鲁塞尔当家庭教师。但她爱上了已婚的雇主，一年内便回来了。勃朗特姐妹私下都写点诗。1846 年，夏洛蒂自费出版了她们的诗，但没有受到欢迎。后来她们开始写小说。1847 年，《简·爱》出版，立即取得了成功。而安妮的《艾格尼斯·格雷》和艾米莉的《呼啸山庄》则几乎没有人关注。1848 年，艾米莉死于肺炎，六个月后安妮死于肺痨。夏洛蒂比兄妹们活得都长。1854 年夏洛蒂嫁给父亲的助理牧师，但几个月后便在孕期因肺炎去世。

Ⅱ. Charlotte Brontë (1816—1855)

1. Literary Style

(1) She writes mainly from a personal perspective, putting her feelings on the main characters. Therefore, she is a subjective writer who tends to describe the lives of characters and show their experiences.

(2) She loves beautiful nature very much, and obviously

Ⅱ. 夏洛蒂·勃朗特(1816—1855)

1. 文学风格

(1) 她主要从个人的角度进行写作，把自己的感情投入在主要人物身上。因此她是一个主观的作家，倾向于描写人物的生活，描述他们的生活和经历。

(2) 她非常热爱美丽的大自然，

despises secular ambitions and success. She only believes in hard work, self-control and extraordinary talents.

(3) The heroines in her novels never have traditional virtues, but are lonely and neglected young women who love life and yearn for love.

明显地蔑视世俗的抱负和成功，因为她只相信努力工作、自制和非凡的才华。

(3) 她的小说中的女主人公(她所有小说中的主人公都是女性)，从来没有传统的美德，而是孤独、被忽视的年轻女性，她们热爱生活、向往爱情。

2. Major Works

Jane Eyre (1847)
Shirley (1849)
Villette (1853)

2. 主要作品

《简·爱》(1847)
《谢利》(1849)
《维莱特》(1853)

3. Selected Work

◆*Jane Eyre*

A. Main Plot

Jane Eyre is recognized as Charlotte's masterpiece, and it is also one of the most popular and important works of the Victorian period. The novel tells the story of Jane Eyre, the orphan of a poor priest. Despite her low status, Jane Eyre is still a representative of the middle-class professional women who are fighting for their basic rights and equality. At the same time, she is also the most outstanding heroine in the novel at that time. The book is considered to be a masterpiece of feminist works that reflects women's experience and protect women's rights.

B. Analysis

A central theme of this book is the criticism of the bourgeois education system. Lowood School is the incarnation of bourgeois educational principles, and its purpose is to cultivate docile slaves for the rich.

Charlotte has a description of the English country squires, she compares them to vulgar people with no education and narrow thinking. However, Rochester is an exception.

This novel explores the status of women in society. Jane Eyre insists that women should have the same rights as men.

3. 选读作品

◆《简·爱》

A. 主要情节

《简·爱》被公认为夏洛蒂的代表作，也是维多利亚时期最受欢迎、最重要的作品之一。小说讲述了一位贫穷牧师的孤女简·爱的故事。尽管身份低微，简·爱仍然是中产阶级为自己的基本权利和平等而奋斗的职业女性代表，同时也是当时小说中最杰出的女主人公。该书被认为是“反映女性经历、保护女性权益”的女权主义作品的代表作。

B. 分析

这本书的一个中心主题是对资产阶级教育系统的批评。洛伍德学校是资产阶级教育原则的化身，它的目的就是为有钱人培养温顺的奴隶。

夏洛特对英国乡绅有描述，她把他们比作没教养、思想狭隘的庸俗之人。但罗切斯特是个例外。

这部小说探讨了女性在社会中的地位。简·爱坚持女性应获得同男性一样的权利。

Ⅲ. Emily Brontë (1818—1848)

◆*Wuthering Heights*

Love in the novel is tragic, morbid and devastating. The charm of the novel comes from the description of the complex

Ⅲ. 艾米莉·勃朗特 (1818—1848)

◆《呼啸山庄》

小说中的爱是悲剧性的、病态的、毁灭性的。小说的魅力来自对两个主人公的复杂心理的描写。艾

psychology of the two protagonists. Emily Bronte's exploration of psychology is profound. She can explore the deepest part of the human soul. At the same time, the novel violently criticizes the bourgeois marriage system, under which the pure love between the hero and the heroine is destroyed by the social prejudice based on wealth. Some critics believe that the story takes place in a wasteland far away from the outside world, with an atmosphere of horror, dramatic exaggeration and bizarre themes, so this novel looks a lot like a Gothic novel in the second half of the 18th century.

Ⅳ. Anne Brontë (1820—1849)

1. Major Works

Agnes Grey (1847)

The Tenant of the Wildfell Hall (1848)

2. Selected Work

◆*Agnes Grey*

This novel exposes the cruel injustice caused by the strict class system in the middle of the 19th century in Britain. Agnes was born in a middle-class family with status, but her family status forced her to make a living as a governess. Beloved at home, she is not ready to face the harsh reality. At the Bloomfields and later the Murrays, she suffers under the snobbery and sadism of the selfish, self-indulgent upper-class adults, as well as the arrogance and rudeness of the spoiled children. To make matters worse, the social and economic status of the governess is special. She is lower than the employer and higher than the servant, which makes her lead a lonely life.

米莉·勃朗特对心理的挖掘是深邃的。她能够深入到人类灵魂的最深处。同时，小说猛烈地抨击了资产阶级的婚姻制度，在这种制度下，男女主人公之间纯真的爱情被建立在财富基础之上的社会偏见所毁灭。一些评论家认为，由于故事发生在远离外部世界的荒原，拥有恐怖的气氛，戏剧化的夸张效果以及奇异的主题，这部小说看起来很像18世纪后半期的哥特式小说。

Ⅳ. 安妮·勃朗特 (1820—1849)

1. 主要作品

《艾格尼斯·格雷》(1847)

《怀尔德菲尔府的房客》(1848)

2. 选读作品

◆《艾格尼斯·格雷》

这本小说揭露了英国19世纪中期严格的阶级体系带来的残忍不公。艾格尼斯生于一个有身份的中产阶级家庭，但家道中落迫使她做家庭女教师来谋生。在家中娇生惯养，她还没做好当家庭教师的严酷现实。在布鲁姆菲尔德家和穆雷家，她遭受上层阶级自私放纵的成人的势利和虐待，还有被宠坏的孩子们的傲慢无礼。更糟的是，家庭女教师的社会经济地位特殊，“低于”雇主又“高于”仆人，使她过着孤独的生活。

29.2 考研真题与典型题详解

Ⅰ. Fill in the blanks.

1. Heathcliff is a character in the novel __________. This novel shows that pure and true love in a class society is impossible of attainment. Its author is Emily Brontë.

2. Different from other heroines, __________ is a plain-looking orphan girl with obscurity and inferiority, but she stands out as a representative of the middle class working women struggling for their basic rights and equality as a human being.

Ⅱ. Multiple Choices

1. The following are the common characters shared by the three Brontë sisters EXCEPT __________.

A. unmarried　B. literary　C. talented　D. dying young

2. __________ is the main hero in the novel of *Wuthering Heights*.

A. Rochester B. Heathcliff C. Manette D. Martin

3. Both Charlotte and Emily wrote about the __________ around them.

A. familiar things B. common people C. neighbors D. evils

4. Emily Brontë wrote only one novel entitled __________.

A. *Jane Eyre* B. *Agnes Grey*

C. *Wuthering Heights* D. *Emma*

Ⅲ. Read the following quotation and answer the questions.

"...What were the use of my creation, if I were entirely contained here? My great miseries in this world have been Heathcliff's miseries, and I watched and felt each from the beginning; my great thought in living is himself. If all else is perished, and he remained, I shall still continue to be; and all else remained, and he was annihilated, the universe would turn to a mighty stranger; I should not seem part of it..."（首师大 2007 研）

Questions:

1. This passage is taken from the novel entitled __________. It is written by __________.
2. Here the speaker "I" is the character named __________.
3. Make a brief comment on the character's philosophy of love.

Ⅳ. Short answer question

Emily Brontë used a very complicated narrative technique in writing her novel *Wuthering Heights*. Try to tell Brontë's way of narration briefly.

Ⅴ. Essay question

In what ways is *Jane Eyre* influenced by the tradition of the Gothic novel? What do the Gothic elements contribute to the novel?

参考答案及解析

Ⅰ. Fill in the blanks.

1. *Wuthering Heights*

（《呼啸山庄》是艾米莉·勃朗特唯一的一部小说。凯瑟琳和希斯克利夫的那种超越自然、刻骨铭心的爱情紧扣读者的心弦，使读者对主人公的遭遇产生很大的同情，对门第观念感到厌恶和憎恨。）

2. Jane Eyre

（简·爱不同于其他女主角，她是个长相普通、默默无闻的贫穷孤女。但她最终凭借自己的努力成为中产阶级女性争取人权平等的代表。）

Ⅱ. Multiple Choices

1. A 勃朗特三姐妹：夏洛蒂、艾米莉和安妮都从事文学，很有才能，英年早逝。三姐妹中，艾米莉和安妮终生未嫁，夏洛蒂嫁给父亲的助理牧师。
2. B 《呼啸山庄》的主人公是凯瑟琳和希斯克利夫(Heathcliff)。
3. A 夏洛蒂和艾米莉小说创作的主要对象都是她们身边熟知的事物。
4. C 艾米莉·勃朗特一生只完成了一部作品，即《呼啸山庄》。

Ⅲ. Read the following quotation and answer the questions.

1. *Wuthering Heights*, Emily Brontë
2. Catherine Earnshaw
3. Catherine's love for Linton is like the foliage in the woods. Time will change it. Her love for Heathcliff resembles the eternal rocks beneath. She once said: "Whatever our souls are made of, his and mine are the same, and Linton's is as different as a moonbeam from lightning, or frost from fire." Her love for Heathcliff is extremely strong, but she marries Linton instead. It is her wrong doing that plunges the two families into misery, violence and despair.

Ⅳ. Short answer question

①Recent Western criticism regards *Wuthering Heights* as one of the greatest novels of the Victorian era. The narrative way of this story is unusual, starting near the ending and spanning a long time.

②The main narrative is told by Nelly, Catherine's old nurse, to Mr. Lockwood, a temporary tenant at Grange. The latter too gives an account of what he sees at Wuthering Heights. In the main narrative by Nelly inserts the sub-narrative told through Isabella's letters to Nelly.

③While the central interest is maintained, the sequence of its development is constantly disordered by flashbacks. This makes the story all the more enticing and genuine.

Ⅴ. Essay question

The Gothic tradition employs elements such as supernatural encounters, remote locations, complicated family histories, ancient manor houses, dark secrets, and mysteries to create an atmosphere of suspense and terror, and the plot of *Jane Eyre* includes most of these elements.

Lowood, Moor House, and Thornfield are all remote locations, and Thornfield, like Gateshead, is also an ancient manor house. Both Rochester and Jane possess complicated family histories—Rochester's hidden wife, Bertha, is the dark secret at the novel's core. The exposure of Bertha is one of the most important moments in the novel, and the mystery surrounding her is the main source of the novel's suspense. Other Gothic occurrences include: Jane's encounter with the ghost of her late Uncle Reed in the red-room; the moment of supernatural communication between Jane and Rochester when she hears his voice calling her across the misty heath from miles and miles away.

Although Brontë's use of Gothic elements heightens her reader's interest and adds to the emotional and philosophical tensions of the book, most of the seemingly supernatural occurrences are actually explained as the story progresses. It seems that many of the Gothic elements serve to anticipate and elevate the importance of the plot's turning points.

第 30 章　托马斯·胡德

30.1　复习笔记

Thomas Hood（1799—1845）	托马斯·胡德（1799—1845）
1. Life Thomas Hood was the son of a London bookseller. When he was young, he engaged in sculpting and learned painting. Later he used this technique to illustrate his own theatrical works. At the age of 22, he began to work as a magazine editor, editing various journals and magazines including *London Magazine*, *The Gem*, *Comic Annual*, and finally *Hood's Magazine*.	**1. 生平** 胡德是伦敦书商的儿子。年轻时从事雕刻，并学习绘画艺术，后来他将这项技术用于给自己的戏剧作品插图。22 岁时，开始从事杂志编辑工作，编辑了各种期刊杂志：《伦敦杂志》《珍宝》《喜剧年鉴》，最后是《胡德杂志》。
2. Poetic Style （1）Most of his works were humorous poems, containing topical comments on contemporary events and manners. （2）Hood expressed his opposition to the injustice of bourgeois society through his poems. （3）As a petty bourgeois humanist, he only lamented for the oppressed and sympathized with their experiences, but did not persuade them to rise up.	**2. 诗歌风格** （1）他的大部分作品是幽默诗歌，包含对当代事件和习俗的评论。 （2）胡德在他的诗歌中表达了他反抗资产阶级社会的不公。 （3）作为一个小资产阶级人道主义者，他只为被压迫者哀叹，同情他们的遭遇，却没有力劝他们奋起反抗。
3. Major Works "Miss Kilmansegg and Her Precious Leg"（1840） "The Song of the Shirt"（1843） "The Bridge of Sighs"（1844）	**3. 主要作品** 《基尔曼塞格小姐和她尊贵的腿》(1840) 《衬衫之歌》(1843) 《叹息桥》(1844)
4. Selected Work **◆"The Song of the Shirt"** This poem commemorates Mrs. Biddell, and her story inspired some people to actively oppose the tragic situation of poor British laborers. These poor laborers work 7 days a week in an inhuman environment, with little chance of surviving and no hope of liberation. This poem is one of the best poems in English literature describing the hard life of laborers in capitalist society.	**4. 选读作品** **◆《衬衫之歌》** 这首诗是纪念比德尔夫人，她的故事激起了一些人积极反对英国贫困劳动者所处的悲惨境地。这些贫苦劳动者每周在非人的环境中工作 7 天，几乎没法幸存，也没希望得到解脱。这首诗是英国文学中描写资本主义社会的劳动者艰苦生活的最好诗作之一。

◆"The Bridge of Sighs"	◆《叹息桥》
"The Bridge of Sighs" was written in 1844. It is a story about a homeless girl who drowned herself in a river. As a representative of realistic poetry, Hood reveals the real situation of the people at the bottom of the city.	《叹息桥》写于1844年，是关于一个无家可归的女孩投河自尽的故事。作为现实主义诗歌的代表，胡德揭示了城市底层人们的真实处境。

30.2 考研真题与典型题详解

Ⅰ. Fill in the blanks.

1. In Thomas Hood's works, he expressed his protest against the social injustice of ________.
2. There is something sinister about Hood's sense of humor, a trait that was to reappear in the "________" of the 20th century.

Ⅱ. Multiple Choices

1. Which poem is written by Thomas Hood?

   A. *Songs of Innocence*　　B. *Maud*

   C. "The Song of the Shirt"　　D. *Deserted Village*

2. Which poem is written to remember Mrs. Biddell?

   A. "Miss Kilmansegg and Her Precious Leg"

   B. "The Song of the Shirt"

   C. "The Bridge of Signs"

   D. *Hood's Magazine*

Ⅲ. Short answer questions

1. What is the poetic style of Thomas Hood's poems?
2. Analyze the theme of "The Song of the Shirt".

参考答案及解析

Ⅰ. Fill in the blanks.

1. bourgeois society

   (胡德在他的诗歌中表达了他反抗资产阶级社会的不公。)

2. black comedy

   (胡德的幽默风格可以说是20世纪60年代黑色幽默写作风格兴起的先兆。)

Ⅱ. Multiple Choices

1. C　《天真之歌》的作者是威廉·布莱克，《莫德》的作者是阿尔弗雷德·丁尼生，《荒村》的作者是奥利弗·哥尔德史密斯，"衬衫之歌"才是托马斯·胡德的诗。

2. B　《衬衫之歌》是纪念比德尔夫人，她的故事激起了一些人积极反对英国贫困劳动者所处的悲惨境地。

Ⅲ. Short answer questions

1. (1) Most of his works were humorous poems, containing topical comments on contemporary events and manners.

(2) Hood expressed his opposition to the injustice of bourgeois society through his poems.

(3) As a petty bourgeois humanist, he only lamented for the oppressed and sympathized with their experiences, but did not persuade them to rise up.

2. With the description of the hard life of the textile women workers under capitalist system in England, the poet showed in his poem deep sympathy for the poor and expressed his mild protest against the exploitation of the laboring people by the capitalists.

第31章 阿尔弗雷德·丁尼生

31.1 复习笔记

Alfred Tennyson (1809—1892)	阿尔弗雷德·丁尼生(1809—1892)
1. Life	**1. 生平**
Alfred Tennyson, the most important poet of the Victorian Age, was born in 1809 at Somersby Rectory, Lincolnshire, the fourth son of an Anglican clergyman. In 1827 he went to Cambridge. He and his brother published *Poems by Two Brothers*, which attracted the attention of "apostles". The leader of this group was Arthur Henry Hallam, who later became Tennyson's best friend. In 1842, Tennyson's *Poems* won the praise of critics for the first time. In 1850, with the publication of *In Memoriam*, which is a tribute to Hallam, he was appointed poet laureate in succession to Wordsworth. Then he finally could afford to marry Emily Sellwood, whom he had loved since 1836. He remained in this position until he died at 83 years old, longer than any other before or after him. In 1884, Queen Victoria admired his poems and talents, and Tennyson was made a baronetcy. He was buried in Westminster Abbey, and a monument was built in England.	阿尔弗雷德·丁尼生是维多利亚时期最重要的诗人。他1809年生于萨默斯比教区，是一位英国国教牧师的第四个儿子。1827年他进入剑桥。他和哥哥发表了《两兄弟诗集》，引起了自称为"使徒"的一个本科生文学社团的注意。这个社团的领袖是亚瑟·亨利·哈勒姆，后来成了丁尼生的挚友。1842年丁尼生发表的《诗集》首次赢得批评界的好评。1850年发表了纪念哈勒姆的《悼念》后，他继华兹华斯成为桂冠诗人。随后他终于能够迎娶深爱了15年的艾米莉·赛尔伍德。他直到83岁去世前一直是桂冠诗人，时间之长前无古人后无来者。1884年因维多利亚女王极其赞赏他的诗作和诗才，丁尼生被封为准男爵。他被葬在威斯敏斯特教堂，英国也建了一座纪念碑。
2. Poetic Style	**2. 诗歌风格**
(1) Tennyson is not only a poet with profound thoughts, but also a poet of the people. He falls deep in his own consciousness and speaks for the national consciousness of Victorian society.	(1) 丁尼生既是一位有深刻反思的诗人，也是一位人民诗人。他深陷自己的意识中，又为维多利亚社会的国民意识发声。
(2) His poems cover a wide range of subjects, including social and political issues, natural and psychological environments, scientific issues, past history and myths.	(2) 他的诗歌涉及题材范围极广，包括社会和政治问题、自然和心理环境、科学问题、过去的历史和神话。
3. Major Works	**3. 主要作品**
"Break, Break, Break" (1842) *The Princess* (1847) *Maud* (1855) *Idylls of the King* (1859—1885)	《溅吧，溅吧，溅吧》(1842) 《公主》(1847) 《莫德》(1855) 《国王叙事诗》(1859—1885)

In Memoriam (1850) "Crossing the Bar" (1889)	《悼念》(1850) 《过沙洲》(1889)
4. Selected Works	**4. 选读作品**
◆*In Memoriam* *In Memoriam* was written in memory of A. H. Hallam, his closest friend and fiancé of his sister. Hallam's sudden death dealt a heavy emotional blow to Tennyson. From 1833 to 1850, Tennyson wrote more than 100 poems to mourn his dead friends. These poems are written in eight syllables and rhyme as "abba", which include 131 lyric poems with a prologue and epilogue. Nearly half of them directly mention the death of Haarlem. In a word, this "poetic diary" shows the poet's views on social issues, death, immortality, and the conflict between religious beliefs and science. He insisted that in the face of new scientific discoveries, we must persist in our faith. Because of its exquisite form and pleasant melody, this collection of poems has been regarded as the pinnacle of Tennyson's poetry achievements by many critics.	**◆《悼念》** 丁尼生为悼念他最亲密的朋友，他妹妹的未婚夫亚瑟·亨利·哈勒姆写下了《悼念》。哈勒姆的突然离世给了他情感上的重击，1833 年至 1850 年，丁尼生写出 100 多首诗悼念已逝的友人。这些诗用八音节写成，押韵为"abba"。这些歌由 131 首抒情诗组成，包括一篇序言和尾声。其中近一半直接提到哈勒姆的死亡。 总体上来说，这部"诗歌日记"展示了诗人对社会问题、死亡、永生及宗教信仰和科学之间的冲突的看法。他坚称，在新的科学发现面前，我们必须坚持信仰。该诗集因其精美的形式和悦耳的旋律被许多评论家推为丁尼生诗歌成就的巅峰之作。
◆*Idylls of the King* From 1859 to 1885, Tennyson devoted himself to creating narrative poems based on the story of King Arthur and his Knights of the Round Table. Each of Tennyson's "Idylls" relates an episode in the legendary romance of King Arthur. He gave up the mere legendary story, but dealt with the real world romantically. The poem is full of hints of contemporary moral and social issues. King Arthur tried to bring civilization to his territory through the efforts of the knights, but ultimately failed because of some evils. Tennyson believed that these evils were the harm in the society at that time.	**◆《国王叙事诗》** 1859 至 1885 年丁尼生致力于创作依据亚瑟王和他的圆桌武士故事构思的叙事诗。每一首"叙事诗"讲述一个亚瑟王的传奇故事。他放弃单纯的传奇故事，而是浪漫化地处理了现实世界，充满了当代道德和社会问题的暗示。亚瑟王试图通过骑士们的努力给他的领地带来文明，但最终因为一些罪恶失败了，丁尼生认为这些罪恶正是当时社会中的危害。
◆"Ulysses" The figure of Ulysses in this poem originates from the ancient hero of Homer's *Odyssey* and the hero of Dante's *Inferno*. "Ulysses" is mainly about transcending the boundaries of one's own vision and ordinary daily life.	**◆《尤利西斯》** 本诗中尤利西斯这一形象来源于荷马史诗中《奥德赛》的主人公尤利西斯在但丁《神曲》中的形象。《尤利西斯》主要是关于超越自己视野的界限和平凡的日常生活。

◆ "Break, Break, Break"	◆《濺吧，濺吧，濺吧》
This poem is written in memory of his close friend A. H. Hallam, who died of a stroke at the age of twenty-two. In this poem, Tennyson expresses his love and mourning for his dead friend. Tennyson puts the images of life and death together: the energetic fisherman's children and sailors symbolize life; the ship sailing into the harbour symbolizes death. The word "break" is Onomatopoeia, which represents the sound of the water hitting the stone. At the same time, "break" has the meaning of "destroy".	本诗是纪念密友哈勒姆的一首诗，他在 22 岁时因为一次中风突然死亡。本诗中丁尼生表达了对亡友的热爱和哀悼之情。丁尼生将生和死的意象放在一起：充满活力的渔家孩子和水手象征生；船舶驶进海港象征死。"break"一词既可以是拟声词，是海水撞击岩石的声音，同时"break"一词还有"毁坏碎裂"的意思。
◆ "Crossing the Bar"	◆《过沙洲》
"Crossing the Bar" is written when the poet is at an old age in 1889. At the request of the poet, this poem serves as the last poem in his anthology. In the poem, the poet compares death to a long journey to sea.	《过沙洲》写于 1889 年丁尼生晚年的时候。应诗人的要求，本诗作为他作品选集的最后一首诗。诗中诗人把死亡比喻成出海远行。

31.2 考研真题与典型题详解

Ⅰ. Fill in the blanks.

1. ___________ was made poet laureate in 1850 when William Wordsworth died.
2. Alfred Tennyson was a great poet in the ___________ Age.

Ⅱ. Multiple Choices

1. ___________ is based on the Celtic legends of King Arthur and his Knights of the Round Table.
   A. *In Memoriam* B. *Ulysses*
   C. *Idylls of the King* D. *The Princess*
2. Which of the following historical events does "The Charge of the Light Brigade" describe?
   A. D-Day B. The Battle of Waterloo
   C. The Battle of Bull Run D. The Crimean War
3. Which of the following poems is not taken from classical mythology?
   A. "Crossing the Bar" B. "Ulysses"
   C. "Tiresias" D. "Tithonus"

Ⅲ. Short answer question

How is the relationship of religion and science explored in the poem *In Memoriam*?

Ⅳ. Essay question

Tennyson said that as a child he was haunted by "the passion of the past." In what ways can Tennyson be considered a poet of the past?

参考答案及解析

Ⅰ. Fill in the blanks.

1. Alfred Tennyson

   (1850 年 11 月丁尼生继威廉·华兹华斯之后，成为桂冠诗人。)

2. Victorian

   (丁尼生是维多利亚时期最重要的诗人。)

Ⅱ. Multiple Choices

1. C 《国王叙事诗》是丁尼生致力于创作依据亚瑟王和他的圆桌武士故事构思的叙事诗，每一首"叙事诗"讲述一个亚瑟王的传奇故事。

2. D 《轻骑兵冲锋》这首诗描写的是 1853—1856 年间的克里米亚战争。D-Day 指第二次世界大战中盟军在法国北部诺曼底海滩对德发起进攻日(1944 年 6 月 6 日)；滑铁卢战役是拿破仑最终被击败的战役；The Battle of Bull Run 是美国内战中的布尔伦河战役(1861—1862)。

3. A 《过沙洲》是丁尼生在海上写的一首诗，时年 80 高龄(1889 年)。暗指诗人在经历了人生的风霜后，平静地迎接死亡的来临，毫无恐惧和哀伤。其他三项都来自希腊神话，提瑞西阿斯是古希腊城邦底比斯的盲人占卜者，奥德修斯(拉丁语尤利西斯)是伊萨卡国王，在特洛伊战争中最贤明的指挥者，提托诺斯是特洛伊城的创建者拉俄墨冬之子。

Ⅲ. Short answer question

In Memoriam connects the despair Tennyson felt over the loss of his friend Arthur Hallam and the despair he felt when contemplating a godless world. He insisted that although there were constant new scientific discoveries and the existence of God could not be proven, it was necessary to maintain the old beliefs. In the end, Denison changed the immortality theory of the soul with the immortality theory of humans through evolution, thus realizing the synthesis between his profound religious beliefs and the new scientific thoughts of the time.

Ⅳ. Essay question

Most of Tennyson's best poems meditate the past. Tennyson looked both to historical and mythological pasts as repositories for his poetry. "The Lady of Shalott" and the poems within *Idylls of the King* take place in medieval England. In addition, Tennyson also explores the mythological past, as articulated in classical works of Homer, Virgil, and Dante. His "Ulysses" draws upon actual incidents in Homer's *Odyssey*. Likewise, his ode "To Virgil" abounds with allusions to incidents in the great poet's *Aeneid*, especially the fall of Troy.

Tennyson's personal past is also noticeable in his work. The sudden death of his closest friend Arthur Henry Hallam when Tennyson was just 24 dealt a great emotional blow to him, who spent the next ten years writing over a hundred poems dedicated to his departed friend, later collected and published as *In Memoriam*. This lengthy work describes Tennyson's memories of the time he spent with Hallam, including their days at Cambridge University. *In Memoriam* also reflects Tennyson's struggle with the Victorians' growing awareness of another sort of past: the vast expanse of geological time and evolutionary history. His treatment of the important scientific issues of his day represents an attempt to compromise with the evolutionary past history of our species and our world. Tennyson can therefore be regarded as a poet of the historical, mythological, personal, and evolutionary past.

第 32 章　罗伯特·勃朗宁

32.1　复习笔记

Robert Browning(1812—1889)

1. Life

Robert Browning was born in 1812 in Camberwell, south London. His education basically came from his erudite father. He was eager to read when he was young. Under the influence of Shelley, he began to write poetry when he was very young. In 1833, Browning anonymously published his first major work, *Pauline*, and in 1840 he published *Sordello*, which was widely regarded as a failure. Between 1840 and 1845, he tried his hand at plays, which were for the most part unsuccessful. In 1846, he eloped with Elizabeth Barrett, who was far more famous than him. The two settled in Italy, and Browning continued to write. After Elizabeth's death in 1861, Browning and his son returned to London. His *The Ring and the Book* finally won him a little fame. The Browning Society was founded in 1881, and he was awarded honorary degrees by Oxford University in 1882 and the University of Edinburgh in 1884. Robert Browning died in 1889.

2. Poetic Style

(1) Browning's principal contribution to poetry lies in the techniques he developed through his dramatic monologue, especially his use of diction, rhythm and symbol, influencing major poets of the 20th century such as Ezra Pound, T. S. Eliot and Robert Frost.

(2) The attraction of his poems lies in the powerful characterization and rich detailed description. In his poems, he explored the relationship between morality and art through historical backgrounds such as the Italian Renaissance.

(3) However, he was criticized for the obscurity of his poems. His poems are difficult to read: conjunctions are omitted; reversed phrases and jumping thoughts will suddenly appear in the poem.

罗伯特·勃朗宁(1812—1889)

1. 生平

罗伯特·勃朗宁 1812 年出生在伦敦南部的坎伯威尔。他受的教育基本来自他博学的父亲。少年时他读起书来如饥似渴，很小的时候就开始写诗，受到了雪莱的影响。1833 年，布朗宁匿名发表了第一部主要作品《波琳》，1840 年发表《索德罗》，被认为是失败之作。1840 年至 1845 年，他试着写戏剧，但都不大成功。1846 年时，他与声名远胜于他的伊丽莎白·巴雷特私奔。两人在意大利定居，勃朗宁继续写作。1861 年伊丽莎白去世后，他和儿子返回伦敦。他的《指环与书》使他赢得一点名气。1881 年勃朗宁会社建立，他在 1882 年被授予牛津大学荣誉学位，1884 年获得爱丁堡大学荣誉学位。1889 年勃朗宁去世。

2. 诗歌风格

(1) 布朗宁的主要成就在于他在戏剧独白中运用的技巧，特别是措辞、韵律、象征、影响了 20 世纪的主要诗人，包括庞德、艾略特和弗罗斯特。

(2) 他诗歌的吸引力在于强有力的人物刻画和丰富的细节描写。他在诗中通过如意大利文艺复兴的历史背景，探讨了道德和艺术的关系。

(3) 然而他因诗歌的晦涩难懂而遭到批评。他的诗歌很难读懂：连词被省略；次序颠倒的短语和跳跃的思维都会突然出现在诗歌里面。

3. Major Works *Pauline* (1833) *Pippa Passes* (1841) *Men and Women* (1855) *The Ring and the Book* (1868—1869) *Dramatic Lyrics* (1842) *Dramatic Romances and Lyrics* (1845) *Dramatic Personae* (1864)	**3. 主要作品** 《波琳》(1833) 《皮帕经过》(1841) 《男男女女》(1855) 《指环与书》(1868—1869) 《戏剧抒情诗》(1842) 《戏剧浪漫诗与抒情诗》(1845) 《剧中人物》(1864)
4. Selected Works ◆***Pippa Passes*** Pippa is an Italian girl who works in a silk factory. During her annual vacation, she travels the whole town and sang happily. She passes a window of a woman who murdered her husband. She then passes a house in which lives a young man who was tricked into marrying an ignorant woman whom he does not love. She passes by a house where an Italian patriot is determined to kill the Austrian king who cruelly rules the Italian people. Finally, Pippa sings and passes the bishop's house. The bishop is planning to sell her to Rome as a prostitute. When Pippa returns home, she is still elated and did not know what happened in the houses she passed by. Her innocence and ignorance are in sharp contrast to the squalor of the social environment at that time.	**4. 选读作品** ◆**《皮帕经过》** 皮帕是一个意大利丝绸厂工作的女孩。在她的年假中，她游历整个小镇，快乐地唱着歌。她经过一个女子的窗口，这个女子伙同情人谋杀了丈夫。她接着走过一栋房子，里面住着一个青年，受骗与一个自己并不爱的无知女子结婚。她又路过一个意大利爱国者居住的房子，这个爱国者决心杀死残酷统治意大利人民的奥地利国王。最后，皮帕唱歌走过主教的住宅，此时，主教正盘算着将她卖到罗马当妓女。皮帕回到家后，仍然兴高采烈，丝毫不知她路过的那些房子里发生的事情。她的天真无知和当时社会环境的肮脏不堪形成强烈对比。
◆***The Ring and the Book*** This is a poetical drama of 20,000 lines, including 12 books or 12 long dramatic monologues. The author asks the characters in the book to tell the story in turn. The story is based on a book that Browning bought from a small book stand, telling the story of a murder trial in Rome in 1689. Count Guido, a wicked nobleman, married Pompilia, an innocent girl, for the purpose of getting her wealth. But he soon found that she was only an adopted child of her parents. Guido determined to get rid of her by way of treating her extremely badly. With the help of a good priest, Pompilia returned to her foster-parents. Guido killed her under the excuse that she had committed adultery with the priest. Then the murderer was arrested and condemned to death.	◆**《指环与书》** 该书是两万行的诗剧，包括12部或者说12篇长的戏剧独白。作者让书中的人物依次讲述故事。故事取材于布朗宁在小书摊上购买的一本小书，讲述了发生在1689年罗马的一次谋杀审判。邪恶的贵族伯爵圭迪娶了天真的少女蓬皮丽娅，以图其钱财。但他很快发现她只是父母的养女，于是决心摆脱她。他虐待她，使她的生活不堪忍受。在一位好心教士的帮助下，蓬皮丽娅逃回到养父母家。圭迪借蓬皮丽娅与教士通奸之名杀死了她。后来谋杀者被捕并被判处死刑。

◆**"My Last Duchess"** "My Last Duchess" is a poem in form of dramatic monologue. This poem is based on a historical event involving Alfonso, the Duke of Ferrara, who lived in the 16th century. The narrator in the poem is the duke, and tells us he is entertaining an emissary who has come to negotiate the Duke's marriage to the daughter of another powerful family. As he shows the visitor through his palace, he stops before a portrait of the late Duchess, apparently a young and lovely girl. The Duke begins reminiscing about the portrait, then about the Duchess herself. His musings give way to a diatribe on her disgraceful behavior. His monologue continues, and the reader realizes that the count must cause the death of the countess. Through irony, the poem exposes the duke's narrow-mindedness, domineering, cruel and hypocrisy.	◆**《我已故的公爵夫人》** 《我已故的公爵夫人》是勃朗宁运用戏剧独白写的典型的一首诗。这首诗是根据文艺复兴时期意大利的费拉拉公爵阿方索二世的一个真实故事创作的。诗中的叙述者是公爵。公爵夫人刚刚去世，随即有人上门提亲，媒人来到时，公爵带媒人参观自己的艺术品，并在公爵夫人的画像前停了下来，开始对已故前妻大加贬斥，然而读者从他的口中得到的却是友善而又开朗的公爵夫人形象。他的独白继续，读者也意识到一定是公爵导致了公爵夫人的死。通过反讽，诗歌揭露了公爵的心胸狭窄，专横霸道，残忍和虚伪。
◆**"Home-thoughts, from Abroad"** This poem was written by Browning when he went to northern Italy in 1845, and is known for his strong homesickness.	◆**《海外思乡》** 本诗为 1845 年勃朗宁去往意大利北部时所写，以浓郁的思乡情调著称。

32.2　考研真题与典型题详解

Ⅰ. Fill in the blanks.

1. ___________ is Robert Browning's masterpiece which tells a horrible story of a man's murder of his beautiful young wife.
2. Robert Browning's poetic experiments transferred the thematic interest of poetry from mere narration of the story to revelation and study of characters' ___________ and brought to the Victorian poetry some ___________ element.

Ⅱ. Multiple Choices

1. What is the Duke arranging in "My Last Duchess"?
   A. The Duchess's funeral.　　B. The painting of the Duchess's portrait.
   C. A new marriage for himself.　　D. The sale of his art collection.
2. What makes "Soliloquy of the Spanish Cloister" a soliloquy?
   A. A speaker who is distinct from the poet, who has no implied audience.
   B. A speaker who is distinct from the poet, who has an audience before him.
   C. The poet is the speaker, and is talking to himself.
   D. The poet is the speaker, and is addressing to a pretend audience.

Ⅲ. Explain the following term.

Dramatic monologue

Ⅳ. Short answer question

What are the advantages of dramatic monologue?

Ⅴ. Read and analyze the following poem.

Meeting at Night

I

The grey sea and the long black land;
And the yellow half-moon large and low;
And the startled little waves that leap
In fiery ringlets from their sleep,
As I gain the cove with pushing prow,
And quench its speed i' the slushy sand.

Ⅱ

Then a mile of warm sea-scented beach;
Three fields to cross till a farm appears;
A tap at the pane, the quick sharp scratch
And blue spurt of a lighted match,
And a voice less loud, thro' its joys and fears,
Than the two hearts beating each to each!

参考答案及解析

Ⅰ. Fill in the blanks.

1. *The Ring and the Book*

(《指环与书》是勃朗宁的代表作。该诗以17世纪末发生在罗马的一个老夫杀少妻的故事为题材，全诗由12组戏剧独白组成。)

2. inner world; psycho-analytical

(罗伯特·勃朗宁的主要成就在于他的诗歌新形式戏剧独白，并且用它鲜明而生动地塑造了各种不同类型的人物性格，深刻而复杂地展示了人的内心世界，赋予了维多利亚时期的诗歌以心理分析的色彩。)

Ⅱ. Multiple Choices

1. C 《我已故的公爵夫人》是勃朗宁早期戏剧独白诗中最著名的一首。公爵因前妻不做他的循规蹈矩的所有物，而把她除掉了；他预备再度结婚，对象是一位伯爵小姐；为了确定嫁妆的数量，伯爵派了一位使者进来谈判；公爵领着这位使者观看他的艺术收藏，中间有他的已故夫人画像。

2. A 这首诗的“独白”指诗歌的主人公自言自语，也是刻画人物形象，揭示道德主题的另一种形式。

Ⅲ. Explain the following term.

(1) A dramatic monologue is a kind of spoken verse that helps to better understand the characters' inner thoughts.

(2) This form was mainly favored by Victorian poets. In the drama monologue, the poem is

mainly composed of the monologue of a character, and the character will start to speak at a specific moment on a specific occasion. This monologue will communicate with one or more listeners, but the answer of these one or more listeners will not appear in the poem. We can guess what the listener said through the words of the monologue. Through this kind of monologue, the poet introduces to the reader the character and qualities of the speaker.

(3) The typical dramatic monologue poems include *My Last Duchess* by Robert Browning.

Ⅳ. Short answer question

Through this kind of monologue, the poet introduces to the reader the character and qualities of the speaker. It also allows readers to enter into the minds of various characters and to see an event from that character's perspective. Understanding the thoughts, feelings, and motivations of a character not only gives readers a sense of sympathy for the characters but also helps readers understand the multiplicity of perspectives that make up the truth. In effect, Browning's work reminds readers that the nature of truth or reality fluctuates, depending on one's perspective or view of the situation.

Ⅴ. Read and analyze the following poem.

This poem does not use passionate expression. Instead, it contains many images and uses different senses, including smell, sight and sound to describe a man's desire and excitement to meet his lover. At the same time, it also shows some of his fear.

第 33 章 伊丽莎白·巴雷特·勃朗宁

33.1 复习笔记

Elizabeth Barrett Browning (1806—1861)	伊丽莎白·巴雷特·勃朗宁(1806—1861)
1. Life Elizabeth Barrett was born in 1806 at Durham, England. Educated at home, Elizabeth had written her first "epic" poem by the age of 12. But when she was fifteen, a fall from her horse injured her spine. Regardless of her illness, she concentrated on learning Hebrew and Greek. She devoutly believed in Christianity and actively participated in the mission of her church. After that, she lived in her father's house in London, living under his father's tyrannical power. After the death of her brother, she was frail and sick, living in seclusion for 5 years. In 1844, her *Poems* attracted Robert Browning's attention and they exchanged 574 letters over the next 20 months. In 1846, the two eloped in spite of Elizabeth's father's opposition and settled in Italy. Elizabeth got better and gave birth to a child. Her father never spoke to her again. Elizabeth's *Sonnets from the Portuguese*, dedicated to her husband and written in secret before her marriage, was published in 1850. She died in Florence in 1861.	**1. 生平** 伊丽莎白·巴雷特 1806 年出生在英国达勒姆。伊丽莎白从小在家受教育，12 岁就写了第一首“史诗”。15 岁因骑马坠落，脊柱受伤。她不顾病痛，专心学习希伯来语和希腊语。她虔诚地信仰基督教，积极参与她所在教堂的传教会。 之后她居于父亲在伦敦的房子，生活在父亲专横的淫威下。弟弟死后，她体弱多病，隐居在卧房长达 5 年。1844 年，她的《诗集》引起了罗伯特·勃朗宁的注意，两人在之后的 20 个月里互通 574 封信。1846 年，两人不顾伊丽莎白父亲的反对私奔，在意大利定居。伊丽莎白身体有所好转，诞下一子。她父亲再没有搭理她。她在婚前秘密写了《葡萄牙十四行诗集》，献给丈夫，于 1850 年出版。1861 年伊丽莎白在佛罗伦萨去世。
2. Poetic Style (1) Her technique is uncertain, and she never gets rid of the typical mistakes of vagueness and indulgence. (2) Her poems embody the approval of the noble cause, her passionate personal feelings, and the best unique expression. Her greatest feature is the expression of intimacy.	**2. 诗歌风格** (1) 她的技巧不确定，她从来都没摆脱模糊和放纵的典型错误。 (2) 她的诗表达了对崇高事业的赞同，她高昂热烈的个人情感，以及最佳的独特表述。她的特征就是对亲密的个人的感情的抒发。
3. Major Works *The Seraphim and Other Poems* (1838) *Poems* (1844) *Sonnets from the Portuguese* (1850) *Casa Guidi Windows* (1848—1851) *Aurora Leigh* (1857)	**3. 主要作品** 《天使及其他诗歌》(1838) 《诗集》(1844) 《葡萄牙十四行诗集》(1850) 《圭迪的窗子》(1848—1851) 《奥罗拉·利》(1857)

<table>
<tr>
<td>

4. Selected Work

◆***Sonnets from the Portuguese***

This collection of poems consists of 44 love poems, written by Elizabeth to her fiancé Robert Browning. The content and tone of the poem changed with the development of her relationship with Browning. Early poems expressed her hesitation and fear of developing a relationship with Browning, and eventually, they took a more accepting and passionate tone. This collection of poems is one of the most widely known collections of lyric poems. Admirers also compare her imagery with Shakespeare, and compare her skill in Italian form with Petrarch.

</td>
<td>

4. 选读作品

◆**《葡萄牙十四行诗集》**

这本诗集由 44 首情诗组成，是伊丽莎白写给他的未婚夫罗伯特·勃朗宁的。诗歌的内容和语气随着她和勃朗宁关系的进展而变化。早期的诗歌表达了她对和勃朗宁展开关系的迟疑和惧怕。随着两人关系加深，她渐渐克服焦虑，最终认可并激情洋溢。这本诗集被普遍认为是最广为人知的抒情诗歌集之一。仰慕者还将她的意象跟莎士比亚做比较，将她运用意大利诗歌形式的技艺与彼特拉克相提并论。

</td>
</tr>
</table>

33.2 考研真题与典型题详解

Ⅰ. Fill in the blanks.

1. Mrs. Browning's poem __________ describes the miserable life of child-workers in the factories and mines.
2. Mrs. Browning's __________ is considered as one of the most widely known collections of love lyrics in English.
3. Political and social themes embody Elizabeth's later work. She expressed her intense sympathy for the struggle for the unification of Italy in __________.

Ⅱ. Multiple Choices

1. Which is not written by Elizabeth Barrett Browning?

   A. *Sonnets from the Portuguese*　　B. *Pauline*

   C. *Casa Guidi Windows*　　D. *Aurora Leigh*

2. For whom *Sonnets from the Portuguese* was written?

   A. Her father.　　B. Her brother.　　C. Her husband.　　D. Her son.

Ⅲ. Read and analyze the following poem by Mrs. Browning.

Sonnet 43

How do I love thee? Let me count the ways.
I love thee to the depth and breadth and height
My soul can reach, when feeling out of sight
For the ends of Being and ideal Grace.
I love thee to the level of everyday's
Most quiet need, by sun and candlelight.
I love thee freely, as men strive for Right;
I love thee purely, as they turn from Praise.
I love thee with a passion put to use

In my old griefs, and with my childhood's faith.
I love thee with a love I seemed to lose
With my lost saints—I love thee with the breath,
Smiles, tears, of all my life! —and, if God choose,
I shall but love thee better after death.

参考答案及解析

Ⅰ. Fill in the blanks.

1. *Cry of the Children*

（勃朗宁夫人对当时英国的社会政治问题予以极大的关注，1844 年发表了短诗《孩子们的哭声》，愤怒抗议资本家对儿童的摧残和剥削。）

2. *Sonnets from the Portuguese*

（《葡萄牙十四行诗集》被普遍认为是最广为人知的抒情诗歌集之一。诗集由美丽的抒情诗组成，表达了一个女子对丈夫真切炽热的爱情。）

3. *Casa Guidi Windows*

（勃朗宁夫人的《圭迪的窗子》表达了她对意大利统一斗争的深切同情。）

Ⅱ. Multiple Choices

1. B 《波琳》是她的先生罗伯特·勃朗宁的作品。
2. C 《葡萄牙十四行诗集》是伊丽莎白写给她的丈夫罗伯特的，诗歌创作时，他们还是未婚夫妇。

Ⅲ. Read and analyze the following poem by Mrs. Browning.

"Sonnet 43" is the most passionate poem, expressing her ardent love for Robert Browning repeatedly. Elizabeth says in the second to third lines that she loves Browning with every aspect of her soul. She then goes onto say that she loves him enough that it meets the needs of every day and every night in lines 5 and 6. Through lines 7, 8, 9 and 11 Elizabeth repeats the phrase, "I love thee..." to build intensity and show emphasis. Line 7 says that she loves him "freely," or willingly, as men who try and reach "Right," which in this case could mean righteousness, or in correlation with the previous word "freely" it may mean freedom. Line 8 means that she loves him, as it says, purely, without any want for praise. Then she expresses her love for him as much as she used to love the saints as a child. At last, her love extends to all her life and even afterlife.

第七部分　二十世纪文学

第 34 章　托马斯·哈代

34.1　复习笔记

Ⅰ. Background Knowledge (1) The rise of imperialism was marked by the Boer War in South Africa from 1899 to 1902. Imperialist countries vied to carve up colonies in backward regions. Two disastrous world wars followed. (2) There was a general demand for drastic social reforms of all kinds. Change bred defiance and despair. Political, economic, and military upheavals of the 20th century have exerted a profound influence on English literature.	**Ⅰ. 背景知识** (1) 帝国主义兴起，其标志是 1899 至 1902 年间发生在南非的布尔战争。帝国主义国家在落后地区争相瓜分殖民地。随后爆发了两次灾难性的世界大战。 (2) 各国普遍要求马上进行各种激烈社会改革。变革孕育了反抗精神和绝望。20 世纪的政治、经济和军事动荡对英国文学产生深刻影响。
Ⅱ. Literary Style of the 20th Century Britain (1) There were conflicting opinions about realism and anti-realism in literature and art at the end of the 19th century. Later English realist writers inherited and developed the tradition of their predecessors in the satirical depiction of capitalist society and psychoanalysis of characters, but those writers were in a state of pessimism and even despair. (2) The whole English-speaking world was crazy about drama. Almost every city had local theatres and some regular playhouses. The Irish Dramatic Movement contributed to the development of the Irish drama. (3) Modernism has gained momentum and popularity among literary circles with new literary techniques emerging in novel and poetry writing. Psychological novels grew in large numbers and wide popularity, emphasizing delicate descriptions of characters' inner world. D. H. Lawrence, James Joyce, and Virginia Woolf (both Joyce and Woolf are writers of Stream of Consciousness) are literary giants of this period. (4) A prominent champion of imperialism was Rudyard Kipling, who celebrated the colonial expansion of the British Empire.	**Ⅱ. 二十世纪文学风格** (1) 19 世纪末的文学艺术出现了现实主义和反现实主义的斗争。英国后期现实主义作者，在对资本主义社会的讽刺性描绘和人物心理分析上，继承和发展了前人的传统，但他们充满了一种悲观情绪，甚至是绝望。 (2) 整个英语世界都狂热地喜爱戏剧。几乎每个城市都有地方剧院和一些固定剧院。爱尔兰戏剧运动给爱尔兰戏剧重新带来了活力。 (3) 现代主义成为文学新倾向，小说和诗歌都出现了新的创作方式。新出现的心理小说强调对人物心理进行细腻描写，典型代表作家是 D. H. 劳伦斯，和同属意识流派的詹姆斯·乔伊斯、弗吉尼亚·伍尔芙。 (4) 帝国主义杰出的拥护者是鲁德亚德·吉卜林，他在作品中颂扬大英帝国的殖民扩张。

(5) During the two world wars, Marxist literary and artistic criticism rose and developed. Marxist literary criticism was closely related to the working-class movement and people's struggle against imperialism and fascism. In the 1930s, two representatives of Marxist literary criticism in England were revolutionary writers Ralph Fox and Christopher Caudwell.	(5) 两次世界大战期间，马克思主义的文学艺术批评得以崛起与发展，马克思主义文学批评与工人阶级运动及人民反帝国主义、反法西斯的斗争密切相关。20 世纪 30 年代，英国马克思主义文学批评的两个代表是革命作家拉尔夫·福克斯和克里斯托弗·考德威尔。
Ⅲ. Literary Term—Stream of consciousness	**Ⅲ. 文学术语——意识流派**
(1) Stream of consciousness is a psychological term for the random flow of the conscious and the subconscious of man at a given time without subjective control.	(1) 意识流是心理学术语，它表示在某一时间里人的想法或观点有意识或不受主观控制地随意流动。
(2) In the early 20th century, under the influence of Freudian psychoanalysis, many writers adopted stream of consciousness as a technique for writing novels. These writers are characterized by their interest in psychological and emotional reactions of characters to external events rather than in the events themselves.	(2) 20 世纪早期，在弗洛伊德心理分析的影响下，许多作家采取意识流作为创作小说的方法。这些作家的特色是关注人物对外在事物的心理和情感反应，而不是关注事件本身。
(3) These writers rejected traditional realistic plot, characterization, and narration. Their works present a series of fluid images that can be seen as reactions to the external, or a thought or a similar image that travels back and forth between present and past memories.	(3) 这些作家摒弃了传统的现实主义情节结构、人物刻画及叙述。他们的作品成为一系列的流动的意象，这些意象可以是对外部世界的反应，也可以是往返于现在和过去的记忆的思绪或者是类似思绪的影像。
(4) The representatives of this school are James Joyce and Virginia Woolf.	(4) 典型意识流派代表作家是詹姆斯·乔伊斯和弗吉尼亚·伍尔芙。
Ⅳ. Thomas Hardy (1840—1928)	**Ⅳ. 托马斯·哈代(1840 - 1928)**
1. Life	**1. 生平**
Thomas Hardy, novelist and poet, is one of the representatives of English critical realism at the turn of the 19th century. He was born in Dorsetshire, in the center of the Wessex country which later figured in his works.	托马斯·哈代，小说家、诗人，19 世纪末英国批判现实主义代表。他生于英格兰南部多塞特郡，是他的威塞克斯小说的中心。
In 1867, he returned to Dorsetshire in poor health and continued to earn a living as an architect and wrote in his spare time. Then he began to write fiction. His first two writings were failures, but later his novels of country life achieved success. Despite his preference for poetry, he had to write stories to support himself, for he got married and gave up architecture in 1874. However, in 1896, Hardy gave up writing	1867 年，他因身体不好返回多塞特，接着靠做建筑师谋生，空闲时写作。之后他转向小说。他的头两部作品都失败了，不过后来描写乡村生活的小说取得了成功。尽管他更偏爱诗歌，他不得不写小说谋生，因为他在 1874 年结婚并放弃了建筑工作。1896 年哈代毅然

Victorian novels and focused on post-Victorian lyrical poetry. His poetry was considered as great as his novels. In his later years, Hardy received many honors. He succeeded Tennyson and Meredith as president of the Society of Authors.

从写维多利亚小说转向后维多利亚抒情诗歌，他的诗作也被认为不亚于小说。晚年哈代所获荣誉颇丰。他接任丁尼生和梅瑞狄斯成为作家协会的主席。

2. Features of Hardy's Works

(1) His literary achievements were mostly his Wessex novels, stories about people and landscape of his home country. Hardy wrote realistically of the poverty and decline of local farmers who are reduced to wage laborers roaming the countryside in search of seasonal work and who are ruthlessly exploited by wealthy landowners. According to Hardy's pessimistic outlook on life, man is governed by a mysterious and hostile destiny that predestines his life to misery.

(2) Hardy's poems express a fatalistic outlook on life, which is miserable in the dark, harsh environment of his hometown of Dorset. He rejected the Victorian belief in a benevolent God. His poems are satirical lamentations about the dismal conditions of human life. He combined rough rhymes with colloquial diction and created a novel style with rich rhymes and stanzaic forms.

2. 作品特点

（1）他的主要作品都是威塞克斯小说，即描写其家乡人与景的故事。哈代真实地描写了小农场主的贫困和衰落，他们沦落成雇佣的田间劳动者，在乡村四处漫游寻找季节性的工作，这些劳动者遭到富裕的农场主的无情剥削。按照哈代的悲观哲学，人类受到充满敌意的神秘命运的主宰，注定了人类生活的悲惨。

（2）哈代的诗歌表达了在家乡多赛特黑暗严酷的环境中，一种宿命论的人生观。他摒弃维多利亚时期仁慈上帝的信仰，因此他的许多诗作是对凄凉的人生境遇的讥讽哀歌。他将粗糙的韵律和口语词汇结合，韵律和诗节形式十分丰富，开创了极其新颖的风格。

3. Major Works

Under the Greenwood Tree (1872)
Far from the Madding Crowd (1874)
The Return of the Native (1878)
The Mayor of Casterbridge (1886)
Tess of the D'Urbervilles (1891)
Jude the Obscure (1896)
The Dynasts (1903, 1906, 1908) (The most important drama)

3. 主要作品

《绿荫下》(1872)
《远离尘嚣》(1874)
《还乡》(1878)
《卡斯特桥市长》(1886)
《德伯家的苔丝》(1891)
《无名的裘德》(1896)
《列王》(1903 – 1908)（最重要的诗剧）

4. Selected Works

◆*Tess of the D'Urbervilles*

Tess of the D'Urbervilles, A Pure Woman is Hardy's most famous book. It tells the tragic life story of a beautiful country girl Tess Durbeyfield. The whole novel is filled with melancholy and fatalism with circumstances and tragic coincidences abound in the book. The bourgeoisie society is to blame for Tess's tragic fate.

4. 选读作品

◆《德伯家的苔丝》

该书讲述了一个美丽的乡村女孩苔丝·德波菲尔德的悲剧。整部小说充满了忧郁和宿命感。宿命的场景和悲剧性的巧合充溢着整部书。但是资产阶级社会才是造成苔丝悲剧命运的根源。

◆***Jude the Obscure*** **A. Main Plot** Jude Fawley is a young Wessex villager who wants to be a man of knowledge and to study at Christminster. But he is seduced into marriage by the handsome and coarse barmaid Arabella Donn, who soon deserts him. He then goes to Christminster, where he earns a living as a stonemason and resumes his studies with the hope of entering university and then becoming a priest after graduation. Then he meets his beautiful and clever cousin Sue Bridehead, who has left her husband, Phillotson, and lives illegally with Jude. Under the double pressure of poverty and social disapproval, their relationship deteriorates. The real tragedy does not begin until Jude's eldest child born by Arabella kills himself and the two children of Jude and Sue in the belief that he and the other two children have no right to be born. Sue leaves Jude in great sorrow and returns to her husband. Jude drinks all day and dies miserably.	◆《无名的裘德》 **A. 主要情节** 裘德·范立是一位年轻的威塞克斯村民，他想要成为一名有知识的人，并且想在基督寺求学。但是他被一位外表漂亮但却粗俗的女招待员阿拉贝拉·唐欺骗成婚。不久她就抛弃了他。裘德前往基督寺，在那里靠做石匠为生，并重新开始学习，他希望可以进入那所大学，毕业之后成为牧师。 这时他遇见了自己美丽聪明的表姐苏·柏瑞和，她离开了自己的丈夫费乐生，与裘德非法同居。在贫困和社会偏见的双重压力下，两人的关系开始恶化。悲剧还未真正开始直至裘德与阿拉贝拉所生的儿子杀死了裘德跟苏所生的两个孩子和他自己，因为这个孩子认为自己和另外两个孩子没有出生的权利。苏在极度悲伤中离开裘德回到丈夫身边。裘德整日喝酒，最后悲惨地死去。
B. Theme In the preface to *Jude the Obscure*, Hardy pointed out that the novel is about the "tragedy of unfulfilled aims". The main theme of the novel is the conflict between the spirit and the body, the life one wants to live in contrast to the dirty reality one is doomed to lead. He also admitted that the novel was an attack on marriage laws as "marriage should be dissolvable as soon as it becomes a cruelty to either of the parties."	**B. 主题** 在小说的序言中哈代指出，这部小说是关于"目标未实现的悲剧"。该小说的主题是灵与肉体的冲突，一个人想要的生活和他注定要过的肮脏的现实生活的比照。他也承认小说是对婚姻法的抨击："一旦任何一方觉得婚姻是折磨，就应该解除婚姻"。
◆**"The Son's Veto"** This story is selected from the collection *Life's Little Ironies*, which tells the life story of its heroine, Sophy. In a society corrupted by egoism and social inequality, Sophy cannot achieve happiness because of her dedication spirit and self-sacrificing personality.	◆《儿子的否决》 该故事选自《生活小玩笑》小说集。该小说集实际上讲述了女主人公索菲的一生，是一本微型小说。在一个充满自大和不平等的社会里，索菲因为奉献和自我牺牲品质而无法获得幸福。

34.2 考研真题与典型题详解

Ⅰ. Fill in the blanks.

1. The 1930s were called __________ because many British intellectuals turned then to the Left, to Marxism and Communism.
2. Thomas hardy is well-known for his __________ novels describing the characters and environment of his native countryside.

Ⅱ. Multiple Choices

1. The lines "At once a voice arose among /The bleak twigs overhead /In a full-hearted evensong / of joy illimited" are depiction of __________.（首师大 2009 研）

   A. thrush　　B. nightingale　　C. reaper　　D. lark

2. Rudyard Kipling was the spokesman for imperialist sentiment. Which one is NOT his work?

   A. *Dubliners*.　　B. *The Jungle Book*.

   C. *The Second Jungle Book*.　　D. *Plain Tales from the Hills*.

3. William Golding's *Lord of the Flies* deals with the conflict between the forces of reason and those of irrationality represented by __________.

   A. Jack　　B. Ralph　　C. Piggy　　D. Simon

4. Which of the following novels is not written by Thomas Hardy?

   A. *Far from the Madding Crowd*.　　B. *The Mill on the Floss*.

   C. *The Return of the Native*.　　D. *The Mayor of Casterbridge*.

Ⅲ. Explain the following terms.

1. The Stream of Consciousness（北航 2008 研；厦门大学 2007 研；西安交大 2008 研）
2. English Modernism in Poetry（北航 2007 研）
3. Psychological novel
4. Interior monologue

Ⅳ. Short answer questions

1. What are the characteristics of modernist literature?
2. Give a brief introduction to the English realistic novels in the early 20th century.

Ⅴ. Essay question

Thomas Hardy's novels, particularly the later ones, are marked by grim determinism shading into pessimism but this is balanced by acute social criticism and a deep sympathy with the plight of the human individual in an indifferent and godless universe. Discuss one of such novels by Hardy.（大连外国语学院 2007 研）

参考答案及解析

Ⅰ. Fill in the blanks.

1. the Red Decade

   （英国的 20 世纪 30 年代被称为是"红色十年"，因为这一时期很多英国知识分子转向左倾，转向马克思主义和社会主义。）

2. Wessex

（哈代的主要作品都是威塞克斯小说，即描写其家乡人与景的故事。）

Ⅱ. Multiple Choices

1. A　题目中所选的是 Thomas Hardy（托马斯·哈代）的“The Darkling Thrush”（《暗夜里的鸫鸟》）中的几行诗。节译如下：霎时间一个声音，/从头顶稀疏的枝条间响起/衷心的晚祷，/充满无边的欢乐。
2. A　*Dubliners*（《都柏林人》）是 James Joyce（詹姆斯·乔伊斯）的作品。
3. A　在威廉·戈尔丁（William Golding）的小说《蝇王》中，拉尔夫（Ralph）代表了社会秩序和文明，他的朋友，戴着眼镜被大家称作“小猪”（Piggy）的胖男孩代表了理性和逻辑思维，而杰克（Jack）则代表了与之相对的野性。
4. B　《弗洛斯河上的磨坊》是乔治·艾略特的小说。

Ⅲ. Explain the following terms.

1. The Stream of Consciousness: William James coined the term in *Principles of Psychology* (1890) to describe the flow of mental experiences. In literature, stream of consciousness refers to a description of characters' thoughts and feelings in their mind without authorial interference or outside interruption. To create the chaotic effect we see and experience in reality, the author presents a seemingly random mix of thoughts, feelings, and sensory impressions of a character at a given time. The style rose in influence following the publication of James Joyce's *Ulysses* and has been widely used by writers such as Virginia Woolf and William Faulkner.
2. English Modernism in Poetry: Modernist poetry in England is generally considered to emerge in the early years of the 20th century under the influence of Imagist painting and writing. In common with many other modernists, poets like W. B. Yeats wrote in reaction against perceived excesses of Victorian poetry, which is obsessed with traditional formalism and ornate diction. Much of early modernist poetry took the form of short, compact lyrics. Nevertheless, longer poems later were preferred.
3. Psychological novel: A vague term for fiction that is concerned with the spiritual, the emotional and the mental aspect of characters rather than with plot and action. Psychological novels have emerged in large numbers during the last two hundred years.
4. Interior monologue: a term for a character's inner thoughts, impressions, and memories presented as if they were directly "overheard" without authorial voice or that of another narrator. The term is often loosely used as a synonym for stream of consciousness.

Ⅳ. Short answer questions

1. (1) Modernist writing deals with the irrational of human mentality .

    (2) The main themes of modernist literature are the distorted, alienated, and ill relationships between man and nature, man and society, man and man, and man and himself.

    (3) Modernist writers value the inside over the outside, the objective over the subjective, the irrational over the rational.

    (4) Modernist writers have a passionate interest in experimentation in literary devices and forms. They break from traditional elements in literature such as story, plot, chronological narration, etc. , creating works characterized as antinovel, antipoetry, and anti-drama.

2. (1) Realistic novelists in the early 20th century continued and developed traditions of Victorian

realistic writing, seeking new ways of revealing the truth of life. In their works criticism of the bourgeois world reached considerable depth and poignancy.

(2) Outstanding realistic novelists of this period include John Galsworthy, H. G. Wells, and Arnold Bennett. They casted insight into and offered criticism of the corrupted capitalist world, revealing their deep distress about social injustice and ruthlessness.

(3) Realistic novels in the early 20th century have significant influence on English literature, though the exposing and criticizing power have faded.

V. Essay question

Tess of the D'Urbervilles is one of the best and most popular works of Hardy. It tells a tragic story of a beautiful, innocent peasant girl Tess. As a pure woman brought up with the traditional idea of womanly virtues, Tess is abused and destroyed by Alex and Angel, agents of the destructive force in society. Through Tess's suffering from poverty, emotional struggle, and tragic ending, Hardy uttered a bitter cry of protest and denunciation of society. The whole novel is filled with melancholy and fatalism with fateful circumstances and tragic coincidences abound in it. The bourgeoisie society is to blame for Tess's tragic fate.

This novel is a fierce attack on the hypocrisy and false morals of bourgeois society and on the capitalist invasion into the rural towards the end of the century. It seems that along with each coincidence, the trap is closing around Tess until she is caught up in a dead end. Holding a determinist outlook on life, Hardy bitterly attacked the irrationality and injustice of Victorian institutions, conventions, and morals, all of which strangle individual will and destroy emotional health and interpersonal relationships. Tess is a tragic figure simply because she is not accepted by society in which the rural, the agricultural, and the innocent are threatened by invading capitalism.

From another perspective, Tess, beautiful and disadvantaged, stands up against ill fate and attempts to escape from all hypocrisy. Hardy expressed great sympathy for those who suffer under similar circumstances.

第 35 章　约翰·高尔斯华绥

35.1　复习笔记

John Galsworthy (1867—1933)

1. Life

John Galsworthy was a prolific novelist, playwright, and renowned social activist born into a wealthy bourgeois family. He traveled extensively and at 28 began to write, at first for his own amusement. As a novelist, Galsworthy is chiefly known for his *The Forsyte Saga*. He was awarded the Nobel Prize for Literature in 1932 "for his distinguished art of narration which takes its highest form in *The Forsyte Saga*."

2. Literary Style

Galsworthy is one of the most prominent of the 20th century realistic English writers. He dwells upon the burning social problems of his time. He has an acute sense of social justice and saw human existence in terms of the hunters and the hunted. Galsworthy is also a great stylist. His style is remarkable for its strength and elasticity, for its powerful sweep, brilliant illustrations and deep psychological analysis.

3. Major Works

The Island Pharisees (1904)

The Forsyte Saga (including: *The Man of Property* (1906), *Indian Summer of a Forsyte* (Interlude, 1918), *In Chancery* (1920), *Awakening* (Interlude, 1920), *To Let* (1921))

A Modern Comedy (including: *The White Monkey* (1924), *The Silver Spoon* (1926), *Swan Song* (1928))

The Silver Box (1906)

Strife (1909)

4. Selected Work

◆ ***The Man of Property***

The Man of Property is a scathing critique of the upper middle class. The central figure of the novel is Soames Forsyte,

约翰·高尔斯华绥(1867—1933)

1. 生平

约翰·高尔斯华绥是一位多产的小说家、剧作家和著名社会活动家。他出生于一个殷实的资产阶级家庭。他游历甚广，28 岁时开始写作，起初只是自娱自乐。作为小说家，他主要是因为《福尔赛世家》出名。1932 年，高尔斯华绥"因其叙述的卓越艺术——这种艺术在《福尔赛世家》中达到顶峰"而获得诺贝尔文学奖。

2. 文学风格

高尔斯华绥是 20 世纪英国最杰出的现实主义作家之一。他主要探讨当时社会热点问题。他敏锐地感知社会正义，并把人类的存在看作猎手和猎物。高尔斯华绥也是一位伟大的文体学家，他的写作风格力透纸背、灵活多变、气势磅礴、叙述明快、心理分析深刻。

3. 主要作品

《岛国的法利赛人》(1904)

三部曲《福尔赛世家》:(《有产业的人》(1906)，插曲《残夏》(1918)，《骑虎》(1920)，插曲《觉醒》(1920)，《出租》(1921))

三部曲《现代喜剧》:(包括《白猿》(1924)，《银匙》(1926)和《天鹅曲》(1928))

《银匣》(1906)

《斗争》(1909)

4. 选读作品

◆**《有产业的人》**

《有产业的人》是对上层中产阶级的严厉批判。小说中心人物是

a man of property. Soames is the spiritual representative of Forsytism, the principle that accumulation of wealth is the only goal of life, and that everything is judged by the amount of personal property. Soames has married Irene, a young and beautiful girl 20 years his junior. Irene loves art and cherishes noble ideals of life, while Soames regards her merely as a piece of his own property. Irene later meets and falls in love with the young architect Philip Bosinney, who is building a country house for Soames and who shares the same interest in art. Soames tries to have his revenge on Bosinney by suing him for spending more money than he needs to build the house. The triangular relationship of Soames, Irene, and Bosinney ends in the tragic death of Bosinney, who has a car accident in a London fog. Irene refuses to have anything to do with Soames then.	索米斯·福尔赛，一位有产业的人。索米斯是“福尔赛主义”的精神代表，即将积累财富作为生活的唯一目标，以个人财产多少来判断一切。 故事开头，索米斯娶了比他小20岁的艾琳为妻。艾琳年轻漂亮，热爱艺术，珍视生活中的崇高理想，但是索米斯只把她当作自己的财产。后来她认识了正在为索米斯建乡间别墅的建筑师菲利普·波辛尼。两人因为对艺术的共同爱好而相爱。索米斯为了报复波辛尼，向法庭起诉他花费的钱物比建房所需的要多。波辛尼在伦敦大雾中车祸身亡，最后三人的三角关系告终。但是艾琳却拒绝跟索米斯有任何关系。

35.2 考研真题与典型题详解

Ⅰ. Fill in the blanks.

1. The central figure in ________ is Soames Forsyte who is the man of property. The story evolves around Soames and his sense of property.
2. ________ was one of the most prominent of the 20th century English realistic writers. *The Man of Property* is one of his works.
3. ________ was awarded the Nobel Prize in Literature in 1932 "for his distinguished art of narration which takes its highest form in *The Forsyte Saga*."

Ⅱ. Multiple Choices

1. Galsworthy was a ________ English writers in the 20th century.
   A. realistic　　B. naturalistic　　C. romantic　　D. humanistic
2. Galsworthy was awarded the Nobel Prize in Literature in 1932 thanks to his great work ________.
   A. *The Island Pharisees*　　B. *The Forsyte Saga*
   C. *The Man of Property*　　D. *In Chancery*

Ⅲ. Short answer question

What is the theme of *The Man of Property*?

参考答案及解析

Ⅰ. Fill in the blanks.

1. *The Man of Property*

（索米斯是《有产业的人》中的主人公，他是有产业的人，故事围绕他和他对资产的态度展开。）

2. John Galsworthy

（约翰·高尔斯华绥（John Galsworthy）是英国20世纪著名小说家、剧作家、批判现实主义作家。《有产业的人》是高尔斯华绥的《福尔赛世家》三部曲中的第一部。书中所描写的福尔赛世家正处于由兴盛到衰落的转折时期。）

3. John Galsworthy

（1932年，高尔斯华绥"因其叙述的卓越艺术——这种艺术在《福尔赛世家》中达到顶峰"而获得诺贝尔文学奖。）

Ⅱ. Multiple Choices

1. A　高尔斯华绥是20世纪最重要的现实主义作家之一。

2. B　高尔斯华绥因为其伟大作品《福尔赛世家》而获得1932年的诺贝尔文学奖。

Ⅲ. Short answer question

The Man of Property is a scathing critique of the upper middle class. The central figure of the novel is Soames Forsyte, a man of property. Soames is the spiritual representative of Forsytism, the principle that accumulation of wealth is the only goal of life, and that everything is judged by the amount of personal property. The Forsytes' obsession with wealth, status, and acquisition manifests itself in the novel. Galsworthy, satirically though not unsympathetically, criticized the hollow insularity in terms of matters of property and marriage and the ideology of the class he was born into.

第 36 章　奥斯卡·王尔德

36.1　复习笔记

Oscar Wilde (1854—1900)	奥斯卡·王尔德 (1854—1900)
1. Life	**1. 生平**
Oscar Wilde, a dramatist, poet, novelist, and essayist, was born in Dublin, Ireland. He studied classics at Trinity College, Dublin and won a scholarship to Oxford University, where he was an excellent student influenced by the aesthetic theory of John Ruskin and became a disciple of Walter Pater. In 1879, he settled in London and soon made a name for himself both as a writer and as a spokesman for "art for art's sake". He was one of the leading authors of the "aesthetic movement". In 1895, charged with a homosexual relationship with Lord Alfred Douglas, Wilde rashly sued for libel but lost the case and was jailed for two years. After the case, the public strongly detested him, and the aesthetic movement suffered a severe setback.	奥斯卡·王尔德是个戏剧家、诗人、小说家和散文家。他出生在爱尔兰的都柏林。他在都柏林圣三一学院主修古典文学，获得了去牛津大学的奖学金，成了牛津大学一名优秀的学生。他受到约翰·拉斯金美学理论的影响，并师从沃尔特·佩特。1879 年他定居伦敦。并成为一名有名的作家和"为艺术而艺术"学派的代言人，紧接着成为美学运动的领导者。1895 年，他被指控与阿尔弗莱德·道格拉斯勋爵有同性恋关系，他鲁莽地起诉对方诽谤，但输了官司，被捕入狱两年。由此一来，公众非常厌恶他，美学运动也受挫。出狱后，王尔德离婚又破产。
2. Major Works	**2. 主要作品**
The Happy Prince and Other Tales (1888) *The Picture of Dorian Gray* (1891) *Lady Windermere's Fan* (1892) *A Woman of No Importance* (1893) *Salomé* (1893) *An Ideal Husband* (1895) *The Importance of Being Earnest* (1895) *The Ballad of Reading Gaol* (1898)	《快乐王子及其他故事》(1888) 《道林·格雷的画像》(1891) 《温德米尔夫人的扇子》(1892) 《无足轻重的女人》(1893) 《莎乐美》(1893) 《理想的丈夫》(1895) 《认真的重要性》(1895) 《里丁监狱歌谣》(1898)
3. Selected Works	**3. 选读作品**
◆***Lady Windermere's Fan***	◆**《温德米尔夫人的扇子》**
Mrs. Windermere suspects her husband of having an affair. When she confronts him, he insists on his loyalty and innocence and inviting Mrs. Erlynne to her birthday ball. Mrs. Windermere, angry at her husband's infidelity, comes to the home of Lord Darlington, who is courting her. Mrs. Erlynne	温德米尔夫人怀疑丈夫有婚外情，她与丈夫对峙，但丈夫却坚持邀请埃尔琳夫人来参加她的生日舞会。温德米尔夫人因为丈夫不忠而生气，来到追求她的伯爵家里。埃尔琳夫人得知后赶来劝解。恰好伯爵和客人回家，两位夫人躲了起

learns about it and comes to help. Just as Lord Darlington and his guest return home, the two ladies go into other rooms to hide themselves, but Lady Windermere's forgotten fan is found. It turns out that Mrs. Windermere is the daughter that Mrs. Erlynne has abandoned twenty years ago. To save her daughter from making a fool of herself, Mrs. Erlynne shows herself up and confesses that the fan is her own to save her daughter's marriage.	来，但温德米尔夫人遗忘的扇子被发现。原来温德米尔夫人是埃尔琳夫人20年前抛弃的女儿。为免女儿出丑，埃尔琳夫人出来承认扇子是自己的，保全了女儿的婚姻。
◆***The Picture of Dorian Gray*** The novel tells of a young man named Dorian Gray, the subject of a painting by artist Basil Hallward. Basil is impressed by Dorian's beauty, which he believes will inspire him in painting. Dorian meets Lord Henry Wotton, a friend of Basil's, and is convinced of his hedonism as a result of which he begins to feel miserable for his fleeting beauty and fantasizes about selling his soul in order to remain young forever. Dorian's wish is miraculously fulfilled with the portrait of him bearing the changes of time in his stead while he remains young and beautiful. So Dorian begins to plunge himself into wicked deeds. He cruelly uses her lover Sibyl Vane, who kills herself at last. When he returns home he finds a cruel expression on the portrait and that the portrait serves as a reminder of the effect each act has upon his soul, with each sin being displayed as a disfigurement of his form, or through a sign of aging. Later Dorian murders Hallward and has a chemist destroy the body. When Dorian decides to stab the frightful portrait, he finally kills himself.	◆**《道林·格雷的画像》** 小说讲述了天生漂亮异常的道林·格雷的故事。画家霍尔沃德为道林的美貌折服，相信他的美赋予他作画的灵感。道林见到霍尔沃德的朋友亨利爵士后，听信了他的享乐主义，开始为自己美貌易逝感到痛苦，异想天开地希望出卖灵魂来永葆青春。他的愿望奇迹般地实现了，那幅肖像代替他自己承担岁月变迁，而他自己却仍旧青春貌美。于是道林开始堕落。一天晚上他粗暴地对待了他所爱的女演员西比尔·苇恩，导致其自杀。回到家里，发现那肖像上出现了残忍的表情。原来那肖像已开始随着道林·格雷心灵的变化而变化了，他的每次恶行都使肖像的容颜扭曲衰老。后来道林杀了霍尔沃德，并让一个化学家毁尸灭迹。当道林决定刺破那个面目狰狞的肖像画时，他竟杀死了自己。

36.2 考研真题与典型题详解

Ⅰ. Fill in the blanks.

1. ________ is the representative among the writers of aestheticism and decadence. *The Picture of Dorian Gray* is a typical decadent novel written by him.
2. Wilde established himself both as a writer and as a spokesman for the school "________".

Ⅱ. Multiple Choices

1. Which of the following plays is not written by Wilde?

A. *Lady Windermere's Fan.*　　B. *An Ideal Husband.*

C. *She Stoops to Conquer.*　　D. *The Importance of Being Earnest.*

2. What's the relationship between Mrs. Erlynne and Lady Windermere?

A. Sisters. B. Mother and daughter.

C. Good friends. D. Enemies.

Ⅲ. Short answer question

Explain Wilde's Aestheticism.

Ⅳ. Essay question

Discuss the character of Lord Henry and his impact on Dorian.

参考答案及解析

Ⅰ. Fill in the blanks.

1. Oscar Wilde

(奥斯卡·王尔德是19世纪末英国唯美派剧作家、诗人、小说家和文学批评家。《道林·格雷的画像》是王尔德最出色的作品，最为详细地阐述了他的颓废主义思想。)

2. Art for Art's sake

(王尔德既是一名作家也是"为艺术而艺术"流派的代言人。)

Ⅱ. Multiple Choices

1. C 《屈身求爱》是哥尔德史密斯的名剧。

2. B 温德米尔夫人和埃尔琳夫人是《温德米尔夫人的扇子》中的角色，两人是母女关系。

Ⅲ. Short answer question

Wilde's Aestheticism is a reaction against the stringent moral boundaries and social conventions in the Victorian age by embracing pure beauty and art, which must be loved for its own sake. As with dandyism and decadence, the Aestheticist movement stresses individuality, freedom, modernity, sensual pleasures, and social theatricality.

Ⅳ. Essay question

Lord Henry's is a man of charm, wit, and intellect. Dorian is convinced of his hedonism as a result of which he begins to feel miserable for his fleeting beauty and fantasizes about selling his soul in order to remain young forever. Lord Henry, regarding Dorian as a potential disciple who lives out his philosophy of hedonism, is cynical about social conventions and morality but passionate for beauty.

Lord Henry is a strong advocate for individualism and freedom, as he believes that man should not be in the yolk of social conventions as a result which he wastes the more valuable such as individuality and secular pleasure. The culprit of Dorian's downfall is more of his ready willingness to surrender himself to others' ideology than of others' negative influence upon him. Following Lord Henry's advice and influenced by the "yellow book" that Lord Henry gives him, Dorian gradually allows himself to fall deep into a life of sin, all in the name of pursuing pleasure. In contrast, Lord Henry himself never seems to act against the conventions detested by him: he carelessly and boldly talks about his cynical ideas around but never puts them into practice. A thinker but no doer, he is uncertain of where his philosophy will carry him if he practices it. The failure to see through his own life philosophy reduces him to ignorance of and indifference to Dorian's degeneration.

第 37 章　乔治·萧伯纳

37.1　复习笔记

George Bernard Shaw (1856—1950)

1. Life

George Bernard Shaw was born in Dublin, Ireland. He had no systematic education because he abhorred organized training. At twenty he moved to London and became a leading music and theatre critic in the eighties and nineties. He was also a prominent member of the Fabian Society (an association founded in 1884 of British socialists in support of moderate and progressive reforms to establish a democratic socialist country), for which he composed many pamphlets. He began his literary career as a novelist. A fervent advocate of the new theatre of Ibsen, he decided to write plays to make public his criticism of the English stage.

2. Dramatic Style

Shaw's radical rationalism, utter disregard for conventions, keen interest in dialectics, and witty language often turn the stage into a forum for clashes of ideas. Shaw's plays are unique in their combination of drama, comedy, and social correction.

3. Major Plays

Widowers' Houses (written in 1885, published in 1892)
Mrs. Warren's Profession (1893)
The Devil's Disciple (1896)
The Man of Destiny (1895)
Man and Superman (1903)
Major Barbara (1905)
Pygmalion (1912)
Heartbreak House (1913)
Saint Joan (1923)
The Apple Cart (1929)

乔治·萧伯纳(1856—1950)

1. 生平

乔治·萧伯纳生于都柏林。他厌恶有秩序的训练，所以没受过系统教育。他 20 岁时搬到伦敦，在八、九十年代成为主要的音乐和戏剧评论家，也是费边社(1884 年成立的英国社会主义知识分子组织，主张采取温和缓进的改革，建立民主社会主义国家)的杰出成员，为其写过很多宣传小册子。他作为小说家初涉文坛，因为是易卜生新戏剧的狂热支持者，他决定写剧本来阐述他对英国戏剧的批评。

2. 戏剧风格

萧伯纳彻底的理性主义、全然不顾常规、他对辩证法的强烈兴趣、以及机智风趣的语言常常使舞台变成思想交锋的论坛。萧伯纳戏剧的独特之处在于融合了戏剧性、喜剧性和社会矫正。

3. 主要戏剧

《鳏夫的房产》(写于 1885 年，1892 年出版)
《华伦夫人的职业》(1893)
《魔鬼的门徒》(1896)
《风云人物》(1895)
《人与超人》(1903)
《芭芭拉少校》(1905)
《卖花女》(1912)
《伤心之家》(1913)
《圣女贞德》(1923)
《苹果车》(1929)

4. Selected Works

◆ *Widowers' Houses*

This play satirizes bourgeois businessmen who make ill-gotten gains by exploiting the poor and the suffering.

Harry Trench, a young English doctor, befriends an English businessman Mr. Sartorius and his daughter Blanche. Trench and Blanche fall in love and are engaged. But Trench learns from Sartorius's clerk Lickcheese that Sartorius is a landlord in London slums, renting out dilapidated houses and exploiting poor tenants for money. Disgusted with his future father-in-law, Trench wants to break his engagement. But Sartorius reveals to Trench the source of his own income. It turns out that Sartorius' houses are built on the land owned by Trench's aunt and that the young man lives on the interest of the mortgage. Therefore, Trench is no better or noble than Sartorius and Lickcheese. After realizing this, Trench marries Blache.

4. 选读作品

◆《鳏夫的房产》

该剧讽刺了资产阶级商人靠压榨穷人和受苦人获取不义之财。

年轻的英国医生哈里·曲兰奇结识英国商人萨托里阿斯和他女儿白朗琪。两人相爱并订婚。但是从萨托里阿斯的书记员里克奇斯那里曲兰奇了解到萨托里阿斯是伦敦贫民窟的房东，出租破旧的房屋，靠压榨穷苦的佃户获得钱财。出于对未来岳父的厌恶，曲兰奇决心解除婚约。但是萨托里阿斯指出曲兰奇财产的来源。萨托里阿斯的房屋就建在曲兰奇婶母的地产上，曲兰奇就是靠地产的抵押利息生活。最后他与白朗琪结婚。

◆ *The Devil's Disciple*

This play derides the much-praised Puritan piety.

The historical background of the play is the national liberation movement of the American colonies against British rule in 1777. The battle comes near Westerbridge where British troops decide to hang Reverend Anderson, the most beloved of the town's citizens, in order to intimidate them. The English soldiers mistake Richard Dudgeon for Anderson and arrest the wrong man. Richard, who proclaims himself to be the "Devil's Disciple", is known to be an enemy of Puritan community. However, his practice proves that he is much braver than those hypocritical Puritans. To save Anderson's life, he bravely takes the place of Anderson to die, which is never expected by Puritans. But at the last moment, Anderson comes to Richard's rescue on behalf of the victorious American army.

◆《魔鬼的门徒》

该剧嘲讽了被赞誉过多的清教徒的虔诚。

戏剧背景是美国1777年反对英国殖民统治的民族解放运动。战争打到韦斯特尔桥附近。英国军队进驻韦斯特尔桥镇，为了恐吓人们，他们决定吊死镇里最受人爱戴的教长安德森。抓捕教长的英国士兵错把该镇公民理查德·达德吉恩误认为安德森。理查德是清教徒公开的敌人，他宣称自己是“魔鬼的门徒”。然而，实践证明他比那些虚伪的清教徒们勇敢得多，为了救安德森的性命，他勇敢代替安德森赴死，这是清教徒们不曾想过的。但在最后一刻，安德森代表胜利的美国军队赶来救了理查德。

◆ *Mrs. Warren's Profession*

A. Main Plot

Mrs. Warren runs a brothel by profession. The old aristocrat Mr. Crofts is her partner in the business. Mrs. Warren's daughter, Vivie, studies at a moral boarding school. Returning

◆《华伦夫人的职业》

A. 主要情节

华伦夫人的职业是经营妓院。老贵族克罗夫茨先生是她生意上的合伙人。华伦夫人的女儿薇薇在一所道德气氛颇浓的寄宿学校学习。毕

home after graduation, she discovers the source of her mother's income. Her conversations with Mrs. Warren and Crofts show the moral depravity of these members of the ruling class. Finally Vivian leaves her mother and tries to make a living by honest labor.	业回到家中的她发现了母亲的收入来源。她与华伦夫人和克罗夫茨的对话表现了这些统治阶级成员的道德败坏。最后薇薇离开母亲，努力靠诚实的劳动谋生。
B. Analysis	**B. 分析**
This play is one piece from the collection *Plays Unpleasant*. Unpleasant it is to the bourgeois public because Shaw attacked the vices of capitalist society. Although Shaw strongly protested against bourgeois exploitation and the British ruling class, he failed to point out a way to change the situation.	该剧是《不愉快的戏剧集》中的一篇。这部戏剧是令资产阶级"不愉快"的，因为剧中萧伯纳攻击了资本主义社会的恶行。虽然萧伯纳强烈抗议资产阶级剥削和英国统治阶级，但是他没能指出一条改变现状的道路。
The play touches upon the fate of poor women among the working masses. Through Mrs. Warren's speeches Shaw showed us that these poor women have only two options: they can either keep their dignity, starve, and die of poverty, or they can give up their moral responsibility and engage in an immoral profession.	剧本触及了劳动群众中贫穷妇女的命运。通过华伦夫人的话语，萧伯纳试图让我们知道，这些贫穷的妇女只有两条路可以走，要么保持自己的尊严，忍饥挨饿并最后死于贫困，要么放弃道德责任，从事不道德的行业。
◆*Major Barbara*	**◆《芭芭拉少校》**
Characters in the story include Barbara, a "major" in the Salvation Army (a reformist Christian organization), her father Andrew Undershaft, a "cannon king" whose actions reveal the truth of monopoly capitalism, and her fiancé Cusins, a professor. Now Barbara wishes to save the souls and the bodies of the poor, and her fiancé shares her views. So there arises the conflict between Undershaft and his daughter plus her fiancé. Undershaft won by buying the Salvation Army. Finally Cusins inherits Undershaft's property, and Barbara believes that in order to oppose capitalism, she has to have a certain strength, which could be obtained by inheriting her father's legacy.	戏剧主人公包括：救世军(基督教改良组织)的"少校"，芭芭拉；她的父亲安德鲁·安德谢夫，一位军火商巨擘(他的所作所为揭示了垄断资本主义的真实嘴脸。)；库森教授，芭芭拉的未婚夫。芭芭拉想要拯救穷人的身体和灵魂，她的未婚夫同她持有一样的观点。这与她父亲的军火理念形成了冲突，最后安德谢夫通过买下救世军的机构获得胜利。库森作为芭芭拉的未婚夫继承了安德谢夫的财产，芭芭拉到她父亲的弹药厂工作，她相信要反对资本主义就必须拥有一定的实力，这种实力可以通过继承她父亲的遗产来得到。

37.2 考研真题与典型题详解

I. Fill in the blanks.

1. In 1926, ________ received the Nobel Prize in Literature "for his work which is marked by both idealism and humanity, its stimulating satire often being infused with a singular poetic beauty".

2. Bernard Shaw was also a prominent member of __________, for which he composed many pamphlets.

3. One of Shaw's greatest contributions as a modern dramatist is in establishing drama as __________, negotiating publication deals for his highly popular plays so as to convince the public that the play was no less important than the novel.

Ⅱ. Read the following quotation and answer the questions.

MRS. WARREN: (piteously) Oh, my darling, how can you be so hard on me? Have I no rights over you as your mother?

VIVIE: Are you my mother?

MRS. WARREN: (appalled) Am I your mother? Oh, Vivie!

VIVIE: Then where are our relatives? My father? Our family friends? You claim the rights of a mother; the right to call me fool and child; to speak to me as no woman in authority over me at college dare speak to me; to dictate my way of life; and to force on me the acquaintance of a brute whom anyone can see to be the most vicious sort of London man about town. Before I give myself the trouble to resist such claims, I may as well find out whether they have any real existence.

MRS. WARREN: (distracted, throwing herself on her knees) Oh no, no. Stop, stop. I am your mother; I swear it. Oh, you can't mean to turn on me—my own child! It's not natural. You believe me, don't you? Say you believe me.

VIVIE: Who was my father?

MRS. WARREN: You don't know what you're asking. I can't tell you.

VIVIE: (determinedly) Oh yes you can, if you like. I have a right to know; and you know very well that I have that right. You can refuse to tell me, if you please, but if you do, will see the last of me tomorrow morning.

MRS. WARREN: Oh, it's too horrible to hear you talk like that. You wouldn't—you couldn't leave me.

VIVIE: (ruthlessly) Yes, without a moment's hesitation, if you trifle with me about this. (shivering with disgust) How can I feel sure that I may not have the contaminated blood of that brutal waster in my veins?

MRS. WARREN: No, no. On my oath it's not he, nor any of the rest that you have ever met. I'm certain of that, at least.

(Vivie's eyes fasten sternly on her mother as the significance of this flashes on her.)(北航 2007 研)

Questions:

1. Identify the author and the title of the play.
2. The sentence "Are you my mother?" is said to her mother by Vivie, which is very inappropriate and therefore unlikely in a congenial conversation between daughter and mother. Why does Vivie say to her mother in this way?
3. Do you know what Mrs. Warren's profession is?
4. Describe the female protagonist, Vivie.

5. What is the theme of the play?

Ⅲ. Short answer question

What are the features of George Bernard Shaw's characterization?

Ⅳ. Essay question

George Bernard Shaw's plays aim at social reforms. He holds that the theatre has a didactic function. Please write a passage to tell us what morals Shaw wants to teach us in his well-known play *Pygmalion*. (天津外国语学院 2009 研)

参考答案及解析

Ⅰ. Fill in the blanks.

1. Bernard Shaw

 (1926 年，萧伯纳因其"作品具有理想主义和人文主义，激动人心的讽刺常充满独特的诗意美"获得诺贝尔文学奖。)

2. the Fabian Society

 (萧伯纳也是费边社的杰出成员，为其写过很多宣传小册子。费边社是 1884 年成立的英国社会主义知识分子组织，主张采取温和缓进的改革，建立民主社会主义国家。)

3. serious literature

 (萧伯纳作为现代剧作家的一项突出成就是把戏剧发展成一种严肃文学，使民众相信戏剧不比小说次要。)

Ⅱ. Read the following quotation and answer the questions.

1. George Bernard Shaw; *Mrs. Warren's Profession.*

2. Suspicious of her mother's profession, Vivie decides to figure it out herself. It seems that she could already vaguely guess the truth. Therefore, she is embarrassed, ashamed, and angry.

3. She runs brothels for profit.

4. Vivie is a new woman intelligent and well-educated, with a strong sense of justice and passion for "honest" work. Therefore, it is unacceptable for Vivie that her mother runs a brothel and practices something against morality, decency, and dignity. That is why she has conflicts with her mother and leaves to earn an honest living in London. Vivie's choice and action show that she is an independent woman eager to find a meaningful life for herself in a world dominated by men.

5. In this play, Shaw proceeds from attacking one of the abuses in the capitalist world to the condemnation of the entire bourgeois, the whole capitalist system. Shaw also exposed the hypocrisy of society, especially that of the ruling class who live in comfort and at ease by exploiting the poor.

Ⅲ. Short answer question

(1) In Shaw's plays, there is a wide range of characters who, though not explored in depth and breadth, are representatives of people at that time.

(2) Shaw often introduced one character in comparison with another, and this characterization is built upon certain attack and exposure of the latter. Usually he would create unconventional and positive images of characters by contrasting them with those of negative ones as means to reveal the latter's hypocrisy, fake courtesy, biases, and dishonesty.

(3) Shaw's characters give different opinions in plays and reveal Shaw's intention through their self-revealing conversations and actions. Shaw is primarily interested in doctrines.

(4) Shaw also frequently added twists to his plays for dramatic effect. For example, a conventional hero as a villain or a conventional villain as a hero will shock the audience and challenge conventional understanding of good and evil, the surface and the reality, and so on.

Ⅳ. Essay question

George Bernard Shaw's play *Pygmalion* is the story of Henry Higgins, a master phonetician, and his mischievous plot to pass a common flower girl, Eliza Doolittle, off as a duchess at the Embassy Ball. In Higgins's experiment, Eliza is the subject taught to speak and act like a lady of polite society.

The play exposes the serious problem of decreasing social mobility in British society in the Victorian age, an extremely class-conscious period in the British history. Shaw depicted British society as divided by people's accent, pronunciation, and manners rather than by their personality and morality. In *Pygmalion*, Eliza's dialect inhibits her from procuring a job in a flower shop. Through the play, Shaw intended to remind the audience that all people, regardless of their social ranks, are worthy of respect and dignity if they have a noble mind and heart. What sets a common flower girl and a duchess apart is not appearance or demeanor but the way she is treated. Besides, *Pygmalion* also looks at the power of identity and middle-class morality through the characterization of Mr. Doolittle, Eliza's father. An ordinary dustman and alcoholic referred to as the best moralist speaker by Higgins, Mr. Doolittle is compelled to behave like a middle-class man who is expected to observe all middle-class conventions despite the fact that he is uncomfortable to live this way. As a result, the transformation only leads to a miserable life. This plot displays Shaw's social criticism.

What's more, the play reflects George Bernard Shaw's socialist views: education available for the working classes. As a member of the Fabian Society, Shaw, confident in the idea of evolutionary or democratic socialism, worked to educate the public through seminars, schools, discussions, and lectures. He held that wealth should be gradually redistributed among all classes through public ownership of industry and business.

第 38 章　戴维·赫伯特·劳伦斯

38.1　复习笔记

David Herbert Lawrence (1885—1930)	戴维·赫伯特·劳伦斯(1885—1930)
1. Life David Herbert Lawrence was born in Eastwood Nottinghamshire. His father was a miner; his mother was an educated genteel woman who had a deep influence upon his life. As a child, Lawrence resented his father's vulgarity and approved of his mother's gentleness. Inspired by his mother, Lawrence won a scholarship to Nottingham High School, where he studied for two years and obtained his teacher's certificate in 1908. From 1908 to 1912, he taught in a school, but finally gave up his job after falling in love with Frieda von Richthofen, a German noblewoman and the wife of a professor at Nottingham. In 1914, after Frieda's divorce, they married and went to Germany together. The outbreak of World War I brought them back to Britain, but Frieda's German heritage and Lawrence's opposition to the war got them into trouble with the authorities. Frustrated, Lawrence sought refuge in many countries. He died of tuberculosis in France, at 44.	**1. 生平** 戴维·赫伯特·劳伦斯生于诺丁汉郡的伊斯特伍德。他的父亲是矿工，母亲是有教养的上流社会女性，对劳伦斯一生产生巨大影响。小时候劳伦斯厌恶父亲的粗俗，认同母亲的文雅。受母亲的鼓舞，劳伦斯赢得去诺丁汉高中的奖学金。他在诺丁汉大学学习了两年，1908年获得了教师资格证。之后的5年内他在学校教书，但在爱上弗丽达·冯·里奇索芬后，放弃了工作。弗丽达是德国贵族，一位诺丁汉大学教授的妻子。1914年，弗丽达离婚后，两人结婚并一起去了德国。一战爆发使两人重回英国，但弗丽达的德国血统和劳伦斯的反战让他们招惹了当局。劳伦斯受挫感到沮丧，便在许多国家寻求庇护。他在法国死于肺结核，享年44岁。
2. Literary Style (1) Lawrence's writing is controversial because he speaks frankly about sex and frankly insists on the need to rebalance the relationship between men and women. (2) Lawrence believes that women are victims. He sees women as capable individuals, but mostly "kept down by men." (3) He is often criticized for the didactic elements and loose structure of his novels. His short stories are generally considered superior in their emotional consistency and artistic form.	**2. 文学风格** (1) 劳伦斯颇具争议性，因为他直白地探讨了性，坦率地坚持需要重新调整男女之间的关系。 (2) 劳伦斯认为女性大多数时候是受害者。他将女性视为独立能干的个体，但多半总是被男人“踩在脚下”。 (3) 他常常因小说中的说教部分和结构松散而被批评。他的短篇小说被普遍认为在情绪的一致性和艺术形式上更胜一筹。

3. Major Works

The White Peacock (1910)

Sons and Lovers (1913)

The Rainbow (1915)

Women in Love (1920)

Lady Chatterley's Lover (1928)

4. Selected Works

◆*Sons and Lovers*

Sons and Lovers, most of which is autobiographical, is one of Lawrence's most important novels. Set in a mining area, the novel is based on the author's early dependence on his mother. The story of the novel is that the demanding mother, feeling hopeless about her marriage, turns to the drudging, possessive love she lavishes on her children. In the novel, Paul's complex relationship with his mother and his two lovers, as well as his psychological activities are described in detail, showing the influence of Freud's psychoanalysis theory, especially that of the "Oedipus complex".

◆*Lady Chatterley's Lover*

This is Lawrence's last novel and the most controversial one. It tells the love story of Lady Chatterley and her husband's gamekeeper. The author's bold description of the sexual relationship between the two lovers is an indictment of upper-bourgeois hypocrisy. He believes that Western society and modern industrial civilization have degraded the relationship between men and women.

The paralysis of Sir Clifford Chatterley symbolizes the moribund power that has ruled the country, whereas his gamekeeper, Mellors, embodies all the qualities the author admires: robust independence, intelligence, and the ability to advance and change.

3. 主要作品

《白孔雀》(1910)

《儿子与情人》(1913)

《虹》(1915)

《恋爱中的女人》(1920)

《查泰莱夫人的情人》(1928)

4. 选读作品

◆《儿子和情人》

《儿子和情人》是劳伦斯最重要的小说之一，大部分是本人自传。小说背景是在矿区，以作者早年对母亲的依赖为蓝本。小说的主题是要求严格的母亲感到自己的婚姻幸福无望，转而向孩子施加单调乏味、占有欲极强的爱。小说中保罗与母亲及两个情人的复杂关系，及其心理活动在书中得到详尽地刻画，显示了弗洛伊德的心理分析理论，特别是俄狄浦斯情结的影响。

◆《查泰莱夫人的情人》

这是劳伦斯最后一部作品，也是他最受争议的一部作品。文中讲述了查泰莱夫人跟她丈夫的猎场看守人的爱情故事。作者大胆描述了两个情人的性爱关系，旨在控诉上层资产阶级的虚伪。他认为西方社会和现代工业文明使得男女关系退化了。

克利弗·查泰莱爵士的瘫痪象征着统治国家的垂死的势力，而他的看林人梅勒斯体现了作者所赞赏的一切特性——强壮而独立，聪明而有创造力，还有带来发展与变化的能力。

38.2 考研真题与典型题详解

Ⅰ. Fill in the blanks.

1. Ursula is the heroine both in *The Rainbow* and ＿＿＿＿＿＿. （首师大2008研）
2. Author ＿＿＿＿＿＿ Title ＿＿＿＿＿＿（南京大学2009研）

Uncle Oscar took both Bassett and Paul into Richmond Park for an afternoon, and there they talked.

3. The statement "A demanding mother turns away from her husband and gives all her affection to her sons" sums up the main plot of D. H. Lawrence's ________.

Ⅱ. Multiple Choices

1. *Sons and Lovers* shows the influence of ________.

   A. Electra complex　　B. apple of discord

   C. Oedipus complex　　D. Damon and Pythias

2. Which is Lawrence's last work?

   A. *Sons and Lovers.*　　B. *The Rainbow.*

   C. *Women in Love.*　　D. *Lady Chatterley's Lover.*

Ⅲ. Read the following quotations and answer the questions.

The moon was high and magnificent in the August night. Mrs. Morel, seared with passion, shivered to find herself out there in a great white light, that fell cold on her, and gave a shock to her inflamed soul. She stood for a few moments helplessly staring at the glistening great rhubarb leaves near the door. Then she got the air into her breast. She walked down the garden path, trembling in every limb, while the child boiled within her. For a while she could not control her consciousness; mechanically she went over the last scene, then over it again, certain phrases, certain moments coming each time like a brand red-hot down on her soul; and each time she enacted again the past hour, each time the brand came down at the same points, till the mark was burnt in, and the pain burnt out, and at last she came to herself. She must have been half an hour in this delirious condition. (北航 2007 研)

Questions:

1. This passage is taken from *Sons and Lovers*. Who is the author of the novel and what are his major works?
2. Comment on the writing style of the author.
3. The author was considered to be the innovator of psychological fiction, and then what is psychological fiction?
4. The author was notorious for his writing about sex in his time, what do you think of his writing about the relationship between the two sexes?

参考答案及解析

Ⅰ. Fill in the blanks.

1. *Women in Love*

   (Ursula 既是《虹》里的主人公，也是《恋爱中的女人》的主人公。)

2. Author: D. H. Lawrence　　Title: "The Rocking-Horse Winner"

   (《木马赢家》是劳伦斯较为著名的短篇小说之一，探讨了劳伦斯所关注的人与人之间的关系。)

3. *Sons and Lovers*

   (这句话是劳伦斯《儿子与情人》里的一句话。)

Ⅱ. Multiple Choices

1. C　《儿子与情人》体现了恋母情绪，即俄狄浦斯情结的影响。

2. D 《查泰莱夫人的情人》是劳伦斯的最后一部作品。

Ⅲ. Read the following quotation and answer the questions.

1. The author is David Herbert Lawrence. His major works include *The Rainbow*, *Women in Love* and *Lady Chatterley's Lover*.
2. Lawrence's combination of psychic exploration with social criticism has contributed to the advancement of the English psychological novel. Well-aware of the desolation of mechanical civilization and its destructive influence on man's mentality, Lawrence showed strong concerns over human relationships, especially that between men and women. Lawrence is a writer of free expression, especially that of sexuality. In terms of writing techniques, his writing is of realism and naturalism, which combine dramatic scenes with an authorial commentary. By mixing traditional realism with symbolism and poetic imagination, Lawrence has managed to probe into the inner world of his characters.
3. A psychological fiction is a work of prose fiction that penetrates the inner world of characters and in this way reveals its themes. Therefore, it not action but what is going on in characters' mind that really matters. The psychological novel is, hence, called a novel of the "inner man". In many novels of this kind, stream of consciousness, flashback, and interior monologue are used to better illustrate the inner workings of human mind.
4. Lawrence boldly wrote about sexuality in his works and even called for a complete emancipation of sex. He believed that any repression of expression of sexuality as a result of social, religious, or moral values of the civilized world would destroy the harmony of human relationships and the psychic health of each individual. Therefore, in many of his novels Lawrence allowed his characters to listen to their heart and follow their sexual instinct. Lawrence's descriptions of sex and human body invite criticisms which accuse his novels of being pornographic.

第39章 弗吉尼亚·伍尔芙

39.1 复习笔记

Virginia Woolf (1882—1941)	弗吉尼亚·伍尔芙(1882—1941)
1. Life Virginia Woolf was the daughter of Sir Leslie Stephen. She was educated at home and in frequent contact with her father's literary and political friends. In 1912 Virginia married Leonard Woolf, a journalist, essayist, and political thinker. They cofounded the Hogarth Press in 1917. From childhood she suffered from fits of nervous breakdown. Her husband encouraged her to write novels. Her house in London was bombed by Nazi planes during the Second World War after which she suffered from relapses of depression and mental illness. In 1941, after completing her last novel, *Between the Acts*, she drowned herself in a river for fear that she would lose her mind and become a burden to her husband.	**1. 生平** 弗吉尼亚·伍尔芙是莱斯利·斯蒂芬爵士之女。伍尔芙在家里接受教育，经常接触父亲所交往的文学界、政治界的名流。1912年，弗吉尼亚嫁给伦纳德·伍尔芙，一位记者、散文家和政治思想家。两人在1917年共同创立霍加斯出版社。她从童年开始就经常遭受精神病的折磨，后来丈夫鼓励她从事小说创作。她在伦敦的住所二战期间被纳粹飞机轰炸，随后她精神忧郁，病情发作。1941年，完成最后一部小说《幕间》之后，她因为害怕会发疯成为丈夫的负担而投河自尽。
2. Literary Style Woolf is skilled in using stream-of-consciousness in her writing. She discussed personal identity, relationships, time, change, and the importance of memory to personality in subtlety. Her great achievement is her elegant prose.	**2. 文学风格** 伍尔芙是意识流写作技巧高超的典范。她十分微妙地探讨了个人身份，人际关系，时间、变化、记忆对人格的重要性等问题。她的杰出成就是最好的小说中雅致诗意的散文。
3. Major Works *Jacob's Room* (1922) *Mrs. Dalloway* (1925) *To the Lighthouse* (1927) *Orlando* (1928) *The Waves* (1931) *Between the Acts* (1941) *The Common Reader* (1925) *The Second Common Reader* (1932) *A Room of One's Own* (1929)	**3. 主要作品** 《雅克布的房间》(1922) 《达洛维夫人》(1925) 《到灯塔去》(1927) 《奥兰多》(1928) 《海浪》(1931) 《幕间》(1941) 《普通读者》(1925) 《普通读者续集》(1932) 《一间自己的房间》(1929)

4. Selected Work ◆***Mrs. Dalloway*** Clarissa Dalloway is an upper-class lady who walks the streets of London and shops for her party in the evening. The fine weather reminds her of her past youth and of Peter Walsh, a previous suitor of her. She wonders if she has made the right decision by marrying reliable Dalloway instead of unpredictable Walsh. Walsh's sudden return to London from India to see her that day adds to her restless thoughts. Septimus Warren Smith, a veteran of World War I, suffers from deferred traumatic stress and spends his day in a park with his Italian-born wife Lucrezia. Smith is inflicted by intermittent fantasies and often has illusions of Ivan, his best friend who has been killed in World War I. When the authorities decide to quarantine him for treatment, he commits suicide by jumping from a building. Clarissa's party that night is a success with many celebrities showing up, including people of her past acquaintances. She hears about Septimus' suicide at the party and gradually comes to admire his unwillingness to compromise and jumping off the building. She feels, with her comfortable position as a society hostess, responsible for his death. Like Septimus, Clarissa feels the pressures in life acutely. However, she chooses to endure and move on.	**4. 选读作品** ◆**《达洛维夫人》** 主人公克拉丽莎·达洛维是一位上流社会的贵妇，她走在伦敦的街道，为自己晚上的派对采买物品。美好的天气使她想起了自己已逝的青春，以及她年轻时的狂热追随者彼得·沃尔士。她思忖自己当初嫁了可靠达洛维，而不是捉摸不定的沃尔士，是不是一个正确的决定。沃尔士当天突然从印度返回伦敦来看望她，更让她突然思绪不宁。 同时，在伦敦的另一角是一战退伍军人塞普蒂默斯·史密斯和他的妻子露西娅。史密斯患有无名的狂想症，经常幻见在一战中牺牲的好友伊凡。当权威医师决定对他实行强制隔离治疗时，他跳楼自尽。 达洛维夫人当晚的派对很成功，名流济济。她在派对上闻知史密斯的自杀事件，心里暗自佩服他不愿妥协而跳楼。身为一个上流社会家庭的女主人，她感到自己对他的死负有责任。和塞普蒂默斯一样，她十分强烈地感受到了生活的压力，然而她选择了忍受。

39.2 考研真题与典型题详解

Ⅰ. Fill in the blanks.

1. ________ represents the much more readable novelists of the stream of consciousness school. She is a fine artist, a woman of sharp sensitivity who, in one of her frequent mental depressions, committed suicide.
2. In *Mrs. Dalloway*, Virginia Woolf adopted a writing technique called ________, in which the whole story was presented with the interior monologues of the characters.

Ⅱ. Multiple Choices

1. ________ belongs to "stream of consciousness" school.（北二外 2010 研）
   A. Virginia Woolf　　B. Thomas Wolfe
   C. Sommerset Maugham　　D. Thomas Hardy
2. Thomas Hardy is a prolific writer whose works include the following except ________.（天津外国语学院 2008 研）

A. *Far from the Madding Crowd* B. *To the Light House*
C. *Under the Greenwood Tree* D. *Jude the Obscure*

Ⅲ. Short answer question

Explain "a room of one's own" as a symbol.

Ⅳ. Essay question

Woolf created Septimus Warren Smith as a double for Clarissa. In what ways are Clarissa and Septimus different? In what ways are they the same?

参考答案及解析

Ⅰ. Fill in the blanks.

1. Virginia Woolf
(弗吉尼亚·沃尔芙是英国现代文学中与乔伊斯齐名的一位意识流小说大师。)
2. stream of consciousness
(意识流是指作品着力展示人物的内心世界采用迥异于传统文学的心理描写方法，伍尔芙是运用意识流的代表作家之一，在《达洛维夫人》中这一写作手法表现明显。)

Ⅱ. Multiple Choices

1. A 弗吉尼亚·伍尔芙是意识流文学的代表人物。
2. B 《到灯塔去》是英国作家弗吉尼亚·伍尔芙的小说。

Ⅲ. Short answer question

In her famous essay "A Room of One's Own" Woolf analyzed previous female writers' inferior status compared with their male counterparts and drew the conclusion that in order to be a great writer, women must have a room of her own which ensures that she has a separate space only to herself. Only in such a room can women write in peace and tranquility without being interrupted by domestic fairs. One example given by Woolf is Jane Austen. Woolf analyzed that because Austen was constantly interrupted by household chores, she could only write novels rich in conversation instead of poetry, the composition of which requires blocks of time. Therefore, Woolf suggested that female writers have a room of their own. During Woolf's time, women rarely enjoyed these luxuries, and consequently their art suffered. Woolf also raised other important issues such as privacy, leisure time, and financial independence. Woolf saw those as prerequisites for women to attain an equal position in society.

Ⅳ. Essay question

Woolf's original design in the novel is to end it with Clarissa's death, but she changed her mind and let Smith die in Clarissa's place.

There are striking differences between Clarissa and Smith. Septimus is a working-class man twenty years younger than Clarissa and a man who suffers from post-war trauma. In contrast, Clarissa is of upper class. Clarissa still finds something of English society that matters, such as the prime minister and expensive cars, while Septimus finds everything meaningless. Septimus's inner world overflows into the public sphere, whereas Clarissa's interior remains contained. The former is seen as insane, while the latter seems normal to others.

Despite their disparities, they have something in common in terms of physical and emotional qualities. Beak-nose, preference for domestic sphere, and apparent interest in Shakespeare are their common features. When Septimus first shows up in the novel, he is observing the car that backfires, just as Clarissa does. Besides, the two both show such strong horror at power-seizers such as Sir William and Miss Kilman. Both believe that people are connected to trees in a spiritual way, and that nature has particular meaning to them. At the end of the novel, in a very direct link, Clarissa feels not only responsible for Smith's death, but also attracted to their similarities. She realizes that Septimus's death is, like her party, an attempt to communicate. At a certain moment, Clarissa feels that there is part of Smith that is also hers.

第 40 章　詹姆斯·乔伊斯

40.1　复习笔记

James Joyce (1882—1941)	**詹姆斯·乔伊斯(1882—1941)**
1. Life	**1. 生平**
James Joyce was an Irishman born into a Catholic family in Dublin. He studied modern languages at University College Dublin. As a child, Joyce rebelled against the shabbiness and philistinism of Dublin. In his final year at Belvedere, he began to reject his Catholic faith to pursue a literary mission which he saw involving rebellion and exile.	詹姆斯·乔伊斯是爱尔兰人，出生在都柏林天主教家庭。后进入都柏林大学学院学习现代语言。小时候乔伊斯就反抗都柏林的破败庸俗。在贝尔维迪学院的最后一年，他开始摈弃自己的天主教信仰，去追求一条他认为包含反抗和放逐的文学使命。
After graduation, he went into "voluntary exile" in France, Italy, and Switzerland. Throughout his 36 years on the Continent, Joyce remained at the center of a literary circle. Life was hard at first, but with the help of some patrons, his financial situation was improved.	毕业后他自愿流放到法国、意大利和瑞典。在欧洲大陆的 36 年间，乔伊斯向来是文学圈的中心。起初生活比较艰难，后来在一些人的资助下，他的经济状况得到改善。
2. Literary Style	**2. 文学风格**
(1) James Joyce is one of the most original novelists of the 20th century. His works show a clever combination of techniques such as realism, stream-of-consciousness, and symbolism. His masterpiece *Ulysses* has been called "a modern prose epic". But for general readers, Joyce's works are too difficult to comprehend; some people may even find his novels unreadable.	(1) 詹姆斯·乔伊斯是 20 世纪最有独创性的作家之一，其作品展示了现实主义、意识流和象征主义的巧妙结合。他的代表作《尤利西斯》被称为“一部现代主义的散文史诗”。但是对于普通读者来说，他的作品很难读懂，有时甚至是不可读的。
(2) His work is always about Dublin. He conceived of ways to extend his description of Dublin into a microcosm of society, of human life, history, and geography for all.	(2) 他的作品总是关于都柏林。他构思出多种方式扩展他对都柏林的描述，使其成为了社会缩影，展现全体人类生活、历史、地理的微观范式。
3. Major Works	**3. 主要作品**
Dubliners (1914) *A Portrait of the Artist as a Young Man* (1916) *Ulysses* (1922) *Finnegans Wake* (1939)	《都柏林人》(1914) 《一个青年艺术家的画像》(1916) 《尤利西斯》(1922) 《芬尼根守灵夜》(1939)

4. Selected Works	**4. 选读作品**
◆*A Portrait of the Artist as a Young Man*	**◆《一个青年艺术家的画像》**
The novel is an autobiographical account of the childhood, youth, and early adulthood of Stephen Dedalus, a highly gifted young Irishman. After a fierce ideological struggle and internal conflict, Stephen abandons his Catholic faith, leaves Ireland, and devotes himself to an artistic career in exile.	这部作品是一部自传体小说，描述了极有天赋的爱尔兰年轻人斯蒂芬·戴德拉斯的童年、青年乃至早期成年的生活故事。经过激烈的思想斗争和内心冲突的煎熬，斯蒂芬放弃了天主教信仰，离开爱尔兰，决心在流放中致力于艺术。
◆*Ulysses*	**◆《尤利西斯》**
The novel took Joyce 7 years to complete. The plot is similar to the wanderings and adventures of the Greek hero Odysseus, or Ulysses, told in Homer's great epic poem "Odyssey".	该书是作者花了7年时间完成的小说。其情节类似于荷马伟大史诗《奥德赛》讲述的古希腊英雄奥德修斯(或称尤利西斯)的流浪和冒险经历。
Joyce's novel tells the story of the vagaries and adventures of a modern-day Ulysses, Leopold Bloom, over the course of 24 hours on 16 June 1904. There are three main characters: Leopold Bloom, an ordinary Jewish businessman in Dublin, his wife Molly, a concert singer, and Stephen Dedalus from *A Portrait of the Artist as a Young Man*, a writer like Joyce.	乔伊斯的小说讲述了现代的尤利西斯——里奥珀德·布鲁姆在1904年6月16日这一天24小时的游荡和历险故事。小说有三位主要人物：里奥珀德·布鲁姆，都柏林一位普通的犹太商人；他的妻子莫莉，一位音乐厅歌手；和《一个青年艺术家的画像》中的斯蒂芬·戴德拉斯，一个类似乔伊斯的作家。
By using the technique of stream-of-consciousness, Joyce revealed characters' inner world. The novel is a record of Leopold's activities: he wanders through the streets of Dublin on his daily business as an advertising agent, is tempted by barmaids and distracted by shop-windows, meets Stephen in drunkenness, and sends him home. In the process, he is constantly worried about his wife Molly, who is carrying on an affair with an impresario.	故事运用意识流手法记载人物的心理活动，讲述了里奥珀德作为一个广告代理商，如何在都柏林的大街小巷游荡而开始他日常的生意，并经受酒吧间女招待的诱惑，橱窗的吸引，遇见醉酒后的斯蒂芬并送他回家，一直惦记着与乐团经理厮混的妻子莫莉。
◆"Araby"	**◆《阿拉比》**
"Araby" is a short story by James Joyce included in his 1914 collection *Dubliners*. The novel tells the story of a little boy vaguely in love with his friend Mangan's sister. On Saturday night he goes to the market to buy her a special present, but in the end he has bought nothing and feels angry. As he stands in the Araby market and the lights go out, he has an epiphany that his obsession is a mere fantasy. Joyce told us through this story that everyone experiences frustrated desire for love or other similar state of mind, and that Dubliners may not feel a sense of fulfillment of wishes or satisfaction.	《阿拉比》是收录到《都柏林人》中的一篇短篇小说。小说讲了一个小男孩朦胧中爱上了朋友曼根的姐姐，星期六晚上专程到阿拉比市场去给她买礼物以示心意，但是最后什么也没买成。小男孩感觉很生气。当他站在阿拉比市场，灯光熄灭时，他顿悟了，自己的迷恋只是个幻想。乔伊斯通过这个小故事告诉我们每个人都会经历对爱情的渴望或其他体验，都柏林人可能感受不到愿望的实现和满足感。

40.2 考研真题与典型题详解

Ⅰ. Fill in the blanks.

1. The title of James Joyce's fiction ___________ shows that the author intends to model his fiction on the Homeric story of __________.（国际关系学院 2007 研）
2. ___________ is the founder of the "Stream of Consciousness" school of novel writing.
3. The novel __________ describes the mental activities of two Dubliners in a single day. This formless, plotless novel records the thoughts, shades and fleeting flashes of the mind.

Ⅱ. Multiple Choices

1. ___________(1922), James Joyce's masterpiece, has become a prime example of modernism in literature.（四川大学 2007 研）

   A. *The Rainbow* B. *Ulysses*

   C. *Little Women* D. *The Virgin and the Gypsy*

2. What did James Joyce intend to expose in *Dubliners*?（大连外国语学院 2008 研）

   A. Greed of the people. B. Paralysis of the people.

   C. Social injustice. D. Snobbery of the people.

Ⅲ. Read the following quotation and answer the questions.

North Richmond Street, being blind, was a quiet street except at the hour when the Christian Brothers' School set the boys free. An uninhabited house of two storeys stood at the blind end, detached from its neighbors in a square ground. The other houses of the street, conscious of decent lives within them, gazed at one another with brown imperturbable faces.

1. Identify the author and the work.
2. What is the meaning of "being blind"?
3. What is the tone and how is it presented in this selected passage?

Ⅳ. Short answer question

What styles does James Joyce use in *Ulysses*?

参考答案及解析

Ⅰ. Fill in the blanks.

1. *Ulysses*; *Odyssey*

   （乔伊斯的小说《尤利西斯》的题目表明作者意在模仿荷马史诗《奥德赛》。）

2. James Joyce

   （乔伊斯被认为是 20 世纪最重要、最具影响力的小说家，被称作"意识流"写作的鼻祖。）

3. *Ulysses*

   （乔伊斯的代表作《尤利西斯》描写了两个都柏林人一天的生活。小说把他们的全部历史、全部精神生活和内心世界表现得淋漓尽致。）

Ⅱ. Multiple Choices

1. B 乔伊斯的代表作是《尤利西斯》。选项 A《虹》和选项 D《吉普赛之恋》的作者都是 David Herbert Lawrence（戴维·赫伯特·劳伦斯）；选项 C《小妇人》的作者是 Louisa May

Alcott(路易莎·梅·爱尔考特)。

2. B *Dubliners*(《都柏林人》)是乔伊斯的一部短篇小说集，包括十五个故事，每一个都在某种程度上代表了“非常肮脏的都柏林”的一个方面，揭露了都柏林人政治上、精神上和道德上的麻痹。

Ⅲ. Read the following quotation and answer the questions.

1. James Joyce's "Araby" from *Dubliners*.
2. "Being blind" implies the dead-end street and the emptiness and hollowness of life.
3. A fine-tuned melancholy. The author depicted the street as "blind" and the Christian Brothers' School as a prison because it "set the boys free". A vacant house is at the dead end with the other houses on the street showing their brown looks. The color brown implies the author's tone, which is insipid due to the desolate and lifeless surroundings and scenes.

Ⅳ. Short answer question

The stylistic features of Ulysses include three aspects. The first is Joyce's original style of being direct, lucid, logical, and relaxing. Joyce's writing is known for its subtlety, accuracy, and conciseness. It is said that in order to truthfully describe the streets in Dublin, Joyce himself wandered through nearly all of them and took detailed notes. The second feature is his use of stream-of-consciousness. Joyce offered detailed and true-to-life descriptions of human thoughts, which are fragmented, shifting, and incomplete in structure and meaning. The third is his mock-heroic style, the essence of which lies in the application of apparently inappropriate styles.